Praise for WILDWOOD

"This book is like the wild, strange forest it describes. It is full of suspense and danger and frightening things the world has never seen, and once I stepped inside I never wanted to leave."
—Lemony Snicket

"*Wildwood* is an irresistible, atmospheric adventure—richly imagined and richly rewarding."
—Trenton Lee Stewart

"Dark and whimsical, with a true and uncanny sense of otherworldliness, *Wildwood* is the heir to a great tradition of stories of wild childhood adventure. It snatched me up and carried me off into a world I didn't want to leave."
—Michael Chabon

"*Wildwood* is a beautiful object and a beautiful read. One part fairy tale, one part coming-of-age story, one part unrepentantly gorgeous work of art, this book is overflowing with gifts."
—Jonathan Safran Foer

"A quick, compelling read, smoothly written with a perfect balance of middle-school-age-appropriate simplicity and more challenging writing that makes the book adult-accessible. An iconic children's novel that embraces fantasy adventure rather than modern dystopian coming-of-age anguish."
—*A.V. Club*

"A satisfying blend of fantasy, adventure story, eco-fable, and political satire with broad appeal."
—*Kirkus Reviews*

WILDWOOD

THE WILDWOOD CHRONICLES, BOOK I

COLIN MELOY

Illustrations by
CARSON ELLIS

BALZER + BRAY
An Imprint of HarperCollins*Publishers*

Balzer + Bray is an imprint of HarperCollins Publishers.

Wildwood: The Wildwood Chronicles, Book 1
Copyright © 2011 by Unadoptable Books LLC

Library of Congress Cataloging-in-Publication Data
Meloy, Colin.
    Wildwood / Colin Meloy ; illustrations by Carson Ellis. — 1st ed.
      p. cm. — (The Wildwood chronicles ; bk. 1)
    Summary: When her baby brother is kidnapped by crows, seventh-grader Prue McKeel
ventures into the forbidden Impassable Wilderness—a dangerous and magical forest at the
edge of Portland, Oregon—and soon finds herself involved in a war among the various
inhabitants.
    ISBN 978-0-06-202468-8 (trade bdg.) — ISBN 978-0-06-202470-1 (pbk.)
    [1. Fantasy. 2. Missing children—Fiction. 3. Brothers and sisters—Fiction. 4.
Animals—Fiction. 5. Portland (Or.)—Fiction.] I. Ellis, Carson, ill. II. Title.
PZ7.M516353Wi 2011   2011010072
[Fic]—dc22   CIP
                                                                                   AC

Typography by Sarah Hoy
13 14 15 16 CG/RRDH 20 19 18 17 16 15 14
❖
First Edition

For Hank, of course

CONTENTS

❧

LIST OF COLOR PLATES

*

WILDWOOD

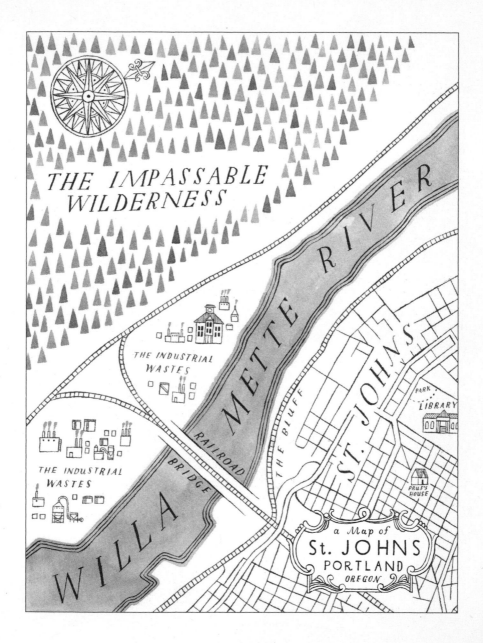

PART ONE

A Murder of Crows

How five crows managed to lift a twenty-pound baby boy into the air was beyond Prue, but that was certainly the least of her worries. In fact, if she were to list her worries right then and there as she sat spellbound on the park bench and watched her little brother, Mac, carried aloft in the talons of these five black crows, puzzling out just *how* this feat was being done would likely come in dead last. First on the list: Her baby brother, her responsibility, was being abducted by birds. A close second: *What did they plan on doing with him?*

And it had been such a nice day.

True, it had been a little gray when Prue woke up that morning, but what September day in Portland wasn't? She had drawn up the blinds in her bedroom and had paused for a moment, taking in the sight of the tree branches outside her window, framed as they were by a sky of dusty white-gray. It was Saturday, and the smell of coffee and breakfast was drifting up from downstairs. Her parents would be in their normal Saturday positions: Dad with his nose in the paper, occasionally hefting a lukewarm mug of coffee to his lips; Mom peering through tortoiseshell bifocals at the woolly mass of a knitting project of unknown determination. Her brother, all of one year old, would be sitting in his high chair, exploring the farthest frontiers of unintelligible babble: *Doose! Doose!* Sure enough, her vision was proven correct when she came downstairs to the nook off the kitchen. Her father mumbled a greeting, her mother's eyes smiled from above her glasses, and her brother shrieked, "Pooo!" Prue made herself a bowl of granola. "I've got bacon on, darling," said her mother, returning her attention to the amoeba of yarn in her hands (was it a sweater? A tea cozy? A noose?).

"Mother," Prue had said, now pouring rice milk over her cereal, "I told you. I'm a vegetarian. Ergo: no bacon." She had read that word, *ergo*, in a novel she'd been reading. That was the first time she had used it. She wasn't sure if she'd used it right, but it felt good. She sat down at the kitchen table and winked at Mac. Her father briefly peered over the top of his paper to give her a smile.

"What's on the docket today?" said her father. "Remember, you're watching Mac."

"Mmmm, I dunno," Prue responded. "Figured we'd hang around somewhere. Rough up some old ladies. Maybe stick up a hardware store. Pawn the loot. Beats going to a crafts fair."

Her father snorted.

"Don't forget to drop off the library books. They're in the basket by the front door," said her mother, her knitting needles clacking. "We should be back for dinner, but you know how long these things can run."

"Gotcha," said Prue.

Mac shouted, "Pooooo!" wildly brandished a spoon, and sneezed.

"And we think your brother might have a cold," said her father. "So make sure he's bundled up, whatever you do."

(The crows lifted her brother higher into the overcast sky, and suddenly Prue enumerated another worry: *But he might have a cold!*)

That had been their morning. Truly, an unremarkable one. Prue finished her granola, skimmed the comics, helped her dad ink in a few gimmes in his crossword puzzle, and was off to hook up the red Radio Flyer wagon to the back of her single-speed bicycle. An even coat of gray remained in the sky, but it didn't seem to threaten rain, so Prue stuffed Mac into a lined corduroy jumper, wrapped him in a stratum of quilted chintz, and placed him, still babbling, into the wagon. She loosed one arm from this cocoon of clothing and handed him his favorite toy: a wooden snake. He shook it appreciatively.

Prue slipped her black flats into the toe clips and pedaled the bike into motion. The wagon bounced noisily behind her, Mac shrieking happily with every jolt. They tore through the neighborhood of tidy clapboard houses, Prue nearly upsetting Mac's wagon with every hurdled curb and missed rain puddle. The bike tires gave a satisfied *shhhhhh* as they carved the wet pavement.

The morning flew by, giving way to a warm afternoon. After several random errands (a pair of Levis, not quite the right color, needed returning; the recent arrivals bin at Vinyl Resting Place required perusing; a plate of veggie tostadas was messily shared at the taqueria), she found herself whiling time outside the coffee shop on the main street while Mac quietly napped in the red wagon. She sipped steamed milk and watched through the window as the café employees awkwardly installed a secondhand elk head trophy on the wall. Traffic hummed on Lombard Street, the first intrusions of the neighborhood's polite rush hour. A few passersby cooed at the sleeping baby in the wagon and Prue flashed them sarcastic smiles, a little annoyed to be someone's picture of sibling camaraderie. She doodled mindlessly in her sketchbook: the leaf-clogged gutter drain in front of the café, a hazy sketch of Mac's quiet face with extra attention paid to the little dribble of snot emerging from his left nostril. The afternoon began to fade. Mac, waking, shook her from her trance.

"Right," she said, putting her brother on her knee while he rubbed the sleep from his eyes. "Let's keep moving. Library?" Mac pouted, uncomprehending.

"Library it is," said Prue.

She skidded to a halt in front of the St. Johns branch library and vaulted from her bike seat. "Don't go anywhere," she said to Mac as she grabbed the short stack of books from the wagon. She jogged into the foyer and stood before the book return slot, shuffling the books in her hand. She stopped at one, *The Sibley Guide to Birds*, and sighed. She'd had it for nearly three months now, braving overdue notices and threatening notes from librarians before she'd finally consented to return it. Prue mournfully flipped through the pages of the book. She'd spent hours copying the beautiful illustrations of the birds into her sketchbook, whispering their fantastic, exotic names like quiet incantations: *the western tanager. The whip-poor-will. Vaux's swift.* The names conjured the images of lofty climes and faraway places, of quiet prairie dawns and misty treetop aeries. Her gaze drifted from the book to the darkness of the return slot and back. She winced, muttered, "Oh well," and shoved the book into the opening of her peacoat. She would brave the librarians' wrath for one more week.

Outside, an old woman had stopped in front of the wagon and was busy searching around for its owner, her brow furrowed. Mac was contentedly chewing on the head of his wooden snake. Prue rolled her eyes, took a deep breath, and threw open the doors of the library.

When the woman saw Prue, she began to wave a knobby finger in her direction, stammering, "E-excuse me, miss! This is very unsafe! To leave a child! Alone! Do his parents know how he is being cared for?"

"What, him?" asked Prue as she climbed back on to the bike. "Poor thing, doesn't have parents. I found him in the free book pile." She smiled widely and pushed the bike away from the curb back onto the street.

The playground was empty when they arrived, and Prue unrolled Mac from his swaddling and set him alongside the unhitched Radio Flyer. He was just beginning to walk and relished the opportunity to practice his balancing. He gurgled and smiled and carefully waddled beside the wagon, pushing it slowly across the playground's asphalt. "Knock yourself out," said Prue, and she pulled the copy of *The Sibley Guide to Birds* from her coat, opening it to a dog-eared page about meadowlarks. The shadows against the blacktop were growing longer as the late afternoon gave way to early evening.

That was when she first noticed the crows.

At first there were just a few, wheeling in concentric circles against the overcast sky. They caught Prue's attention, darting about in her periphery, and she glanced up at them. *Corvus brachyrhynchos*; she'd just been reading about them the night before. Even from a distance, Prue was astounded by their size and the power of their every wing stroke. A few more flew into the group and there were now several, wheeling and diving above the quiet playground. *A flock?* thought

Prue. *A swarm?* She flipped through the pages of Sibley to the back where there was an index of fanciful terms for the grouping of birds: a sedge of herons, a fall of woodcock, and: a murder of crows. She shivered. Looking back up, she was startled to see that this murder of crows had grown considerably. There were now dozens of birds, each of the blackest pitch, piercing cold empty holes in the widening sky. She looked over at Mac. He was now yards away, blithely toddling along the blacktop. She felt unnerved. "Hey, Mac!" she called. "Where ya going?"

There was a sudden rush of wind, and she looked up in the sky and was horrified to see that the group of crows had grown twentyfold. The individual birds were now indiscernible from the mass, and the murder coalesced into a single, convulsive shape, blotting out the flat light of the afternoon sun. The shape swung and bowed in the air, and the noise of their beating wings and screeching cries became almost deafening. Prue cast about, seeing if anyone else was witnessing this bizarre event, but she was terrified to find that she was alone.

And then the crows dove.

Their cry became a single, unified scream as the cloud of crows feinted skyward before diving at a ferocious speed toward her baby brother. Mac gave a terrific squeal as the first crow reached him, snagging the hood of his jumper in a quick flourish of a talon. A second took hold of a sleeve, a third grabbing the shoulder. A fourth, a fifth touched down, until the swarm surrounded and obscured the view of his body in a sea of flashing, feathery blackness. And then, with seemingly perfect ease, Mac was lifted from the ground and into the air.

Prue was paralyzed with shock and disbelief: *How were they doing this?* She found that her legs felt like they were made of cement, her mouth empty of anything that might draw forth words or a sound. Her entire placid, predictable life now seemed to hinge on this one single event, everything she'd ever felt or believed coming into terrible relief. Nothing her parents had told her, nothing she'd ever learned in school, could possibly have prepared her for this thing that was happening. Or, really, what was to follow.

"LET MY BROTHER GO!"

Waking from her reverie, Prue found she was standing on top of the bench, shaking her fist at the crows like an ineffectual comic-book bystander, cursing some supervillain for the theft of a purse. The crows were quickly gaining altitude; they now topped the highest branches of the poplars. Mac could barely be seen amid the black, winged swarm. Prue jumped down from the bench and grabbed a rock from the pavement. Taking quick aim, she threw the rock as hard as she could but groaned to see it fall well short of its target. The crows were completely unfazed. They were now well above the tallest trees in the neighborhood and climbing, the highest flyers growing hazy in the low-hanging clouds. The dark mass moved in an almost lazy pattern, stalling in motion before suddenly breaking in one direction and the next. Suddenly, the curtain of their bodies parted and Prue could see the distant beige shape of Mac, his cord jumper pulled into a grotesque rag-doll shape by the crows' talons. She could see one crow had a claw tangled in the fine down of his hair. Now the swarm seemed to split in two groups: One stayed surrounding the few crows who were carrying Mac while the other dove away and skirted the treetops. Suddenly, two of the crows let go of Mac's jumper, and the remaining birds scrambled to keep hold. Prue shrieked as she saw her brother slip from their claws and plummet. But before Mac even neared the ground, the second group of crows deftly flew in and he was caught, lost again into the cloud of squawking birds. The two groups reunited, wheeled in the air once more, and suddenly, violently, shot westward, away from the playground.

Determined to do *something*, Prue dashed to her bike, jumped on, and gave pursuit. Unencumbered by Mac's red wagon, the bike quickly gained speed and Prue darted out into the street. Two cars skidded to a stop in front of her as she crossed the intersection in front of the library; somebody yelled, "Watch it!" from the sidewalk. Prue did not dare take her eyes off the swimming, spinning crows in the distance.

Her legs a blue blur over the pedals, Prue blew the stop sign at Richmond and Ivanhoe, inciting an angered holler from a bystander. She then skidded through the turn southward on Willamette. The crows, unhampered by the neighborhood's grid of houses, lawns, streets, and stoplights, made quick time over the landscape, and Prue commanded her legs to pedal faster to keep pace. In the chase, she could swear that the crows were toying with her, cutting back toward her, diving low and skirting the roofs of the houses, only to carve a great arc and, with a push of speed, dart back to the west. In these moments Prue could catch a glimpse of her captive brother, swinging in the clutches of his captors, and then he would disappear again, lost in the whirlwind of feathers.

"I'm coming for you, Mac!" she yelled. Tears streamed down Prue's cheeks, but she couldn't tell if she'd cried them or if they were a product of the cold fall air that whipped at her face as she rode. Her heart was beating madly in her chest, but her emotions were staid; she still couldn't quite believe this was all happening. Her only thought was to retrieve her brother. She swore that she would never let him out of her sight again.

The air was alive with car horns as Prue zigzagged through the steady traffic of St. Johns. A garbage truck, executing a slow, traffic-stalling Y-turn in the middle of Willamette Street, blocked the road, and Prue was forced to hop the curb and barrel down the sidewalk. A group of pedestrians screamed and dove out of her way. "Sorry!" Prue shouted. In an angular motion, the crows doubled back, causing Prue to lay on the brakes, and then dove low in an almost single file and flew straight toward her. She screamed and ducked as the crows flew over her head, their feathers nicking her scalp. She heard a distinct gurgle and a call, "Pooooo!" from Mac as they passed, and he was gone again, the crows back on their journey westward. Prue pedaled the bike to speed and bunny-hopped the wheels of the bike back onto the black pavement of the street, grimacing as she absorbed the bump with her arms. Seeing an opportunity, she took a hard right onto a side street that wound through a new development of identically whitewashed duplexes. The ground began to gently slope and she was gathering speed, the bike clattering and shaking beneath her. And then, suddenly, the street came to an abrupt end.

She had arrived at the bluff.

Here at the eastern side of the Willamette River was a natural border between the tight-knit community of St. Johns and the riverbank, a three-mile length of cliff simply called the bluff. Prue let out a cry and jammed on the brakes, nearly sending herself vaulting the handlebars and over the edge. The crows had cleared the precipice and were funneling skyward like a shivering black twister cloud, framed by the rising smoke from the many smelters and smokestacks of the Industrial Wastes, a veritable no-man's-land on the other side of the river, long ago claimed by the local industrial barons and transformed into a forbidding landscape of smoke and steel. Just beyond the Wastes, through the haze, lay a rolling expanse of deeply forested hills, stretching out as far as the eye could see. The color drained from Prue's face.

"No," she whispered.

In the flash of an instant and without a sound, the funnel of crows crested the far side of the river and disappeared in a long, thin column into the darkness of these woods. Her brother had been taken into the Impassable Wilderness.

CHAPTER 2

One City's Impassable Wilderness

As long as Prue could remember, every map she had ever seen of Portland and the surrounding countryside had been blotted with a large, dark green patch in the center, stretching like a growth of moss from the northwest corner to the southwest, and labeled with the mysterious initials "I.W." She hadn't thought to ask about it until one night, before Mac was born, when she was sitting with her parents in the living room. Her dad had brought home a new atlas and they were lying in the recliner together, leafing through the pages and tracing their fingers over boundary lines and sounding out the exotic place names of far-flung countries. When they arrived at a map of Oregon, Prue pointed to the small, inset map of Portland on the page and asked the question that had always confounded her: "What's the I.W.?"

"Nothing, honey," had been her father's reply. He flipped back to the map of Russia they had been looking at moments before. With his finger, he traced a circle over the wide northeastern part of the country where the letters of the word *Siberia* obscured the map. There were no city names here; no network of wandering yellow lines demarking highways and roads. Only vast puddles all shades of green and white and the occasional squiggly blue line linking the myriad remote lakes that peppered the landscape. "There are places in the world where people just don't end up living. Maybe it's too cold or there are too many trees or the mountains are too steep to climb. But whatever the reason, no one has thought to build a road there and without roads, there are no houses and without houses, no cities." He flipped back to the map of Portland and tapped his finger against the spot where "I.W." was written. "It stands for 'Impassable Wilderness.' And that's just what it is."

"Why doesn't anyone live there?" asked Prue.

"All the reasons why no one lives up in those parts of Russia. When the settlers first came to the area and started to build Portland, no one wanted to build their houses there: The forest was too deep and the hills were too steep. And since there were no houses there, no one thought to build a road. And without roads and houses, the place just sort of stayed that way: empty of people. The place, over time, just became more overgrown and more inhospitable. And so," he said, "it was named the Impassable Wilderness and everybody knew to steer clear." Her father dismissively wiped his hand across the map and brought it up to gently pinch Prue's chin between his thumb and finger. Bringing her face close to his, he said, "And I don't ever, *ever* want you to go in there." He playfully moved her head back and forth and smiled. "You hear me, kid?"

Prue made a face and yanked her chin free. "Yeah, I hear you." They both looked back at the atlas, and Prue laid her head against her father's chest.

"I'm serious," said her father. She could feel his chest tighten under her cheek.

So Prue knew not to go near this "Impassable Wilderness," and she only once bothered her parents with questions about it again. But she couldn't ignore it. While the downtown continued to sprout towering condominium buildings, and newly minted terra-cotta outlet malls bloomed beside the highway in the suburbs, it baffled Prue that such an impressive swath of land should go unclaimed, untouched, undeveloped, right on the edge of the city. And yet, no adult ever seemed to comment on it or mention it in conversation. It seemed to not even exist in most people's minds.

The only place that the Impassable Wilderness would crop

up was among the kids at Prue's school, where she was a seventh grader. There was an apocryphal tale told by the older students about a man—so-and-so's uncle, maybe—who had wandered into the I.W. by mistake and had disappeared for years and years. His family, over time, forgot about him and continued on with their lives until one day, out of the blue, he reappeared on their doorstep. He didn't seem to have any memory of the intervening years, saying only that he'd been lost in the woods for a time and that he was terribly hungry. Prue had been suspicious of the story from her first hearing; the identity of this "man" seemed to change from telling to telling. It was someone's father in one version, a wayward cousin in another. Also, the details shifted in each telling. A visiting high school kid told a group of Prue's rapt classmates that the individual (in this version, the kid's older brother) had returned from his weird sojourn in the Impassable Wilderness aged beyond belief, with a great white beard that stretched down to his tattered shoes.

Regardless of the questionable truth of these stories, it became clear to Prue that most of her classmates had had similar conversations with their parents as she had had with her father. The subject of the Wilderness filtered into their play surreptitiously: What once was a lake of poisonous lava around the four-square court was now the Impassable Wilderness, and woe betide anyone who missed a bounce and was forced to scurry after the red rubber ball into those wilds. In games of tag, you were no longer tagged It, but rather designated the Wild Coyote of the I.W., and it was your job to scamper around after your fleeing classmates, barking and growling.

It was the specter of these coyotes that made Prue ask her parents a second time about the Impassable Wilderness. She had been awakened one night in a fright by the unmistakable sound of baying dogs. Sitting up in bed, she could hear that Mac, then four months old, had awoken as well and was being quietly shushed by their parents as he wailed and whimpered in the next room. The dogs' baying was a distant echo, but it was bone-shivering nonetheless. It was a tuneless melody of violence and chaos and as it grew, more dogs in the neighborhood took up the cry. Prue noticed then that the distant barking was different from the barking of the neighborhood dogs; it was more shrill, more disordered and angry. She threw her blanket aside and walked into her parents' room. The scene was eerie: Mac had quieted a little at this point, and he was being rocked in his mother's arms while their parents stood at the window, staring unblinking out over the town at the distant western horizon, their faces pale and frightened.

"What's that sound?" asked Prue, walking to the side of her parents. The lights of St. Johns spread out before them, an array of flickering stars that stopped at the river and dissolved into blackness.

Her parents started when she spoke, and her father said, "Just some old dogs howling."

"But farther away?" asked Prue. "That doesn't sound like dogs."

Prue saw her parents share a glance, and her mother said, "In the woods, darling, there are some pretty wild animals. That's probably a pack of coyotes, wishing they could tear into someone's garbage somewhere. Best not to worry about it." She smiled.

The baying eventually stopped and the neighborhood dogs calmed, and Prue's parents walked her back into her room and tucked her into bed. That had been the last time the Impassable Wilderness had come up, but it hadn't put Prue's curiosity to rest. She couldn't help feeling a little troubled; her parents, normally two founts of strength and confidence, seemed strangely shaken by the noises. They seemed as leery of the place as Prue was.

And so one can imagine Prue's horror when she witnessed the black plume of crows disappear, her baby brother in tow, into the darkness of this Impassable Wilderness.

🌿

The afternoon had faded nearly completely, the sun dipping down low behind the hills of the Wilderness, and Prue stood transfixed, slack-jawed, on the edge of the bluff. A train engine trundled by below her and rolled across the Railroad Bridge, passing low over the brick and metal buildings of the Industrial Wastes. A breeze had picked up, and Prue shivered beneath her peacoat. She was staring at the little break in the tree line where the crows had disappeared.

It started to rain.

Prue felt like someone had bored a hole in her stomach the size of a basketball. Her brother was gone, *literally* captured by birds and carried to a remote, untouchable wilderness, and who knew what they would do to him there. And it was all her fault. The light changed from deep blue to dark gray, and the streetlights slowly, one by one, began to click on. Night had fallen. Prue knew her vigil was hopeless. Mac would not be returning. Prue slowly turned her bike around and began walking it back up the street. How would she tell her parents? They would be devastated beyond belief. Prue would be punished. She'd been grounded before for staying out late on school nights, riding her bike around the neighborhood, but this punishment was certain to be like nothing she'd ever experienced. She'd lost Mac, her parents' only son. Her brother. If a week of no television was the standard punishment for missing a couple curfews, she couldn't imagine what it was for losing baby brothers. She walked for several blocks, in a trance. She found that she was choking back tears as, in her mind's eye, she witnessed anew the crows' disappearance into the woods.

"Get a grip, Prue!" she said aloud, wiping tears from her cheeks. "Think this through!"

She took a deep breath and began assembling her options in her mind, weighing each one's pros and cons. Going to the police was out; they'd undoubtedly think she was crazy. She didn't know what police did with crazy people who came into the station ranting about murders of crows and abducted one-year-olds, but she had her suspicions: She'd be carried off in an armored van and thrown into some faraway asylum's subterranean cell, where she'd live out the rest of her days listening to the lamenting of her fellow inmates and trying hopelessly to convince the passing janitor that she was not crazy and that she was falsely imprisoned there. The thought of rushing home to tell her parents terrified her; their hearts would be irretrievably broken. They had waited so long for Mac to come along. She didn't know the whole story, but understood that they'd wanted to have a second child sooner, but it just hadn't come about. They had been so happy when they found out about Mac. They had positively beamed; the entire house had felt alive and light. No, she couldn't be the one to break this terrible news to them. She could run away—this was a legitimate option. She could jump on one of those trains going over the Railroad Bridge and split town and travel from city to city, doing odd jobs and telling fortunes for a living—maybe she'd even meet a little golden retriever on the road who'd become her closest companion, and they'd ramble the country together, a couple of gypsies on the run, and she'd never have to face her parents or think about her dear, departed brother again.

Prue stopped in the middle of the sidewalk and shook her head dolefully.

What are you thinking? She reprimanded herself. *You're out of your mind!* She took a deep breath and kept walking, pushing her bike along. A chill came over her as she realized her only option.

She had to go after him.

She had to go into the Impassable Wilderness and find him. It seemed like an insurmountable task, but she had no choice. The rain had grown heavy and was pelting down on the sidewalks and the streets, making huge puddles, and the puddles became choked with flotillas of dead leaves. Prue devised her plan, carefully gauging the dangers of such an adventure. The chill of evening was draping over the rain-swept neighborhood streets; it would be unsafe to attempt the trip in the dead of night. *I'll go tomorrow,* she thought, unaware that she was mumbling some of the words aloud. *Tomorrow morning, first thing. Mom and Dad won't even have to know.* But how to keep them from finding out? Her heart sank as she arrived at the scene of Mac's abduction: the playground. The play structure was abandoned in the sheeting rain, and Mac's little red wagon sat on the asphalt, a heap of soggy blanket sitting inside, collecting water. "That's it!" said Prue, and she ran over to the wagon. Kneeling down on the wet pavement, she started to mold the sopping blanket into the form of a swaddled baby. Standing back, she studied it. "Plausible," she said. She had started to attach the wagon to the back axle of her bike when she heard a voice call:

"Hey, Prue!"

Prue stiffened and looked over her shoulder. Standing on the sidewalk next to the playground was a boy, incognito in a matching rain slicker and pants. He pulled the hood back on his slicker and smiled. "It's me, Curtis!" he shouted, and waved.

Curtis was one of Prue's classmates. He lived with his parents and his two sisters just down the street from Prue. Their desks at school were two rows apart. Curtis was constantly getting in trouble with their teacher for spending school time drawing pictures of superheroes in various scrapes with their archenemies. His drawing obsession also tended to get him in trouble with his classmates, since most kids had abandoned superhero drawing years before, if they hadn't abandoned drawing altogether. Most kids devoted their drawing talent to sketching band logos on the paper-bag covering of their textbooks; Prue was one of the only kids who'd transitioned away from her superhero- and fairy-tale-inspired renderings to drawings of birds and plants. Her classmates looked askance at her, but at least they didn't bother her. Curtis, for clinging to his bygone art form, was shunned.

"Hey, Curtis," said Prue, as nonchalantly as possible. "What are you doing?"

He put his hood back on. "I was just out for a walk. I like walking in the rain. Less people around." He took his glasses off and pulled a corner of his shirt from beneath his slicker to clean them. Curtis's round face was topped by a mass of curly black hair that sprang from beneath his slicker hood like little coils of steel wool. "Why were you talking to yourself?"

Prue froze. "What?"

"You were talking to yourself. Just back there." He pointed in the direction of the bluff as he squinted and put his glasses back on. "I was sort of following you, I guess. I meant to get your attention earlier, but you looked so . . . distracted."

"I wasn't," was all Prue could think to say.

"You were talking to yourself and walking and then stopping and shaking your head and doing all sorts of weird things," he said. "And why were you standing on the bluff for so long? Just staring into space?"

Prue got serious. She walked her bike over to Curtis and pointed a finger in his face. "Listen to me, Curtis," she said, commanding her most intimidating tone. "I've got a lot on my mind. I don't need you bothering me right now, okay?"

To her relief, Curtis appeared to be easily intimidated. He threw up his hands and said, "Okay! Okay! I was just curious is all."

"Well, don't be," she said. "Just forget everything you saw, all right?" She started to push her bike away toward home. As she straddled the bike seat and put her feet in the toe clips, she turned to Curtis and said, "I'm *not* crazy." And she rode off.

To Cross a Bridge

It was nearing seven o'clock as Prue approached her house, and she could see the light on in the living room and the silhouette of her mother's head, bowed over her knitting. Her father was nowhere in sight as she crept around the side of the house, moving slowly so as not to disturb the pea gravel of the walk. The soggy blanket in the wagon made a convincing slumbering one-year-old but definitely wouldn't withstand close inspection, so Prue held her breath in hope that she wouldn't encounter an inquisitive parent. Her hopes were dashed as she rounded the back corner of the house and saw her dad fumbling with the garbage and recycling bins. The following day was garbage day; it had always been her father's task to wrestle the bins curbside. Seeing Prue, he wiped hands together and said, "Hey, kiddo!" The porch light spread a hazy glow across the darkened lawn.

"Hi, Dad," said Prue. Her heart was racing as she slowly walked the bike over to the side of the house and rested it against the wall.

Her dad smiled. "You guys were out late. We were starting to wonder about you. You missed dinner, by the way."

"We stopped at Proper Eats on the way in," said Prue, "shared a stir-fry." She stepped awkwardly sideways so as to stand between her dad and the wagon. She was painfully aware of her every movement as she tried to feign nonchalance. "How was your day, Dad?"

"Oh, fine," he said. "Fairly hectic." He paused. "Get it? Craft fair? Fairly hectic?" Prue let out a loud, high-pitched laugh. She immediately second-guessed the reaction; usually she groaned at her father's terrible puns. Her father seemed to notice the inconsistency as well. He cocked an eyebrow and asked, "How's Mac?"

"He's great!" Prue sputtered, maybe too quickly. "He's sleeping!"

"Really? That's early for him."

"Um, we had a really . . . active day. He ran around a lot. Seemed pretty tuckered out, and so after we had food I just wrapped him up in his blanket and he fell asleep." She smiled and gestured at the wagon behind her. "Just like that."

"Hmm," said her father. "Well, get him inside and into his

jammies. He might be down for the count." He sighed, looked back at the recycling bins, and began dragging them along the side of the house toward the street.

Prue let out a breath of relief. Turning around, she carefully scooped the wet blanket out of the wagon and walked into the house, bouncing and shushing the bundle as she went.

The back door let into the kitchen, and Prue walked as softly as she could across the cork flooring. She had almost made it to the stairs when her mother called from the living room, "Prue? Is that you?"

Prue stopped and pressed the wet blanket against her chest. "Yes, Mother?"

"You guys missed dinner. How's Mac?"

"Good. He's sleeping. We ate on the way home."

"Sleeping?" she asked, and Prue could imagine her bespectacled face turning to look at the clock on the mantel. "Oh. I guess get him—"

"In jammies," Prue finished for her. "I'm on it."

She tore upstairs, skipping every other step, and rushed into her room, dumping the soaked blanket in her dirty clothes hamper. She then walked out into the hall and headed into Mac's room. She grabbed one of his stuffed animals—an owl—and placed it in his crib, carefully shrouding the toy with blankets. Satisfied that the lump, at a glance, would suggest a sleeping baby, she nodded to herself and turned off the light, then headed back into her room. She closed the door and threw herself onto her bed, burying her head in her pillows. Her heart was still beating wildly and it took several moments to get her breath under control. The rain made a quiet rattle against the glass of her window. Prue lifted her head from the bed and looked around her room. Downstairs, she could hear her father shutting the outside door behind him and walking into the living room. The shushed murmur of her parents' voices followed, and Prue rolled

out of her bed and set about preparing for tomorrow's adventure.

Pulling her messenger bag from beneath her desk, she upended it and dumped everything out onto the floor: her science book, a spiral notebook, and a clutch of ballpoint pens. She grabbed the flashlight she kept under her bed and took the Swiss Army knife her dad had bought her for her twelfth birthday from her desk drawer and stuck them in the bottom of the bag. She stood for a moment in the middle of her room and chewed on a fingernail. What did one pack for a trip into an impassable wilderness to retrieve one's brother? She would get food from the pantry in the morning. For now, all she needed to do was wait. She thumped back down on her bed, pulled *The Sibley Guide to Birds* from inside her peacoat, and flipped through the pages, trying to clear her mind of the frantic thoughts that were racing through her head.

After an hour or so, she heard her parents walk up the stairs, and her heart started pounding again. There was a knock at her door.

"Mm-hmm?" she said, again feigning nonchalance. She didn't know how much longer she'd be able to keep this act up, all this nonchalance-feigning. It was exhausting work.

Her dad cracked the door and peeked in. "G'night, sweetheart," he said. Her mom added, "Don't be up too late."

"Uh-huh," said Prue. She turned and smiled at them, and they closed the door.

Prue frowned as she heard their footsteps on the hardwood floor, moving toward her brother's room. The sound of Mac's door creaking open sounded like a peal of thunder to Prue's hyperattentive ears, and her breath caught in her throat. Thinking quickly, Prue leapt from her bed and ran to her door, peeking her head out from around the jamb. "Hey, Mom? Dad?" she whispered loudly.

"What's that?" said her father, his hand on the doorknob. The light from Mac's night-light spilled into the hall.

"I think he's really wiped out. Maybe try not to wake him?"

Her mom smiled and nodded. "Sure thing," she said, before poking her head into Mac's room and saying quietly, "Good night, Macky."

"Sweet dreams," whispered her father.

The door creaked shut, and Prue smiled at her parents as they passed her on the way to their bedroom. Seeing the door close behind them, she returned to her bed and let out her breath. It emerged from her chest as if she'd held it in all day long.

That night, Prue slept restlessly, her sleep fraught with dreams of great flocks of giant birds—owls, eagles, and ravens—in dazzling plumage, swooping down and carrying away her father and mother and leaving Prue alone in their emptied house. She had set her alarm for five a.m. but had been awake for a while when it finally went off. She rolled out of bed, careful not to make too much noise. The house was silent. The world was still dark outside and the neighborhood had yet to wake up, the only sound being the occasional car whispering past the house. Prue slipped into her jeans and threw on a shirt and a sweater. Her peacoat was still draped over her desk chair from the night before, and she cinched a scarf around her neck before putting on the coat. She wiggled her feet into her black sneakers and padded out into the hall. She put her ear to her parents' door and listened for the sawing snore of her father. Her parents were fast asleep. She figured she had an hour before they would be up, which would be plenty of time to make her escape. She walked down to her brother's room and pulled the stuffed animal from his crib and upset the blankets; she picked a set of warm clothes from Mac's red chest of drawers and stuffed them into her messenger bag. Tiptoeing downstairs, Prue wrote a hasty note on the dry-erase board by the refrigerator:

> *Mom, Dad:*
> *Mac was up early. Wanted to go adventuring.*
> *Back later!*
> *Love, Prue*

She opened the pantry and puzzled over the potential rations she might bring along, settling on a handful of granola bars and a bag of gorp left over from the summer's last camping trip. By the camping staples was the family's emergency first aid kit, and Prue slipped the plastic case into her bag. An air horn, a kind of canister with a plastic belled horn on the top, caught her attention, and she picked it up, inspecting it. A picture of a menacing grizzly bear graced the label.

The words BEAR-BE-GONE made an arc in the air above him. Apparently the noise was loud enough to scare away wildlife, something she imagined would come in handy in an impassable wilderness. She dropped it into the messenger bag and scanned the kitchen before slipping out the back door to the yard. The air was brittle and cold, and a slight breeze disturbed the yellowing leaves in the oak trees. Prue pushed her bike, the Radio Flyer wagon still attached, quietly out into the street. The first glimmers of dawn could be seen to the distant east, but the streetlights still illuminated the leafy sidewalks as Prue pushed her bike a safe distance from her house before climbing on. The scarf her mother had knit for her the prior winter clung snugly to her neck as she gained speed over the pavement, heading southwest through the streets and alleys. Lights in the houses began flickering on, and the hum of cars on the streets grew as the neighborhood awoke to the morning.

Following the path of her pursuit the day before, Prue made her way through the park to the bluff, the wagon jumping and clattering behind her. A heavy mist hung over the river basin, obscuring the water completely. The lights of the Wastes on the far banks of the river flashed under the cloud. An inscrutable clanking noise was carried across the wide trough of the river, echoing off the cliff walls of the bluffs. It sounded to Prue like the grinding gears of a giant's wristwatch. The only thing beyond the bluff that was exposed above the bank of clouds was the imposing iron lattice of the Railroad Bridge.

It seemed to float, unmoored, on the river mist. Prue dismounted her bike and walked it south along the bluff toward an area where the cliff side sloped down into the clouds. The world around her dimmed to white as she descended.

When the ground below Prue's feet finally evened out, she found she was standing in an alien landscape. The mist clung to everything, casting the world in a ghostly sheen. A slight wind was buffeting through the gorge, and the mist occasionally shifted to reveal the distant shapes of desiccated, wind-blown trees. The ground was covered in a dead yellow grass. Just beyond a line of trees, a span of railroad tracks carved a straight line east to west, disappearing into the haze on either end. Assuming the tracks would lead over the bridge, Prue began following them westward.

Ahead, the mists lifted, and she could see the spires of the Railroad Bridge. As she made her way toward it, she suddenly heard the sound of footsteps in the gravel behind her. She froze. After a moment, she cautiously looked over her shoulder. There was no one there. She had turned and kept walking when she heard the sound again.

"Who's there?" she shouted, searching the area behind her. There was no response. The railroad tracks, flanked by the line of strange, squat trees, disappeared into the mist; there was no sign of a pursuer.

Prue took a deep, shuddering breath and began walking faster toward the bridge. Suddenly, the footsteps sounded again unmistakably, and she spun around in time to see a figure dart off the tracks and through a gap between two of the trees. Without thinking, she dropped her bike to the ground and gave chase, her shoes sending up a small plume of gravel as she took the corner into the trees.

"Stop!" she yelled. She could now see the person through the mist—it was rather short and wore a heavy winter coat. A stocking cap was pulled down over the figure's head, obscuring his face. When Prue yelled, the person momentarily looked behind him—and slipped in a patch of loose dirt, slamming shoulder-first into the ground with a hoarse yell of surprise.

Prue dove onto the prostrate form of her pursuer and yanked the figure's stocking cap away. She gave a startled cry.

"Curtis!" she yelled.

"Hi, Prue," said Curtis, out of breath. He squirmed underneath her. "Can you get off of me? Your knee is really pushing into my stomach."

"No way," said Prue, regaining her composure. "Not till you tell me why you were following me."

Curtis sighed. "I w-wasn't! Really!"

She jammed her knee farther into his ribs, and Curtis let out a cry. "Okay! Okay!" he shouted, his voice quavering on the edge of crying. "I was up early taking the recycling out and I happened to see you riding by and I just wondered where you were going! I heard you talking to yourself last night about your brother and how you were going to get him, and then I saw you leave your house so early this morning and I figured something had to be up, and I just couldn't help myself!"

"What do you know about my brother?" Prue asked.

"Nothing!" said Curtis, sniffling. "I just know he's . . . he's missing." He blushed a little. "Also, I don't know who you were trying to fool with that wet blanket in the wagon."

Prue released the pressure on his ribs, and Curtis let out a breath of air.

"You scared the crap out of me," said Prue. She stepped off his body, and Curtis sat up, dusting off his pants.

"Sorry, Prue," said Curtis. "I didn't really mean anything by it, I was just curious."

"Well, don't be," said Prue. She stood up and began to walk away. "This is none of your business. This is my mess to deal with."

Curtis scrambled to his feet. "L-let me come with you!" he shouted, following after her.

Back at the railroad tracks, Prue pulled her bike up from the gravel and started walking it toward the bridge. "No, Curtis," she said. "Go home!" The riverbank sloped in toward the first abutment of the bridge, creating a kind of peninsula, and the track followed a gentle slope to meet the lattice of the bridge. Prue led her bike up the middle of the tracks while she balanced on the rail. As she climbed, the mists began to clear to reveal the first spire of the bridge. The spires housed the pulley mechanism that lifted the middle section when taller boats crossed under it, and they were topped with flashing red beacons. Prue breathed a sigh of relief to see that the lift span was down, allowing her to cross.

"Aren't you worried that a train's going to come?" asked Curtis, behind her.

"No," said Prue, though in truth it was one thing she hadn't really considered. Between the track and the truss of the bridge there was barely three feet of space, and the loose gravel was not too friendly to pedestrian traffic. As she arrived at the middle section of the bridge, she looked over the edge and gulped. The mist sat heavily on the river basin and created a floor of clouds that hid the water below, giving the illusion that the bridge sat at a tremendous height, like one of those delicate rope bridges spanning some cloudy Peruvian chasm Prue had seen in *National Geographic* magazine.

"I'm a little worried that a train's going to come," admitted Curtis. He was standing beneath one of the spires in the middle of the track.

Prue stopped, leaned her bike against the bridge truss, and picked up a rock from the gravel bed. "Don't make me do this, Curtis," she said.

"Do what?"

Prue threw the rock, and Curtis leapt out of the way, nearly tripping on the rail of the track.

"What'd you do that for?" he yelled, couching his head in his hands.

"'Cause you're being stupid and you're following me and I told you not to. That's why." She bent down and selected another rock, this one sharper and bigger than the previous one. She juggled it in her hand as if gauging the weight.

"C'mon, Prue," Curtis said, "let me help you! I'm a good helper. My dad was den leader of my cousin's Webelos group." He let his hands fall from his head. "I even brought my cousin's bowie knife." He patted the pocket of his coat and smiled sheepishly.

Prue threw the second rock and swore as it glanced off the ground in front of Curtis, missing his feet by inches. Curtis yelped and danced out of the way.

"Go HOME, Curtis!" Prue shouted. She crouched down and selected another rock but paused as she felt the ground give a sudden tremble below her. The rocks began to clatter in place as the bridge gave a long, quaking shudder. She looked up at Curtis, who was frozen in place in the center of the track. They stared at each other, wide-eyed, as the trembling began to grow stronger, the steel girders of the truss lowing in complaint.

"TRAIN!" shouted Prue.

C H A P T E R   4

The Crossing

From the quick glance that Prue was afforded of the train, she could tell it was not a long one, but it was moving at a fairly steady pace, puffing up the incline of the hill they had climbed minutes before. She turned and bolted for her bike, lifting it from where it rested against the side of the bridge and tossing it between the rails of the track. She vaulted the seat and jammed down on the pedals, sending the back tire into a free spin against the loose rock between the railroad ties.

"Wait for me!" screamed Curtis from behind her.

The metal of the bridge was now heaving and rattling under the weight of the oncoming locomotive. Prue was already in motion and threw a fast glance over her shoulder to measure the distance between her bike and the train. Backdropped by the ominous iron face of the train bursting through the mist, Curtis was running toward her, his arms swinging in frantic arcs. The bike frame jolted with every wooden tie she crossed, and she had to keep a studied eye on the space in front of her in order to keep the bike upright on the unsteady ground. The Radio Flyer in tow hopped from tie to tie, threatening to upend at each pedal. "Jump in the back!" shouted Prue over the deafening hiss of the train.

"I can't! You're moving too fast!" shouted Curtis.

Prue swore under her breath and pumped the handle brakes, her back tire fishtailing in the gravel. The train, now reaching the middle section of the bridge, let out a staccato burst of whistle, the tracks audibly groaning under its weight. Curtis dove for the Radio Flyer and let out a bone-numbing *"OOF!"* as his body met the metal floor of the wagon. He grasped the sides of the wagon and hollered, *"Go!"* and Prue was off, peeling a wake of shale from the track and firing down the far side of the bridge.

On the other side of the bridge, the tracks split into a Y at a dense, deep green bank of trees. Prue was picking up speed on the gradual incline as the end of the bridge came into view, and her bike leapt and kicked against the pounding of the tires on the ties. The wagon, now freighted with Curtis's writhing body, held to the ground much better, though Prue was panting to keep her momentum up. The train was getting louder behind them. She couldn't bring herself to steal a glance to mark its progress; her eyes were intent on the far side of the river.

"Hold on, Curtis!" she shouted over the din as she reached the spot where the tracks split and angled away from the bridge in either direction. She shoved her right foot down on the pedal and hopped her front wheel over the track, sending the bike over the rail and into the deep, loose gravel of the ditch that fell away from the track at the bridge's end. The back tire and the wagon followed quickly after, and the whole bike pitched forward in a violent spasm, sending both occupants over the handlebars and into a dry bed of scrub brush on the other side of the ditch. The train went screaming by, the steel rails wailing under the weight of the train as the engine rolled southward into the bank of clouds.

Prue lay flattened against the cold ground, rapidly panting. Her every limb felt charged with electricity. She pushed herself onto her knees and spat, wiping a smear of mud from her cheek. She looked around her; she was sitting in a shallow culvert in a drab field of

dead grass. Just beyond stood the Industrial Wastes, a bizarre and imposing neighborhood of windowless buildings and silos; beyond that lay the first rise of a steep hill, blanketed thickly with a dizzying retinue of towering trees. They were on the borderlands of the Impassable Wilderness. She shuddered. A grumble issued from the bed of grass beside her, and she looked over to see Curtis struggling to his knees, the red Radio Flyer wagon obstinately clinging to his back like a turtle's shell. He threw it off and rubbed at the nape of his neck.

"Ow," he said. He looked at Prue mournfully and repeated, "Ow."

"Maybe you shouldn't have followed me, then," said Prue, bringing herself to her feet. The wreckage of the bike and wagon lay in a crumpled mess next to them. Prue grunted as she pulled the frame of her bike from the grasp of the culvert's sticker bushes and studied the remains: Most of the bike had withstood the impact well enough, but the front wheel was irretrievably bent, its twisted spokes jutting from the rim at desperate angles.

Cursing loudly, she dropped the bike and kicked at a clump of thistles, sending up a spray of dirt.

Curtis was sitting cross-legged, marveling at the bridge behind them. "I can't believe we made it," he wheezed. "We outran that train."

Prue was not listening. She was standing with her hands on her hips, staring at the twisted remnants of her front bike wheel, her brow deeply furrowed. She'd worked all summer on tuning up the bike. The front rim, now disfigured beyond repair, had been practically brand-new. Her mission was clearly not getting off to a very good start.

"We did pretty well back there," Curtis was saying. "I mean, we worked together really well. You were riding the bike and I was . . . on the wagon." He laughed as he massaged his temples with his fingers. "We were like partners, huh?"

Prue's messenger bag had been thrown to the ground during the crash, and she stooped and picked it up, fitting the strap over her shoulder. "Bye, Curtis," she said. Leaving behind the bike and the wagon, she began walking through the Wastes toward the steep hill of trees.

The tawny field of dried and burned grass led into the tight grid of the mysterious buildings. Some appeared to be warehouses, paneled in corrugated metal, while others had the aspect of massive boxy silos and had doors at wild heights that seemed to open to nowhere and yards of metal ducting snaking out of them, leading to their neighboring buildings. A few of the buildings had windows that glowed and flickered red, as if great fires were raging within them. All along, this "city" rang with an insistent metallic clanging and the gaseous belching of smokestacks, giving it the strangest appearance of being completely abandoned yet perfectly active. Far off, the grunts and shouts of stevedores, their bodies lost to the low-lying mist, rang from the metal walls. As Prue walked, she cast her eyes about her; no one she knew had ever ventured here before. So soon in her journey, she already felt like the first explorer of some alien world. The fog continued to dissipate. Recessed in the grid of the gravel-paved avenues was a gray stone mansion, its mossy roof topped by a clock tower. A bell tolled the hour; Prue counted six bells.

After a time, the boxy structures of the Wastes gave way to a slope of deep green brush; Prue stepped across the northbound branch of the train tracks and found herself immersed in a lush, knee-deep thicket of ferns. The ground continued to slope upward toward the first trees that marked the boundary between the outside world and the Impassable Wilderness. Prue took a deep breath, adjusted the bag at her shoulder, and began walking into the woods.

"Wait!" shouted Curtis. He had pulled himself up and was stumbling after her. He stopped at the barrier of trees. "You're going in there? But that's . . . that's the Impassable Wilderness."

Ignoring him, Prue marched on. The ground was soft beneath her feet, and leaves of salal and fern whipped at her calves as she walked. "Uh-huh," she said. "I know."

Curtis was at a loss for words. He crossed his arms and shouted as

Prue ventured farther up the slope and into the forest: "It's *impass-able*, Prue!"

Prue paused and looked around. "I seem to be passing through it okay," she said, and kept walking.

Curtis scampered forward so as to remain within earshot of Prue. "Well, yeah, right now, maybe, but who knows what it's like once you're farther in there. And these trees . . ." Here he paused and scanned one of the taller trees on the hillside, top to bottom. "Well, I have to tell you I'm not getting a very friendly vibe from them."

His warnings had no effect on Prue, who kept marching up the wooded slope, steadying herself on the trunks of the trees as she hiked.

"And coyotes, Prue!" continued Curtis, scrambling up the incline but stopping at the first tree of the boundary. "They'll tear you apart! There has to be another way to go!"

"There isn't, Curtis," said Prue. "My brother's in here somewhere, and I have to find him."

Curtis was shocked. "You think he's in *here*?" Prue was far enough into the woods now that Curtis could barely make out the red of her scarf through the bramble of trees. Before she disappeared completely from view, Curtis took a deep breath and stepped into the woods. "Okay, Prue! I'll help you find your brother!" he shouted.

Prue stopped and leaned against a fir tree, taking in her verdant sur-roundings. As far as the eye could see, it was green. As many shades of green as Prue could imagine were draped across the landscape: the electric emerald of the ferns and the sallow olive of the drooping lichen and the stately gray-green of the fir branches. The sun was rising higher in the sky, and it streamed through the gaps of the dense wood. She looked back at Curtis, panting up the hill behind her, and kept walking.

"Wow," said Curtis, between gasps for breath, "the kids at school are not going to *believe* this. I mean, no one's ever been in the Impassable Wilderness before. Least I've never heard. This is wild! Look at these trees, they're so . . . so . . . tall!"

"Try to keep it down, Curtis," said Prue finally. "We don't want to alert the whole Wilderness that we're here. Who knows what's out there?"

Curtis stopped and gaped. "You said 'we,' Prue!" he shouted, and then caught himself, repeating in a hoarse whisper, *"You said 'we'!"*

Prue rolled her eyes and turned around, jabbing a finger at Curtis. "Like I have a choice. But if you're going to come along, you've got to stick by me. My brother was lost on my watch, and I'm not about to lose a stupid schoolmate too. Is that clear?"

"Clear as . . . ," Curtis began. He grimaced, remembering Prue's instruction, and whispered the rest: *". . . as crystal!"* He raised his hand to his brow, apparently imitating some kind of specialized salute. He looked like he was tending an eye injury.

They walked in silence for a while; a deep gully in the trees opened up to their left, and they scrambled down the bank to the bottom, skidding on the mossy loam of the forest floor. The small trickle of a creek had cut a wash down the valley of the ravine and no trees grew, only short plumes of fern and shrubs. The walking was easier here, though they occasionally were forced to struggle underneath some of the low fallen trees that crisscrossed the ravine. The sunlight dappled the ground in hazy patterns, and the air felt pure and untouched to Prue's cheeks. As she walked, she wondered at the majesty of the place, her fears subsiding with every step in this incredible wilderness. Birds sang in the looming trees above the ravine, and the underbrush was periodically disturbed by the sudden skitter of a squirrel or a chipmunk. Prue couldn't believe that no one had ever ventured this far into the Impassable Wilderness; she found it a welcoming and serene place, full of life and beauty.

After a time, Prue was pulled from her meditations by the voice of Curtis, whispering, "So what's the plan?"

She paused. "What?"

He whispered louder, "I said, *what's the plan?*"

"You don't have to whisper."

Curtis looked nonplussed. "Oh," he said, in his regular voice, "I thought you said we had to keep our voices down."

"I said to keep it down, but you don't have to whisper." She looked around her and said, "I'm not quite sure what we'd be hiding from anyway."

"Coyotes, maybe?" offered Curtis.

"I think coyotes only come out at night," said Prue.

"Oh, right, I read that somewhere," Curtis said. "Do you think we'll be done before night comes?"

"I hope so."

"Where do you think your brother is?"

The question, simple as it was, made Prue blanch. It was dawning on her that the job of finding Mac might be harder than it had initially seemed. On second thought, had she even considered what she was going to do once she'd made it *into* the Impassable Wilderness? It was one thing to brave the journey but—what now? Improvising, she said, "I don't really know. The birds disappeared around—"

Curtis interrupted her. "Birds? What birds?"

"The birds that kidnapped my brother. Crows, actually. A whole flock of 'em. A *murder*. Did you know that? That a flock of crows is called a murder?"

Curtis's face had dropped. "What do you mean, birds kidnapped your brother?" he stammered. "Like, *birds*?"

Prue flared her eyes and said, "Try to keep up here, Curtis. I have no idea what is going on, but I'm not insane and I have to believe what I saw. So if you're going to come along, you're going to have to believe this stuff too."

"Wow," said Curtis, shaking his head. "Okay, I'm there. I'm with you. Well, how are we going to find out where these birds went?"

"I saw them dive into the woods in the hills above the Railroad

Bridge, and I didn't see them fly back out, so I have to assume they'd be around here somewhere." She studied the world around her: The forest seemed limitless and unchanging, the ravine ascending along the hill as far as the eye could see. The word *hopeless* suddenly sprang to mind. She pushed it away. "I guess we'll just have to keep searching and hope for the best."

"Does he understand English?" asked Curtis.

"What?"

"Your brother. If we called for him, would he answer?"

Prue thought for a moment and said, "Nah. He speaks his own weird language. He babbles pretty loudly, but I'm not sure he'd respond if we started yelling his name."

"Tough," said Curtis, scratching his head. He looked up at Prue sheepishly. "Not to change the subject or anything," he said, "but you didn't happen to bring any food along, did you? I'm kinda hungry."

Prue smiled. "Yeah, I've got some stuff." She sat down on a broken tree limb and swung her messenger bag over her shoulder. "You like gorp?"

Curtis's face brightened. "Oh yeah! I'd *kill* some of that right now."

They sat on the log together and scooped handfuls of the trail mix into their mouths, looking out over the brambly ravine. They talked about school, about their sad, boozy English teacher, Mr. Murphy, who had teared up while reading Captain Cat's opening monologue in *Under Milk Wood.*

"I was out that day," said Curtis. "But I heard about it."

"People were so cruel about it, behind his back," said Prue. "I didn't get it. I mean, it's a really pretty bit, huh?"

"Hmm," said Curtis. "I didn't get that far."

"Curtis, it's like in the first ten pages," snorted Prue, tossing another handful of peanuts into her mouth.

They started talking about their favorite books. Curtis briefly profiled his favorite X-Men mutant, and Prue playfully teased him before admitting a certain envy for Jean Grey's telekinesis.

"So why'd you stop?" asked Curtis after a pause.

"What do you mean?"

"Well, remember, in fifth grade, we used to pass pictures to each other? Of superheroes? You did really good biceps. I totally ripped off your bicep technique." Curtis was shyly looking down into the bag of gorp, fishing through the raisins and peanuts for the M&Ms.

Prue felt castigated. "I don't know, Curtis," she said finally. "I guess I just lost interest in that stuff. I still like drawing, I like drawing a lot. Just different stuff. Getting older, I guess."

"Yeah," said Curtis. "Maybe you're right."

"Botanical drawing, that's sort of my thing now. You should try it."

"Botanical? What, like drawing plants and things?" He was incredulous.

"Yeah."

"I don't know. Maybe I'll try it sometime. Find a leaf to draw." He spoke quietly, almost despondently.

Prue glanced down at the log they were sitting on. A wild tangle of ivy had claimed the territory; scarcely any of the wood's bark could be seen below the green leaves. It looked as if the ivy itself had been the reason for the tree's toppling. "Look at these ivy leaves," she said, trying on the tone of an art teacher. "How the little white lines make designs against the green of the leaf. The more detail you get into, the more fun it gets."

Curtis shrugged. He tugged at one of the vines. It clung to the bark tenaciously, like some obstinate animal. Letting go, he quietly reached back into the bag of gorp for another handful.

Prue tried to lighten the mood. "Hey," she said pointedly. "Stop picking through for the chocolate. That's *so* illegal."

Embarrassed, Curtis smiled and passed the bag back to her.

After they'd finished half the bag, Prue produced her bottle of water and took a slug. She handed it to Curtis, and he took a drink too. The early morning light dimmed as a gray bank of clouds blew in above the trees and covered the sun.

"Let's keep moving," said Prue.

They continued marching up the ravine, grabbing fistfuls of ivy to steady themselves as the ground steepened below them. The creek bed, which seemed like it would carry a lot of water during the winter and spring, was shallow and mostly dry, and they soon found the going easier if they used it as a makeshift trail. The wash flattened out

Prue stopped and leaned against a fir tree,
taking in her verdant surroundings.

at the crest of a hill, and they were again standing in the midst of the trees on a slight plateau.

"I have to pee," said Prue.

"Okay," said Curtis, distractedly staring back down the ravine.

"So go over there," said Prue, pointing to a thicket of bracken, "and don't look."

"Oh!" said Curtis. "Yeah. Okay. I'll give you some privacy."

Prue waited until he was out of sight through the branches, found a spot behind a tree, and squatted. Just as she was finishing she heard an unintelligible rasp coming from the thicket. She quickly buttoned her jeans and cautiously came around the tree; there was no one there.

"Prue!" repeated the rasp. It was Curtis.

"Curtis, I said you didn't have to whisper," she said, relieved it was him.

"C-come here!" Curtis sputtered, still whispering. "And keep *quiet*!"

Prue walked over toward his voice, pushing her way through a tangle of vines. On the other side of the thicket, Curtis was hunched down and staring into the distance.

"Look there!" he whispered, and pointed.

Prue blinked and stared. "What—" she began, before she was interrupted by Curtis.

"Coyotes," said Curtis. "And they're talking."

CHAPTER 5

Denizens of the Wood

The ground fell away from the edge of the thicket at a steep grade, creating a kind of promontory over a small meadow amid the trees. In the middle of the clearing was a gathering of roughly a dozen figures, collected around the remnants of what appeared to be a campfire. From the distance, it was difficult to make out details, but the figures were definitely coyotes: They were covered in a matted gray fur and their haunches were thin. Some prowled around the smoldering campfire on all fours, while others stood on hind legs and sniffed at the air with their long gray snouts. However, there were two rather startling aspects of the scene: One, they all seemed to be wearing matching red uniforms with tall, plumed helmets on their heads, and two, they were definitely talking to one another. In English.

The coyotes spoke in a brittle, yapping timbre, and they punctuated their sentences with snarls and barks, but Prue and Curtis could occasionally make out what they were saying.

"You're pathetic!" shouted one of the larger coyotes, baring his yellow teeth at one of his smaller compatriots. "I request a simple fire and you *idiots* can't get a single ember alight." Some of the animals had what appeared to be sheathed sabers attached to belts around their waists, while others stood leaning against tall, bayonet-topped rifles. This larger coyote rested his paw on the ornate pommel of a long, curved sword.

The coyote to whom this tirade was addressed was skulking in the grass and whinging little yelps in response.

"This platoon is not fit to serve," continued the larger one, "if it cannot complete a simple routine scouting drill." He looked about him at the rest of the group.

Curtis whispered to Prue: "Are they . . . soldiers?"

She nodded slowly, still deeply in shock.

"And look at the filthy condition of your uniforms," howled the larger coyote, who Prue assumed to be a commander of some sort. His dress was marginally cleaner than that of his soldiers, and his shoulders were ornamented with epaulets. He wore a kind of large feathered hat that Prue thought she recognized from a documentary about Napoleon their world history teacher had shown them. The commander continued, "I should bring you before the Dowager Governess in this state and see how she'd receive you." He snapped his jaws at another coyote, who was cowering on the ground behind him. "She'd cast you out of Wildwood, is what she'd do, and we'd see how you fared without your pack." He stiffened and adjusted his sword handle at his side and said, "I have half a mind to do it myself, but I'd rather not soil my hind feet booting you out into the brush."

The coyote at whom the commander had been yelling finally spoke words between his abashed yelps: "Yes, Commandant. Thank you, Commandant."

"And where was your confounded guard detail?" the commander barked, pacing the ground. "I walked up without a single soul batting an eyelash. You are an embarrassment to the corps, a stain on the legacy of every soldiering coyote who's come before you."

"Yes, Commandant," was the response from the cowering coyote.

The commander sniffed the air and said, "It'll be dark soon. Let's finish this drill and head back to camp. You, and you!" Here he pointed at two of the soldiers who were standing at attention by the campfire. "Get into the brush and start collecting firewood.

I'll get this fire started if I have to throw one of you into the pit for kindling!"

The group burst into activity with this command. Curtis and Prue eased themselves flat to the ground and froze under the fronds of a particularly large stand of ferns. A few coyotes began circling out from the group in search of firewood while others stood in formation in the center of the meadow and continued to be berated by the commander.

"What do we do if they see us?" hissed Curtis as a few of the coyotes walked closer to them.

"Just keep quiet," whispered Prue. Her heart was racing in her chest.

Two of the coyotes wandered over to a pile of scrub right below Curtis and Prue's perch and began collecting branches of deadfall in their spindly arms. They were snapping at each other while they worked, and Prue held her breath as she listened to their canine bickering.

"It's your fault we're in this mess, Dmitri," said one coyote to the other. "My usual detail is never this incompetent. It's embarrassing."

The other, bent down among the branches, said, "Oh, shut up, Vlad. You were the one who insisted everyone 'mark the territory' everywhere. Never seen so much pee in one place. No wonder the stupid fire wouldn't start."

Vlad waved a birch branch in Dmitri's face, his eyes wide in anger. "That's—that's the *blasted* protocol! Check your field manual. Or can you even read?"

Dmitri dropped his load of firewood and bared his teeth. The coyotes were close enough now that Prue could see his lips snarl back to reveal a frightful set of chipped yellow teeth emerging from his bright red gums. "I'll show you protocol!" shouted Dmitri. They both stood silent for a moment until Vlad spoke up.

"What is that supposed to mean?" asked Vlad.

Dmitri barked sharply and leapt at his compatriot's throat, his teeth flashing.

Through the mossy ground cover, Curtis crept his hand along until it met Prue's, and he squeezed her fingers. She squeezed back, not daring to take her eyes off the battling coyotes. The two soldiers had fallen to the ground and were thrashing about in a desperate whirl of motion, their jaws locked on to each other's throats. Their pained and angered yips caught the immediate attention of the rest of the platoon, and the commander roared as he ran over to the tangle of the two soldiers. He had drawn his saber from its sheath, and when he arrived at the warring coyotes, he grabbed the first one he could get his hands on—Vlad—and yanked him from the scrum, his blade's edge at Vlad's throat.

"I'll have your heads on tree branches!" swore the Commandant. "I'll see you strung limb from limb, so help me God." He threw his captive to the ground and swiveled, swinging his sword point so that it was a mere hairbreadth from Dmitri's muzzle. He spoke more slowly. "And you, you raggedy, snot-snouted, pathetic excuse for a coyote: I'm prepared to end this right here, right now." Dmitri whimpered at the point of the blade, and the commander brought the sword up to swinging height. From above, Curtis gaped and Prue buried her head in her hands to avoid witnessing the gruesome scene to come.

Suddenly a breeze picked up and whispered down through the trees, traveling over Prue and Curtis's bodies from their feet to their neck, out over the promontory and down into the meadow below.

The violent scene playing out below them froze into stillness as each of the coyotes' ears flinched and their snouts sniffed the air. The commander huffed, his saber motionless above his head in mid-swing. Dmitri, his sentence temporarily commuted, let out a rush of breath and looked around him. Prue lifted her head from her hands. Slowly, the Commandant lifted his nose and took a deep, lingering inhalation.

"HUMANS!" the Commandant shouted, breaking the silence and swinging his sword to point at the stand of ferns above them. "IN THE TREES!"

In an eruption of action, several soldiers who had been flanking the Commandant broke away and started clambering up the embankment toward Prue and Curtis.

"RUN!" shouted Curtis, pushing himself up from the ground. Prue scrambled to her feet and dove out of the bushes, away from the embankment. The coyotes were baying frantically behind her as they crested the lip of the plateau and tore through the ferns. She sprinted back through the trees until she arrived at the ravine they'd been following. She took one wild step over the edge, caught a foot on a tangle of briar, and was thrown headlong into the gully.

Curtis had plowed in a different direction, choosing instead to make his way up the hillside in the direction they had been walk-ing. The grade was steep and unrelenting in this densely wooded area, and the birch branches and blackberry vines thrashed at his face and arms, hampering his scrabbling sprint. The coyotes, accustomed to the terrain, raced through the underbrush on all fours, and Curtis had barely made it ten yards from the embankment before the first coyote lunged on his back and brought him to the ground.

"You're mine!" hissed the coyote, and Curtis's arms and legs were pulled taut and pinned to the ground as more soldiers arrived at the scene of his capture.

"C-Curtis?" Prue mumbled, gaining her bearings. It was clear she'd been knocked momentarily unconscious; she found herself lying facedown in the bracken of the ravine with a splitting headache and the metallic taste of blood in her mouth. She heard a distant howling and was jolted into her present circumstance. Staying close to the ground, she dragged herself through the underbrush and peeked over the lip of the ravine. Apparently, the soldiers had not seen her headfirst vault into the gully and had chosen to take down Curtis instead. From her vantage, she could see the soldiers hauling Curtis to his feet. She watched the Commandant slowly approach, grab Curtis by the scruff of his coat, and shove his muzzle into either side of Curtis's throat, sniffing. She could see the fear in Curtis's eyes. He was surrounded by a group of coyote grunts who were skulking around his feet on all fours, whining and snapping. The Commandant barked a series of orders, and their captive was bound by rope and thrown over the back of one of the larger coyotes, and the party disappeared into the woods.

Prue fought the urge to cry; she could feel the sobs coming from the pit of her stomach, and her eyes started to well with tears. Her fingers clenched around a tussock of grass and squeezed as she willed her mind to quiet. She felt with her tongue the spot on her lip where there was a small bulb of blood and licked it clean. The air was still and the light was flat as the early afternoon sun began to dim. She thought about the note she'd left for her parents that morning. *Back later*, it had said. Despite the gravity of the situation, she couldn't help but stifle a laugh. She pulled herself up from the ground and sat on the edge of the ravine, dusting the stain of dirt from the knees of her jeans. A squirrel popped its head from behind a rotted tree stump and looked at her quizzically.

"What do you want, squirrel?" she jeered. She laughed to herself and said, "I suppose I should watch what I say. You probably talk too. Do you?"

The squirrel said nothing.

"Great, that's actually a bit of a relief," she said, propping her chin in her hands. "Though you might just be the quiet type."

She scanned her surroundings and then looked back at the squirrel, which had cocked its head to the side, studying her. "So what do I do now?" asked Prue. "My brother was kidnapped by birds. My friend was captured by coyotes." She snapped her fingers. "And I nearly forgot: My bike is broken. Sounds like a country song. If country songs were really, really weird."

The squirrel suddenly straightened and froze, its ears twitching. Beneath the hush of the breeze in the tree branches came an unexpected sound: the putter of a car engine. As it grew louder, the squirrel dove from its perch and disappeared. Prue jumped up and started running toward the sound, fighting her way through the fallen tree branches and brush. "Stop!" she shouted as the sound seemed to grow louder. The woods were particularly dense here and the hillside steep, and Prue's run became more of a desperate stagger as she tried to reach the sound. A hedgerow of blackberry brambles bloomed in front of her and she dove into them, feeling the thorns tear at her coat and hair. Her eyes closed, she fought through the bushes, flailing at the stinging branches until suddenly she was released from their clutches and she fell forward onto the first level, empty ground she'd seen since entering the woods. She looked up to find she had fallen onto what appeared to be a *road*. And quickly approaching along this road was what appeared to be a *van*. Prue leapt up and waved her arms frantically, and the driver slammed on the brakes, the vehicle's tires skidding in the dirt of the road.

It was a bright red cargo van, and it looked like it had seen better days. It was of an indeterminate age, though the amount of rust and scraped paint on the sides suggested it had seen its fair share of punishment. The side of the van was emblazoned with a strange crest that Prue did not recognize.

As she stared in disbelief at this mysterious vehicle, she heard the distinctive *click* of a shotgun being cocked. She looked to see the driver's-side window being hastily rolled down, and a grizzled, balding head emerged, eyes squinting down the sight of a massive double-barreled rifle that looked to be of Civil War vintage.

"Make one move, missy, and I'll fill you full of holes," said the driver.

Prue threw her hands into the air.

The driver cautiously lowered the rifle and gaped at Prue.

"Are you . . . ," spluttered the driver, "are you an *Outsider*?"

Prue wasn't quite sure how to respond; the question was bizarre. She stared blankly for a moment before hazarding a response: "I live in St. Johns, in Portland."

The shotgun was now lowered at a much less threatening angle, and Prue's pounding blood relaxed in her chest. "Is that what you call it?" asked the man in the van.

"I guess so," responded Prue.

The man continued to gape at Prue. "Incredible," he said. "Just incredible. In all my years, I never in my life thought I'd ever run into one of *you*. From the *Outside*."

Now that the shotgun was no longer at his eye, Prue had a better view of the driver. He was an elderly man—his skin was pale and weathered and two great plumes of wiry hair were his eyebrows—but there was something Prue couldn't put her finger on that seemed to exude from him, something that made him seem like no one she'd ever met before. It was a kind of aura or shine, like the way a familiar landscape is transformed in the light of a full moon.

Prue summoned her courage and spoke. "Sir, can I put my hands down?" When he nodded consent, she dropped her hands to her sides and continued, "I'm in a little bit of a jam. My little brother, Mac, was kidnapped yesterday by a flock of birds—crows, actually—and brought somewhere in these woods. On top of this, my classmate Curtis stupidly followed me into the woods, and we were attacked by what I think were coyote soldiers. I managed to escape, but he was captured. I'm really tired and a little confused by all that's happened today, and if you wouldn't mind helping me, I'd really, really appreciate it."

The speech seemed to render the man at a loss for words. He pulled the shotgun back into the cab of the van and looked behind him, down the road. Then he looked back at Prue and said, "Okay, get in the van."

Prue walked around to the side of the van, and the driver opened it from the inside. She climbed into the cab and extended her hand to the man, saying, "My name's Prue."

"Richard," said the man, shaking her hand. "Pleasure to make your acquaintance." He turned the key in the ignition, and the van grumpily sputtered to life. Behind the cab was a metal gate leading into the cargo area. Through the gate Prue could see piles of manila-colored boxes and crates teeming with neatly tied stacks of envelopes.

"Wait," said Prue. "You're a . . . mailman?"

"Postmaster general, miss, at your service," said Richard. He wore a tattered uniform: a royal-blue blazer with dirty yellow piping. A patch on his chest sported the same emblem as Prue had seen on the side of the truck. His chin bristled with a week's worth of white, unshaved stubble, and his face was etched with wrinkles.

"Okay," said Prue, assessing the situation. "Well, it'll have to do.

Now: My friend Curtis was taken just back there. They can't have gotten far. Between you and me and that shotgun of yours, I figure we can probably devise some sort of plan . . . where are you going?"

Richard had gunned the van, and it lurched forward, moving bumpily along the uneven road. He had to shout his response over the roar of the engine: "No way we're going back there," he hollered. "It's way too dangerous."

Prue's eyes widened. "But—sir! I have to help him! He's on his own out there!"

"I've never seen these coyote soldiers you're talking about, but I've heard about 'em, and believe me, your friend is beyond help at this point. No sense in us getting killed as well over it. No, best we get back to South Wood and report this to the Governor-Regent."

"The *what*?" stammered Prue, and then, before waiting for Richard to respond, "Listen: Those coyotes might look scary, but they've only got swords and old-looking rifles. You've got a really big gun. With you waving that shotgun around, I'm sure we could get in and out of there without a scratch."

"I've got a job to do," said Richard, gesturing to the piles of mail in the cargo hold. "And I'm not about to jeopardize it over some boyo who gets himself nabbed by coyotes. This is Wildwood, kid, and I can't afford to stop for anything. You're lucky you jumped in my way. Otherwise, I'd have left you on the side of the road."

"Fine," said Prue, and she started fumbling at her side for the door handle. "I'd like to be let out, please. I'm going to save him myself."

Before she could swing the door open, Richard shot his hand across her lap and held the door closed, the van swerving nearly into the roadside ditch. A single wheel hopped over a stray tree branch, and Richard yelled, "Don't go out there if you value your life—I ain't joking around!" Prue retracted her hand and crossed her arms over her chest grumpily.

"Listen to me," said Richard calmly. "This is no place for a young girl to be out alone. And an *Outsider* one at that. Those animals will catch your scent from a mile away. I don't know how you got this far on your own but I can tell you, your luck wouldn't likely last much longer. If the coyotes didn't get you, the bandits who camp in these parts would. In the cab of this van is the safest place you could be right now. I've got to take you straight to the Governor-Regent. It's protocol."

"Who is the Governor-Regent?" asked Prue. "And why does everyone keep calling this place Wildwood? I heard the coyotes say that too."

Richard pulled a half-chewed cigar from the ashtray and put it between his teeth, leaning out the window to spit a few flecks of tobacco onto the road. "The Governor-Regent," he said, talking around the stogie in his mouth, "is the leader of South Wood. His name is Lars Svik." He suddenly lowered his voice. "Though, between you and me, he's got enough snakes around him hissing advice into his ears to populate a sultan's salon." He glanced at Prue. "Figurative snakes, that is. Bureaucrats and the like.

"Wildwood," Richard continued, "is the uncivilized country." Using the dashboard as a map, he traced his finger along the vinyl. "It stretches from the northernmost border of the Avian Principality all the way to the border of North Wood. I found you about halfway in the middle of nowhere, right smack in the center of Wildwood where there ain't nothing but wolves and coyotes and thieves living off what they can scavenge from the ground or loot from the occasional passing supply truck. Or mail truck—which is why I carry that piece of iron down there." He pointed at the shotgun. "Being the postmaster general, it's my job to deliver mail and supplies and whatnot from the folks in South Wood to the country folk in North Wood and vice versa, and I do that by driving this blasted road— it's called the Long Road, which is a no-brainer of a name—back and forth between the two places, braving this madness and putting my life and limb at great risk every week. And I tell you one thing, Port-Land Prue, being a state employee is not a pathway to wealth and riches."

"You can just call me Prue," was all she could think to say. She was dumbstruck by Richard's monologue. She had so many questions swirling around her head, begging to be asked, she was barely able to sort them out. "So there are other people. Living here. In these woods. Where I come from, this place is called the Impassable Wilderness."

This made Richard laugh so hard his cigar flew out of his mouth, and he had to fumble around at his feet to find it again. "Impassable Wilderness? Oh boy, would that it were. I might have a little more time at home. Nah, I don't know who told you that, but you Outside folk have got it all wrong. 'Course, you're the first of your kind I've ever seen here, so it stands to reason that no one ever made an effort to find out about the Wood—Wild, North, or South." He looked at Prue and smiled. "Seems like you just might be our first pioneer, Port-Land Prue."

The Warren of the Dowager;
A Kingdom of Birds

The ropes stung Curtis's wrists, and his chest ached from being bounced against the coyote's bony spine. The pack moved quickly through the forest, undaunted by each sword fern and low-hanging tree branch that lashed at Curtis's face. The forest floor was a blur below the feet of his coyote captor, but Curtis kept his eyes open, trying to register any change in the environment that might allow him to retrace their tracks. This endeavor seemed hopeless until the pack broke through a particularly dense patch of brush onto what appeared to be a wide dirt road. The coyotes picked up speed here over the level ground, and Curtis looked sideways at the oncoming terrain. The pack was approaching what appeared to be a very large wooden bridge. They hit the bridge at breakneck speed, and Curtis gave a little yelp as he looked down over the edge, through the ornate railings of the bridge: A massive chasm yawned below them, stretching downward into blackness. Just as quickly as they'd arrived at the bridge, they made the other side and scrambled back off the road and into the trees. Curtis strained to see behind him, to catch another sight of this awesome gap they'd crossed, but the towering firs swallowed up the landscape, and he returned to staring down at the forest floor.

He wasn't sure how long they'd traveled, but the afternoon was waning when finally the pack emerged into a wide glade in the woods. In the center of the glade was a small hill, covered in ivy and deadfall, where a man-sized hole had been burrowed into the earth. Without a word, the party hustled through the hole and began following a long, dark tunnel down into the ground. Twines of ivy and tree roots supported the roof of the tunnel as it descended, and here and there, burning torches affixed to the dirt walls provided a hazy light. The unmistakable smell of wet dog was everywhere, though Curtis thought he smelled something like cooked food and gunpowder as well. Finally, the tunnel opened into a massive chamber bustling with activity. He was in the coyotes' warren.

A group of soldiers in the center of the room made a tight phalanx

and were being commanded in a drill by a menacing sergeant. A host of aproned coyotes were preparing a dinner in a black iron cauldron resting on a raging fire, where a line of eager soldiers waited patiently with tin plates extended in their paws. A crude stone chimney carried the smoke from the fire upward into the central trunk of a giant tree, whose roots provided the structural bones for the room. The winding root tendrils of the gargantuan tree framed the openings to a myriad of grottos and tunnels leading off this main room. The walls were lined with wooden racks where rested a massive arsenal of weapons: rifles, halberds, and sabers. Upended crates, their packing hay spilling out, littered a corner of the room, and a small troop of soldiers was busily checking their contents. Ancient-looking muskets were being inspected; sacks of gunpowder were unloaded and safely stowed in a nearby hollow.

A line of tattered banners on pikes led to a large, circular door at the far end of the room, made of a single wide slice of a giant cedar tree. In front of the door stood two rifle-bearing coyotes. It was to this doorway that Curtis was finally dragged, his bound wrists freed with a *swik* of the Commandant's sword.

"Hold him fast," ordered the commander as he stepped forward and spoke to the guards in front of the door. Two coyotes wrangled Curtis to his feet, holding his arms in their clammy paws. One of the door guards nodded to the Commandant and heaved the door open, disappearing within. After a short time, the guard returned and gestured for the commander and his prisoner to enter. Curtis was shoved forward, and he stepped over the threshold into the room.

The light was very dim inside, the only visible sources being a few flickering braziers and what little light was allowed inside via several crude skylights dug into the ceiling leading to the ground above. Dark woody roots snaked across the ceiling and walls; the white tendrils of plant roots dangled above their heads, and the room smelled distinctly of onions. At the far end of the chamber was an elaborate dais, decorated with long vines of ivy and plush cushions of gathered moss. In the center of the dais was a chair unlike any Curtis had seen before: Seemingly hand carved from a single massive tree trunk, it looked as if it had grown from the earth itself. The armrests snaked around the cushioned seat and were capped by carved talons; the legs were clawed at the bottom with what looked to be coyote paws. The seat back towered over the room, and the two posts on either side of the back rose to meet at the top, where the wood had been carved into the ominous shape of a single spiked crown. Curtis stared in wonder at the scene until he heard a voice behind him ask:

"What do you think?" It was a woman's voice, and Curtis found himself soothed by its sonorous music. "A marvel of craftsmanship, yes? I had it made especially for the room. Took *ages.*"

Curtis turned and clapped eyes on the most beautiful woman he'd ever seen in his life. Her face was ovoid and pale, though her lips shone red like the freshest late summer apples. Her hair was an electric copper-red and it hung in braided tresses, brocaded with mottled eagle feathers. She wore a simple floor-length gown of tawny leather, and a heavy stole was draped over her shoulders. She was discernibly human, yet she struck Curtis as being entirely otherworldly, as if she'd been pulled from the face of some cathedral's faded, ancient fresco. She towered over her court of coyotes, and they scurried in her wake as she moved toward Curtis.

"It's very nice," he said.

"We've done our best here," she continued, waving at her surroundings. "It was difficult at first to gather the basic comforts—those *creature* comforts—but we managed. It's miraculous, really, considering that we started from nothing." She smiled in thought and let her slender hand caress Curtis's cheek. "An Outsider," she said thoughtfully. "An Outsider child. How beautiful you are. What's your name, child?"

"C-Curtis, ma'am," he stammered. He'd never called anyone *ma'am* before. It just seemed appropriate now.

"Curtis," said the woman, retracting her hand, "welcome to our warren. My name is Alexandra, though most call me the Dowager Governess." She stepped up to the dais and draped herself over the seat of the throne. "Are you hungry? Thirsty? You must have traveled far today. Our stores are meager, but you are welcome to whatever we can offer."

"Sure," said Curtis. "I am pretty thirsty."

"Borya! Carpus!" she said loudly as she snapped her fingers at two loitering coyotes. "A bottle of blackberry wine for our guest. And greens! Dandelion and fern fiddles. And a bowl of the venison stew for the Outsider child Curtis! Quickly!" She flashed a broad smile at Curtis and gestured at the pile of freshly gathered moss that surrounded the throne. "Please, have a seat," she said.

Curtis, surprised to be treated with such hospitality, settled himself into the deep cushion of the moss.

"We're simple folk, Curtis," began the Governess. "We protect our own, and we ask little of the forest. You might call us the wardens of Wildwood. We've made this untamed wilderness our own and imposed an order on it that it was sorely lacking. Our intent is to cultivate a beautiful flower from this stark and infertile ground. For example, when I arrived here in Wildwood, these coyotes you see were a hardscrabble, desperate lot. Practically anarchistic in their organization, they were constantly at war with one another and reduced to the lowest form of forest dweller: the scavenger. But I brought them to order."

A coyote attendant appeared at the door and made his way to Curtis, carrying a wide tin plate heaped with fresh greens, a bowl of stew, and a wooden mug of a dark purple liquid. He set it in front of Curtis. The attendant then produced a corked bottle from underneath his arm and placed it next to the tray. The Governess nodded, and the coyote bowed deeply and walked from the room.

"Please, eat," said the Dowager Governess, and Curtis dove into the food, slurping down the venison stew with relish. He took a healthy gulp from the wooden mug, and his face flushed as the warm liquid rolled down the back of his throat.

The Governess was watching him intently. "You remind me of a boy I knew," she said thoughtfully. "He must've been not much older than you. How old are you, Curtis?"

"I'll be twelve in November," said Curtis between bites.

"Twelve," she repeated. "He was just a few years older, this boy. His birthday would've been in July. He was born in the full throat of summer." Her eyes trailed off to stare at some fixed point over Curtis's shoulder. Curtis paused in his chewing and looked behind him; there was nothing there.

The Governess smiled and, remembering herself, looked back at Curtis. "How is the food?" she asked.

He had a mouth full of greens, and he had to quickly swallow them to answer. He pulled an errant fiddlehead from between his teeth and set it down on the plate. "Oh, very good," he responded finally. "Though these ferns are a little weird. I didn't know you could eat them." He dipped his spoon back into the hearty stew and brought it, full, to his mouth.

The Governess laughed and then, turning serious, said, "But Curtis, I'm very curious as to what brought you into these woods. You Outside folk haven't thought to visit for such a long, long time."

Curtis paused mid-slurp, set his spoon down, and swallowed. It hadn't occurred to him in the chaos of his capture what explanation he should give for his presence in the woods. He decided it would be best not to give away Prue's mission until he had a better sense of the Governess's intentions. "I was just out walking, actually, and I wandered into the trees. I got lost, and that's when your . . . your coyotes found me." He could only hope that the soldiers hadn't seen Prue.

"Just out walking?" asked the Governess, arching an eyebrow.

"Yeah," said Curtis. "I'll be totally honest with you: I was skipping school. I was skipping school and thought I'd go on a little adventure. You're not going to report me to the principal, are you?"

Alexandra threw her head back and laughed. "Oh no, dear Curtis," she said between fits, "I'd never report you. Then I wouldn't have the pleasure of your company!" She reached down and picked up the bottle of wine. Pulling the cork from the top, she poured more of the dusky liquid into Curtis's cup. "Please, drink more. You must be so parched."

"Thank you, Miss Dowag——" He fumbled over her title and corrected himself: "Alexandra, ma'am. I will have a little more. It's really good." It was sweet and strong, and when he drank it, he felt his stomach radiate warmth to the rest of his body. He took another large swig. "I've never really drunk wine before—I mean, I've had a little Manischewitz at Passover, but it's nothing like this." He took another drink.

"So you were out walking. In these woods," repeated the Governess.

Curtis swallowed the wine and picked up a pile of dandelion greens and shoved it in his mouth. He nodded.

"But Curtis, my dear," said Alexandra. "That is simply not possible."

Curtis munched his greens and stared at the Governess.

"Literally impossible," she said, turning serious. "You see, Outsider child Curtis, there is a thing called Woods Magic that protects this wood from the curiosity of the outside world. It is the thing that separates our kind from yours. Every being in this forest has the Woods Magic running through their veins. If one of your kind, an Outsider, was to find his way into these woods—I think you charmingly refer to it as the 'Impassable Wilderness'—they would find themselves immediately and irretrievably caught in the Periphery Bind, a maze in which every turn is a dead end. The forest becomes like a hall of mirrors, its image repeated in illusion into the horizon, you see, and at every turn one would find oneself exactly where one had started. If you were lucky, the woods would spit you out somewhere back to the outside world, though it is just as likely that you would forever be lost, wandering the forest's infinite reflection until you either died or went mad."

Curtis slowly finished crunching the dandelion greens and swallowed them with a loud gulp.

"No, my sweet Curtis," the Governess said, thoughtfully toying with one of the eagle feathers pinned in her hair, "the only way you would have been able to cross the border and travel in these woods would be if you were born of the Magic yourself."

Curtis stared at the Governess, a chill running up his spine.

"Or," she continued, "if you were *accompanied* by someone of Woods Magic."

The Dowager Governess looked directly into Curtis's eyes, the steel blue of her irises flashing in the light of the flickering fires, and smiled.

☙

The sun was setting, and Prue grew sleepy as the mail van trundled bumpily down the Long Road, occasionally swerving to avoid the felled tree branches and muddy potholes that littered the road. The conversation quieted, and Richard had stubbed his cigar in the ashtray and was whistling to himself. Prue rested her head against the door and stared out the window, watching the woods change from a knot of dense scrub and gaunt trees to wide groves of massive, ancient cedar and fir trees, their wizened limbs reaching out over the road.

"The Old Woods," said Richard as they passed under the canopy of the giant trees. "We're getting closer."

Prue smiled and nodded at Richard, and a great wave of tiredness overcame her, and she felt herself drifting off to sleep, the rattle of the van lulling her into a deep slumber. She woke suddenly when she felt the van shudder to a stop. It was dark now, and she didn't know how long she'd slept. In the crooked light projected from the van's headlights, Prue thought she saw birds, though her vision was too foggy from sleep to be sure. Richard heaved the emergency brake with both hands and let the van idle as he turned to Prue and said, "Checkpoint. You might have to get out of the van." He pushed open his door and stepped outside onto the road.

Prue rubbed her eyes clear and squinted through the dirty windshield. A strange flickering was occurring just outside the edge of the headlights, and she strained to make sense of it when suddenly a pair of scaly talons alighted on the hood in front of her. She shrieked with surprise and fell back in her seat. A gigantic golden eagle (*Aquila chrysaetos*—she recognized it immediately from *The Sibley Guide*) craned his head down and looked curiously into the cab of the van. Abruptly, the headlight glare behind him was teeming with birds of every feather: thrushes, herons, eagles, and owls, some flying in and out of the headlights, some landing on the ground, some scrambling for a grip with their claws on the van's hood. Prue pushed herself farther back into the seat as the eagle on the hood continued his probe of the cab. Richard appeared in the midst of the squall, making his way into the shine of the headlights. He was brandishing a small book, opened and held at arm's length. The eagle on the van's hood turned from the windshield and hopped into the air to land on a branch in front of Richard, his powerful wings fanning in quick, mighty beats.

"You'll find it's all in order, General," said Richard to the eagle, who was intently studying the booklet in Richard's hand. Satisfied, he flew back to his former perch on the hood of the van. He upset a flurry of nuthatches as he landed and turned his steely eyes again to Prue.

"And who is your companion, Postmaster?" asked the eagle.

Richard smiled and laughed. "Well, I was going to get to that, sir," he said, walking to the driver's-side window. He tapped at the glass and gestured for Prue to get out. "An Outsider child, sir. A girl. I found her on the road."

Prue opened her door and stepped out onto the gravel. She was immediately met by a host of smaller birds, finches and jays, who flew around her head and shoulders in frantic circles, skimming her hair and picking at her peacoat.

"An Outsider?" asked the eagle, incredulous. He flew to the other side of the van and, landing, let out a loud *squawk* that sent the smaller birds flying into the trees. He looked intently at Prue and said, "Incredible. How did you find your way, girl?"

"I . . . walked," responded Prue, aghast. She'd never been so close to an eagle before. It was stunning.

"You *walked*?" asked the eagle. "Ridiculous. What's your business in Wildwood?"

Prue was speechless. The eagle craned his head forward until his beak was inches from her face.

"She's looking for her brother," interjected Richard. "And her friend, come to think of it."

81

"The Outsider girl can answer for herself!" squawked the eagle, not taking his eyes off Prue.

"It's t-true," stammered Prue finally. "My brother, Mac. He was taken by crows and, as far as I can tell, taken somewhere in these woods. So I came here to find him. And on the way, I was followed by my friend Curtis, and he was captured by a group of coyotes."

The eagle stared at Prue in silence for a moment. "Crows, you say," he said. "And coyotes." He cast a meaningful look at his fellow birds and shuffled his talons along the hood of the van.

"Right," said Prue, gathering her courage. "Any help in finding Mac and Curtis would be much appreciated. Sir."

Evidently satisfied, the eagle ruffled his feathers and looked behind him at Richard. "Where were you planning on taking her, Postmaster?"

"To the Governor-Regent," answered Richard. "That's the best option I could think of."

The eagle snorted and looked back at Prue. "The Governor-Regent," repeated the eagle, an acid tone creeping into his voice. "I'm sure he'll be very helpful. I hope you're not in too much of a hurry to find your brother and your friend, Outsider. If I recall correctly, Request for Aid in Search of Human Abduction by Crow is a standard H1 sub 6 slash 45E document, to be signed in triplicate by all reigning Metro Commissioners."

The flurry of birds surrounding the eagle began to titter with laughter. Prue didn't get the joke. Richard smiled nervously and said, "I'm sure he'll be very sympathetic, General. Unless you have a better idea."

"No, no," said the eagle, "I suppose that is the best tack. Besides, her story, if it is true, may lend credence to our plea when the Crown Prince visits South Wood."

"The Crown Prince," said Richard, in surprise. "In South Wood?"

"Himself," replied the eagle. "The birds are sick of waiting for your commissioners to act while the safety of the Principality is at risk. Our ambassadors have been ignored, if not altogether shunned; our entreaties for aid and alliance brushed off. If the Crown Prince can't achieve results, then it is one eagle's humble opinion that the Wildwood Protocols be considered null and void. There is a gathering storm in Wildwood. I have seen it. We can't sit back any longer and wait for these barbarians to overrun us."

"Understood, General," said Richard. "Now if I'm cleared to go . . ." He gestured at the van. "I have a lot of mail to deliver."

The General raised his wings to their full span and pushed himself aloft from the van's hood. With only a few robust wing beats he was in the air, alighting on a tree limb overhead. "Yes, Postmaster," said the eagle, "you are free to go. Let other Long Road couriers know, however: We will continue to detain travelers on the road until the safety of the Principality is assured." The rest of the birds circled in the air above the van before disappearing into the dark of the tree line. "And you, Outsider girl," continued the eagle, "to you I say good luck. I hope you find what you've lost." With that, the eagle unfurled his wings and vanished into the trees, producing a gust of wind that shook the branches and rustled the leaves.

After the birds were gone, Richard smiled at Prue from across the van and mimed a relieved wipe of his forehead. "Well!" he said, opening the driver's-side door and climbing in. "That checkpoint is getting more challenging every day. Get in. Let's get going before they change their minds."

Prue, a little stunned, returned to the passenger seat. Richard revved the van's engine and started driving, arduously grinding the gears into place.

"What was that all about?" asked Prue.

"Oh, it's complicated, Port-Land Prue," said Richard. "We're passing through the Avian Principality, a kingdom of birds. It's a sovereign country between South Wood and Wildwood; they've been pressuring the Governor-Regent to allow them to move into Wildwood to defend themselves against attacks that have been made on their borders."

"What's stopping them? Why do they need the Governor-Regent's permission?" asked Prue.

"What he said: a thing called the Wildwood Protocols, which basically states that any signatory of the treaty is forbidden from expanding into Wildwood—and that includes military excursions,"

Richard explained. "Which is ridiculous, if you think on it. Why anyone would want to move into Wildwood is beyond me. The place is wild. Overgrown. Treacherous. Unruly. You couldn't pay your citizens to try and settle in that place."

"But who is attacking the birds? Obviously, somebody's living in Wildwood."

"They've been claiming that troops of coyotes, probably the same as your coyote soldiers, have been attacking bird sentries along the border. They believe that these coyotes—typically a disorderly lot—are under the leadership of the deposed Dowager Governess, the former leader of South Wood." He chuckled under his breath, as if the story were some inside joke. "Crazy birds."

Prue turned to him, saying, "Wait; who?"

"The Dowager Governess. She was the wife of the late Governor-Regent Grigor Svik. Came to power after his death. Terrible ruler. She was removed from the seat about fifteen years ago and exiled to Wildwood like a common criminal. Gone. Out of the picture."

"Richard!" said Prue, her face alight. "The coyotes! They mentioned her name!"

"Whose, the Dowager Governess's?" asked Richard. He stared at her.

"Yes!" said Prue. "When Curtis and I first came on the coyotes, they were arguing. One of them threatened to turn the other over to the Dowager Governess. I'm certain of it."

"Can't be," Richard said. "There's no way that woman survived. Dropped into the middle of Wildwood. With naught but the clothes on her back."

Prue smarted at Richard's disbelief. "I swear to you, Richard," she said, "one of the coyotes said he was going to report another to the Dowager Governess. I heard it very clearly. And I don't even know what that title means."

Richard swallowed hard. "Well, Governess—she was the female heir to the seat of governorship. And Dowager—that means she was made a widow. When her husband died, see." He let out a low whistle between his lips. "Hoo, boy. If she's alive—and putting together an army, no less—I gotta think that bodes ill for Governor-Regent Svik and the folks of South Wood. I'm sure the Governor-Regent will want to hear your story. So far, no one's come forward to give witness to what the birds are claiming. He's not buying it from the birds alone." Richard pulled another cigar from his jacket pocket and began chewing on the end thoughtfully.

"Maybe the Governor-Regent can help me after all," said Prue. "I mean, if this Governess woman is really a threat to his country, he'll have to help me get Curtis back! And then, who knows; maybe she can lead us to Mac." She put her forehead in her hand. "I can't believe I'm saying this stuff. I can't believe I'm here, in this weird world. In this mail van. Contemplating talking birds and a Dowery Governess."

"Dowager," corrected Richard.

"Right. And her army of coyotes." Prue looked imploringly at Richard, the only friendly face she'd seen since arriving in this strange land. A flood of emotion overcame her. "What am I doing here?" she asked weakly.

"I suppose," responded Richard, "things tend to happen for a reason. I have a suspicion that you being here ain't an accident. I tend to think you're here for a reason, Port-Land Prue." He spit a wad of tobacco out the window. "I just don't think we know what that reason is yet."

CHAPTER 7

An Evening's Entertainment;
A Long Journey Ended;
Going for a Soldier

Despite the fact that it was now nightfall and he was as far away from his parents as he'd ever been, deep in an underground coyote warren and the captive of an army of talking animals and their strange and mysterious leader, Curtis was feeling pretty good. He'd had seconds of the venison stew, which he'd found to be incredibly tasty, and he'd lost track of how many times his mug of blackberry wine, which he found to be equally wonderful, had been refilled. His present circumstances, he reasoned, would seem pretty strange and frightening if he were to look at them in the cool light of day, but there, in the warm confines of the earthy burrow with the braziers burning and the moss below him so comfortable, everything looked particularly rosy. He was captivated by his host, the most beautiful woman he'd ever met, and fancied that with every refill of his mug, he grew more charming and charismatic himself. He was regaling her with the true story of how he and a classmate had broken an entire row of fluorescent lights while pounding nickels flat on an anvil in metal shop. He had struck one nickel at a bad angle, and it had shot up like a bullet and "blew out the whole light! BOOOOSH! And, like, everyone was going 'WHAAAAT?'" He paused for effect while Alexandra laughed heartily. She motioned to an attendant to refill his mug of wine. "And I just walked over to the . . . oh, sure, I'll have a little more . . . over to all the broken glass and just picked up the nickel and was all like, 'I'll be keeping this, *thank you very much.*'" He laughed and mimicked slipping the nickel into his jeans pocket. He slurped down more of the wine, spilling some on his coat. "Oh boy, that'll leave a stain!" He laughed so hard he had to set the mug down and collect himself.

The Governess was laughing with him as well, though her laugh trailed off as she began speaking. "Oh, Curtis, how *charming*. How *excellent*. You are truly one of a kind. No *wonder* you braved these woods alone. You are a singularly independent spirit, aren't you?"

"Oh, well, yeah," said Curtis, attempting sobriety. "I . . . well, I was always kind of a loner, I guess. Kept to myself, you know. But that's sort of how I, um, roll. You know, looking out for number one. *Et cetera, et cetera.*" He sipped at his mug. "But I'm good in a team, too. Really. I mean if you're ever in need of a partner, I'm your man. Prue didn't believe me at first, but we made a pretty good team for a bit—we were, like, real partners."

"Who?"

"Who? Did I say someone's name? Prue? I think I said, *who*, as in: 'Who wouldn't believe me?'" Curtis turned pale. "Wow. This stuff is really strong." He fanned himself with his hand and set his mug down.

"Prue. You said the name Prue," said the Governess, her face growing serious. "So maybe you weren't alone after all in your little foray into the woods."

Curtis clasped his hands between his knees and breathed deeply, exhaling loudly. The wine had had an unexpected effect on him: He had totally lost track of what he was talking about. He found himself struggling to return to his senses. "Okay," he said finally, "I might not have been totally straight with you on that front."

The Governess arched an eyebrow.

"It was Prue's idea to come into the woods—she's my, well, friend, I guess. She's a classmate. She sits two rows over from me in homeroom. And we have honors English and social studies together. We've never really hung out that much, though, outside of school."

Alexandra impatiently motioned her hand for him to continue. "And what brought you into the woods?"

"Well, I followed her this morning. See, she was coming into the woods to look for her . . . her baby brother, who was . . ." Here he trailed off, glancing around the room. "I would say that this would sound crazy, but considering all that I've seen today, it seems pretty ordinary actually. Her brother was, I guess, kidnapped by crows. A bunch of 'em. Swarming around. They just picked the kid up and took him into the woods here, and so Prue went after them."

The Governess was staring at Curtis intently.

"And I went after her. Thinking she could use the help. And here we are," Curtis finished. He looked at Alexandra pleadingly. "Please don't be angry. I know I said I came here alone at first, but I wasn't sure what was going on or if you guys were, y'know, trustworthy." Massaging his belly, he puffed his cheeks and blew through puckered lips. "I don't feel very well."

There was a long silence. A cold, musty breeze blew through the room, guttering the flames of the braziers. A coyote attendant in the corner coughed, cleared his throat, and excused himself.

"Oh, we're very trustworthy, Curtis," said the Governess, breaking the reverie. "I think you should not be afraid to tell us anything. This must be quite a shock for you, having grown up in the mundane Outside, with your everyday experiences and your domesticated animals, so short on intelligence they haven't the capacity to speak.

I can understand your reticence in trusting me, especially after my Commandant and his brutish underlings handled you so disrespectfully. They can be a miserable bunch. I can only offer my humblest of apologies. We're just not used to visitors here." The Governess was tracing her finger along the eddying grain of the armrest's wood. "And I can tell you directly that this is not the first time we've heard complaints about those meddling crows. Their species as a whole tends toward this sort of mischievous activity. I can't imagine they mean to do anything untoward with your friend's brother. It's likely that they'll keep him around for a bit and play with him like some bauble, and once they've tired of his company, they'll return him to the place from whence he was stolen."

"P-play with him? Really?" asked Curtis.

"Oh yes," replied the Governess. "Though I don't imagine they'll do him any *real* harm." She thought for a moment and continued, "As long as he doesn't fall from one of their nests."

"Fall? From their nests?"

"Yes, I would expect that's where they'll be keeping him. Notoriously, they make them rather high in the trees. But he should be fine; crows are very protective of their possessions. He'll be perfectly safe provided he doesn't get stolen by a neighboring buzzard or something."

"A buzzard would steal him?"

She nodded. "Oh yes, and then, dear Curtis, I'm not sure anything could be done. Buzzards *adore* human flesh."

Curtis's body convulsed, and he clasped his hand to his mouth. He had grown considerably paler over the course of the last few minutes.

"But don't worry, Curtis!" said the Governess, leaning forward. "I will personally see to it that a battalion is devoted to the search and rescue of your friend's brother. We've dealt with these crows before; I have no doubt we will have ferreted out that boy in a few days' time, trust me."

The low light of the warren shivered in Curtis's vision, and the dirt walls began to revolve slightly, sending a sickening feeling into his stomach. The feeling was stanched when he closed his eyes, so he rasped, "I think I might just rest my eyes a little, if that's okay," and shuttered his lids, reclining farther back on the bed of moss.

"You must be exhausted, my dear boy," came the voice of the Governess, sounding closer now in the darkness. "You should rest. We'll speak again in the morning. Until then, lie back. Sleep. Sleep and dream."

And Curtis did just that.

Asleep, he did not see the Governess looking down on him fondly. He did not feel her lay a fur blanket over his body and tuck the hem tidily under his chin. He did not hear her sigh deeply to watch him sleep.

The first broken rays of dawn were filtering up through the trees when the mail van came to a halt at a massive stone wall. A towering pair of wooden doors provided a gateway through the wall, and a carved placard reading NORTH GATE was affixed to the keystone. Prue rubbed sleep from her eyes, exhausted after their nightlong drive, and looked out the window at the imposing wall as it stretched in either direction away from the road until it was swallowed by distant trees. A soft haze dusted the vegetation of the forest floor, and the green was cast in a crystalline shimmer by the early morning's remaining dew. A few birds sang. Richard stubbed his third cigar of the night into the overflowing ashtray and waved at the two armored guards who stood on either side of the doors. They walked over to the van window and peered through the glass. When they saw Prue, their eyes widened, and Richard rolled the window down.

"An Outsider," he explained wearily. "I'm bringing her to the Governor-Regent."

"We had heard," said one of the guards, an older man. His gray-whiskered beard protruded between the chinstraps of a tin helmet that closely resembled an overturned dinner plate. "We caught word from the Avians. You can go through." The other guard was younger and appeared more aghast by Prue's presence in the van. As the oaken doors of the gate were slowly heaved open and Richard drove beneath the wide stone arch, Prue caught a glimpse through the side-view mirror of the younger guard, standing stone-still in the middle of the road, watching the van. The look made her uncomfortable; she felt overly scrutinized, like some strange insect under a magnifying glass. Prue returned her attention to the road in front of the van as it widened on the ground beyond the gate.

"South Wood," said Richard. "Home at last."

The forest here had a completely different aspect than the wild scrub and crooked, looming trees of Wildwood: Prue began to see odd structures appearing in the woods along the road, what appeared to be modest houses and buildings. Some stood dramatically apart from the trees, built of rough stone and brick, while some seemed to grow from the trees themselves, shingled in branches and layers of moss. Others bolted up from the ground like burrows with colorful wooden doors and small porthole-like windows and sprouted crooked tin chimneys that belched wisps of smoke into the arbor eaves. A lattice of walkways and bridges linked the higher boughs of the trees together, and Prue craned her neck upward to see that they led to more houses, shacks, and outbuildings in the tops of the trees. People moved in and out of the buildings and populated the walkways and doorways, but not just people: animals, too. Deer and badgers, rabbits and moles walked among the humans in this miraculous world. Other roads appeared and intersected with the Long Road: arterial roads, side streets, and alleys, some paved with flagstones and brick, others covered in gravel and dirt and pockmarked with puddles remaining from the previous night's rain.

The Long Road itself, after a time, became a grand avenue through the trees, and smooth, ancient ruts were worn into its paving stones.

Lavish residences began to line the Road, multistory townhouses built of pale white granite and deep red brick with graceful porticos and mullioned windows. Some of the houses seemed to be built around the trees themselves, dramatic cedar trunks extending from the center of the roofs or out the side of the walls. The acrid smell of burning coal and creosote slightly tainted the air, a striking change from the clear, crisp air of Wildwood. The Road here became choked with traffic, even: Sputtering cars and battered old motor scooters vied for space along the flagstones among bicyclists, pedestrians, and clattering carts drawn by (literally) complaining oxen, horses, and mules.

"This is incredible," Prue finally murmured once she'd recovered from her shock at seeing the forest come to life. "I can't believe this has been here all along and I never even knew it."

Richard, his arm resting on the open van window, had just finished castigating a wobbly cyclist for cutting him off. He looked over at Prue and smiled. "Yup, here it is. South Wood in all its glory. A little cluttered, for my taste. The quiet of the North Wood is a bit more my speed. Country folk. Simple things."

The section of road they traveled on now cut across the side of a hill, and a knobby stone bridge allowed passage over a rushing brook before the road began carving switchbacks up another hillside, this one rimmed with the wooden and stone facades of buildings gaudy with carnivalesque signs advertising cafés and taverns, shoe shops and soda fountains. The traffic was thickest here, and the van heaved

jerkily forward along the steep and busy streets, Richard swearing
under his breath every time he was forced to slam on the brakes for a
stopped car or passing pedestrian. Finally, they topped the hill, and
the traffic cleared and the buildings receded behind them as the forest
fell away to reveal an extraordinary sight: a glorious granite mansion
in the middle of a pristine park, its windows glinting in the bright
morning sun. Prue drew in her breath; it was truly beautiful.

"Pittock Mansion, built centuries ago by a William J. Pittock to
serve as the seat of power for South Wood—it has changed hands
many times over the years, mostly peaceably, though sometimes by

97

force," explained Richard, in tourist guide mode, "as you can see from the many pockmarks in the granite from cannon and bullet fire. This country was forged in the clashing of divisions, Port-Land Prue, and not a lot of those disagreements have been forgotten, I'm sad to say." Sure enough, Prue could see the divots in the stately stone, though they did not diminish the grandeur of the place, its two north-facing corners capped with red-roofed turrets bordering a handsome balcony on the second floor.

The grounds of the Mansion suggested an immaculately tended English garden, hedges and flowering trees (denuded by the season) fanned in symmetric patterns away from the central hub of the Mansion—a stark contrast to the cluster and chaos of the busy streets in the woods below. A few couples strolled along the gravel paths; a family of beavers fed breadcrumbs to enthusiastic geese paddling in a resplendent statue-crowned fountain. The van exited the Long Road here and followed a circuitous stone road into the Mansion's inner compound. A wrought-iron gate was thrown open at the end of the drive, and Richard navigated the van through the tumult of carriages and state vehicles that clogged the driveway. He eased to a stop in front of a pair of glass-paned French doors.

"And 'ere we are," said Richard, letting the van idle noisily in front of the Mansion.

"And here we go," Prue muttered as she threw the door open and stepped down onto the cobblestone drive.

Curtis, on the other hand, did not have such a nice introduction to the morning.

Just prior to waking, he had the clearest sensation of being home, in his bed, pillowed in his duvet with its Spider-Man duvet cover. As he woke, his eyes still closed, he marveled at the bizarre and vivid dream he'd been having, something involving him and Prue McKeel and a voyage into the Impassable Wilderness; it had been at times a terrifying dream, but now he felt a distant, nagging reluctance to reawaken into his normal life. When he did finally acquiesce and open his eyes, he screamed.

Above him stood a headless figure, clothed in an officer's coat, its arms and legs made of the branches of a leafy tree. It loomed over him, inspecting him, ready to strike. Curtis grasped for his duvet and found it wasn't there; his hands sank into the mossy loam of the dais. His surroundings came into focus: the ornate throne, the root-lined ceiling, the cracked mud of the walls. He immediately realized where he was: the throne room of the Dowager Governess. He scrambled backward, pressing himself against the rough wall, and readied himself for his attacker. The figure did not move.

A voice came from the middle of the room. "Good morning, Master Curtis," said the voice, growling, gruff, and brittle. Curtis looked over to see one of the coyote soldiers, fresh from his dream, walk into the light of the braziers.

A sinking feeling of nausea was creeping up on Curtis. His mouth felt uncomfortably dry. He quickly glanced back over at the uniformed figure by the moss bed and realized, to his relief, that it was only a dummy.

"The Dowager Governess wished you to have this uniform. She instructed me to dress you and to make sure it fit correctly," said the coyote, gesturing to the dummy. The slightest tone of resentment colored his voice.

The uniform slung over its shoulders looked newer than the tattered apparel of the coyote soldiers he had seen the day before: The coat was dark blue and held closed by bright brass buttons. The shoulders were crested with epaulets, and the hems of the sleeves ended in bright red cuffs, delicately brocaded with golden cording. The chest of the jacket was festooned with important-looking medals and badges. A wide black leather belt had been draped over one of the dummy's stick-arms, and on it hung a scabbard encrusted with small river stones; a sword hilt, glinting gold and topped in a river-pebble pommel, jutted out from one end. A pair of dark tapered pants with silver piping clung to the dummy's legs.

Curtis stared at the sight. "For me?" he asked. His surprise had sent a jolt up through his body, and his stomach turned. The coyote nodded and began pulling the uniform from the dummy. Once he had removed it, he shook it at the shoulders, the medals jingling, and waited patiently for Curtis to stand.

The room felt unsteady as he stood, and he had to brace himself on the arm of the throne. The soft throb of a headache pushed at the insides of his skull. It occurred to him that this might be a consequence of the beverage the Governess had served him the night before. His tongue felt like it had been beveled with a rasp. However, the feeling soon became secondary as the reality of the situation dawned on him.

"Why does she want me to wear it?" he asked, eyeing the uniform. Back home, he had a poster detailing the anatomy of a British hussar's uniform from the Crimean War above his bed. The prospect of wearing what was being offered to him was nothing short of thrilling.

"You'll have to ask her," responded the coyote impatiently. "I'm just doing as I was told."

Curtis was suspicious. "I don't suppose I'll have to fight anyone, will I?" he asked, envisioning a Thunderdome-style melee with some brute from the warren. It seemed to him that this sort of thing was constantly happening in movies and comic books. "I can't do that. I'm a pacifist," he said. A younger and meeker friend of his, Timothy Emerson, had once used that excuse to explain why he hadn't fought back when a few of the older kids from the grade above pushed him off the monkey bars during recess. It had seemed impressive at the time.

The coyote said nothing. He shook the outfit again and cleared his throat.

"That *is* a pretty sweet sword," admitted Curtis, admiring the sheathed sword on the belt. "Can I see it?"

The coyote laid the coat down on the dais and pulled the sword from its scabbard, presenting it to Curtis hilt-first with professional aplomb. Curtis took hold of it and swung it into the air—it was heavier than he'd imagined it to be. The blade was roughly the length of his forearm and was made of highly polished silver steel. The lights of the chamber's smoldering torches reflected in the metal as he carved a figure eight in the air with the blade. Though alien, the weight of the sword in his hand released a torrent in his imagination—at that instant, he was no longer Curtis Mehlberg, son of Lydia and David, resident of Portland, Oregon, comic-book fanboy, persecuted loner; he was Taran Wanderer, he was Harry Flashman. He massaged the grip of the hilt in his palm and narrowed his eyes at the coyote. "Okay," he said, "help me get that uniform on."

CHAPTER 8

To Catch an Attaché

The relative quiet of the driveway was broken as soon as a pair of liveried attendants threw open the French doors and ushered Prue and Richard into the foyer of the Mansion. They both immediately froze. The foyer was a cauldron of frenzied activity. An ocean of figures, animal and human, occupied the large main room of the building, some milling about, involved in heated conversation, others speeding across the granite floor in an array of directions. What sounded like a million voices echoed throughout the chamber, and Prue's head spun trying to pick them apart.

The figures, clothed primarily in dress blacks and ties, each carried sheaves of paper under their arms and were each flanked by other, similarly dressed figures trying desperately to keep up with the pack. The only obstacle to this perpetual blur of movement was a brilliant white central staircase that wound up from the polished checkerboard floor. A warthog in a three-piece green corduroy suit was holding court from the middle landing of the staircase; a small retinue of observers huddled around him as he spoke, his cloven thumbs tucked into the armholes of his waistcoat. A pair of black-tailed deer, the ties on their oxford shirts matching their tails, argued vehemently by the marble bust of an important-looking man; a squirrel stood on the edge of the bust's plinth, nodding.

Occasionally the collective attention of the room would be swayed to follow one single character, a graying man in bifocals, as he sped across the room, a daunting pile of papers and manila file folders precariously embraced to his chest. When this man appeared, entering the room from one pair of doors and exiting at the opposite end through another, many of the figures in the room would drop whatever they had been doing and would desperately entreat him for attention. Invariably, the man ignored all advances, and, after he had disappeared behind another pair of doors, the room would return to its former chaotic buzz of activity. Richard finally spoke. "I think that's the guy you need to see—the Governor's attaché." Prue looked up at him and saw that he was just as shell-shocked as she was. She took a deep breath and extended her hand to him.

"I think I'm good from here," she said. "You've got mail to deliver."

Richard looked relieved. He took her hand and shook it. "It was very nice meeting you, Port-Land Prue. I hope our paths cross again. I wish you the best of luck."

Turning to leave, he hesitated at the door and turned around. "If you ever need anything, I'm at the post office—just southwest of the Mansion here. That is, if I'm not on the road." He smiled warmly.

"Thanks, Richard," said Prue. "Thank you for everything."

After Richard had left, Prue stood for a time and watched the busy current of life in the room as it ebbed and flowed. She nodded to an aged black bear as he hobbled past her to the outside door; she smiled politely at a woman wearing cat's-eye glasses who nearly ran into her, her focus was so intent on a pile of papers in her hands. Finally, Prue heard the telltale sound of the room's attention diverted again to a far set of double doors as they were thrown open and the bespectacled attaché emerged and began his foray into the cluttered antechamber.

Prue stepped forward, raised her hand, and began to speak, but was immediately silenced as the room erupted with every imaginable sound of the animal kingdom: yelled entreaties from the humans, deafening roars from the bears, and shrill birdsong from the jays, swallows, and nuthatches that furiously winged around the room. Undaunted, the attaché dove headlong into the crowd and began making his way to the opposite end of the room. Prue looked on in despair as he was immediately swallowed by the crush of humans and animals, all vying desperately for his attention. As the crowd passed within a few feet of where she was standing, she feebly raised her hand again and said, "Sir!" but it had come out so meekly that it was indistinguishable from the hubbub.

"You're going to have to do better than that," said a voice by her side.

She looked over and saw no one.

"Down here," the voice said.

Prue looked down and saw a field mouse, calmly chewing on a split filbert. He appeared to be on his lunch break. He was sitting against the base of one of the room's columns, and a kerchief laid out in front of him displayed a tidy selection of foods: a chunk of carrot, a tiny wedge of cheese, and a thimble of beer. He washed down a mouthful of the filbert with a swig of beer, cleared his throat, and said, "Are you on the list?"

"List?" asked Prue, nonplussed. "What list?"

The mouse rolled his beady black eyes. "I expect you're here to see the Governor-Regent. And anyone who wants an audience with

Governor Svik needs to be registered with the Governor's office. Once you're registered with the Governor's office, your name is put on a waiting list. When your name is at the top of the list, you will be contacted by the attaché and an audience with the Governor will be scheduled." The mouse said all this while inspecting the wedge of cheese in one of his spindly-fingered hands. Evidently satisfied, he popped the whole thing into his mouth.

"But . . . ," began Prue, dismayed. "How long does that take?"

"Well," answered the mouse, sounding the words around the massive chunk of cheese in his mouth, "the registrar's office is in the south building, just down the road. That's where you register for an audience. I believe their office hours are noon to three, Wednesdays and Fridays."

"W-Wednesdays and Fridays?" stammered Prue. By her best reckoning, today was Sunday.

"Mm-hmm," responded the mouse casually. "Get there early, there's always a line. And then once you're on the list, it's usually a five- to ten-business-day turnaround before you're contacted to schedule an appointment—usually about three to four weeks out at the earliest, depending on the season."

Prue was devastated. She could feel tears welling up in her eyes. "But my brother! My brother was abducted and I have to find him! He's out in the woods somewhere—there's no way he'll survive that long!"

The mouse shrugged, unmoved by her story. "We've all got problems, miss." He tossed the remaining carrot chunk into his mouth, washed it down with the rest of the beer, and began cleaning up his diminutive picnic.

Prue swallowed hard. She looked out into the room at the loitering hordes of humans and animals. The attaché had exited the chamber again, and the creatures had resumed their prior activities as they waited for him to return.

"What about them?" she asked the mouse. He was wiping the corners of his mouth with the kerchief.

"Them?" he asked.

"Yeah—if there's a waiting list and the governor's office contacts you to schedule an appointment, why are they all trying to get the attention of the secretary?"

The mouse stuffed the kerchief into his vest pocket and wiped his hands together. "Well, it's an imperfect system. Sometimes it works if you just yell loud enough to be noticed. Who knows?" He shrugged, gave a little salute, and walked off into the foyer.

Prue waited for a moment and studied the crowd in the room thoughtfully. She wondered where the best vantage point might be; where she might get the harried secretary's attention the easiest. While she didn't mind crowds—the anonymity they granted gave her a kind of weird confidence—this one was awfully intimidating. Finally gathering her courage, she walked over to the spot where the stairway began and stood, her hand resting on the ivory banister. A middle-aged man and a badger who were standing next to her engaged in a hushed discussion glanced over when she arrived and nodded, then did a double take. Prue smiled and waved faintly.

The man who had been talking to the badger turned to Prue and said, "Excuse me, miss. My friend and I were just talking—and we were wondering if you weren't from the Outside." He had a long, gray-flecked beard and, from his outfit, appeared to be a naval officer of some sort.

"Yes," responded Prue. "Yes, I am."

"Incredible," said the officer. "And you have an audience with the Governor-Regent?"

"Well, not exactly," said Prue. "I don't have an appointment or anything. But I really need to see him, and so I figured maybe they'd just slip me in somewhere."

The officer frowned and shook his head. "Good luck. I've had an appointment scheduled for weeks now, and I still haven't been able to get in to see the Governor. My ship is in dockside with an impatient crew, and all I need is these blasted papers stamped and I'm on my way." He angrily shook a sheaf of paper in his hand. "I tell you . . ." Here the officer looked around the room conspiratorially. "This country still hasn't recovered from the coup, all those years ago. These fools don't know how to run a government, not by a long sight." He straightened and ironed the front of his jacket with a palm and looked at Prue. "Is this how things are run on the Outside? Do you have to deal with this madness?"

Prue thought for a moment. Her only struggle with bureaucracy was when she'd been on the waiting list for a particularly popular book at the library. "I guess so," said Prue. "But I don't really know. I'm only twelve."

The officer had barely time to respond with a dissatisfied *"Hrrrm"* before the double doors at the other end of the foyer were thrown open and the attaché blazed into the room, a long line of assistants and hangers-on trailing in his wake. The room again descended into cacophony, with all the various parties who had been waiting in the room jumping into action, fighting to get to the attaché before he disappeared again. The officer and the badger next to Prue sprang away from the staircase and began shouting their pleas to the frazzled secretary. Prue, caught off guard, gained her bearings and dove into the fray, pushing aside a red-tailed fox who was hopping up and down, trying to see above the scrum of people. "Sorry!" she cried as she was practically picked up off her feet and whisked along the marble floor by the rush of the pack. "Mr. Secretary!" she shouted, waving an arm above her head. Most of the creatures in the crowd were much larger than Prue, and it was all she could do to keep her eye on the center of the storm, where the embattled attaché could be seen with his pile of papers, doing his best to ignore the pleading cries of the mob that beset him. A brightly colored halo of birds circled his head, squawking for attention. "Mr. Secretary!" she repeated, a little louder. She could feel the sharp jab of elbows in her ribs as others joined in and competed for ground.

"Mr. Secretary!" she hollered as loudly as she could muster. "I need to talk to the Governor! My brother was kidnapped! Mr. Secret—*oof!*" Her plea was cut short when a squat flailing beaver, shoved back from the center, head-butted her directly in the stomach and all the air blew out of her lungs. She and the beaver went flying headlong out of the throng and spilled in a tumbling mass to the floor. Prue swore, pushing herself to her feet. She stared determinedly at the attaché and his teeming horde, who had by now reached the double doors. She suddenly remembered the emergency air horn she'd put in her bag. She quickly whipped the bag over her shoulder and, ripping the flap open, pulled out the can.

"MR. SECRETARY!!!" she screamed one last time before she squeezed the handle of the horn.

The room filled with sound. Ear-shaking, hair-rattling sound. The burst lasted a few seconds.

Everyone froze.

Someone's pen clattered to the floor.

A black bear in a gabardine waistcoat panicked and ran out the front door.

The entire crowd, silenced by the immense volume of the horn, turned slowly to look at its source. Prue stood alone in the middle of the foyer floor, momentarily stunned by the horn's power. She cleared her throat. "Um," she intoned quietly, "Mr. Secretary. I . . . um . . . need to speak with the Governor." The swarm surrounding the attaché stood transfixed, and Prue found it eerily unsettling to have the attention of the entire room. Finally, the mass of people began to move as a figure forced its way through the bodies. It was the attaché. His brow deeply furrowed, he was looking down his nose through his bifocals at Prue as he hobbled clear of the crowd. Pausing, he studied her intently, alternately over and through his glasses.

"Are you . . . ," he began. "Are you . . . an *Outsider*?"

"Yes, sir," responded Prue. She slipped the air horn back into her bag.

"I mean—I mean—" stammered the attaché. "From the *Outside*?"

"Yes, sir," said Prue. "And the reason I've come is because—" She was interrupted by the attaché. "*How* did you get here?"

Prue smiled uncomfortably, suddenly struck shy by her rapt audience. "I walked, sir," she replied.

"You *walked?*" asked the attaché, in disbelief. "But—but—you *can't do that!*"

Prue, at a loss for words, stood silently.

The attaché, evidently deeply flustered, shook his head and rubbed his brow with his free hand. "I mean—I mean—it's absolutely impossible! Or it *should* be absolutely impossible, unless—unless—" He stopped and stared at Prue and then, changing his mind, he shook his head and continued, "There must be a rift somewhere or a break in the Bind. A lesion in the spell. Those confounded Northerners. Backwoods idiots!" He snapped his brittle fingers, and an assistant scurried to his side. Speaking out of the side of his mouth, the attaché began dictating his directions: "Get me a form 45 slash C—they should have them down in accounting—and let the Secretary of the Exterior know that I'll be needing it signed immediately. Better yet: Contact the Office of North Wood Relations and let him know that—"

Prue, regaining her footing, interjected, "Sir, I have a serious problem."

The attaché, looking away from his assistant, laughed nervously at Prue. "Mademoiselle, you *are* a serious problem."

Prue continued, undaunted, "Sir, my brother, Mac, was taken yesterday by crows. I saw them take him into the woods. Into Wildwood." The congregation in the foyer listened spellbound. "And I'd really just like to get him back." She could feel tears of desperation welling up in her eyes. "And I promise, I cross my heart, that if I can just get him home, I'll never ever come here again." She weakly traced an X across her chest with her finger. "Promise."

The room remained stalled in silence as the attaché stared in disbelief. Finally, the assistant at the attaché's side leaned in and whispered something in his ear. The attaché nodded silently, never taking his eyes off Prue. "Very well," said the secretary, after what seemed to Prue an eternity. "Since you are in a unique position, we'll see if we can fit you in. Follow me."

The crowd surrounding the attaché fell away, and he led Prue up the alabaster staircase.

🌿

Though there were no clocks hung in the Governess's cavernous hall, Curtis could tell that the morning was nearly gone by the time he had finished sashaying around the room in his new garb,

"I can't believe this has been here all along and I never even knew it."

thrusting and parrying his saber in the sort of grand and dramatic fashion of the swashbuckling dragoons he had seen in movies and read about in books. The decorations on his chest jingled deliciously with his every move, and the sword made a terrific *whish* every time he swung it through the air. The coyote attendant, apparently accustomed to attending to eccentric masters, waited patiently by the throne, moving only to flinch at one of Curtis's wild ripostes.

"Very nice, sir," said the attendant after Curtis's energy had flagged. "You are a gifted swordsman. For a *pacifist*."

Curtis stood in the center of the room and kicked his feet in the dirt. "Well, I would never, you know, *fight* anyone." He was panting slightly from the exertion. "But . . . ," he continued. "You think so?"

"Oh, certainly," said the coyote.

"It kind of wears you down, doesn't it?" Curtis asked. He managed a final thrust before he let the sword fall to his side. He massaged his arm with his free hand.

"You'll get used to it, sir," said the coyote.

Curtis eyed the coyote suspiciously. "What's your name?" he asked.

"Maksim, sir," said the coyote.

"Maksim, huh?" said Curtis, turning the sword in his grip. "You guys sure have funny names."

Maksim merely raised an eyebrow.

"So what do you do around here, Maksim?" asked Curtis.

"I am the Governess's aide-de-camp. I have been assigned to oversee your orientation."

"My orientation."

"Yes," the coyote replied. "The Governess would seem to have auspicious plans for you."

Curtis, trying to divine the meaning of the word *auspicious* (was it like *suspicious*?), chewed on this information for a moment before replying, "Where is the Governess?"

"In the field, sir," said Maksim. "Awaiting your company."

"The field?" asked Curtis. "What's the field?"

Maksim ignored the question. "I was instructed to wake you, fit you, and send you to her as soon as you were ready." He paused. "Are you ready?"

Curtis cleared his throat and nodded. "I suppose so," he said, and then, in a voice as adult as he could conjure, "Lead the way, Maksim." He slid his sword into the sheath at his belt.

Exiting the room, Curtis noticed the warren was strangely devoid of the previous day's hubbub: Absent was the throng of coyotes that had huddled around the central cauldron and whose military drills had tattooed the dirt floor. A few soldiers milled about, patching crumbling walls and hauling firewood, but compared to the day before, the warren felt practically uninhabited. Curtis felt the clawed fingers of Maksim adjust the shoulders of his uniform, which had slid off to one side.

"You'll grow into it," said Maksim finally, apparently unsatisfied with the fit. He then began leading Curtis through one of the many tunnels leading from the main room. "This way."

Back above ground, Curtis winced at the brightness of the air. The low early morning clouds had burned away and the light was crisp in the grove, and the brilliance washed a second wave of nausea down his spine from brain to belly. Maksim led the way through the open glade and into the thick of the trees that surrounded the clearing. A small group of soldiers at the tree line, laboring over a stake that refused to be hammered into the ground, abruptly stopped their activity when Maksim and Curtis approached, and snapped to attention, their hands locked in salute. As they got closer, Curtis realized that the soldiers were saluting *him*, not Maksim. Curtis awkwardly saluted back as they passed, and the coyotes returned to their work.

"What was that about?" whispered Curtis when they were out of earshot of the soldiers.

"Showing proper respect to rank. You're an officer, after all," said Maksim. He stopped and pointed to one of the brooches that was pinned to Curtis's chest. It was simple: a taut weave of blackberry brambles topped by the broad petal of a trillium flower, cast in a dark bronze. Curtis pushed at it curiously with his finger, adjusting its place on his jacket. "An officer," he repeated quietly. Maksim continued walking into the woods.

"Whoa. Wait a second," said Curtis. "An off-officer? What did I do to deserve that?"

"You'll have to ask the madam."

"I'm not sure if you're, you know, familiar with the *human species* or not," Curtis said, "but I am not technically an adult. I'll be twelve this November. I don't know what that is in coyote years, but in human years it's a kid. A boy. A child!" He was walking briskly to keep up with Maksim. Curtis waited for a reply, and when there was none, he continued, "So what does this mean? Do I have to do anything? I told you guys, I'm a pacifist. I can't really use this sword. Whatever *swordsmanship* I was showing off back there was totally, totally accidental. Just some stuff I cribbed from, like, Kurosawa movies."

"I expect all will be made clear when we see the Governess," responded Maksim, batting branches from his path, not attempting to hide the irritation in his voice.

Curtis glanced back, trying to find the entrance to the warren amid the woods' thick bracken. He was astonished to see how all signs of the coyote encampment completely disappeared into the forest as they traveled farther away.

"Like, will I have to command . . . something?" asked Curtis.

"I have no idea," Maksim said. "I'm a little surprised myself."

They walked in silence for a moment. The wood grew darker, the canopy oppressive.

"How did you become an . . . aid of camp?" asked Curtis.

"Aide-de-camp? I was appointed."

"What did you do to deserve that?"

"I suppose I distinguished myself," responded Maksim, "in battle."

"Oh boy," said Curtis, his worry growing.

"Though I was not born a fighter. In truth, I owe my life and my destiny to the Dowager Governess. I was born to a poor pack in the bush; my father had been killed in a mudslide and my mother slaved to raise my five siblings and myself. We were starving when the Governess found us. She brought us to the camp; she fed us and taught us to build and to fight." Maksim told his story without a shade of sentimentality. "And so: I would gladly lay my life down for the Governess. She elevated our entire species from our lot as scavengers and scroungers; she brought us coyotes to a place of honor among the beasts of the wood. And we'll enjoy a seat at the table when Wildwood is ours."

"Yeah," said Curtis. "Listen, Maksim. I can totally see how that works for you and I appreciate your commitment, but, you see, I don't know if I'm quite there yet, you know, officer material. I've only been here for a day and I'm still kind of figuring everything out."

A voice, a woman's voice, sounded from above them. "And that's why we're here, dear Curtis."

Curtis looked up and saw Alexandra, the Dowager Governess, astride a jet-black horse, emerge from over a hillock between two massive cedars. She extended a willowy hand. "Come," she said to him, "I'll show you the world."

CHAPTER 9

A Lesser Svik;
To the Front!

"Step this way, Miss . . . ?" prompted the attaché when they had reached the far end of the landing and were standing in front of a massive oaken door. He was looking through the smeared glass of his bifocals at his clipboard; he'd written down the details of her circumstances on a single-sheet dossier.

"McKeel," said Prue distractedly. She peered around the edge of the door as it was prized open by one of the attaché's aides. A wide hallway was revealed, lined with dark wooden wainscoting topped by panels of dusky green damask. The door pulled wide, Prue could see that the hallway terminated at the far end at another large door, which was hinging open and closed like a giant clam. With every out-breath, it emitted men in black suits carrying sheaves of paper and file folders, its in-breath receiving more of the same.

"Don't mind the activity, Miss McKeel," said the attaché. "While it resembles chaos, I can assure you, the government is running as smoothly and efficiently as ever." He smiled widely at her, revealing two crooked rows of long, mustardy teeth. He took a deep breath, frowned, and ushered her into the hallway.

"Excuse me. Pardon me. Sir, if you'll allow us . . . ," the attaché called out with every step as they dodged the coming-and-going current of government agents. Prue felt the hallway bending in her vision as she navigated her way toward the far door, the whirl of bodies pushing in and out of her periphery like a plague of insects. "Just a little farther—excuse me, sir!—and here we are," said the attaché as they arrived at the door. "I won't be a moment." When the door breathed open again, the secretary slipped through the opening and disappeared. The door remained closed for a few quiet moments before it was thrown open and the attaché beckoned for Prue to enter.

The room was stately; hunters chased stags in a pastoral frieze along the top of the wall, illuminated by a giant crystal chandelier hanging from the ceiling. The chamber seemed, however, to be in serious disuse. Large framed paintings, evidently intended to be hung, were leaning against the wall in a haphazard fashion, and the ornate rug that covered the wooden floor was worn with abuse and neglect. In the center of the rug, the floor bore the weight of a huge wooden desk, piled so high with stacks of paper that the person sitting at it was completely obscured by the mess. In fact, you wouldn't even know there was someone sitting at it if it weren't for the huddle of black-suited men standing around, competing for the attention of the person behind the piles of paper. When the attaché arrived at the front of the desk, the black-suited men all snapped to attention.

"Sir," said the secretary, "meet Prue McKeel. Of St. Johns, the Outside."

The pale, balding crown of a head appeared over the mountain of paper. The man to whom it belonged followed close behind, wearing a pair of huge tortoiseshell glasses and a wide mustache on a jowly face. His skin was wet with perspiration, and his lips quivered as he spoke.

"How do you do?"

Prue was taken aback by the man's disheveled appearance. This was the Governor-Regent? His suit was wrinkled, and little blossoms of sweat bloomed from the armpits of his jacket. His tie, a plain burgundy, was loosely knotted and hung askew above a shirt unbuttoned to just below his Adam's apple. Apparently noting Prue's surprise, the Governor made an attempt to tidy himself by adjusting the knot of his tie and smearing a few strands of oily hair over his bald patch.

"My name's Lars. Lars Svik. The Governor-Regent of South Wood." Finding an opening between two of the towering stacks of paper, Lars put out his hand, and Prue stepped forward to shake it.

"How do you do, sir," was her reply. "I'm Prue."

"Yes, yes," said the Governor-Regent, looking back down at his desk at the sheet of paper that the attaché had given him. He pushed his glasses back from the tip of his nose and began studying the paper. "Prue McKeel, human girl," he read aloud in a humming monotone. "Of Port-Land, the *Outside*. Parentage unknown. Discovered by postmaster in Wildwood, Area 12A, Long Road. In apparent distress. Complaining of lost brother, Mac, and abducted friend, Curtis Mehlberg. Suspects: crows, coyotes respectably. Respectably?" He looked up at Prue quizzically.

"Respectively, sir," corrected an attendant at his side, a thin man with a neat, close-cropped beard and a pince-nez. "Crows in the case of the brother, coyotes in the case of the friend."

"Ah yes," said Lars, looking back down at the paper. "Of course. Thank you for that clarification, Roger."

"Think nothing of it, sir." Roger smiled.

Lars continued reading from the dossier: "Suspects: crows, coyotes *respectively*. Seeks aid of government of South Wood in recovering said abductees. Has made passing reference to the Dowager Governess in initial—" Lars stopped suddenly and stared at the paper. He pushed his glasses back and reread the sentence, mouthing the words silently. When he was finished, he looked up at Prue and gawked.

"The Dowager Governess?" he asked. "Are you *sure* you heard that?"

Before Prue had a chance to answer, Roger, the thin man, interrupted. "Entirely hearsay, sir. Before listening to the insinuations of an Outsider girl, I would remind you that there is no substantial evidence whatsoever that would lead us to believe that the Governess has survived."

Prue glared at the man. "I can only tell you what I heard, *sir*," she said. "And I specifically heard those coyotes say that."

Roger challenged, "And what makes you so sure they were coyotes, Miss McKeel? They could've been dogs or . . . anything! In the haze of the forest, a mild-mannered mole could be mistaken for a—"

"They were coyotes, sir, I'm sure of it. And they were wearing uniforms and carried swords and rifles and things," snapped Prue.

Roger paused and studied Prue. "I'm given to understand that you had a rough crossing at the border. You had a bit of a, how shall I say, *confab* with the bird sentries."

Prue paused, attempting to guess the aide's intentions. "Yes," she said, "I guess."

"What was the nature of your dealings?"

"They, um, wanted to know what I was doing. They said they were looking out for coyotes."

Roger turned to Lars. "You see, sir? It's just as likely she's been

put up to this by the birds. She's a pawn. A paid shill for their agenda."
He looked back at Prue. "And rather clever, I must admit. Just in time
for their Avian *Eminence*'s great arrival."

Prue was speechless. The aide had an incredible ability to manipu-
late the circumstances. "That's not true," she muttered.

"My dear," soothed Roger, his tone icy, "you must be very agitated. You are likely suffering from some sort of culture shock being
here in the Wood. I would recommend a hot bath and a warm com-
press on your forehead. Our world is very different from your own.
Which reminds me"—here he turned to the Governor-Regent—
"the Outsider girl's presence here is *unprecedented*. Under subsection
132C in the Boundary Law Code, it clearly states that Outsiders are
not legally allowed to cross over from the Outside without proper
permit in the event that the boundary magic, the Periphery Bind, is
somehow compromised, which I can only assume—"

Prue interrupted angrily, "I know I'm not supposed to be here. And
I'll be perfectly happy to leave and never bother you again, but I can't
do that without bringing my brother and my friend Curtis with me."

The Governor-Regent still appeared stunned. A few fresh beads
of sweat had collected on his massive forehead, threatening to fall.
He massaged his carrotlike fingers together nervously. "You're certain you heard them refer to the Dowager Governess? Those very
words?" he asked.

Prue replied, "Yes, sir. Certain."

Lars gritted his teeth and pounded his desk with a clenched fist. "I knew it!" he said. "I knew exile was too lenient. We should've foreseen this!"

Roger spoke in low, firm tones. "Sir, these are unsubstantiated rumors from a delusional little girl."

Lars ignored him. "And to think she's managed to bring the coyotes to her side. Unthinkable!" His eyes widened. "Does this mean that what the birds are saying is true? Could it be?" His voice trailed off as he became lost in thought, his eyes staring unblinking into the distance.

Roger's face grew beet red. "P-pqppycock!" he shouted, before collecting himself. "If you'll excuse the expression." He brought his thin fingers to his mustache, smoothed his whiskers, and then dropped his hand to the Governor's shoulder in a consoling caress. "Sir, calm yourself. There is absolutely no reason to get upset over this. If the Governess were alive, we'd have heard long before now. There is absolutely no possible way a woman such as herself could survive in the wild for that long. These *coyote soldiers* the girl has seen are apparitions, illusions—the product of a traumatized mind." Before Prue could object, he held out a hand. "*But*," he continued, "if it would put the Governor at ease, might I suggest we send a small platoon, a few dozen men, into this area of Wildwood and see what sort of information they can glean from the natives. It's an unorthodox approach and I am hesitant to recommend it, but if it would satisfy the girl's supplication and dispel any fears you might have, Mr. Svik, I think it would be the best course of action. Think of your *condition*, sir."

Lars grunted in agreement and began calmly, deliberately measuring his in- and out-breaths in a meditative way, his eyes fluttering closed.

"And Curtis?" asked Prue. "You'd look for Curtis?"

Roger smiled. "Of course."

"And what about my brother? My brother Mac?"

"Right, the *other* Outsider you've lost in your adventures," Roger replied. "Abducted by *crows*, you say?"

"Yes. From a park in St. Johns. In Portland—the Outside, I guess." She was distracted by the rhythmic pumping of breath emanating from the Governor-Regent, who now had a finger at his wrist, monitoring his pulse.

"Well, that may be out of our jurisdiction. A case for your friends in the Avian Principality, I'd say. Though it is highly suspicious that any avian creature should be involved in the abduction of a human child from the Outside. Highly suspicious." Roger paused and tapped his finger against his chin in thought. "This may be very valuable intelligence, Miss McKeel." He leaned down and whispered something in the Governor's ear, during which Lars briefly halted his breathing exercise. When Roger had finished, the Governor nodded gravely and looked at Prue.

"If what you're saying is true," said the Governor, Roger's hand still resting on his shoulder, "this could mean very serious things for the relationship between South Wood and the Avian Principality."

Roger interjected, "What the Governor is trying to say, Miss McKeel, is that any sojourn a bird or birds may have taken into the Outside, not the least the suggestion that they may have returned with someone *in tow*, is quite clearly a violation of any number of citations in the Periphery Laws, and we would thank you for bringing this information to our attention."

"And my brother?" asked Prue impatiently, her brain reaching capacity for political talk.

"It would be in the South Wood's best interest to help find your brother so that we might bring the perpetrators to justice more swiftly," replied Roger.

Prue breathed a sigh of relief. "Oh, thank you!" she cried. "Thank you so much. I know he's out there; I know he's still alive."

Roger had rounded the side of the desk and walked to Prue's side, placing an arm around her shoulder. He gently guided her back toward the door. "Of course! Of course!" he consoled. "We'll do *everything* in our power to find your brother, I promise."

"And you'll let me know when you have?" asked Prue.

"Absolutely," said Roger as they neared the door. "You'll be the first to know."

"He's wearing a brown corduroy jumper," she stammered. "A-and he doesn't really have any hair."

"Brown jumper," repeated Roger soothingly. "No hair. Got it."

They arrived at the far end of the room, and Roger nodded to the attaché, who had been waiting at the door. The door was opened for them.

"We would be honored to have you as a guest of the Mansion," said Roger as they stood at the open doorway. "You'll find comfortable lodgings awaiting you in the North Tower. Wait at your chambers and we'll alert you as soon as we know anything more about your brother or your friend Constance."

"Curtis," corrected Prue.

"Curtis," Roger repeated, and then added: "Please don't hesitate to let the secretary know if there's anything else we can do to make your stay here in South Wood more enjoyable." His hand at the small of her back ushered her gently into the hallway. "Good-bye, Prue. It was very nice to meet you."

The door closed behind her.

The attaché smiled his mustardy smile and motioned the way down the hall.

🌿

The horse's hooves pounded the soft ground as the stallion vaulted berm and tree trunk and Curtis held tight to the Governess's slender waist. Throwing the leather reins back and forth across the horse's broad neck, the Governess nimbly navigated her mount through the wild vegetation of the forest.

"Hold tight!" Alexandra would occasionally remind Curtis when they would leap a particularly large fallen tree or dive into a deep gulch.

"Where are we going?" hollered Curtis, ducking the branches that swung at his face and shoulders.

"To the front!" shouted the Governess, urging the horse to run faster. "I want to give you a glimpse of our struggle, our fight for justice!" The forest blew by at a furious pace, the soft echo of their every hoof-fall resounding through the woods. Curtis gaped up at the towering trees flying by, their tops enshrouded in a veil of mist.

"Okay!" shouted Curtis in response. "So long as I don't have to fight!"

"What's that?" yelled Alexandra.

The cool air whipping at his face brought tears to Curtis's eyes. "I said, AS LONG AS I DON'T HAVE TO FIGHT!"

The Governess pulled back on the reins and the horse reared as they crested a ridge, a steep fern-laden valley stretching out before them. Steam blew from the horse's nostrils, and it whinnied to feel the Governess's caress at its neck. "Good boy," Alexandra chimed. Curtis gazed down at the blanket of deep green that covered the valley floor, a canyon of moss and stone erupting from either side of a gushing brook. The gap was crisscrossed with ancient deadfall,

and colonnades of soaring fir and cedar trees rose majestically from the opposing hillsides.

"It's really beautiful," Curtis said.

Alexandra smiled and looked back at him. "My thoughts exactly when I first arrived here in Wildwood. I immediately knew that this was my home; this wild country was where I belonged."

"How long have you been here?" asked Curtis, uneasily adjusting his perch on the back of the horse. The horse made a kind of box step on the forest floor, shifting its footing below the two riders. "Did you move here from somewhere?"

"Let's just say, sweet Curtis, that I did not come here of my own free will," the Governess responded, "and initially I was deeply unhappy—but I soon realized that my exile here in Wildwood was predestined, that there were greater machinations at work. I began to see my persecutors as my liberators."

Somewhere, distantly, a bough broke, and the ensuing crash of its landfall echoed through the wood. A bird sang its full-throated warble in a nearby bush.

"I saw in Wildwood, this forsaken country, a model for a new world. An opportunity to return to those long-forgotten values that are programmed deep within us, the draw of the wild. I thought if I were able to corral and focus this powerful law of nature, I could bring to the Wood a sort of order out of disorder and govern the land as it was always intended to be governed."

"I'm not totally sure I'm following you," Curtis said.

The Governess laughed. "In due time," she said. "In due time, all will be made clear." She turned and looked at Curtis again, her steely eyes bright and piercing. "I need people like you, Curtis, on my side. Can I count on you?"

Curtis gulped. "I guess so."

Alexandra's smile turned wistful. Her eyes lingered over Curtis's face. "Such a boy," she said quietly, as if she were speaking to herself. "Is it a coincidence, the resemblance?"

"Pardon?" asked Curtis, his confusion redoubling.

The Governess blinked rapidly and furrowed her brow. "But we're wasting time here! To the front!" She dug her heels into the horse's flank and it burst into movement, leaping down into the ravine and charging up the far side. Curtis gripped his hands together at Alexandra's waist and gritted his teeth as the horse made quick time through the trees.

They had traveled for the better part of an hour when they arrived at a small clearing at the top of a hill. There, a group of coyote soldiers had gathered and a small village of tents had been assembled in a circular formation. One of the soldiers, seeing Alexandra and Curtis's approach, ran up to the horse and grabbed its reins, allowing the Governess to vault to the ground. Unaided, Curtis threw one leg over the rump of the horse and awkwardly slid off, nearly falling as he did so.

"Battalion is in place, ma'am," reported a soldier, saluting them both. "Awaiting further instruction."

"Any sign of the bandits?" asked the Dowager Governess, knotting a belt around her waist that had been given her by another soldier. A long, thin sword hung in its scabbard through the weave of the belt. The soldier also presented to her a timeworn rifle, which she hefted to her shoulder, peering down the barrel and checking the sights.

"Yes, ma'am," replied the soldier. "They are grouping on the far ridgeline."

Dropping the rifle to her side, the Governess smiled. "Let's show these ruffians the true law of Wildwood."

Curtis, meanwhile, was standing by the horse, still jarred from the horseback ride. He snapped from his trance to notice one of the coyote soldiers still standing at attention in front of him, saluting. "As you were," said Curtis, a line repeated from countless war movies he had seen. Satisfied, the soldier moved away and left Curtis, suddenly exhilarated, a smile creeping across his face. "As you were," he repeated in a whisper to the air.

"Curtis!" shouted the Governess, standing amid a crowd of soldiers. "Stay by me!"

Holding his sword pommel, Curtis jogged over to where Alexandra stood.

❧

The room was plain and simple and, being the lone room at the top floor of the Mansion's North Tower, was in the shape of a half circle. A few framed etchings decorated the drab papered walls. In one, a square-rigged sailing ship, its keel exposed, was navigating around a giant rock in a wild gale. Another etching showed a pastoral scene of a wooded clearing, in the center of which rose a massive gnarled tree that dwarfed its surroundings. A line of figures encircled the base of the tree, their heads barely cresting the tree's exposed roots. Prue studied these pictures for a while, admiring the line work, before a wave of tiredness overcame her and she walked to the bed and threw herself down. The box spring gave a complaining squeak. She grabbed the bed's only pillow and hugged it to her face, breathing in its musty scent. She hadn't realized how exhausted she was until this moment. Before she had any further chance to reflect, she felt herself drifting into a deep sleep.

She was awoken by what initially sounded like a colossal, lingering gust of wind, like the sudden onset of a summer thunderstorm. She soon realized that the sound was instead the collective rustling of a hundred birds' wings. "The crows!" she cried, in half sleep. She leapt from the bed and ran to the window, in time to see the largest and most varied flock of birds she'd ever seen, swirling in a liquid, eddying pattern against the sky. A dizzying panoply of birds, nuthatches and jays, swifts and eagles, all volleyed for air space in the sudden swarm. Amid their squawks and titters, Prue could hear the words "Make way!" and "He approaches!" and she craned her neck to see what the fuss was about. Below the tower, she could see that the entranceway to the Mansion was alight with movement, the full retinue of the Mansion's staff running in and out of the double doors in panicked chaos. Looking up, she saw a procession approaching along the drive that curved through the estate's luxuriant lawn. This procession, however, was entirely in flight, a multitude of small brown finches surrounding a central figure: the largest and grandest great horned owl Prue had ever seen.

As the procession flew nearer to the entrance of the Mansion, the double doors were thrown open, and Prue recognized the figures of the Governor-Regent and his aide, Roger, as they stepped forward to meet it. The owl, nearly the size of the corpulent Governor, arrived at the entrance, and the hovering finches dispersed into the trees and the cornices and eaves of the Mansion's exterior. The Governor-Regent bowed deeply. The owl, all mottled brown, white, and gray, alighted on the pavement and nodded his head, his two wide yellow eyes glowing amid his plumage. Roger bowed his head slightly and made a welcoming gesture, motioning the great owl through the doors. Together, the group walked forward and disappeared into the Mansion.

"Wow," breathed Prue finally. "He's beautiful."

"Owl Rex," said a girl's voice behind her. "He really is, ain't he?"

Prue jumped. Turning around, she saw that a maid had entered while she had been at the window and was busy laying towels and a bathrobe at the foot of the bed. She looked about nineteen and was dressed in a very old-fashioned-looking apron and dress.

"Oh!" said Prue. "I didn't hear you come in."

"No worries," the girl said. "I'll be out of your way in a tick."

Prue looked out the window, watching the ebb of activity at the entranceway below. "That was some entrance," she said finally. "The birds, I mean."

"Oh yeah," responded the maid. "I never seen that before, the owl coming to the Mansion. Usually it's some lower bird or other who comes for the Principality's business. Don't know that Owl Rex has ever set foot in South Wood. Or would you say 'set

claw'?" She laughed and shrugged. "Hey, I don't mean to pry, but . . . you're that Outsider girl, huh? The one that everyone's talking about."

"Yeah," Prue responded, "I guess that'd be me."

"I'm Penny," said the girl. "I live down in the Workers' District. I can see the tops of your buildings from my bedroom back home.

I always wondered what it was like on the Outside."

"It's pretty different from here," said Prue. "So no one's ever been—to the Outside? From here?"

"Not that I know of," was Penny's answer. "Way too dangerous." She walked to the bed frame and began turning down the hem of the quilt. "How'd you get in here?"

"I just walked in," answered Prue. "But I guess I wasn't supposed to be able to. Something about a boundary?"

"Yep," said Penny. "There's a thing called the Periphery; keeps us safe from the Outside. You can only get through if you're, you know, *from* here." She paused and thought for a moment. "But you're not from here."

"Definitely not," said Prue.

The two girls stood quietly in the room, each privately considering that paradox.

"So I heard you lost your brother?" asked Penny finally.

Prue nodded.

"I'm real sorry to hear that," said Penny. "I have two brothers at home and I hate 'em to death sometimes, but I can't imagine what I'd do if they ever left." Suddenly fearing she'd overstepped her bounds, Penny retreated to the doorway with her satchel of cleaning supplies. "Is there anything I can get for ya, miss?" she asked.

"No, I'm good," said Prue, smiling. "I don't suppose you know how soon they'll come for me, do you? I mean, regarding any news they find out."

Penny smiled sympathetically. "Sorry, dear," she said. "I don't know nothing about what goes on down there. I just clean up."

Prue nodded and watched as the girl walked out into the hall-way and closed the door behind her. Crossing over to a mirror that sat atop an ancient-looking vanity, Prue tousled her hair and stared at her reflection. She looked tired; there were bags under her eyes and her hair was tangled with bedhead. She stood there and let time slowly cascade over her, thinking of her parents and how devastated they must be, she and Mac now two days gone. She bet they'd been reported as missing to the police, and a search team would be assembled, combing through the parks and alleyways of St. Johns and downtown Portland. She wondered how long it would be before they gave up, declared them missing, and their pictures started showing up on the backs of milk cartons and in the foyer of the post office. Maybe, in time, they'd take old school photos and digitally age them like she'd seen on TV, creating a weird approximation of the influence of age and time on a young girl's face, a baby boy's toothless smile. She sighed heavily and walked from the mirror and into the bathroom, grabbing a towel and the bathrobe on her way. Maybe a hot bath would cure everything.

CHAPTER 10

Enter the Bandits;
An Ominous Note

"Hold to the line! Keep in formation!" barked the Dowager Governess as she stalked back and forth behind a long line of coyote soldiers who were installed at the edge of a deep, wide wash. Curtis struggled to keep pace. The sides of the wash fell gradually away from the ridgeline, allowing several distinct rows of the soldiers to find their ground. The first row was made up of fusiliers, armed with muskets, who were crouched in the tufts of maidenhair fern that blanketed the slope. Directly behind them was a long row of archers, their bows at the ready, the ground at their feet bristling with the fletching of their arrows. A third, wider row stood behind these two ranks, and these were the infantry dogs, the grunts who were sparking with anticipation at the battle ahead, yapping at one another and nervously stamping the ground with their hind paws.

"Make way for the cannons!" shouted a soldier, and Curtis looked behind him to see a row of cannons—ten at least—being pushed up the rear hillside above the clearing where the soldiers' camp was made. Each cannon had four soldiers laboring over its movement, the unruly forest floor an uncooperative surface for the cannons' heavy wooden wheels. When they finally arrived at the rear row of infantry, the coyotes shuffled out of the way so that the cannons could be placed, every fifteen feet or so, at the highest point on the ridge. The soldiers who had pushed the cannons collapsed when they reached their goal, only to be yapped at by their commanding officers and shoved into formation.

While Alexandra stood apart and upbraided a sergeant whose column was in disorder, Curtis crept through the rows of soldiers (intoning "as you were" to every soldier who turned and saluted) to the front of the line. Arriving at the row of archers, he peered behind their shoulders, trying to catch a glimpse of the enemy that would warrant such an impressive display of military might.

The far side of the gully was empty.

Curtis looked to either side of him, down the seemingly endless row of coyotes that populated the hillside, at the soldiers as they stared with steely eyes at the ridge on the other side of the wash, and wondered what they could possibly be seeing that he wasn't. He looked back at the far side of the gully and squinted. Still nothing; only trunks of hemlock and oak sprouting from a mossy floor of fern and salal. He whispered to the nearest archer next to him, "So who are we fighting?"

"The bandits," replied the soldier before adding, "sir."

Curtis nodded knowingly. "Okay," he whispered. He still couldn't see anything.

A moment passed.

"Where are they?" asked Curtis.

"What, the bandits?" asked the soldier, clearly uncomfortable having an officer speak to him this way.

"Yeah," said Curtis.

"They're in the trees, over there, sir," said the archer, pointing to the far hillside.

"Ah, okay," said Curtis, still unclear. "Got it. Thanks. As you were." Muttering excuses, he pushed his way back to the rear of the formation and found the Governess speaking to a small group of officers. When she saw Curtis, she turned and smiled.

"Curtis, just in time," she said. "We are about to begin our advance. I was thinking of depositing you in one of these high tree limbs, that you might have a better view of the battle. Would you like that?"

Glancing up at the looming branches, Curtis nodded. "Yeah," he said. "Maybe that would be best."

A small group of soldiers helped Curtis into the lower limbs of an obliging cedar, and from there he scaled up to the thicker branches that sprouted at the ancient tree's gnarled midsection. Selecting a particularly hearty branch, he scooted himself out along the woody surface until he found a spot where the branch split and he was able to couch himself in the intersection, looking out over the ravine. From this vantage, he could see the entire legion of coyotes stretching away down the ridge. He still could not, however, see anything on the other side of the ravine. He heard a command below and watched as the fusiliers lifted their muskets to their shoulders in taut unison. The orderly rows of soldiers behind the rifles ceased their restless movement and stood vigilantly at the ready. The barking of orders came to a stop and there was silence in the ravine, save the slight whisper of the wind and the rustle of the high tree branches. Curtis found himself holding his breath as he searched the opposing hillside for sign of movement.

Suddenly, the trees came alive.

🌿

Prue leapt out of her bath, hearing the mirage of a knock at the door. Hoping it would be one of the Governor's attendants, come to give her good news, she threw on the bathrobe and ran to the door, peeking out into the hallway beyond. Her heart sank to see no one was there.

"Hello?" she called.

Her eyes fell on the figure of a large dog, a mastiff, clad in dress blues, standing against the wall at the very end of the hallway. He glanced at her briefly before looking back down at his paws. He lifted a cigarette to his teeth. The glow of a lit match suddenly illuminated the smooth fur of his face as he brought it to the end of his cigarette. He took a ponderous drag and looked back at Prue. He nodded.

"Oh, hi," said Prue.

The mastiff said nothing. Prue squinted, making out a patch on the shoulder of his jacket. There, the word SWORD was spelled out in all capital letters.

"Excuse me," called Prue. "Do you work here?"

The dog gave no answer.

"I don't suppose you know anything about my brother, do you? Did the Governor send you here?"

Still, silence. The dog shrugged his shoulders and looked away down the hall.

Well, that's pretty rude, thought Prue. She was about to ask what the dog *was* doing there when a tall man in a suit rounded the corner and greeted the dog. They shook hands and began speaking to each other in low voices.

He was just waiting for someone, thought Prue despondently. *That's all.*

She closed the door and returned to the bathroom, where she began toweling her wet hair. Some song from the radio snuck into her head and she began humming it, singing an approximated version of the chorus when it came around. Absently running the towel over her neck and nape, she wandered the room in the early evening's dimming light.

The better part of an hour had passed before a sudden sound from below brought her to the window. She arrived in time to see the multitude of finches she had seen earlier swing down from their nooks in the building and hover before the double doors of the Mansion's entrance. After a few moments, the doors were heaved open and out walked the resplendent Owl Rex, attended by Roger, the Governor's aide. Prue watched transfixed as the massive owl turned and nodded to his companion. Roger repeated his shallow bow and walked back into the Mansion, the doors closing behind him. Alone in the courtyard, the owl hesitated before taking flight; he scanned the horizon and seemed to savor the air for a moment before, astonishingly, he craned his horned head around to gaze directly up into Prue's window.

Prue jumped back from the glass with surprise. His bright yellow eyes continued to hold in place as she stared back. Finally, after what seemed an eternity, he swiveled his head back around, crouched low, and unfurled his immense dappled wings. With a tremendous lunge, the owl launched himself into the sky. He wheeled twice above the driveway, almost prehistoric in his carriage, before flying off into the forest, the mass of finches gliding in his wake like static against the graying sky.

Prue shook her head, unnerved by the experience. Had he been looking at her? He couldn't have been, she decided; why would an owl prince have any interest in a human girl? It must've been pure coincidence, an illusion that he looked up into her window, nothing more.

Something caught her eye on the windowsill, just outside the glass. It was a small white envelope. The words *Miss Prue McKeel* were written on the front in a delicate, elaborate hand. She quickly threw open the sash and grabbed the letter from the sill. She looked out at the vista beyond the window; the birds were gone. Tearing open the seal of the envelope, Prue removed a piece of ivory paper, which, unfolded, revealed a short note written on the Mansion's own embossed letterhead. It read:

Dear Miss McKeel,

It is of vital importance that I meet with you tonight. Please come to my rooms at the White Stone House, 86 Rue Thurmond. Make certain that no one follows you.

You may be in grave danger.

Yours, Owl Rex

Prue reread the note in stunned silence. She wandered the room, turning the piece of paper over and over in her hands, a pang of fear blossoming in her chest. She read the note again, this time in a hushed whisper, intoning the last sentence several times over before she folded the note into a small square.

She walked to the door and slowly cracked it open, peering out into the hall. The mastiff in the blue suit was still there at the end of the corridor. His attention was focused on his forepaws; he was picking at his claws with a little file. Prue saw him begin to turn his great, jowly head toward her, and she quietly pushed the door closed, retreating back into the room.

In a trance, she walked over to the bed, where her jeans lay. She stuffed the note into the front pocket. The light was slowly fading in the room, and she turned on the small bedside lamp. She sat on the bed and felt her heart pounding through her rib cage as if it were exploding.

❧

Curtis had, at one point, been an avowed Animal Planet buff. Couldn't get enough of it. Starting when he was two, he was told, his parents would set him down in front of the television after dinner and he would sit, transfixed, absorbing anything the cable channel would broadcast, regardless of the featured species, habitat, or climate. The obsession wore off eventually (to be replaced by a series of things: Robin Hood, ancient Egypt, Flash Gordon— the list went on) but he always remembered the images that first carried his fascination. One of them was the scene, ubiquitous in any program involving creatures that numbered camouflage among their evolutionary advantages, where the camera would be trained on a tranquil, empty meadow or veldt and you, the viewer, would be baffled as to why these professional wildlife documentarians would waste precious film on animal-less grassland—when all of a sudden, a lion or a snake or a panther would move out of the grass or scrub and you would be shocked at your own inability to detect it.

This is what popped into Curtis's mind as he watched the forest on the far side of the gully breathe into life.

It started imperceptibly; the gentle movements of the swaying fern fronds and low-hanging branches slowly seemed to take on a more threatening, deliberate aspect, and Curtis thought he saw a flash of metal from behind a small pile of deadfall. Then, it was as if the undergrowth sprouted limbs and began to move, unmoored from the forest floor. The bodies of humans soon began to distinguish themselves from the background, and Curtis gasped to see a few figures emerge from the greenery, their dark faces savagely streaked with brown and green paint. As Curtis watched, more and more bodies joined these few until the entire far ridge was crowded with people, a people swathed in tattered clothing and holding a strange and wild variety of weapons: rifles, knives, clubs, and bows. The crowd continued to grow, and Curtis estimated their number to be well over two hundred—at least as many people as he'd remembered seeing in his school's gymnasium during a rally. Their movements made no sound, save the clicking of rifles engaging and the yawning creak of arrows being drawn.

Below him, the Governess appeared, back astride her horse. She fearlessly cantered the horse to the front of the line, drew her sword, and pointed it at the emerging army across the ravine.

"Bandits!" she shouted. "I'm giving you one last chance to drop your weapons and concede defeat. Those who surrender will be treated with fairness and leniency. Those who don't will face death!"

The horse sidestepped and whinnied on the lush slope. There was no response from the other side. A breeze disturbed the quiet tree

branches. The afternoon light came through the woods sideways, casting long, looming shadows on the ground.

"Very well!" continued Alexandra. "You have chosen your fate. Commandant, prepare your—"

She was interrupted by the *snick* of an arrow, speeding past her cheek and lodging itself with a woody *pop* into a nearby tree. Her horse reared and she struggled to calm it, all the while training her eyes angrily across the ravine.

A man stepped forward from the throng on the opposing ridge. He wore a thick red beard and what looked to be the salvaged remnants of an officer's coat, its red cloth and decorative braiding defaced by dirt and ash. Finger-wide streaks of paint scarred the cheeks of his weather-beaten face. He held a gnarled yew bow in his gloved hand, its sinewy string still quivering from the shot. A crown of ivy and salal was tangled in his matted, curly red hair, and his forehead was branded with a tattoo of some totemic aboriginal design.

"This country ain't yours for the taking!" shouted the man. "You'll be queen of Wildwood when we're dead and laid in the dirt!" The army of bandits surrounding him let out a boisterous cheer in response to the man's defiance.

The Governess laughed. "Couldn't agree more!" she cried, finally steadying her horse. "Though I am unclear as to what authority crowned you king, Brendan!"

The man, Brendan, grumbled something under his breath before shouting, "We follow no law, accept no governance. They call me the Bandit King, but I've as much right to that title as anyone here, any animal, avian, or man who follows the bandit code and creed."

"Thieves!" shouted Alexandra, furious. "Low thieves and brigands! King of the Beggars is your rightful mantle!"

"Shut it, witch," was Brendan's steady reply.

The Governess laughed and clicked her tongue at her horse, spurring it away from the ravine. Passing the Commandant, she turned to him and said flatly, "Wipe them out."

"Aye, madam," said the Commandant, smiling. Standing at the front of the line, he raised his saber and shouted, "Fusiliers! Aim!"

The line attended his command; together, their rifles were raised to their shoulders.

"FIRE!"

An erratic staccato of cracks followed, and the air of the ravine was filled with a dense, acrid smoke as the fusiliers fired into the opposing bandit forces.

Through the clearing haze, Curtis watched as several bandits toppled into the gully, their lifeless bodies rolling down through the ferns, while others crowded into their abandoned posts. There was a sort of half second of shocked silence that seemed to Curtis to last an eternity before the quiet was broken by a collective, impassioned cry from the entire hillside and the bandit line burst into action, tearing down the ravine, their swords, clubs, and knives brandished savagely above their heads. A loosely organized line of archers behind them let fly a dense volley of arrows into the coyotes' forces, and Curtis gaped to see the line of fusiliers decimated, dozens of the coyote riflemen keeling over into the gully with arrows lodged in their chests.

Before the bandit ground forces had a chance to reach the other side of the ravine, the coyote archers, on command, stepped forward into the fusiliers' position, their arrows nocked. "Archers!" shouted the Commandant, standing in their midst. "FIRE!"

The wash was again bridged by a tight weave of arrows in flight, this time in the opposite direction, and the gully became littered with the bodies of those unfortunate bandits who should find themselves in the arrows' path. The bandit archers, reaching for more ammunition, allowed a straggling few riflemen to step forward and fire into the coyote formation; many shots struck home and more bodies of coyotes began to join the bandits' in the smoky ravine. Curtis stared at the growing number of dead and wounded, and the battle had scarcely begun.

"Infantry!" came the Commandant's holler. "MARCH!"

The grunts in the rear of the formation marched forward past the archers and fusiliers, just in time to meet the bandits as they clambered up the gradual incline of the ravine. The two forces crashed together in an explosion of sound: clashing sabers, wild howls, fiery shouts, and cracking bones. Curtis grimaced, his stomach turning. The romance he'd associated with these sorts of battles, chiefly from historical novels he'd recently taken a liking to, was beginning to tarnish. The reality was proving much uglier.

The two warring forces became a tangle of bodies, fur and flesh, metal and wood, as their respective artilleries fired round after round of arrow and bullet into the opposing ridgeline. But however many bandits spilled over the edge and into the gully, more appeared from the forest to replace them, and for a moment it seemed as if the coyotes would be horribly outnumbered.

That was when the cannons were called in.

With four coyotes to each gun, they were heaved through the remaining line of archers and fusiliers to stand at the top of the ridge. One coyote stood beside the cannon and howled commands to the others, who in turn packed powder and ball into the cannon's wide shaft with a disciplined efficiency. When the guns were loaded, the commanders raised their sabers and, on the Commandant's mark, yelled "FIRE!" and the forest resounded with a series of thunderous booms.

The cannonballs smashed into the bandits' line, sending bodies flying in every direction. The balls, hitting their mark, sent up giant plumes of dirt and splintered even the most massive of tree trunks as if they were toothpicks. Ancient, sky-tall trees that looked as if they'd been born when the earth was new came lumbering to the ground, crashing into their neighboring trees and sending splintered branches and limbs flying in every direction. More than a few unlucky fighters in the ravine, in heated battle, were crushed by these falling behemoths.

Curtis's ears were still ringing from the cannon fire when he saw the bandits regrouping on the hillside. The fusillade had temporarily disarmed them, but they were growing again in number, their forces continually feeding from the woods behind the ravine. Their line of archers was pulling back for another deadly volley. In an attempt to capitalize on the artillery's initial success, the Commandant quickly ordered that another round be fired. Curtis watched the coyotes' movements intently, fascinated by the quickness of the artillery team below him.

Just as the Commandant barked his order to fire, an arrow shot over the ravine and directly into the neck of the coyote tasked to light the wick. He fell back, dead, and the smoldering slow match in his hand toppled into a pile of dried vines at the foot of the tree in which Curtis was cradled. The rest of the artillery team was suddenly beset by bandits as a wave of them crested the slope, and the coyotes were forced to leave their posts, locked in combat.

The ember from the match quickly caught fire in the dried vegetation, and little flames began licking at the base of Curtis's tree. Curtis flinched, staring down at the growing fire.

"Darn," he muttered. "Super darn, darn, darn."

He hastily pushed himself back from his perch on the branch and slid down the trunk of the tree, the rough bark scraping through his uniform at his knees and elbows. Landing on the ground, he grabbed the slow match from where it lay and began stamping out the fire at the roots of the tree.

"Darn, darn, darn," he repeated incessantly.

The dried leaves quickly crumbled beneath his shoes, and the fire was extinguished. The tip of the lit slow match glowed in his hand. He stood for a moment, paralyzed by the action around him, and then looked over at the abandoned cannon, its tenders still blade-to-blade with their bandit foes.

"Might as well . . . ," his internal voice decided.

He ran to the cannon and held the lit match to the wick. In an instant, the fuse caught, the cannon fired, and Curtis was thrown as the gun mule-kicked backward and a shower of smoke and sparks filled the air and the world around him was silenced save for a slight, distant high-pitched ring.

"Wow," he felt himself whisper, though he couldn't hear a thing.

Prue couldn't remember ever being as impatient for the sun to go down as she was now. She sat at the window of her room in the Mansion and watched the big orb descend behind the distant peaks of the Coast Range until the forest was dark. With the dimming of the day, the activity in the Mansion seemed to ease and calm, and the comings and goings she had witnessed all afternoon at the front doors came to a quiet end. The clatter of footfall in the hallway outside her door had ceased, and the Mansion seemed to fall into a silent nocturnal slumber. Prue figured her chance was now.

She padded quietly into the bathroom and turned the sink faucet on full blast. The rush of water spattered against the white tile of the floor. She then returned to the main room and grasped the handle of the door. Taking a deep breath, she turned the knob. *Here goes nothing*, she thought.

The door creaked open, revealing the long hallway. A few hanging light fixtures illuminated an ornate Persian runner that led from her room. As she'd expected, the mastiff still stood sentry at the far end of the hall. Hearing the door open, he briefly looked up. Wisps of smoke drifted from a lit cigarette in his paw.

"Excuse me!" called Prue. "Excuse me, sir?"

The dog, apparently surprised to be spoken to, looked around. Once he realized she was talking to him, he grumbled uncomfortably and stood up from his leaning position against the wall. "Yes, miss?" he asked.

"I was wondering—I just need some help," said Prue, conjuring her best damsel-in-distress routine. "I can't seem to get the sink in the bathroom to shut off. I think the faucet is broken. I'm afraid it's going to overflow."

The dog paused, evidently weighing the propriety of his helping. He shifted in his suit, which clung tightly to his large, hairy body.

"Please?" asked Prue.

The mastiff gave a little *huff* and stepped away from the wall. He ground the cigarette out on the wood of the floor. When he came closer to Prue, he said, "I ain't no plumber, mind," his voice low and gruff. "But I'll see what I can do." Prue got a better look at the badge on his shoulder; below the word SWORD was the grim image of a blade surrounded by what looked to be barbed wire.

Prue let the dog into the room and followed him as he walked toward the bathroom. He swung the door open and entered, approaching the sink. Prue stayed behind in the room. Reaching over, he gave the spigot a quick turn and the faucet stopped. Before he had a chance to raise any kind of surprised objection, Prue had slammed the bathroom door closed behind him.

"Hey!" the dog cried, his voice muffled behind the door.

The ornate bow of a skeleton key could be seen protruding from the keyhole in the door. With a swift flick of her wrist, Prue had thrown the lock, hearing the weighty *click* of the deadbolt engaging.

"HEY!" the dog cried again, now angrier. He began frantically trying the doorknob. "Let me outta here!"

"Sorry!" cried Prue, feeling genuine anguish that she'd tricked the mastiff. "I'm really super sorry. I'm sure someone will be along to help you. I put a bag of gorp by the bathtub if you get hungry. I've got to go. Sorry!"

She quickly exited the room, hearing the echoes of the mastiff's angered barks fade behind her down the hallway. As she walked, she breathed a quick benediction to the patron saint of sleuthing.

"Nancy Drew," she whispered, "be with me now."

At the end of the hall was a door. She opened this to find herself looking down another long hallway. The corridor before her was empty. Prue cautiously stepped one foot out onto the rug, paused at the floorboards' first complaint, and then started tiptoeing down the hallway.

The wing seemed particularly vacant, and Prue gained confidence with every step that she would not be caught; until a door suddenly flew open and a young bespectacled man walked out, carrying a briefcase with an overcoat slung over it.

"Good night, Phil," he said to someone inside the room he had exited.

"G'night," came the response from within.

Prue froze in place. With nowhere to conceivably hide, Prue had no choice but to stay stock-still in the middle of the hallway, praying the young man would not turn and see her. To her great relief, he didn't. Apparently so occupied in leaving, he simply walked down the hall and disappeared around a corner. Not moving, Prue looked out of the corner of her eye into the room, the door now opened to the hallway. Another man sat at a desk, busily intent on his work. A green anglepoise lamp illuminated the papers in front of him. Occasionally he dabbed a nib pen into an inkwell.

Prue hurriedly stepped through the block of light on the floor cast from the open room, hardly daring to breathe until she had cleared the doorway. When she heard no calls for her to stop, she started walking faster.

The rug ended at a large wooden door, and Prue cracked it open and peeked through. Beyond the door was the stairway landing and below it, the foyer, now eerily absent of all the manic activity she had witnessed that afternoon. The double doors to the east wing were closed, and what appeared to be a Labrador in khakis slumbered noisily in a chair outside.

Prue pushed the door open and snuck out onto the landing. Reaching the stairs, she carefully began descending, counting each step until she made the bottom. Upon reaching it, she half walked, half ran across the checkerboard marble of the floor and was nearly to the front door when she suddenly heard a man's voice, loud and reproachful:

"What do you think you're doing?"

Prue's body seized up, mere steps from the freedom of the front door.

"How many times have I told you, the Governor takes *cream* with his chamomile tea?" continued the voice.

Prue looked over to the source of the scolding and saw, through a door off the foyer, a man—a butler of some sort—giving a stern lecture to a girl who Prue saw, in the faltering lamplight of the small room, to be none other than her maid, Penny. The man was holding a tray with a teacup and a kettle on it.

"Sorry, sir," was Penny's sheepish reply. "It won't happen again."

Penny's eyes looked up and in an instant she saw Prue, frozen in the foyer. Her eyes widened. So did Prue's. They stared at each other for a moment before the butler spoke.

"Well, I don't expect you'll make the mistake again. Otherwise, it's back to the scullery with you—and that's going easy!"

Penny looked back at the man. "Yes, sir," she said. "Understood, sir. Give me the tea, sir, I'll bring it to the Governor."

The butler huffed his approval and handed the tray to Penny, exiting the small room through a door in the rear, his back to Prue all the while. When he had gone, Penny looked at Prue, her eyes again wide with surprise.

"What are you doing?" she whispered.

Prue realized she had no choice but to be honest.

"I have to go see Owl Rex," Prue whispered back. "He sent me a note. He said I should come see him. Tonight!" She toed the ground in front of her ashamedly. "And, oh gosh, I kind of locked someone in my bathroom, this dog who I think was guarding me. I might be in a bit of trouble."

"You did what?" whispered Penny, appalled.

"I . . . locked him in my bathroom. It's okay, I left a bag of gorp in there, in case he gets hungry."

Penny was momentarily speechless. Finally, she hissed, "Well, don't go that way! There are sentries every fifteen feet out the front door!"

Prue looked at the doors in front of her, bowled over by the fact that that had not occurred to her. "Oh."

Penny rolled her eyes. "What were you gonna do, lock them up in your bathroom too? Come this way."

Prue joined Penny in the small room, which appeared to be a kind of servants' staging area. Penny set down the tea tray and opened the small door through which the butler had left. She peeked her head around the corner and, satisfied that all was clear, motioned for Prue to follow.

Penny led Prue down a tight labyrinth of passageways, lit by the occasional flickering gaslight. At some points, the passageways seemed to be just arteries connecting other corridors, where others appeared to be in use as pantries or larders, their walls covered

in shelves holding bags of flour and rows of strange vegetables in jars. Prue lost track of their bearing after the fifth intersection was crossed, and she simply started following Penny blindly, acquiescing wordlessly to the maid's every hushed "this way" and "follow me." They finally arrived at a particularly ancient-looking door and Penny opened it, revealing a worn flight of stone steps leading down into darkness. Penny fetched two candles from a box on the floor and, lighting them both on an obliging gas lamp, she handed one to Prue.

"What's this?" Prue whispered.

"The tunnels," said Penny. "They run everywhere. We can take them into town."

"What about the tea? Isn't the Governor expecting you?" asked Prue.

Penny smirked. "That old insomniac? He'll get by."

Prue paused at the doorway. "Thank you," she whispered. "For helping. I don't know what to say."

"Listen," replied Penny, "I could get in big trouble for this. But I'm a firm believer that you gotta do what you gotta do. And if the Crown Prince wants to see you, you go. God knows you'll likely be better off than collecting dust in that guest room." She studied Prue intently. "As soon as I saw you, my heart went out. To imagine losing a brother." She sighed and held her candle into the doorway, illuminating the steps. The slightest breeze, cold and still, crept from the opening and it smelled of musty, damp stones. "Go ahead."

Prue stepped down onto the smooth stone of the stairs, worn by what looked like a forgotten eternity of footsteps. The dankness of the stairwell was bone-chilling, and she shivered as she descended. Penny followed, closing the door behind her as she went. The candles in their hands projected flickering shadows against the brick walls, their flames quivering in the stagnant air.

At the bottom of the stairs, the corridor linked up to a single passageway that led in either direction into pitch-blackness. The walls of the tunnel radiated a wet chill, the expanse stained here and there by rivulets of water dripping from the arched ceiling. The ground was of ashy dirt, and Prue could feel the cold seeping through her shoes.

The construction of the tunnel changed as they traveled farther along; the red brick and mortar of the walls gave way to rough-hewn stone and granite. Sometimes, the tunnel seemed to be carved out of the earth's rock itself. The ceiling towered above them and took on the aspect of a cavern; other times, they were forced to crouch over and shuffle through low passageways. After what seemed like an eternity, they arrived at an intersection, and Penny pointed her candle down this new corridor. "This is as far as I go," she said. "I have tea to deliver. Follow this passage. After a bit you'll come to a ladder—take that to the surface. From there, you're on your own."

"Thank you so much," said Prue. "I don't know what I'd have done without you."

"Don't mention it," replied Penny. "I know you'll find him, your brother." She smiled and turned to leave, the halo of light cast by her candle fading into the darkness of the tunnel.

Prue began walking down this new passageway. Before too long, she arrived at the ladder Penny had described. Its rungs were splintered and worn, and they bowed with the weight of Prue's feet as she gingerly climbed. The ladder carried her up through a long cylindrical duct in the ceiling of the tunnel that ended at what looked like a manhole cover. Bracing herself against the rungs of the ladder, Prue heaved the cover up and slid it to the side of the opening. A brisk breath of fresh air caught her by surprise, and she inhaled deeply. She cautiously pushed her head up through the opening and looked around.

She was back in the woods.

CHAPTER 11

A Soldier Distinguished;
Audience with an Owl

Curtis, lifting himself up on his elbows, surveyed the damage he had wrought. The coyote soldiers who had, just moments earlier, been in the throes of battle stood frozen in surprise, their adversaries having miraculously vanished. The course of the cannonball had ripped a tidy pathway through the underbrush, crossed the gaping ravine, and continued its path onto the other side. Several bandits, immobile, lay in its wake. Curtis blinked rapidly.

The soldiers raised their sabers in a brief cheer before a new wave of bandits appeared over the ravine edge, and they leapt back into the fray. Curtis heard the sound of hoofbeats behind him.

"Curtis!" came the voice of the Governess. "Come with me!"

He turned to see Alexandra above him, her hand extended. They locked hand-to-forearm, and he was carried over the horse's flanks. Curtis's hearing was only now returning.

"Did you see that?" he shouted over the ruckus of the ongoing battle. He could feel himself beaming, as much with astonishment as with pride.

"I did!" was Alexandra's response. "Very nice work, Curtis! We'll make a warrior out of you yet!"

One hand holding her sword, the other holding the reins, she urged the horse to a gallop as it deftly slalomed through the trees. Her horsemanship was second to none, and woe betide the bandits who attempted to raise a rifle or saber to her as she rode: They were certain to be cut down.

"Where are we going?" asked Curtis, his face nuzzled into the fur of her stole.

"You'll see!" shouted Alexandra.

They arrived at the far end of the ridge, where the wash was at its deepest and the gully's walls rose from the bottom like the sheer face of a canyon. The ridge was all a-tangle with bandits and coyotes, toe to toe, their bayonets and swords clashing. Alexandra leapt from the horse, quickly dispatched a charging bandit with a thrust of her sword, and ran to the edge of the ridge. Curtis gulped loudly and followed. When he had arrived at her side, the Governess pointed to the trough of the draw, where a group of bandits was laboriously pushing a giant howitzer up the gully.

"There," she said softly. "If that gun gets much farther, our battalion will be at the mercy of these savages."

The massive howitzer made the coyotes' cannons look like Roman candles; its mouth was easily three feet in diameter and the bore was of such a length that two men, end to end, could lie inside. The iron of the gun was ornately decorated with the vicious form of a dragon, the gun's maw framed by the dragon's barbed fangs. One shot from that, Curtis surmised, and you could take out an entire hillside.

"What can we do?" Curtis asked.

"Start shooting," Alexandra replied. She thrust a rifle into his hands before hefting her own to her shoulder, squaring her sights with the howitzer crew below.

Curtis blanched, and the pit in his stomach grew. He had fired the cannon, sure, but it had felt so anonymous and random. He wasn't sure he'd actually be able to *shoot a gun* at someone. Paralyzed, he simply stood, holding the rifle in his arms.

The Governess, meanwhile, had fired several shots into the crowd surrounding the giant cannon, felling two bandits who were quickly replaced as more reinforcements came hurrying up the draw. Stamping the rifle butt on the ground, she cursed as she unscrewed the ramrod from the rifle and busily began repacking a round.

Desperate for an alternate strategy, Curtis scanned the ridgeline. His eyes fell on something that made his heart catch in his throat. "Hold on!" he shouted to Alexandra, dropping his rifle to the ground. He sprinted over to a mossy outcrop overlooking the gully, where a massive cedar tree had fallen, its rough bark overgrown with ivy and ferns. It lay in the underbrush, perilously balanced on the edge of the ravine, its midsection cantilevered on another fallen tree. Curtis gauged the distance and height of the overhang, all the while looking back and forth between the bandits and the dead tree. Satisfied, he vaulted back over the tree and threw himself to the ground, lifting his feet to find purchase against the bark of the tree's trunk. With a pained grunt, he began pushing with all the power he could muster. The trunk began to tip on its axis, the living earth below it ripping away, before he exhausted his energies and the tree tipped back to its resting place. He took a deep breath and, grunting louder, began pushing again. The trunk lifted a little farther this time, but still not enough to be unanchored from its perch.

"Alexandra!" he shouted. "Come help me!"

The Governess, who had been firing her rifle into the amassing bandits below to no appreciable effect, looked over and, catching on to Curtis's plan, ran over to where he lay. Dropping to the ground, she too began pushing at the tree trunk with her moccasined feet.

"One . . . two . . . three!" counted Curtis, and they both pushed with all their might. The tree trunk gave a terrific groan before it toppled from its moorings and pitched over the edge of the ravine with a deafening crack. Alexandra and Curtis leapt up from the ground in time to see the giant tree go crashing down the steep wall of the gully, gaining speed with every roll. A scant few of the bandits, those that were alert, managed to dive out of the way before the tree collided with the howitzer, sending a spray of splinters and bark into the air. The howitzer collapsed from its carriage and tipped over onto the ground, the massive cedar trunk finally coming to rest on top of its muzzle. The bandits who made up the howitzer crew, the few that remained, ran off down the gully and disappeared into the bush.

Curtis started jumping up and down. "Holy . . . holy . . . ," he sputtered. "Holy SMOKE! Did that really just happen?" Alexandra looked on and smiled.

The inimitable sound of a conch shell being blown distracted them from their celebration, and suddenly the tide of bandits was retreating from the hillside, desperately scrambling up the far side of the ravine and back into the woods. The surviving coyote soldiers gave brief chase, picking off a few of the stragglers as they went, before raising their arms in a collective cheer. The ravine was theirs.

***

Prue pulled herself from the manhole and, sitting on the edge, surveyed the landscape; the knot of the forest's canopy loomed over her, and the few stars in the early evening sky glimmered through the branches above. She found she was in a small clearing, surrounded by a dense weave of trees.

She scarcely had time to ponder the presence of a manhole (its face was minted with the words PROPERTY OF SOUTH WOOD, DRAINAGE RESOURCES COUNCIL) in this remote clearing when she heard a strange, woody clattering behind her. She turned to see a bright yellow rickshaw making its way toward her. It was being pulled by a badger.

"Hello," said the badger when he arrived at Prue. He slowed to stop.

"Hi."

The badger blinked and looked down at the manhole. "Did you just climb out of there?" he asked, puzzled.

Prue looked back at the hole. "Yes."

"Oh," said the badger, and then added, as if suddenly remembering his trade, "Need a ride?"

"I do, actually," Prue said, pulling the owl's note from her pocket. "I need to get to Rue Thurmond. Number Eighty-six. Is that far?"

"Nah, not far at all," he said. "Just up the road." He jerked his head, gesturing to the rickshaw. "Hop in, I'll give you a ride."

"I don't have any money," said Prue.

The rickshaw driver paused for a moment before responding. "Don't worry about it. Last fare of the night. You're on my way home."

Prue thanked him kindly and hopped into the rickshaw's cushioned chair. The carriage's garish coat of yellow paint was accented with bright red designs and little knitted baubles dangled from the roof. With a quick word of warning ("It might be bumpy") from the badger, the rickshaw burst into movement, and in no time they were bumping along the forest floor at a quick clip. Taking a few quick turns, the rickshaw began following a well-trod path, and little ramshackle hovels started appearing in the woods. After a time, the dirt of the path gave way to cobbled streets, and the woods were upstaged by an impressive row of posh town houses, their mullioned bay windows refracting the light of candelabras down onto the pavement.

"Fancy place, this," commented the driver wryly. "Your friend is doin' all right for himself."

The street began inclining gradually, and the badger put his head down in concentration as the rickshaw climbed the hill. When they had arrived at the top, the carriage came to a stop in front of the grandest house on the block—it was a three-story behemoth of alabaster-white stone, and twin cherubs carrying trumpets met in a relief carved into the ground floor window's ornate molding. A warm light bathed the drawn curtains in front of the window, and the number

86 was written on a placard over the front door.

"Here ya go," said the badger, catching his breath. "Eighty-six Rue Thurmond."

Prue climbed down from the carriage. "Thank you so much," she said. The badger nodded and drove off.

She climbed the marble stairs to the front door and took a moment to admire the knocker that hung there: a brass eagle's head with a heavy golden ring in its beak. With more than a little trepidation, she lifted the ring and let it fall onto the oak of the door. It gave a resounding bang and she stood back, waiting. There was no answer. She tried the knocker again and still no one came to the door. Stepping back, she looked up at the placard a second time, reaffirming that this was, in fact, house number 86. She let the great golden ring fall a few more times before she started to get worried.

Suddenly, the door creaked open a few inches and stopped. She was about to step forward when the door slammed closed, only to inch a little farther open than it had before. Puzzled, Prue peered into the space between the door and the jamb and called, "Hello?"

The sound of feathers fluttering in a desperate manner answered her greeting, and she could see that two sparrows were trying, fairly unsuccessfully, to turn the doorknob.

"Sorry! Sorry!" one of them said, his talon striking at the polished brass.

"Oh!" said Prue. "Let me help you!" She carefully pushed the door wide and walked into the entryway.

"Thank you!" said one of the sparrows, hovering before Prue. "We're not used to these sorts of bipedal contraptions."

"You must be the Outsider girl, McKeel," said the other sparrow. "The Prince is expecting you."

The sparrows, after effortlessly taking her coat and flying it up to hang on a hook by the door, led Prue through one, down a short hallway, and into an enormous sitting room.

An open fire roared in the hearth below an ornate wooden mantel at the far end of the room, and its light projected whirling shadows against the towering ceiling. The furniture was, for the most part, draped in white cloth, save for two tall-backed wing chairs that were angled facing the fireplace. The walls were lined with high bookcases, the thousands of book spines lining their shelves giving the illusion of a multicolored tapestry. The draping on a framed portrait above the mantel had fallen to the side a little, revealing the figure of a blue jay in an austere robe, and it struck Prue that the room exuded a kind of cozy melancholy.

"Good evening," said a wizened voice from behind one of the chairs. "I hope you found your way here safely. Please, sit."

A giant wing appeared from behind the chair, its innumerable brown and white feathers articulating open to gesture to the chair opposite.

Prue whispered a thank-you and walked across the room toward the chair. The warmth of the fire greeted her as she reached it, and she found herself sitting, her jeans absorbing the heat of the flames, staring into the eyes of Owl Rex.

He was even more impressive in person, the hornlike feathers extending from the gossamer feathers of his head, and his brown speckled body easily filled the cushions of the chair. He wore a soft velvet waistcoat, and a tasseled cap was perched on his crown between the two feathered tufts. His gnarled talons were resting on an ottoman, and his piercing yellow eyes stared intently at Prue.

"I apologize for the state of the rooms," he continued. "We've scarcely found the time to make ourselves at home here. More pressing things demand our attention. But I should be offering you some refreshment. You must be parched from your travels. Tea or coffee?"

"Tea, sure," responded Prue, still getting over her amazement. "I mean, herbal tea. If you have it. Peppermint or something."

"Mint tea!" shouted the owl, swiveling his head to the side of the chair. A sudden flapping of wings behind them suggested the order had been received. He turned to look back at his guest, the beads of his eyes burrowing into Prue's. "A girl. An Outsider girl. Quite fascinating. I'm told you . . . you simply walked in?"

"Yes, sir," replied Prue.

"I've flown over your Outside city many times, but I can't say that I've had any interest in stopping. Do you enjoy nesting there? Is it comfortable?" asked Owl Rex.

"I guess so," said Prue. "I was born there and my parents live there, so I guess I don't really have a choice. It's a pretty nice place." She paused, thinking, before continuing: "Most people—and animals—I've met were pretty surprised I was here. You don't seem to be that weirded out by it."

"Oh, Prue, if you live to be as old as I, you'll see many, many strange and wonderful things. And the more strange and wonderful

things you see, the less likely you are to be, as you say, 'weirded out' by them." Owl lifted one of his dappled wings and lightly pecked at the underside with his beak before returning it to his side.

Prue, in the conversation's pause, hazarded the question she'd been dying to ask since she'd arrived at the house: "Mr. Rex, do you know what the crows have done with my brother?"

The owl sighed. "I am very, very saddened to tell you that I do not. If it is true, as you say, that the crows are responsible for your brother's abduction, then I have as much authority to find and prosecute his kidnappers as I would if the salamanders were to blame."

Prue didn't quite follow.

"You see," continued the Crown Prince, "the crows—the entire subspecies, mind you—defected from the Principality some months ago. They had always been a troubled lot, prone to mischief and petty thievery, and seemed to suffer under the delusion that they somehow stood above their avian brethren. A separatist streak developed. Naturally, we fought them on the issue many times over many years, but that did not stop them from leaving our Principality en masse one afternoon in July. And I'm disheartened to say that we've heard very little from them since."

The rhythmic flutter of wings from behind the chair alerted Prue to the arrival of her tea, and she graciously accepted the cup and saucer from the claws of the two attending sparrows. A tea tray was brought and placed delicately on a small table next to her chair; one of the sparrows hefted a teapot and poured the dark liquid into Prue's proffered cup. Thanking the bird, she despondently stirred a lump of sugar into the translucent brown liquid, crestfallen that yet another potential lead had been stamped out.

Owl Rex, detecting her despair, spoke up. "But that's not to say we aren't eminently concerned about their whereabouts. Rather, their tomfoolery is a bit of a thorn in our side at present. You see, over the last several months the isolated settlements to the north—at the border of Wildwood—have been threatened on numerous occasions by roving bands of what our citizen birds describe as 'coyote soldiers.' Coyotes— the most infamously disorganized, ragtag creatures in the forest, mind you—who have somehow pulled themselves together enough to form a cohesive military force. If I weren't so dedicated to the well-being of my subjects, I would be the first to dismiss such reports as absolutely implausible. But I have heard the stories, Prue, I have seen the anguished families, their nests destroyed, their home trees cut down, their foraging grounds despoiled. They cannot be ignored.

"Now, our emissaries have appealed to the Mansion over and over that we be allowed to defend our subjects and the strength of our border by retaliating against these bands of coyotes—but they have always been stonewalled. I have come myself to entreat that the amendments to the Wildwood Protocol that prohibit us from military action within Wildwood be suspended until our borders are made safe again. And here come reports of crows, ungrateful, meddling crows, carrying away an Outsider child and depositing him within the borders of Wildwood, clearly illegal activity that reflects very poorly on the Avians in general. I am as angered and disappointed with this situation as you, Prue. Since the Mansion doesn't recognize the breakaway status of the crows, their actions have the potential of completely derailing our case." He paused, searching for words. "The Mansion has, for years now, been looking for ways to curtail the freedoms of the Avians. It worries me that this may give them even more reason."

"Why?" asked Prue.

The owl shrugged. "Distrust. Intolerance. Fear. They dislike our ways."

This was baffling to Prue. The birds she'd met so far in this strange place seemed very kind and accommodating.

Owl Rex abruptly raised his wings and, with a few brisk flaps, carried himself to the stack of wood by the fireplace; the fire was now smoldering. He gripped a fresh log in his talons and threw it onto the coals, and the fire started anew. He returned to his seat, adjusted his cap, and continued.

"Gone are the days when the Mansion could be seen as a place of wise counsel and just governance. It is now a den of political opportunists and would-be despots, each grabbing desperately for every possible shard of power. It is the void that has remained since the coup."

"The coup?" asked Prue. She had been stirring her tea the entire time, transfixed by the owl's story. She caught herself and laid the spoon down on the saucer with a tiny clink.

The Crown Prince nodded gravely. "All this requires a bit of explanation. The coup in which the Dowager Governess, the widow of the deceased Governor-Regent Grigor Svik, was deposed and exiled to Wildwood."

"Grigor Svik—Lars's dad?" asked Prue.

"Uncle," replied Owl Rex. "And what a ruler he was. A gracious man, a kind man. As understanding of other species as one could hope. He and I were great friends. When we assumed our respective seats of power, we agreed on the sovereignty of the Avian Principality and the country of North Wood, countries that had existed for centuries but had not yet been recognized by their neighbors. We allowed free and safe passage for all subjects between these nations. And, most importantly, we authored the Wildwood Protocols—that very treaty I am now attempting to undo—which set aside the vast, untamed country of Wildwood as free and wild space, safe from the industrial barons who would seek to spoil it for their own ends. When Grigor died, I was . . . bereft." The Crown Prince lowered his head.

Prue shifted in her seat uncomfortably. "How did he die?" she asked softly.

Owl Rex composed himself, staring into the flames of the fire. "Heartbreak, I suppose. He and his wife, Alexandra, had a son, an only child. His name was Alexei. They adored him. From an early age he had been groomed to assume the governorship after his father, so it was a crushing blow to the country as well as the family when he was thrown from a horse, shortly after his fifteenth birthday. He did not survive the fall. Grigor and Alexandra, naturally, were devastated. After a private funeral, Grigor went to his bed in the Mansion and never left it.

"Alexandra handled these two unfathomable tragedies as well as could be expected, and she assumed the governorship, gaining the title Dowager Governess—but her grief was eating her from the inside out, and she became distant and withdrawn to those who knew her best. She isolated herself in the Mansion and kept very strange company: soothsayers, gypsies, and practitioners of the black arts. Her aides were powerless to stop her. Finally, she called the two most renowned toy makers in South Wood and, behind the Mansion walls, commanded them to create a mechanical replica of her dead son, Alexei.

"In a secluded Mansion garret, the two toy crafters slaved over their creation for months until they presented to the Governess the final product, and it was seen to be a very remarkable facsimile of the late young governor-in-waiting. It was, however, still a toy. It required winding at regular intervals and did little more than walk stiffly around, making metallic clicks and buzzes."

"Creepy!" interjected Prue. "I mean, how could she think that would replace her son?"

Owl Rex nodded soberly, saying, "She had other plans. Using magics learned from her attendant dark mystics, she placed Alexei's full set of teeth—which she had salvaged from his corpse—into the mouth of the automaton. Weaving a powerful spell into the machinery, she brought forth the deceased soul of Alexei into this mechanical child."

Prue gasped. The fire crackled in the hearth. A clock on the mantel gently chimed the hour.

Curtis had never been so elated in his life. The surrounding forest took on an unearthly glow and the air tasted like ambrosia and he was being buoyed along on the shoulders of a multitude of cheering coyote soldiers, their overjoyed cries occasionally conjoining to chant, "CURTIS! CURTIS! CURTIS!" This rowdy parade marched through the woods, the soldiers' crackling torches illuminating the way.

Their victory had been decisive, their losses minimal. The afternoon's battle had been a resounding success, and Curtis the crowned hero of the day. Alexandra trotted her horse alongside the procession, smiling proudly on.

When they arrived at the warren, the great hall was alight with burning braziers, and the smell of a hearty stew drifted from the burrow entrance. A crooked, brazen melody was struck up by a motley brass band and the procession marched Curtis in five circles around the Governess's throne room before depositing him, with much fanfare, on the moss of the throne's dais. A mug thrust into his hand was filled to the brim with blackberry wine before he had a chance to demur.

The Commandant quieted the room with a loud bark.

"Listen up, curs!" he shouted when the clamor in the room began to calm. "You stinking mongrel dogs!" He grabbed a nearby soldier and with a free arm—the one not holding an overflowing mug of wine—ensnared him in a savage headlock. "I've not seen a more putrid, fetid stink of mange in all my days." The room paused, unsure of what to expect from the commander. The Commandant smiled and snarled, "And we gave 'em *what for* today!"

The room exploded in a cheer, and the Commandant planted a sloppy kiss on the forehead of his imprisoned soldier before letting him go. Then, staggering over to brace himself on the shoulder of another coyote, he stiffened and grew serious.

"The woods will resound with our victory. In time every animal will be talking about our actions. Our presence will no longer be ignored. And when we march into South Wood, those pasty pansies will have no choice but to lay down their arms, and the gilded halls of Pittock Mansion will resound with the echoes of our celebrations."

He was interrupted by Alexandra, who had strolled through the celebrants to seat herself on the ornate throne. "What's left of the Mansion," she said coolly.

The Commandant, sensing he had overstepped his bounds, bowed deeply, his mug raised high.

"When we're done with South Wood, there won't be two walls standing to support an echo," Alexandra hissed.

"Aye, madam," said the Commandant. The tone of the room had chilled considerably.

"But tonight, we celebrate our victory!" the Governess shouted, rising to stand before the throne. "And we raise our mugs to Curtis, cannon killer, bandit vanquisher, *tree crusher*." She had turned to Curtis and was smiling, her wooden chalice proffered in a toast. He blushed and raised his mug in return. The room solemnly joined in, a sea of rough-hewn cups raised in salute. "Strike up the band!" she hollered, looking back out into the hall, and the drawling buzz of a trumpet launched the brass band into another drunken tune. The soldiers cheered loudly and returned to their celebrations. Grinning ear to ear, Curtis tapped his hand on the knee of his navy britches to the beat of the music.

"They're never going to believe me back at school," shouted Curtis over the band's manic playing. "Never in a million years."

"Perhaps you shouldn't return to school," Alexandra replied, her eyes wandering the room of celebrating coyotes.

"What, drop out? My parents would . . . ," started Curtis. He then blanched momentarily. "Oh," he continued thoughtfully. "You mean . . ."

"Yes, Curtis," said Alexandra. "Stay with us. Join our fight. Leave your plain, simple human life behind. Join the Wildwood brigade and

185

savor the taste of our inevitable victory."

"Well," said Curtis, "I don't know. I think my parents would be pretty upset, for one thing. They already had my spot reserved for sleepaway camp next summer, and I think they might've even paid a deposit."

Alexandra rolled her eyes and laughed. "Oh, I cherish you, Curtis. I really do. But there are more important things at stake here. The salvation of Wildwood hangs in the balance. You have proven yourself today; you have shown us all that within that little frame beats the true heart of a warrior." She gestured to the room full of soldiers. "I have tremendous respect for the coyotes. They took a remarkable risk when they came to my side. But one longs for the company of *humans*. And I do not expect to build a cabinet of advisers from these ragtag canines—they're far too impetuous." She took a small sip of her wine and fixed her gaze on Curtis, her tone growing serious.

"I want you to be my second in command, Curtis. I want you to be by my side when we march on the South. I want you to sit next to my throne when it is laid on the smoldering rubble of the Mansion. And together we could rebuild this land, this beautiful wild country." Here she paused, her eyes drifting slowly away from the activity to fix on some distant, elusive point. "We could rule together, you and I."

Curtis was speechless. Finally, setting down his mug of wine, he found his voice. "Wow, Alexandra. I mean, I don't know what to say. I might have to think about it. It's kind of a big thing to just ditch out on my parents and my sisters and my school like that. I mean, don't get me wrong: This is amazing. Everybody's been really kind to me, and I have to say, today was pretty epic. I didn't really think I had it in me, either." He shifted uncomfortably in his seat. "Just give me a moment, is all."

"Take however much time you need, Curtis," said Alexandra, her voice softening. "We have all the time in the world."

One of the coyotes who had witnessed Curtis's impromptu firing of the cannon came wobbling over to the dais, gesturing to Curtis. "Curtishh! Shir!" he slurred, after sloppily saluting both Curtis and Alexandra. "I'm telling the sh-sh-shtory of your cannon sh-shot. Those mongrels don't believe me! You gotta back me up here!"

Alexandra smiled and nodded to Curtis, mouthing, *Go.* Laughing, Curtis accepted the soldier's paw to help him up from the moss. The coyote slung his arm over Curtis's shoulder, and they walked off together over to a group of soldiers who were gathered by the wine barrel. Alexandra watched him intently as he wandered away, her finger scratching absently at the wood of the throne.

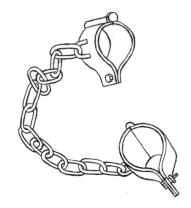

CHAPTER 12

An Owl in Irons;
Curtis's Conundrum

"Really?" asked Prue in disbelief. "His teeth?" A sparrow flew over the shoulder of her chair and, picking up the poker in its claws, began stirring the glowing embers of the fire.

Owl Rex nodded.

"That's disgusting."

"Never underestimate the power of grief, Prue," said the owl.

"So suddenly Alexei was back to life? Just like that?"

"Yes," answered Owl. "His death had been kept secret from the people of South Wood, explained away as a period of convalescence as the young prince recovered from injuries sustained in the accident. Much fanfare greeted his return to public life. Alexandra, for her part, did everything in her power to conceal the fact that he was an automaton—she even went so far as to exile the two toy makers responsible for his creation to the Outside. Even the boy Alexei was unaware that he was mechanical. As for the period of his death, he merely thought he had been unconscious from the fall. He was naturally in despair over the unexplained demise of his father, but the grief eventually passed and he took on the governorship with enthusiasm and aplomb. Until one day, while he was working in the Mansion's garden (a particular passion of his), he chanced to knock open a plate in his chest that exposed the inner workings of his, well, chassis. Bowled over by this revelation, he confronted his mother, who revealed the truth behind his death. He was horrified. He retired to his rooms in the Mansion and, opening the door in his chest, removed an indispensable piece—a little brass cog—from the clockwork of his body and destroyed it. The machine seized up, and the boy was again rendered lifeless.

"Her enterprise was laid bare. The Governess was dragged before a high court and, in a protracted trial, all was revealed. She was sentenced to exile in Wildwood for criminal use of black magic. The prosecution even suggested that she'd been responsible for the death of her husband, Grigor. It was expected that she would not survive her banishment; she would be torn apart by coyotes or killed by roving bandits." Owl locked eyes with Prue and raised a feathery eyebrow. "It appears that neither of those fates befell her."

Prue nodded in agreement.

Looking back to the fire, Owl continued, "In the vacuum that followed the Governess's deposition, Lars Svik, then a young peon in administrative affairs, was propped up by the military as the rightful heir to the governorship. Many opposed him. However, rather than risk a civil war, the progressives abdicated, and Svik and his cronies assumed the office of Governor-Regent."

A wind was steadily picking up outside, and a branch whipped against the windowpane of one of the room's windows. Owl Rex started at the sound before turning back to Prue and saying, "Since then, fifteen years on, the political climate of South Wood has steadily changed. Dissenters are no longer suffered. Vocal opponents to Lars's ham-handed rule have been demoted, imprisoned, or, in some cases, have simply disappeared. Their blatant disrespect toward the sovereignty of the independent countries of the Wood is clear. Their intolerance of others, plain. Which brings me to why I've called you here. I'll be the first to admit that I've become a bit of a windbag in my dotage, but I urge you to listen closely to what I say now."

Prue leaned in, listening intently. The owl began speaking in a hushed, conspiratorial tone.

"There are people in South Wood who can help you. There are

people who are trustworthy, who are trying to change the rule of law from the inside out. But they are the minority. As for the Governor and his aides, they are not to be trusted. If it is in their interest, Prue, and you are a *problem* to them, they will *make that problem go away.* Is that clear?"

Dazed by the insistence of the owl's question, Prue looked on.

"I said: *Is that clear?*"

"Yes," said Prue quickly. "Totally clear."

"And after speaking with them today," continued Owl, "I fear that your presence here has the potential of becoming *problematic.*"

Prue's mind flashed to the mastiff sentry she'd locked in her bathroom.

Owl Rex leaned back into his chair and stared into the fire's trembling flames, their light reflected in the shine of his eyes. "I can't tell you how hard it is for me to witness all this; the slow and certain despoiling of everything that Grigor had built. I fear it has broken my heart." He held the tip of his wing to his chest and heaved a great sigh. He looked back at Prue with a sidelong glance. "I hope I haven't frightened you too much—and you strike me as a very bright girl. I have no doubt that you will be able to navigate these issues with courage and wisdom. I just felt it imperative that you understand what kind of people you are dealing with."

"What should I do?" asked Prue, feeling desperate. "I don't know who else to turn to."

The owl was silent for a moment. The ticking of the mantel clock filled the quiet room. "I suppose," began Owl, "if all else failed, you could visit the Mystics."

"The Mystics?"

"Of North Wood," explained the owl. "They have little dealing with the South—they are a reclusive people. But they may have an insight into your problem. They are responsible for the Periphery Bind—the protective spell woven into the trees on the edge of the Wood that protects and separates us from the Outside—that thing that you managed to disregard when you just walked in here." Here, the owl smirked a little at Prue.

"Sorry," whispered Prue sheepishly.

He went on, "The North Wood Mystics share a connection with the woods that no one else has. The great Council Tree, whose roots reach us even here in the South, registers every footstep in the Wood. It is around this tree that the Mystics meet; it is how they derive their power. It's a long shot, but if you've no other choice, they may have clues to the whereabouts of your brother. And perhaps your friend as well." He shook his head gently. "But it's a long journey; one that is rife with danger. And you are not necessarily guaranteed to receive a gracious welcome—the Mystics are protective of their seclusion. However, even if you were able to convince them to help you, they do not have a military to speak of—it's inconceivable that they would have the ability or manpower to forcibly recover your brother or your friend." The owl's chest rose in a deep sigh. "You are truly at an impasse, Prue. I wish I could be of more assistance."

A sudden frantic explosion of squawking violently disrupted the calm of the room, and the air was alive with the flapping of wings. The two attendant sparrows swooped around the sides of their chairs and made a hasty landing on the lip of the mantel in front of Prue and Owl Rex, a small flurry of lost feathers floating to the ground in their wake.

"Sir!" shouted one. "Sir! You must hide yourself! You must—"

"What he's trying to say, sir," sputtered the other, "is that they are—the street is—we don't think we'll be able—"

The other interjected, "It is vital that you hide yourself because—"

This last sentence was interrupted by the unmistakable sound of the front door of the house being kicked open.

"THE SWORD!" shouted one of the sparrows. "THEY'RE HERE!"

Prue shot a panicked look at Owl Rex. "The *what?*" she asked.

"The Mansion's secret police," Owl said, desperately searching the room. "The South Wood Office of Rehabilitation and Detention. They've acted faster than I suspected. Quickly! We must hide you."

Owl Rex lifted his wings and carried himself out of his chair. Prue leapt up and followed him as he flew in a quick, frantic arc around the room. He stopped at a large wicker hamper by one of the book-cases and, knocking the lid open with his talons, urged Prue to climb inside. The racket from the entryway was now spilling over into the dining room—a staccato of boot heels against floorboards and the overturning of chairs polluted the air, while the sparrows desperately tried to waylay the intruders with squawked objections. Prue dove into the hamper and nestled into a pile of musty old newspapers, while Owl Rex threw the lid closed and she was in darkness, her hand at her chest in an effort to stay her agitated heartbeat.

Just as the lid snapped shut and Owl Rex had flown to a safe distance from the hamper, the double doors at the end of the room were savagely kicked open and the room was filled with the sound of hammering jackboots.

"Where is she, owl?" shouted one of the voices. Prue sucked her breath into her chest, her heart a caged hummingbird within her ribs.

"I'm afraid I have no idea to whom you are referring," responded Owl Rex civilly.

The man laughed. "Just like you birds, playing stupid."

A sparrow interjected: "This is an outrage! No one speaks to the Crown Prince this way!"

Owl Rex waved away the sparrow's objection. "If you're referring to the Outsider girl, Prue, she was here earlier, yes, but left some time ago. I haven't the slightest idea where she's gone."

There was a short silence before the man spoke again. "Is that so?" Prue could discern the sound of the SWORD officers milling about the room. A few footsteps approached the hamper before stopping, and Prue could hear the sound of a book being opened, pages flipped.

When the owl gave no answer, the man at the bookcase cleared his throat and said in a loud, authoritative tone, "Owl Rex, Crown Prince of the Avian Principality, we are putting you under arrest for the violation of the Wildwood Protocols, Section Three, the harboring of an illegal, and for conspiring to overthrow the government of South Wood. Are the charges clear to you?"

Prue choked a gasp in her throat, her eyes wide. The silence that followed prompted her to push the lid of the hamper open a crack to get a view of the room. Owl Rex was standing in front of a small group of men who were dressed in identical black rain slickers and policemen's caps. Two of them, while Prue looked on, drew small pistols from their coats and pointed them at the owl.

"Your law is a sham," said the owl defiantly, "and a gross distortion of the founding principles of South Wood."

"I'm sorry you feel that way, owl," came the voice of the man standing at the bookcase by the hamper. He threw something heavy—Prue guessed it to be a book—onto the top of the hamper, forcing the lid to slam closed. She stifled a shriek of surprise, a squeal that was thankfully masked by the quick creak of the closing lid. "But go ahead: Spit your invectives. Proclaim injustice! Shout it to the rooftops! You're only going to make things worse for yourself. Now: You can come easy or you come fighting."

A hush fell over the room. "Very well, I submit," came the owl's voice. Pushing the hamper lid slightly open again, Prue saw Owl Rex extend his wings to his would-be captors, as if in pious supplication.

"Lock him up, boys," said the man, and one of the other officers stepped over and fastened a pair of large iron manacles around the owl's wing tips. Another pair locked his two talons together by a short link of chain. Owl Rex's head sank against his chest.

"What about the girl?" asked one of the officers.

"Search the building," said the man. "She can't have gotten far."

Prue breathlessly retreated back to the bottom of the hamper and listened to the sound of Owl Rex being dragged from the room, the chain of his shackles scraping along the wooden floor.

Curtis watched his fellow soldiers dive headlong into their celebrations. His prior experience with the Governess's blackberry concoction was still branded on his brain, and rather than actually imbibe the stuff, he went to great effort to merely mime drinking. The rest of the troop was evidently eschewing this strategy. A barrel of wine rolled into the hall would scarcely have been tapped before another appeared through one of the tunnels that led into the main room of the warren. Several soldiers, their uniforms unbuttoned to the waist, exposing the gray matted fur of their spindly rib-carved chests, lolled in mangled lumps below the barrel spigots, greedily lapping up every drop that fell. Curtis did his best to remain an active participant in the celebrations. His feet grew tired from treading around the room to every group that beckoned to him, asking him to retell the story of the battle—the firing of the cannon, the loosing of the tree trunk on the bandits' howitzer. He found himself, after the seventh or eighth telling, allowing the other coyotes to finish his sentences and punch up the climaxes of the stories. Eventually, his voice grown hoarse, he found an upended keg in the corner of the room and sat, smiling politely at every soldier who stumbled over to him, each bearing a new, full mug of wine, until his feet were surrounded by a small army of untouched drinks.

A lieutenant, his uniform's sash tied raffishly around his forehead, had climbed to the top of a short tower of emptied wine crates and was waving his saber as if it were a conductor's baton. He cleared his throat and began singing a melody, which the rest of the room took up with a swaggering, throaty familiarity:

> *I was born a hangman's cub*
> *Whelped and weaned on maggoty grub*
> *Torn right from my dead pa's whiskers*
> *So listen close, my brothers and sisters.*

Hey! Hey! Catch that rat!
Tie him up and boil 'im in his fat.
Loose one finger if he is feckless
Wear it as a noose or wear it as a necklace.

Way down yonder in the brambly bog
I saw my girly with another dog.
Took 'er by the ear to the old town well
And that's where my girl-y does dwell.

Hey! Hey! Catch that rat!
Tie him up and boil 'im in his fat!

Curtis politely tapped his finger on his pant leg and even made a halfhearted attempt to join in on the chorus when it came back around, making his neighbors cackle and lift their mugs to him.

"The boy's getting a hang of the dog shanty!" howled one.

"There's a good jackal!" shouted another.

A coyote who had plopped himself down next to Curtis and his array of untouched wine mugs ribbed him clumsily, nearly sending them both falling backward.

Curtis laughed shyly and pushed himself up. "Excuse me, guys," he said. "Might go get a little air." The activity in the room was beginning to get a little too clamorous for his taste. He tiptoed around the rows of mugs and the chains of arm-linked coyotes singing in full throat, toward one of the many tunnel entrances leading from the room. A few torches attached to the wall of the tunnel lit the way, the knobby ground below his feet alive with the winking shadows cast by the partyers. As he followed the curve of the tunnel, the song continued behind him, fading:

Liar! Liar!
Furze and briar!
Bind his feet and hang 'im with a wire!

A shiver running up his spine, Curtis was glad to hear the noise of the manic crowd bleed away as he descended farther into the tunnel. He wasn't sure where he was going—he was simply following this sudden instinct to find somewhere he could sit by himself and reflect on all that had transpired during the last two days.

Several side tunnels, through which Curtis could see the torch-illumined walls of antechambers and storerooms, broke away from this main corridor, and he took extra care to mentally mark his every turn so as to be able to return to the Governess's hall. The noise from the party was a distant echo now, the ashy smoke from the central fire a mere hint in the musty air. The plant roots dangling from the earthen roof of the tunnel caressed his head as he went like long, downy fingers. Curtis was overcome by a warm closeness here, the feeling of being cocooned in this labyrinthine warren, and he wondered if this was a place where he could stay. The aching anxiety with which he faced every school day, the quiet loneliness of the playground and the overwhelming authority of his teachers, disappointed coaches, and fretful parents—all seemed to recede like the singing of the coyote soldiers behind him. He had never been so embraced by a group of people in his life; he had always found himself on the outside, desperately striving for the approval of his peers. Alexandra's suggestion of their relationship—she would be a new mother to him! How many kids were afforded that opportunity?—was thrilling to Curtis, and the idea of their dominion in this strange new world seemed intoxicating.

Whish.

The unmistakable sound of a flutter of wings came from the distant dark of the tunnel.

Whish.

The smile dropped from Curtis's face, replaced by a puzzled frown.

Again, the noise replayed: a distinct whip of feathered wings, the sound of a bird briefly circling before landing.

He kept walking toward the sound. A bat? No: He had heard bats wheeling above the patio at his house at dusk. They barely made a flutter. But what could a bird possibly be doing in an underground warren? So far, he hadn't seen any other animal included in the Governess's forces. He followed the sound through a passageway leading off the tunnel—a small light could be seen at the end. This ceiling here was lower than the main one, and Curtis bowed his head as he walked. The pinprick of light at the end of the tunnel flickered like a movie projector, its tiny gleam occasionally being blotted by the sudden appearance and disappearance of a number of quick black shapes. Curtis narrowed his eyes, the sound of flapping wings now growing in volume.

"Hello?" he called.

The brittle agitation of the wings started at the sound of his voice, and Curtis now guessed there must be hundreds of birds, the noise of their flying, circling, and diving massing together.

Suddenly he felt something sweep over his shoulder, skirting the fabric of his uniform. He instinctively dove out of the way, landing uncomfortably on his saber's scabbard against the raw dirt of the tunnel wall. A single black feather drifted lazily to the ground where he had been standing.

Curtis righted himself and drew his saber from its sheath.

"Seriously! Who's there?" he called, unnerved.

And that was when he heard the sound of a baby crying. A sharp, short wail from an infant, bubbling up from below the harried noise of the birds' wings. His heart froze at the sound.

"Oh man," whispered Curtis, walking faster down the passageway.

The tunnel opened into a tall chamber—almost egglike in shape—and it was filled to the ceiling with crows. Pitch-black, tar-black crows. Dozens, hundreds, all wheeling and hovering, sparring and cawing. The few lit torches on the wall illuminated their oily black feathers. The apex of the room was crowned with a small opening, through which more crows arrived and departed.

In the center of the room, on the dirt floor, sat a small, simple bassinet made from the mossy boughs of beech saplings. And in this bassinet lay a chubby, burbling baby, his eyes vacillating between fear and amazement at the whirling cloud of crows above his head. He wore a brown corduroy jumper, badly stained with dirt and what appeared to be bird droppings.

Curtis gaped. "Mac?" he stammered.

The child looked at Curtis and cooed. A single crow broke away from the hovering mass and landed on the side of the cradle, a long fat worm writhing in his beak. To Curtis's disgust, the crow dropped the worm into Mac's open mouth. Mac munched it contentedly.

"Gross," whispered Curtis, his stomach churning.

Curtis's mind was racing; did the Governess know about this? Did the company know that there were these intruders in the warren? He was certain Alexandra, once informed, would not stand for this trespass.

"Mac, I'm getting you out of here," said Curtis, snapping from

his spell. Raising his saber above his head, he began moving in on the strange bassinet. The crows, threatened by this usurper, began cawing and crying madly. Several dive-bombed him as he arrived at the cradle, their talons ripping at the fabric of his uniform. Swinging his saber about his head to thwart the birds' attacks, he arrived at the cradle and, with his free hand, scooped Mac into his arms. Mac gurgled happily, a speck of half-chewed worm still on his lip. The crows, now incensed, redoubled their attacks, and Curtis and Mac were enshrouded in a veil of black feathers, beaks, and talons. Their claws scratched at his face and their beaks tore through his clothing, pinching blood through his revealed skin. Curtis stumbled across the floor, his saber waving haplessly in the air before him. Mac began crying. Curtis could feel the crows' talons tangling in his hair, their wings batting him in the face until he was practically blinded. He shouted, at once in frustration and in pain. Suddenly, a voice cleared the racket of the room.

"STOP!" shouted the voice. Curtis immediately recognized it to be Alexandra's.

"OFF!" she commanded.

The storm of crows abated slightly, and Curtis was able to lift his head and open his eyes. Through the diminishing sea of feathers, he could make out the form of Alexandra, standing by the entrance to the chamber.

"Alexandra!" he shouted. "I got Mac! I got Prue's brother!"

He paused. As Alexandra stood, taking in the scene, a few crows alighted on her shoulders. One landed on her arm, and she petted the feathers absently with her ringed fingers.

"He was . . . here," continued Curtis, the wind leaving his sails as the reality of the situation began to dawn on him.

Alexandra, looking away from Curtis, lifted her arm so as to bring the crow perched there to eye level. The crow squawked a reprobation, to which Alexandra calmly smiled, cooing soothingly. Satisfied, the crow returned its steely gaze to Curtis.

"What are you doing in here, Curtis?" asked Alexandra.

He stuttered a response: "I was j-just wandering and I . . . well, I heard the sound of a baby so I came to, um, check it out."

Mac was still crying.

Alexandra walked forward, confidently, sternly. The crow on her arm flew off. Alexandra pulled Mac from Curtis's arms and cradled him, quietly shushing his crying. "There now," she said. "Shhhh."

"You . . . ," began Curtis. "You knew about this?" A trickle of blood from his scalp had descended the distance of his forehead and was clotting in his eyebrow.

Alexandra rocked back and forth, her eyes on the child in her arms, and Mac began to quiet.

"You knew about this?" repeated Curtis, louder.

His raised voice startled Mac, who began to cry again.

Alexandra shot Curtis an angered look. "Curtis, keep your voice down," she said, resuming the rocking motion. "You've already upset the child enough." The crow on Alexandra's shoulder snapped its beak at Curtis.

"But," he objected impotently, "why have you—how did you—" Despondent, he punctuated this slurry of words with: "I'm just confused."

Alexandra half smiled at Curtis and walked past him to the vacant bassinet. Whispering calming assurances to the unquiet baby, she placed him down in the mossy heather that lined the bottom of the cradle. Touching Mac's lips with a finger, she mouthed a final *shhhh* before returning to Curtis, taking him by the arm.

"I wasn't quite prepared to show this to you, Curtis," she said, walking him away from the baby. "But since you've forced my hand, I have no choice." The crowd of crows above them, in the presence of the Governess, had calmed, and many had exited the room via the opening in the ceiling.

"These are difficult times," continued Alexandra. "Difficult, confusing times. Eventually, it will all make sense to you—but I can understand your present bewilderment."

"W-why didn't you tell me?" pleaded Curtis. "I mean, you knew why I was here in the first place. Why did you keep it a secret?"

"I couldn't have told you, Curtis," said the Governess. "Think of what a shock it would've been—before you'd been properly *acclimated* to Wildwood. No, I needed to give you time before revealing this to you—and believe me, I was intending to. I would've hoped you'd enjoyed your night of celebration a little longer but no matter: Now is as good a time as any."

Alexandra stopped short of the opening to the chamber and turned to Curtis, putting her hands on his shoulders and looking him squarely in the eye. "Sometimes," she began, her tone turning from dulcet to firm, "you are forced into a position against your own wishes, a position that requires you to retaliate with any given weapon at your disposal—even if it is at the expense of others. Those reprobates in South Wood have done this to me. They have taken from me my dignity, my power. And not only do I intend to get it back, but I also intend to strip the same from those who stole from *me*. Any action I take to further this end that might be construed as immoral or antagonistic is a consequence of their foolhardy decisions. Do you follow?"

Curtis sniffled. "No, not really."

Alexandra smiled. "That child is rightfully mine. He is owed to me. I have waited thirteen long years for this moment. *Thirteen* bitter years. Curtis, the child is the key to my—to *our*—success in this campaign. Do you remember, earlier this evening, you and I were talking? We were talking about ruling, you and I. On the rubble of South Wood. Returning the natural order, the natural rule, to this country, with me as its queen and you by my side.

Do you remember that?"

Curtis nodded dolefully.

"Well, that is not possible without that child, that babbling incoherent thing there." She pointed over to Mac, who was idly toying with a small twig in his rustic cradle. She looked back at Curtis and gripped his chin between her thumb and forefinger. "That child is our ticket to victory."

Curtis nodded again before adding, "How?"

"The ivy, Curtis. We need him to harness it."

"The ivy? Like, the plant?"

Alexandra closed her eyes briefly and took a deep breath. "Curtis," she said, "this may be difficult for you to hear." Her fingers drifted from his chin to caress his cheek. She wiped a small drop of blood from his skin. "The child must be given as offering. As offering to the ivy."

"W-what does that mean?" stammered Curtis.

Her voice became a meditative monotone, as if she were reciting primeval scripture: "On the autumnal equinox, three days hence, on the Plinth of the Ancients, the body of the second child will be laid. At my incantation, the vines will come forward and consume his flesh and drink his blood. This will confer upon the ivy an inestimable power, the human blood coursing through its stalks, and what's more it will render the plant in thrall to my command. When we march on South Wood, we need only follow the path of destruction laid in the wake of the ivy." Lifting her hand from Curtis's cheek, Alexandra poised to cap this neat explanation with a snap of her fingers.

"Simple," she said.

Snap.

"As that."

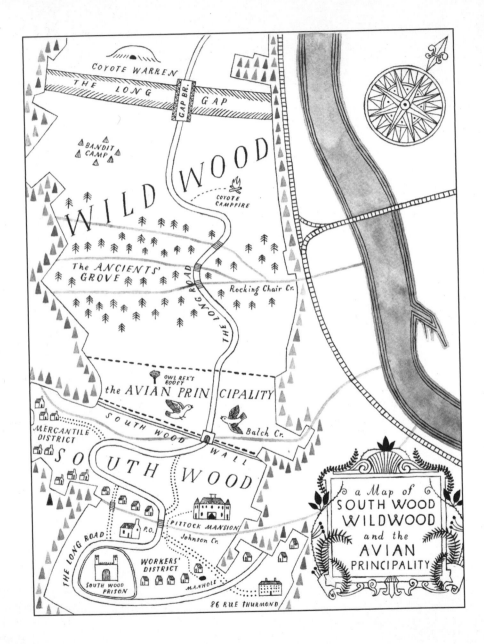

PART TWO

CHAPTER 13

To Catch a Sparrow;
Like a Bird in a Cage

A wild flutter of wings. The piercing shatter of glass. The gruff dismissal of a sparrow's squawked reproach. All these things created a vivid collage in Prue's mind as she squatted, frozen, at the bottom of the wicker hamper and listened to the sounds of Owl Rex's living room being violently dismantled. The searchers, the remaining SWORD officers, seemed to be working in a methodical manner; overturning chairs, slamming doors, and upending bookcases on the other side of the room, slowly making their way to where Prue was hidden. She had little time.

Using the eruptions of sound as concealment, she shifted her weight on the pile of old newspapers below her and began sliding the top few from underneath her feet. During the silent breaks between the officers' work, she would halt her efforts and stare silently, breathlessly, at the ambient strands of light coming in through the slats of the hamper until the noise of their searching began again. Finally, just as the footsteps grew closer, she managed to get several folded stacks of newsprint up from beneath her shoes to rest on her head. She had no sooner achieved this when a voice shouted, "What about there?"

"Where?" came another voice, mere inches from where Prue sat.

"Under your nose, idiot! That hamper!"

"Oh," responded the voice. "I was just going to look there."

Light poured in above Prue, and she squeezed her eyes closed and willed herself disappeared.

"Well, well, well," the voice said. "What *have* we here?"

Prue's eyes shot open.

A hand reached down into the hamper and fumbled with the pile of papers balanced on her head. Suddenly, the hamper lid slammed shut again. Prue noticed that the weight of paper on her head had grown a little lighter.

"It's Jonesy and his *pwetty wittle garden!*" announced the officer, his voice dripping with unbridled sarcasm. "Front page of the *illustrious* House and Home section."

"What?" said another voice from across the room.

"Yeah, take a look: Jonesy got a nice shiny medal from the Governor-Regent last week for his, get this, *award-winning peonies*."

The room erupted with laughter as the sound of boot heels echoed, moving toward the man's voice. A litany of mirthful shouts followed:

"Nice one, Jonesy!"

"Ooh! That's a fancy little apron you're wearing!"

"The way you cradle those peonies, Jonesy, *very* maternal."

Finally, the object of all this laughter, Jonesy, made it over to the side of the hamper and, judging by the sound, whipped the incriminating object from the joker's hand. "My wife put me up to it!" was the man's feeble explanation.

The room exploded with more laughter, and Prue could practically feel the crimson redness of poor Jonesy's cheeks through the hamper walls. "I—I—" he stammered. "Well—you know—" Finally, he gave up. "Oh, STUFF IT! All of you!" More laughter. In the flash of a moment, the hamper lid was thrown open and the newspaper was heaved, powerfully, back onto the stack on Prue's head. The lid slammed closed. "Back to work!" shouted Jonesy. "Enough of this horseplay."

The river of laughter eddied down to a trickle as the sound of footsteps and voices spread back out across the room. More doors were slammed, more furniture was disturbed, and more sidelong comments regarding Jonesy were whispered, but Prue scarcely paid attention; she was too busy counting out a thousand thank-yous to the Fates, the Goddess, or whatever pantheon of deities had somehow granted her this reprieve.

Minutes passed. Prue's left foot was starting to fall asleep, and she began trying to ignore the incessant needling pain by practicing her Pranayama. It was a technique for controlling breathing; she'd learned it in her beginning yoga class. No matter how much control she was gaining over her breathing, however, it didn't change the fact that her foot felt like it was about to fall off her body. Finally, a voice came from beyond the hamper walls.

"No sign, sir," said the officer. "We've searched the whole building."

Prue exhaled a sigh of relief out her nose.

"Everywhere?"

"Yes, sir."

"She must've escaped. Someone tipped her off," said the commanding officer. "Well, no matter. She'll turn up in the sweep."

"Yes, sir," responded the other officer. "And the sparrows? What should we do with them?"

"Arrest them," was the answer.

Another voice sounded from the far end of the room. "There's only one, sir."

"What happened to the other?"

"Must've flown away, sir, in the excitement."

There was a brief silence in the room. "Flown away? Just . . . flown away?"

"That's my guess," another officer quietly replied.

"Idiots! Brain-dead idiots!" shouted the commander. "Incompetent brain-dead . . ."

"Idiots, sir?" offered an officer.

"IDIOTS!" The commander regained himself and said in a level voice, "Head office is not going to stand for this. We can lose one collar, but they'll have our jobs if they see we've lost two." He thought for a moment before instructing, "Write up in the report that there was *one*, I repeat, *one* sparrow attending to the incarcerated on arrival."

"And the girl?" quavered a subordinate officer.

Another pause. "Write that the Outsider girl is suspected to have been tipped off to SWORD's arrival and was not to be found at the scene."

"Yes, sir," replied another officer.

"And you, bird," spoke the commander, "you're coming with us. We'll see how well you're soaring after a few weeks in the hoosegow."

There was a pause in the room. An officer chimed in, "The what, sir?"

"Hoosegow. Pokey. Slammer." No response. "PRISON, idiots! Now let's hop to it before the place is full. Lord knows the prison warden's hands'll be full tonight." A thunder of boot steps followed this proclamation, and in moments the room was empty of sound. The front door slammed in the distance, and the growl of a car's engine could be heard, starting up and grinding away down the street. After counting out thirty Mississippis, Prue slid the pile of newspapers from off her head and cautiously opened the lid to the hamper. Peeking over the lip and seeing no one, she stood up straight in a gust of energy, feeling the blood course from her neck down to her toes in an ecstatic rush. She shook her numb foot and carefully stepped out of the hamper.

She was alone in the room. The two high-backed chairs where, only minutes before, she and the owl had been sitting were carelessly toppled on their sides, and the fine tall bookcases that had stood against the wainscot of the walls had been thrown to the ground, their contents strewn about the room in a great scatter of warped spines and splayed pages. A few mottled feathers lay in the center of the room, and Prue's heart broke at the sight. What had she done? It was all her fault; the police had come for *her*. And yet he had protected her. Guilt washed over her as she knelt down and picked up one of the feathers. "Oh, Owl," she gushed. "I'm so, so sorry."

She was startled by a flustered flap of wings sounding from the hearth. Looking over, she saw one of the sparrow attendants, his light gray belly marred with soot, emerge from the fireplace flue.

The bird clumsily flew over to where Prue was standing and landed on the edge of one of the upended bookcases. He shook a mist of ash from his left wing and looked haplessly at Prue. "He's gone," said the sparrow, his voice as ashen as his plumage. "The Crown Prince. Gone."

Prue could only nod sympathetically. She was still gutted by the events. "How did you escape?" she asked. "I thought for sure you'd all be taken."

"Likewise. I thought they had you—when they opened the hamper," he said before motioning his head to the fireplace. "And in the fuss I managed to swoop into the chimney." He dropped his beak and stared at the ground. "But what's the use? Our Crown Prince, imprisoned!" He then turned his imploring eyes, all sad and tearful, to meet Prue's: "Was it cowardly of me? Shouldn't I have given my life, or at least my freedom, in defense of my Prince?"

"No, no, no," soothed Prue. She reached out a hand and brushed a smudge of soot from the sparrow's head. "He wouldn't have wanted that. You did what was best." She sat down on the edge of the bookcase and laid her chin in her palms. The braying whistle of a siren sounded in the distance.

The sparrow shuddered. "I never thought I'd see the day," he said quietly. "All our work, our careful diplomacy to create this fragile alliance. Dashed." The siren, now joined by another, grew louder. Prue stood and walked toward the window, where a flashing red light was playing against the pane. Kneeling down and carefully peeling back the curtain, Prue could see, several doors down the street, a gang of jackbooted SWORD officers escorting a small flock of birds out of a building and into an armored van. "What's going on?" said Prue.

The sparrow, not getting up, guessed at her horror. "I expect they're rounding up the lot. All birds, South Wood folk and members of the Principality alike." He repeated solemnly, "Never thought I'd see the day."

More sirens sounded; more clanking paddy wagons trundled down the cobblestones of Rue Thurmond. Farther down the street, Prue watched as a small group of egrets, their bright white feathers painted crimson in the siren's glow, were led out to a waiting truck. Before they arrived at the armored doors, however, one broke away from the group and, its long spindly legs beating the paving stones, unfurled its great wings and took to the sky. No sooner had it done so than a SWORD officer pulled a rifle from over his shoulder, took aim, and fired. Prue clapped her hand over her mouth to stop a shriek. The egret plummeted to the cobbles in a limp jumble of white feathers. A few cursory words were exchanged between the officers and the truck was off, rumbling down the street. The body of the egret lay where it fell, motionless. After a few moments, a stray SWORD officer who had emerged from one of the other buildings casually kicked the egret's body out of the middle of the street and into the gutter.

Prue gritted her teeth and slammed her fist down on the windowsill. "Murderers!" she hissed. She looked back at the sparrow, expecting to see him moved by the sound of the gunshot, but instead saw him sitting where she had left him, his head inclined even farther into his breast.

"We have to do something!" shouted Prue, marching back over to where the sparrow sat. "This is an injustice! How can anyone stand for this?"

"Fear," the sparrow responded quietly. "Fear rules the day. The powerful, for fear of losing that power, have become blinded. Everyone is an enemy. Someone has to bear the brunt."

Prue groaned angrily and began pacing the room. "Well, one thing's for sure, I'm not just going to sit here and wait till they run out of ideas and come back here to arrest us. THAT'S crazy."

"I don't know what to tell you," he murmured.

Prue stopped her pacing. "North. Go North." She shot a look over at the sparrow. "That's what Owl said. Just before the police came in. He said if all else fails, I could go to North Wood and see those . . . magicians."

"Mystics," corrected the sparrow, looking up.

"Yeah," said Prue, now wagging her index finger in thought. "I'd be safe there. And they might know where my brother is."

"*Maybe* you'd be safe there; the North Wood folk do value their isolation."

Prue shrugged. "It's worth a shot, though, isn't it?"

The sparrow had by now perked up considerably. "Maybe. Maybe. But how on earth would you get there?"

Frowning, Prue absently scratched her cheek. "That's the thing. I have no idea."

"You could fly," said the sparrow.

"Yeah, that's no problem at all," Prue scoffed.

"I mean," said the sparrow, standing on his claws and shaking out his wings, "you could be flown."

"Flown?" Prue was beginning to see an answer.

"You must weigh nothing," said the sparrow, studying her body. "To a golden eagle, anyway. If we could only get you to the Principality, there are plenty of birds who could carry you."

Even in the darkness of this dire situation, Prue couldn't help but be quietly thrilled at the proposition. "Okay," she said. "That sounds pretty good. So how do I get there?"

"We'd have to sneak you to the border somehow," said the sparrow, his energy having returned. "It's too far to walk, and the streets are crawling with secret police—no, we'd have to find a vehicle, something we could conceal you in—it's the only way."

Prue snapped her fingers, interrupting the bird's thought. "Got it," she said.

🌿

In another part of the Wood, deep underground, another finger snap had just finished echoing off the walls of a cavernous warren. Curtis stared blankly at Alexandra. Mac cooed quietly in the cradle in the center of the room. Far off, the blare of a brass band colored this quiet, tense moment with a comical soundtrack.

Curtis swallowed deeply, loudly.

Alexandra, her arms now folded, tapped a ringed finger against a pewter bracelet clasped around her bicep. The noise made a hollow *ting* that reverberated through the chamber.

Ting.

"Well, I . . . ," started Curtis.

Ting.

He shifted uncomfortably in his boots. The stiffness of the uniform suddenly became hyperapparent, the rough wool fabric chafing against his shoulders. His right toe dug a little too closely into the leather of his boot. The heat in the room swelled, and little beads of perspiration broke out at his hairline. "I think that . . . ," he began.

Ting.

"Are you with me, Curtis?" asked Alexandra, finally. "Or are you against me? It's one or the other."

Curtis tittered uncomfortably. "I realize that, Alexandra, I just—"

He was interrupted: "Easy decision, Curtis."

Curtis silently waited for another *ting* to unsettle the quiet of the room, but when it did not come (Alexandra's finger remained poised in the air above the bracelet) he gave his reply.

"No."

"What was that?"

Curtis straightened his spine and looked directly into Alexandra's eyes. "I said no."

"No, what?" asked the Governess, her eyebrows carving a sinister angle on her brow. "You *won't* return home? You *will* join me?"

"No, I won't join you. I will not." The saliva that had been robbed from his mouth in his initial terror was now beginning to return, and speaking was growing easier and easier. "No way." He gestured to the baby in the cradle behind him. "This is *wrong*, Alexandra. I don't care who did what to you, but I can't just sit here and let you take this baby and, well, *sacrifice* him just so you can get your measly revenge. No, no, no. Maybe you can use something else; a squirrel or a pig or something—maybe that ivy won't really know the difference—whatever. All I know is that I'm done here, thanks very much, so I'll just get my things and leave, if you don't mind."

The Governess remained strangely silent during this speech, and Curtis attempted to fill the awkward stillness with more talk. "You can have the uniform back, the saber too. I'm sure there's another coyote or someone who it will fit, and I know you're in need of equipment, so don't even think about it—this will definitely stay with you. Though I don't know where my clothes are that I wore in here; maybe someone could find them for me?"

The Governess remained silent, studying Curtis as he fidgeted with his uniform.

"Or whatever. I don't *need* my other clothes. One thing, though," Curtis said, "is that I'm going to take the baby. I'm going to have to take Mac with me. I owe this to Prue."

This was where Alexandra broke her silence. "I can't let you do that, Curtis."

Curtis sighed. "Please?"

"Guards!" shouted Alexandra, turning slightly to call down the corridor behind her. Within moments, the sound of shuffling feet announced the arrival of a group of uniformed coyote grunts. Appearing at the opening to the chamber, they were initially surprised to see Curtis. "Madam?" asked one, confused.

"Seize him," was Alexandra's command. "He's a turncoat."

Immediately Curtis was beset by coyotes, his arms pinned behind him, manacles snapped in place around his wrists. He gave no resistance. One of the coyotes yanked the sword from Curtis's scabbard, raising the blade to his face with a menacing sneer. Alexandra watched the proceedings calmly, her eyes never wavering from her captive's.

"Don't do this, Curtis," said Alexandra, her face now belying a sadness beneath her stony countenance. "I'm offering you a new life, a new direction. A world of riches awaits you, and you would throw it away to save this *thing*? This babbling *thing*? You'd have a seat at the table, Curtis. You'd be second in command. And, perhaps one day, an heir to the throne." She paused before saying, "A son to me."

The coyotes at Curtis's side smelled of matted fur and stale wine. They huffed threateningly in his ear, their muzzles snapping. The manacles bit into the flesh of his wrists.

Curtis stiffened his resolve. "Alexandra, I'm asking you to stop this; let me and the baby go. I . . . uh . . . command you."

Alexandra stifled a laugh. *"Command?"* she said icily. "You *command* me? Oh, Curtis, don't get ahead of yourself. Has the blackberry wine given you delusions of grandeur? You're not quite in a position to be commanding anyone, I'm afraid." The half smile disappeared from her face and she moved closer, her cheek rubbing Curtis's cheek, her lips at his ear. Her breath smelled unworldly, like a sweet poison, rare and deadly. "Last chance," was all she whispered.

"No," repeated Curtis in a firm voice.

Scarcely had the response left his lips when Alexandra snapped back and clapped her hands. "Take him away," she shouted, now breaking eye contact with Curtis. "To the cages!" Her finger traced the brocade of his uniform collar to rest on the medal, the bramble and trillium, at his chest; with a flick of her wrist, she tore the badge from the cloth and threw it to the ground.

"Aye, madam!" barked the coyotes, and Curtis was roughly dragged from the room. He was afforded a quick backward glance: the tall, thin silhouette of the Governess, backlit by the torches of the room, darkened the entry to the room, a witness to his rough removal. The ghostly light behind her flickered from the flapping of a host of crows' wings, and she solemnly began to turn back to the room, to the baby in the cradle—and Curtis's jailers took a dogleg corridor and the haunting scene was gone.

He struggled to keep up with the coyotes' pace. The corridor they followed snaked through the earth, wandering in every direction to accommodate the occasional gnarled tree root and boulder. The air grew cooler and denser as they moved farther from the central compound of the warren, and the tunnel slowly began sloping downward.

"Listen to me," Curtis said after a moment. "You don't have to follow her. Do you know what she's doing? She's kidnapped a baby—a baby boy—and she's going to *kill* him. An innocent baby! Does that seem right to you?"

No response.

"I mean, what if one of your, your"—he struggled to find the word—"*whelps* was kidnapped by some person or animal or whatever. And they were going to *sacrifice* him? Would you stand for that?" Not receiving an answer, he proffered one himself: "NO! No, you wouldn't. It's not right!"

The tunnel was filled with the noise of the coyotes' labored panting; in the half-lit distance, something vaguely arachnid scurried across the tunnel floor, disappearing into a large hole in the wall.

"What was that?" shrilled Curtis.

"Who knows what lives down here," responded one of the coyotes.

Another took up the game. "Never been this far into the warren, myself. Heard stories, though—they say there're things down here ain't never seen the light o' day. Things that are dyin' for a lump of good meat to sink their teeth into."

"Good *human* meat," intoned another coyote.

"Feed a rat to the rats," said one. "That's how we deal with turn-coats around here."

"Listen, just let me go," said Curtis. "No one has to know—I'll just go on my way and . . ." The words froze in his mouth as the coyotes turned a sharp corner and the tunnel opened up into a large room and Curtis saw the cages.

"Oh," he said flatly. "Oh man."

It appeared as if the room had formed naturally: The floor was knobbed with rubble and rock and the walls sloped down from the towering ceiling in an irregular fashion—but this was by far the least remarkable thing about the room. The thing that instantly demanded Curtis's attention was the massive twist of roots that hung from the ceiling—what a tree must be above this system of limbs!—and the ominous array of rickety wooden cages that hung from the thick tendrils. The viney maple boughs that made up the cages' bars joined in a crown at the top; they looked like birdcages in a giant's aviary. Thick hempen cables attached the cages to the root system above, and they issued whining creaks as they twisted around on their lines. Inside, Curtis could make out a few figures—the cages looked to be big enough to imprison several unfortunate souls apiece—while many remained empty. He didn't have time to count them, but they looked to number in the dozens.

"Warden!" shouted one of his captors, and a bloated and graying coyote appeared from behind a jagged rock below the dangling cages.

A cord around his neck carried an impressive assemblage of keys of all different sizes and shapes. As he shuffled toward them, he blandly mumbled a recitation:

"Abandon hope, ye prisoner, abandon hope. The cages' bars, impenetrable. The cages' locks, unbreakable. The distance to the ground, unjumpable. Abandon hope. Abandon hope." He sniffled between sentences, barely looking up from the ground. Curtis, horrified, noted that the ground appeared to be littered with the bleached and broken bones of former captives, dropped to their deaths.

"Yes, yes, we know," one of the coyotes holding Curtis's arm said impatiently. "Enough with the ominous speeches. We got a traitor here. Cage 'im high."

As the warden approached, a voice could be heard from one of the cages above. "What? Is that another biped? I thought this was a coyote-only brig."

Curtis looked up at the source of the complaint and saw a coyote muzzle sticking out between the wooden bars of one of the cages nearer to them.

"Quiet!" hollered the warden suddenly, breaking from his monotone.

A distinctly human-sounding voice rose up from one of the cages farther up. "You jackals'll pay for this! I swear!" Curtis couldn't make out the speaker through the snarl of the branching roots.

"See?!" shouted the coyote prisoner. "Do you hear that? I'm a soldier and I'm thrown in here with bandit scum! I thought this was an exclusively military prison!"

"QUIET!" the warden shouted again, now louder. "Or I'll cuff the lot of ya."

The bandit, now enlivened, began chanting, "Free Wildwood! FREE WILDWOOD!" A few other prisoners, apparently bandits as well, stood up in their cages and took up the call, screaming and shaking the bars of their enclosures.

The warden sighed and walked over to Curtis. "Lively bunch," he said under the din. "Sure you'll enjoy the company."

While Curtis was still being held, the warden walked over to the wall and fetched what looked to be the longest, ricketiest ladder Curtis had ever seen. Carefully balancing it upright, the warden walked the ladder over to the center of the room, weaving its topmost rungs through the tree roots. Arriving at a vacant cage, he hooked the top against the bars and steadied the bottom on a large rock on the cavern's floor.

"Up we go," said the warden. He climbed first; arriving at the cage, he undid the lock and climbed back down. At a nod from the warden, Curtis's wrists were uncuffed and he was shoved rudely toward the ladder. The ladder swayed and bowed beneath his weight as he climbed. When he finally arrived at the cage, he swooned slightly at the height: He was easily sixty feet above the chamber floor, and the ground was strewn with boulders, stones, and toothy stalagmites; the

fall did not look inviting. Once he had been pushed into the cage, the warden returned to the top of the ladder and fixed the door closed with a large iron padlock. Before returning to the ground, he looked directly at Curtis and said, "Don't even *think* about escaping."

"Wasn't going to," said Curtis.

The warden seemed temporarily caught off guard by the answer. "Oh," he said. "Good." And with that, he disappeared down the ladder. Curtis let out a sigh of despair as the top rung lifted away from the bars, and the wooden cage swung freely, the anchor cable above creaking and groaning under the weight of its new resident.

The gas lamps, positioned as they were on every corner, cast pallid cones of light on the cobbled intersections of the streets; shadows ruled the in-between spaces. It was within these shadows that Prue found concealment as she and the sparrow made their way through the neighborhood. Prue stayed hidden behind an obliging rain barrel or mailbox while the sparrow (whose name was Enver, Prue had come to find out) stealthily flew ahead, scouting the area from the roof eaves and weathervanes of the majestic houses that dotted the landscape. When the sparrow warbled an all-clear, Prue would leave her hiding place and rush to the next available cover. The pace was slow, but they made steady progress up the street. Their momentum was only ever stalled when the inevitable SWORD van would come wailing down the street, its flashing siren tinting the houses in garish red, and Prue and Enver would have to hold their positions until the sparrow was satisfied that their movement would not be detected.

"I think it's a left up here," Prue whispered loudly from behind a garbage bin. Enver was perched atop a gaslight that lit a four-way intersection. The cobblestones here were slowly being replaced by dirt and pine needles as the upscale Rue Thurmond neighborhood gave way to the smaller hovels of the forest, their mossy roofs enshrouded by the overhanging fir boughs in the near distance.

"You sure?" asked Enver, uncertainly scanning the horizon.

"No," whispered Prue. "Kind of just guessing."

"Where did you say we should be headed?" asked the sparrow.

"Just southwest of the Mansion," said Prue. "That's what I was told."

The sparrow clucked his beak. "One sec," he said, giving a quick look down the four ways of the intersection. Once he saw the way was clear, he unfurled his small gray wings and shot upward, corkscrewing between the looming tree branches until he was out of sight.

Prue waited calmly, the sour smell of the garbage bin staining the air around her. The howl of a police siren sounded far away, and she froze as a small group of SWORD officers rounded the corner and marched down Rue Thurmond. Prue snuck a look from behind the bin as they walked away and noticed that each was carrying birdcages. Between the metal bars of the cages, Prue caught sight of bird feathers, all downy and gray.

Minutes passed. Finally, a flutter of wings sounded from above. She looked up to see Enver, out of breath, land on top of the Dumpster.

"Sorry," said Enver. "I had to wait till they'd gone by." He shook one of his wings and leaned into Prue. "I saw the top of the Mansion. It's pretty far still, but we're moving in the right direction. Judging from the stars"—and here Enver pointed his beak to the heavens; it was a rare clear night and the blackness was pinpricked by constellations—"we stay straight to keep southwest."

"Great," whispered Prue. "Let's keep moving."

"Have you ever been to this place?" asked the sparrow. "Do you know what it looks like?"

"No, but I think we'll know it when we come to it," said Prue before adding, "I expect if you've seen one post office, you've seen them all." And with that, Enver nodded and took wing, flying ahead to find another perch from which to guide Prue to her next hiding place.

CHAPTER 14

Among Thieves

"I insist I see an attorney!" shouted the coyote, his voice cracking midsentence. "This is an OUTRAGE!" He rattled the cage bars with his paws. Curtis watched him curiously from above; the coyote's cage was much farther down the root-ball than Curtis's.

"Oh, keep it down," shouted one of the bandits. His cage was above and to the left of Curtis, and he was sitting against the bars, picking at his fingernails. "They're not listening to you. Habeas corpus doesn't really apply here."

"Habeas corpus?" snarled the coyote. "Where'd you learn those fancy words, you half-wit?" He had turned to face the bandit, and at that moment Curtis had a chance to see his face; he was one of the coyotes he had first seen with Prue—one of the privates who had been fighting below their hiding place. Curtis seemed to remember that his name was Dmitri.

"Oh, we know a lot more than you jackals would believe," responded the bandit, tapping a finger against his temple. "Some of us might seem thick, but don't be fooled. We're smart as whips. Which is why you'll never put us under. No matter how many battles you win, no matter how much our numbers fall, there'll always be bandits to keep up the fight."

"Oh, please spare us your little rallying cries," responded Dmitri. "You're wasting 'em on me. I was drafted. I could care less if you bandits overran the place; I'd rather be in my home warren anyway, minding my own business. What bothers me is that I'm stuck up here like a common criminal—I thought I'd just get a few demerits and be on my way. Instead, I'm in the bandit ward, having to listen to you lot."

"*I'm* not a bandit," Curtis chimed in. "I'm a soldier." He paused and looked down at his uniform, at the torn fabric where his brooch used to be. "Or I *was.*"

The coyote huffed and turned away.

"You," said another bandit, this one farther away. His cage dangled from one of the larger root branches, at a similar height to Curtis's.

"So you're the Outsider, huh? You fought alongside the Dowager, didn't you?"

Curtis frowned and nodded. "I did, yeah," he said, abashed. "But I wish I hadn't now. I didn't know what she was doing."

"What'd you expect?" said the bandit from above, his venom now directed downward. "She was the rightful Queen of Wildwood? Just cleaning up shop a little bit? Making sure everyone remembered who was the boss? And you just waltz in from your Outside world and decide to help out?"

"Well, I didn't have much of a choice," said Curtis, hackles rising. "I mean, she captured me and the next thing I know she's feeding me and clothing me and telling me I'm her second in command!"

"Sucker," came a voice. It issued from a cage directly above Curtis. Another bandit was staring down at Curtis, sitting cross-legged with his cheeks propped in his hands.

"Seriously," continued Curtis, "I had no idea what she was up to; I would've never agreed to go along with her if I'd known."

"Yeah?" The bandit farther out on the root branch scoffed. "What was your first hint? Her conscription of an entire species of animal? Or maybe the fact that she was steadily wiping out every natural-born resident of Wildwood one after another? What was it, boy genius?"

Something wet dripped down on Curtis's forehead, and he winced to look up and see that the bandit in the cage directly above him had just dropped a big ball of spit on him. The bandit's face was visible between his bent legs, and Curtis could see he was preparing for a second lob. Groaning, Curtis ducked and moved to another side of the cage.

"You Outsiders," said another bandit, one who had remained silent during all the invective. "You're always looking for a way to conquer and despoil things that ain't by rights yours, huh? I heard about what you do. Don't think we don't know that you'd be all over this Wood— that you'd have beat the Governess to her own game if she hadn't been at it first. I heard you about ruined your own country, nearly ran it into the ground poisoning your rivers and paving over your wild lands and such." His cage was a bit lower and off to the right; Curtis watched as the bandit came close to the cage bars and glowered up at him. He wore a dirty checkered scarf around his neck and a loose linen tunic. A ratty bowler was perched on his head. "Bet you thought this place'd be all yours, didn't ye. Well, I expect it'll just chew you up and spit you out—if you don't end up just rotting here first."

Curtis shivered and sat down on the floor of his cage, squeezing his knees to his chest. He could feel the glare of all the prisoners boring into his very bones. He wished now, more than ever, that he could be back home with his mother and father and his two niggling sisters. The ropes creaked and shuddered and the cages twisted slightly back and forth in the great cavern. Dmitri, the coyote, offered his sympathy: "Get used to it. They don't really let up."

Before long, Prue and Enver had arrived at the post office, a small redbrick building nestled into a dense scrub of hemlock trees. A tumbledown wooden fence, gray and mossy, made an enclosure behind the building, and Prue could see a few dilapidated red vans sitting idle in the yard as she climbed the steps to the door. A flat brass panel was fastened to the brick above the door, and the words SOUTH WOOD POST OFFICE were engraved into the metal.

A light from one of the windows illuminated a cluttered room, stacked floor to ceiling with brown packages and envelopes, and Prue could make out the figure of Richard, his body half-obscured by the piles of parcels and paper.

"Here goes nothing," she whispered to Enver, who stood balanced on a nearby tree branch, nervously standing vigil over the deserted, darkened road.

Prue rapped her knuckles quietly against the wood of the door. When no response came, she knocked again.

"We're closed!" came Richard's voice from within. "Come back during business hours, please!"

Prue cupped her hands against the door and, bringing her lips to her fingers, rasped, "Richard! It's me, Prue!"

"What?" came Richard's response; his voice, loud and impatient, seemed to rattle the hinges of the doorjamb.

Enver warbled anxiously from above.

"It's Prue. Y'know, *Port-Land Prue!*"

After a moment she heard slow footsteps and the hollow *clunk* of a deadbolt being undone. The door cracked slightly and Richard, his eyes bleary and gray hair all a-muss, appeared through the opening.

"Prue!" he hollered, clearly oblivious to Prue's hushed approach. "What in heck are you doing here?"

Enver warbled again, louder, in warning, and Prue threw her finger to her lips. "Shhhh!" she hissed. "You have to keep your voice down!"

Richard, eyes wide, glanced out at the sparrow on the tree and back at Prue. He matched Prue's volume, saying, "And you've got a bird with you—y'know, the coppers were here, not but two hours ago, looking for you. I don't rightly know what's going on!"

"I need your help," said Prue, hesitating before saying, "it's way too long and complicated to explain here on the porch—can I come in?"

Richard stood in thought for a moment. "Well, all right," he said. "But mind no one sees you. This ain't regular."

"Exactly!" agreed Prue. She turned and whistled to Enver, who flew down from his perch. Ushering them quickly inside, Richard shot a quick glance down both ends of the street before carefully closing the door and throwing the deadbolt.

A windowed partition divided the interior room in half, separating the public part of the post office from the private, and Richard led

Prue and Enver through a gate to the back room. Towers of packages created a maze of Lilliputian city streets, and Prue navigated the boulevards gingerly, as the cardboard and brown paper skyscrapers quaked at her every footstep. In the corner of the room, a small hearth enclosed a smoldering coal fire.

Richard cleared his throat in embarrassment as he set about clearing away some of the detritus. "I know there's another chair around here somewhere," he mumbled, sifting through the stacks. Finding no chair, he slid a few empty crates from underneath a desk and set them down in the clearing before the fireplace. "Have a seat," he offered.

Prue thanked him and sat down, relieved to be off her feet. Enver settled on a pile of boxes near the desk, fluttering his wings nervously when the pile swayed under his weight.

"So what's the deal? Why all the hullabaloo?" asked Richard, sitting on an overturned basket before the fire.

Prue took a deep breath and began to recount all the events since she and Richard had parted ways. "They're rounding up all the birds in South Wood," she explained, finally arriving at the end of her adventures. "Who knows where they're taking them? So I'm stuck there wondering what to do, and Enver and I figured we'd come to you and maybe ask a favor."

Richard took in the whole story with wide-eyed amazement. It took a moment before he realized a question had been asked him.

"A—a favor?" he asked, rubbing a temple with his knobby fingers. "What'd that be?"

"Well," continued Prue, "the owl, just before the police showed up, said if all else fails I should go to North Wood. To see the Mystics. Enver here seems to think I can catch a ride with an eagle, if I could just get myself across the border to the Avian Principality. And since the whole South Wood is searching for me and any bird that happens to be in the vicinity, I'd need to do that undetected." She bit her lip. "Like, I need someone to sneak me out."

Richard caught on. "So you want me to smuggle you. Across the border."

"Yep," said Prue.

"I can only imagine: in the van. In the government's own mail van."

"Uh-huh," said Prue.

Rubbing his hand across the stubble of his chin, Richard stood up and walked to the fireplace. He absently stirred the coals in the hearth with a poker.

"Well," said Richard carefully, "I can say that I have no love for the Governor-Regent and his buddies, that's for a long sight. And these SWORD goons, just waltzing all over town, arresting folks for no reason—it ain't right. This country ain't what it used to be, least not since Grigor died. I've outlived a lot of Governors-Regent in this place, and I can say that Lars is just about the worst we ever come up against. But me taking you across the border in a post office vehicle, well, if we got caught, that'd cost me my job, and my job is all I got right now, since my Bette took ill—that's my wife, understand. She's counting on me for this paycheck. Worse yet, that'd probably land me in jail for a time, and that just can't happen."

Prue was crestfallen. Enver whistled dispiritedly and looked out the window.

"So I guess we're just gonna have to not get caught," said Richard.

Prue leapt up from her crate. "So you'll do it?" she asked.

"Yeah, I s'pose so," he said, sighing.

Prue grabbed his hands and, squeezing them, led Richard into a kind of impromptu, maniacal dance in the small clearing before the fire. "I knew you'd do it!" she shouted, forgetting herself. "I knew you'd say yes!" Enver had left his perch and was making quick figure eights in the air of the room, twittering joyously.

"Now slow up," cautioned Richard, pulling Prue to a stop. "Let's not get ahead of ourselves. And we've got to keep our voices down—those SWORD officers are like little termites when they want to be: coming out of the woodwork. They could be anywhere." He let go of Prue's hands and walked over to a paraffin lamp on the mantel, the sole source of light in the room, and lowered the wick. Shadows extended into the room. He gave a hasty look out the window before returning to Prue, saying, "I said before you were likely here for a reason; maybe you were sent here to make rightful change in this place—get folks back up on their feet. That's a kind of cause I can stand for."

Prue smiled, tears welling in her eyes. "Thank you so much, Richard," she said. "I can't tell you how much this means."

Richard nodded before scanning the room. "Now," he said, "we just have to find a box that'll fit the cargo."

Curtis had a difficult time finding a comfortable spot to sit in his cage; the floor was made of closely woven maple boughs, and the knobby surface did not make an inviting sitting area. He settled for a spot opposite the cage door, where a depression in one of the branches created a kind of seat; this was where he stayed, waiting out the bandits' derision. They had made good sport of Curtis for the better part of an hour until, their tormentee remaining silent, they turned their attention elsewhere: first to the coyote Dmitri, who spat more insults back at them, and then to one another, berating their neighboring prisoners over boasted feats of strength and derring-do.

"Ten feet?!" challenged one. "I've leapt farther in my sleep! Ten feet."

"Oh yeah?" responded another. "Would love to hear your best jump, Cormac."

Cormac, farther out the same branch as Curtis, replied casually,

"Thirty, easy. The distance of about five trees. And not just little saplings, mind you, these were full mature firs we're talking about. During that big raid, last August. Connor saw me. I'm on the crown of this massive cedar and all of a sudden a big gust comes up and I hear this *crack* and I look down and the whole top of the tree is splitting, right in two. Well, I'm high enough up that there's no real tree to get to, just these firs that are well down below from where I was. In a flash, I look over and see—I swear to you here, five fir trees apart, thirty feet, easy—another cedar, same size. So I grab hold of the treetop, set my foot in the crotch of the topmost branch, and I just jump, hell-for-leather, just as that old cedar gives way, and the next thing I know I'm scrambling for a grip in the far tree. Sure as I'm standin' here, gentlemen. Thirty feet."

A snort came from the bandit below Curtis's cage. "Right," he scoffed. "I heard from Connor that that cedar top just tipped over and fell straight into the other tree—ye'd as easily walked from branch to branch if ye'd not had your eyes clapped closed in terror!"

Cormac shouted a reproach. "Eamon Donnell, so help me, I'll string you from your toes as soon as we're out of here—the second we're out of here, you and me are going blow for blow."

"Save your breath, gents," advised the bandit up and to the left of Curtis's cage. "We won't be seein' the light of day anytime soon."

"You may be right there," said another. "Hey, Angus, don't suppose your old lady's going to wait around?"

Angus, a bandit with a raspy voice whose cage was the farthest out, its weight straining the root branch, sighed a reply. "Hope she does. That bairn'll be born any day now, I expect. Had half a hope that I'd be there for the birthing." He kicked impotently at the wooden bars, setting his cage slowly rocking. "Blasted cages. Blasted coyotes. Blasted war."

Dmitri had remained mostly silent during this exchange; here he interrupted, "Now hold on, some of us coyotes don't want any more a part of this than you all do. I'd let you know that I happen to have a litter of pups at my home warren, waiting for me. Haven't seen them in ages! I imagine they'll be just about full grown by the time I get back. If I get back."

The bandits gave no rebuttal to this honest admission; the cages fell silent for a moment as each prisoner fell into a reverie. Finally, Angus spoke up. "Hey, Seamus," he called.

"Yeah?" was the response.

"Give us an air," said Angus. "Nothing too sad, mind you—something to kick the mood a bit."

The surrounding bandits murmured approval with a chorus of "Aye, aye."

Seamus, the bandit directly above Curtis—the expectorator himself—turned and spoke to the other prisoners. "What," he said, "like 'The Wildwood Maiden'?"

Cormac groaned. "God, no—not the treacly, maudlin stuff. Something to take our minds off o' things."

Eamon shouted his suggestion: "How 'bout the one about the lawyer—the lawyer and Jock Roderick?"

The request was popular; the other bandits chimed in with their approval.

Seamus nodded his agreement and then, shifting in his cage, straightened his chest and began singing, his voice sweet and tuneful:

Sawyer the Lawyer was plying his trade
Clacking and stacking the money he made
Robbing the poor and deceiving the meek
Leaving 'em naught but the tears on their cheek.
Jock Roderick, the Brave Bandit of Hanratty Cross.

As Sawyer was trav'ling the Long Road in May
A client to see for to free from his pay
Who should arrive at the top of the heath?
Young Jock, with his pistols and a blade in his teeth.
Jock Roderick, the Brave Bandit of Hanratty Cross.

Says Sawyer, "I'll give you a piece of the deal
I've a widow in South Wood who's lost an appeal.
Sure, there's money to make of us both millionaires!"
But Jock with his pistols just fixes a stare.
Jock Roderick, the Brave Bandit of Hanratty Cross.

"You're a savvy young man," says Sawyer, "quite right.
But I'm suing a blind man for not having sight.
We'll split up the settlement, right down the middle!"
But Jock, he don't move, he don't flinch in his saddle.
Jock Roderick, the Brave Bandit of Hanratty Cross.

"But let's not be tidy, whatever's your druther,
I'm suing an orphan for having no mother.
We'll share all the proceeds! Whatever the figure!"
But Jock, he just sits there, a-twitch at the trigger.
Jock Roderick, the Brave Bandit of Hanratty Cross.

Says Sawyer, "O tell me what would thee entice
Ev'ry man has a weakness, we each have our price.

248

Name that one thing and I swear to make good."
Says Jock, "You marched naked down into South Wood."
Jock Roderick, the Brave Bandit of Hanratty Cross.

So Jock's robbed the lawyer his gold and his store
He's taken the horses and deeds and what's more
He's marched him all naked for South Wood to stare
How a lawyer's a lawyer whatever he wears.
Jock Roderick, the Brave Bandit of Hanratty Cross.

The cavern erupted into laughter and applause at this last verse, and the cages shook beneath the weight of the guffawing bandits. Curtis cracked a smile despite himself. The coyote, Dmitri, shouted acidly from his cage, "Beautiful song, guys, real beautiful."

The Delivery

The pounding of the hammer ceased, the last nail driven into the wood of the crate, and Prue was alone in the darkness, listening intently to the sounds outside. She'd said her good-byes to Enver with a promise to reunite on the other side of the border; she'd thanked Richard again and had sat calmly while he prepared to encase her in the packing crate. Suddenly, there was a loud *thunk*, the sound of wood hitting metal, and she felt herself tipped sidelong, the world moving underneath her—she guessed the box had been lifted onto a dolly and she was being moved toward the—*bang!* The back of the van. The crown of her head had hit the top of the box, and she stifled a cry. She heard Richard whisper a "Sorry!" through the wood before saying, "See you on the other side!" A metallic slam. Footsteps. The wheeze of the van engine igniting, and a grinding rattle as the van was thrown into gear and began moving.

Prue shifted her weight in the box, trying to ignore the pressure she was already feeling in the joints of her bent knees. She shared the space with a small clutch of wooden shavings and paper scraps, remnant packing material from the crate's previous contents. The box smelled faintly of wax.

The van hit a pothole and the box gave a great shake and she fell sideways against the wall of the crate. This time she yelled out loud, "OUCH!" her knee slamming into the floor. She braced herself against the walls of the box and shifted back upright, prepared for any further convulsions.

She felt the shocks of the van lighten as the surface changed from rough gravel to smooth paving stones. The engine shuddered into a higher gear, and the mail van picked up speed. Prue could hear the whistle of wind blowing alongside the vehicle. A quarter of an hour passed this way and Prue eased into the journey, her breath settling into a calm rhythm. The white noise of the van's engine was only ever eclipsed by the occasional whine of a distant siren—it was clear that the SWORD's house-by-house avian roundup was continuing apace.

Time passed. The realization that she had not slept more than a few hours in two days dawned on her; she was suddenly aware that she was fighting to keep her eyelids open. Surrendering to the impulse, she fell into an immediate slumber—the anxiousness of her present predicament seemed to melt away like candle wax.

Until the van jerked to a halt.

Her eyelids flew open. Her heartbeat accelerated, a racing horse released from the starting gate. The sound of footsteps, murmured voices. The noises came closer to the back of the van and suddenly, with a clang, the doors of the van could be heard being thrown open, the voices now muffled only by the thin veneer of wood that separated her from the interior of the van.

". . . this time of night," sounded one of the voices. "Regulations, you understand. We're instructed to be vigilant tonight, what with the crackdown. Border patrol, especially."

"Of course, Officer." This was Richard's voice. It was calm, assured. Its confidence instilled a newfound bravery in Prue. She hitched her breath and waited.

"Now, let's see," said the other voice, which Prue assumed to be that of a border guard. The van gave a shrug as she felt the officer's weight climbing into the cargo hold. "Envelopes, packages," intoned the officer, his footsteps sounding against the metal floor. "Mmm-hmm, all seems to be in order."

Suddenly, there was a loud, hollow *crack* against the side of the box. The officer had kicked the crate! Prue threw her hand to her mouth.

"What's in this one, Postmaster?" asked the officer.

The assurance had dropped from Richard's voice. "Toilet paper," he said, stumbling over the first consonants. "Towels and, um, ladies' undergarments."

What? screamed Prue's mind.

"What?" said the officer.

"Undergarments, y-yes," stuttered Richard. "And toilet paper. Some socks, yes, some socks are in there. And, wouldn't you believe it, old . . . old dryer lint."

Prue put her face in her hands.

"*Old dryer lint?*" asked the officer incredulously. "What kind of package is that?"

"A very, um, strange one," said Richard. "I guess."

The game was up. Prue knew it. She was already trying to imagine how well she would handle prison life. Would they let her have a TV? Would the food be any good?

"Open it," commanded the officer.

"What was that?" asked Richard.

"You heard me, Postmaster. Open it. Open the box. I want to see this . . . this dryer lint."

Richard grumbled something under his breath and walked along the side of the van, presumably to fetch a crowbar. While he did this, the officer drummed his fingers impatiently on the top of the crate. Through the wood, it sounded like peals of thunder. Finally, Richard returned, and the van shifted again as Prue felt him climb into the hold.

"Now, which one was it?" asked Richard. Prue heard the hollow *thok* of something being tapped against wood, but this sounded from the far end of the van. "Was it this one?"

"NO," said the officer impatiently. "The one I am currently standing next to, thanks very much."

"Ah yes," said Richard, his voice trembling slightly. "That one. Thing is, I've a customer who's expecting that package, and I can't imagine that they'd be too happy if—"

He was interrupted by the border guard. "Open it, Postmaster. I promise I won't sully their *dryer lint* too much." He was beginning to take on the tone of a cat toying with its prey. "There better not be anything *illicit* in that package, or you'll be wishing there really were towels and toilet paper and ladies' undergarments in there—quite the currency, I'm given to understand, in *prison*."

Richard laughed uncomfortably

Prue prepared herself for the big reveal.

"What about the one next to it?" asked Richard suddenly. "Perhaps you'd like better what was inside." He spoke in a suggestive tone.

"Listen, old man, I'm getting tired of your—" said the officer, before stopping abruptly. "Wait. What does that say?"

"I believe you can read it," said Richard.

"It's not . . . can it be?" asked the officer. There seemed to be a tremble of excitement in his stern voice.

"Allow me," said Richard, his confidence returning. A creaking wheeze was followed by a loud *crack*, suggesting the crate just adjacent to Prue's had been pried open, and Prue heard the officer catch his breath.

"All yours," said Richard. "But I really must be on my way. I do have quite a bit of mail to deliver."

"Quite right," said the officer, his tone professional and short. "Quite right. Sorry to have bothered you." Prue heard the sound of a terse hand clap, and a bevy of footsteps approached the van. "Jenkins! Sorgum! Please see to it that this box here is delivered safely to my quarters." These instructions were followed by the sound of a box being dragged across the metal floor of the van.

"Very well," said the officer. "Thanks for your time. Sorry for the inconvenience."

"Think nothing of it," said Richard. The shocks on the van groaned slightly as the two men left the cargo hold and *bang*, the doors were closed behind them. Someone—Prue imagined it to be Richard—gave a quick series of knuckle raps on the door, and she smiled widely.

The van roared back into life and, with a clatter of the transmission, heaved down the road and over the border into the Avian Principality.

After a time, the van took a sharp turn and drove for a stretch up a rough section of road before slowing to a stop. The doors were noisily thrown open, and Prue was greeted by the sound of a crowbar prying the top off the crate. In a moment, the lid had been tossed aside and Prue cautiously looked up to see Richard smiling down at her, the valleys of his wrinkled face illuminated by the hazy light of the van's dim overhead lamp.

"Dryer lint? Undergarments?" These words emerged from Prue's mouth like water breaking through a dam, though she immediately began laughing as soon as she'd said them.

"Oh, Prue," he said, his smile giving way to an embarrassed frown, "I don't know what came over me! All the preparation, and

I'd given no thought to what I'd say was in the box. Undergarments, indeed! Thank the heavens that I still had that case of poppy beer from the North—quite a commodity, and banned in South Wood, no less. No soldier worth his salt would pass over a treasure like that!"

Prue leapt up and threw her arms around Richard's neck. "Oh, thank you, thank you, thank you!" she shouted.

Richard returned the embrace briefly before saying, "Come on, you've still got a long ways to go." He helped her climb from the box, and, brushing a few petals of packing material from her jeans, she walked toward the door of the van. They had stopped in a kind of natural cul-de-sac, enclosed in a dense shroud of black-berry and western hazel bushes. The light was a deep blue-gray as the first glimmers of dawn filtered through the trees. Birdsong was everywhere here; the sound practically showered from the treetops. A flutter of wings heralded the arrival of Enver as he landed on a nearby branch.

"Enver!" cried Prue. "We made it!"

The sparrow nodded. "And not a moment too soon. They've closed the border to all travelers." Enver looked up to the sky, the dewy air of morning ruffling his feathers. "He should be here any moment."

"Who'd that be?" asked Richard.

"The General," said Enver, and, as if the words were an

incantation, a giant bird dove into the clearing, its wing beats disturbing the foliage like a small hurricane. It was a golden eagle, and Prue recognized him to be the same one she'd seen when they had first been on their way to South Wood. He landed on a low-hanging hemlock branch, dramatically setting the whole tree to shaking.

"Sir," said Enver, bowing his head slightly.

The General steadied himself on his perch and glared down at Prue. "Is this the human girl? The Outsider?"

"Yes, sir," replied Enver, nodding to Prue.

"Hello, sir," said Prue. "We met before, I think. I saw you—"

The General interrupted her. "Yes, I remember." He shifted his great talons on the branch and the leaves rustled wildly. "You were with the Prince when he was arrested?"

Prue nodded sadly. "Yes, sir."

The General watched her, silent. The light was still dim and the air hazy; the eagle's tawny plumage was a stark contrast to the wall of green that surrounded him. He scratched the underside of his wing with his beak, briefly, before turning back to Prue. His yellow eyes bore into Prue's.

"He was really brave, sir," she offered quietly. "I don't know what else to say; I owe him my life, I guess. They came for me, not him. And he protected me. I don't know why, but he did."

The eagle finally broke his steady gaze. He stared off into the distance, his face seemingly devoid of emotion. Finally, he spoke.

"I've sworn allegiance, as a general of the Avian army, to the throne of the Crown Prince. My orders come directly from our monarch. And now he's gone; imprisoned. In the absence of his authority, I can only infer what the Crown Prince would command." Here, he looked back at Prue, a steely reserve settling over his feathered brow. "If he has protected you, then I must protect you. If he has risked his life for you, I am duty bound to do likewise."

Enver warbled in agreement. The General unfurled his massive wings, the wingspan stretching easily as wide as Prue was tall, and leapt from his perch to land gracefully on the ground before Prue's feet.

"If it is your wish to fly to North Wood, then I would be honored to be your carriage," said the General, and he bowed his head low.

Prue, at a loss for words, made an awkward curtsy. Turning to Richard, she extended her hand in thanks. He took it and shook it firmly, his face set in a grave frown. "Another good-bye between us, Port-Land Prue," he said. "Let's hope it's the last."

She smiled. "Thanks again, Richard. I won't forget it." She turned to Enver. "And you," she said, reaching out her hand to run a finger along his smooth black head. "The best attendant a Crown Prince could hope for. I'm sure he'd be really proud of you, if he was here."

Enver cooed and sidestepped shyly on his roost.

Prue heaved a deep breath and turned to the General, his head still bowed low. "Okay," she said. "Let's go." The eagle shifted his talons and turned so Prue could climb onto his back, her fingers running through the down of his feathers to find a grip at the crook of his shoulder. She could feel the taut sinew of his muscle shift and shudder as he flexed his wings in preparation for flight.

"Hold on," he said.

Prue pressed her body against the General's back, her cheek nestled against his soft feathering, and the eagle took a few nimble steps before shoving off from the ground. And they were flying.

Curtis had been immersed in some strange circumstances since he'd made that fateful decision to follow Prue into the Impassable Wilderness, but surely nothing was as bizarre as this, sitting in a giant birdcage dangling from a root-ball in an underground warren, trying to remember the words to "Mustang Sally."

Mustang Sally
You probably should slow the mustang down
Mustang Sally
You probably should slow the mustang down
One of these . . . something . . . mornings
Hmmm guess you something something something something eyes.

"Something eyes?" asked Seamus, incredulous. "Whatever does that mean?"

"No, no, no," said Curtis, scratching his head. "I forget the words. Something about eyes, though. Sleeping eyes? Oh boy, I'm really sorry, guys. I thought I knew it better." The song had been one of his parents' favorites and was a perennial family road trip sing-along classic. He was now mining the dregs of his pop song repertoire in an effort to match the bandits' last offering, a tuneful song about a gypsy kidnapping a lord's daughter. They'd been at it for hours now, trading song for song, and time was flying by. The cavern rang with the voices of the prisoners.

"But I'm a little confused," said Angus. "So she's a horse, this Sally? And yet there's another mustang she has to slow down?"

Before Curtis had a chance to correct this misreading, another bandit joined in. "Angus, ya fool, it's *clearly* a love song from a man to a horse. The man loves the horse, this Mustang Sally." This caused the entire prison block to erupt in laughter.

"Aye, Curtis," shouted another, between gales of laughter. "You Outsiders have some fairly odd ways about ya!"

Curtis tried to stem the laughter, shouting, "Guys, it's a *car!* A kind of *car!*" But the bandits would have none of it. Rather than fight it, Curtis started laughing right along with them. One of the bandits, Cormac, managed to speak through the din. "Another, Curtis! Give us another Outsider song!" But before Curtis had a chance to insist that it was, in fact, the bandits' turn, there came a loud banging noise from below.

"Shut yer holes, maggots!" shouted a voice. It was the warden. He stood on the floor of the cavern, banging his giant key ring against a round soot-black cauldron. "Gruel time!" A group of four soldiers had entered the cavern; two carried the wooden spit from which the cauldron hung, two stood guard by the door. The warden walked over to where the giant ladder was leaning up against the cavern wall and grabbed a pole, of similar height, on the top of which was tethered a large wooden ladle.

"Get yer bowls ready!" came the next shouted instruction.

The prisoners grumbled and shifted in their barred enclosures, causing the array of cages to twist and swing like ornaments on a Christmas tree after it's been shaken. From between the bars of the cages emerged single arms, blackened with dirt, holding wide tin bowls. Curtis looked over to his side and noticed for the first time that his cage, too, came with a tin bowl, and he picked it up and held it out of the cage like his fellow prisoners. The warden dipped the ladle end of the pole into the cauldron and, carefully paying out the length of the wooden shaft into the air, filled each of the prisoners' proffered bowls, one by one. A little of the gruel splashed onto Curtis's hand as it was poured, and he flinched at the expectation that it would be hot; he was chagrined to discover that it was pretty tepid.

After the warden had finished, he put the ladle pole back in its resting place (with the ladle end down and planted in the dirt, Curtis couldn't help but notice) and ushered the soldiers from the room. The warden, too, exited the cavern, though not before turning and issuing a sardonic *"Bon appétit!"* to his prisoners.

Curtis looked deep into his bowl; the "gruel" appeared to be a pale milky broth of some sort in which bobbed a flotilla of foodlike objects. Curtis picked at one such object with a finger; it appeared to be the cartilage of some indeterminable beast.

Seamus, in the cage above, hollered down at Curtis, "Don't look at it too closely, man! Just eat the stuff."

Curtis looked up and winced before carrying the bowl to his lips and taking a sizable slug of the stuff. It was more disgusting than anything he had tasted in his life—and he'd had the displeasure of tasting his mother's collard greens. It wasn't so much the taste that offended, however, but the appreciable *lack* of taste—it allowed the textures of the floating cartilage and who-knows-what to really come forward on the palate. Curtis gagged loudly. The bandits, who had apparently been waiting to hear his reaction, erupted into laughter.

"Get used to it, kid!" one shouted.

"Nothing like home cooking, huh, Outsider?" yelled another.

"Bleagh!" said Curtis, setting the bowl down on the cage floor. "What is this stuff?"

"Squirrel brain, pigeon's feet, skunk tendons—all served up in a healthy broth of spoiled milk," shouted Angus.

Dmitri, the coyote, couldn't help but intercede. "It ain't so bad—I've had worse in the mess hall, believe me!"

Curtis frowned at his leftovers. "Might just hold off," he said to no one in particular. "Not really hungry right now." He sat back against the bars and gazed out to the cavern floor below, listening to the ravenous slurpings from his neighboring cages. *God forbid*, he thought, *I should stay in here long enough to get used to that stuff.*

To Curtis's great surprise, a voice suddenly sounded from somewhere inside his cage. "You gonna finish that, then?"

Curtis leapt up, scanning the cage for the owner of the voice. In the far side of the enclosure, standing on his hind legs, was a tall and wiry gray rat. He was licking his chops and rubbing his spindly fingers together in anticipation. "Well, are you?"

"Who are you?" demanded Curtis. "And what are you doing in my cage?"

Seamus, above, cried down between mouthfuls, "That's Septimus. Septimus the rat. Septimus, meet Curtis, our new friend."

Cormac added onto the introduction, "He's a loiterer. Not even

a prisoner. Hangs out here of his own volition."

Septimus made a dramatic bow. "How do you do?" he said.

"Very well, thanks," said Curtis. "And no, I don't think I'm going to finish it."

The rat took a step forward and extended a hand. "Would you mind if I did?"

Curtis thought for a moment—troubled at the idea of voluntarily sharing food with a rat, of all creatures—but finally capitulated. "Go ahead."

Septimus cracked a smile and smoothed back the matted fur on his head. "Don't mind if I do," he said, before diving headlong into the bowl of gruel, lapping it up with a ferocious intensity.

Having finished, Septimus let out a diminutive belch before reclining lazily against the bars of Curtis's cage. He put his hands behind his head and closed his eyes. "Aaaah," he said. "Nothing like relaxing after a good meal." After a moment, he cracked an eyelid and looked over at Curtis. "So what are you in here for?"

Curtis sat back down. He had to admit, it was nice having some company in the cage. "I'm a turncoat, I guess," he said. "A deserter, of sorts. I saw what the Governess is going to do and I couldn't let it happen. So she threw me in here."

"Ooh," said Septimus. "That's pretty bad." He paused before saying, "What's she going to do?"

"She's going to sacrifice my friend's baby brother to the ivy so she can control it and take over the whole country."

A collective murmur arose from the surrounding cages. "What?" one of the bandits whispered.

"Oh," said Septimus, "that *is* bad. Ivy, huh? Evil stuff." Another pause. "Is it English ivy? Or the other stuff? I can't remember; I think one is more invasive than the other—"

He was interrupted by Cormac, who'd been listening in. "Septimus, if the ivy needs to *consume a human child* to become all-powerful, it's safe to assume it's the invasive stuff."

Septimus nodded gravely. "Tenacious plant, that ivy."

"And let's not forget the tenacious WITCH whose plan it is to feed it human blood and make it do her bidding!" shouted Seamus, casting his food bowl aside with a metallic clunk. "That evil woman is going to get what's coming to her, believe you me!"

Dmitri the coyote sounded from below. "And what are you gonna do about it now, all locked up in your oversized birdcage?"

Seamus leapt up and shook the bars of his cage, shouting, "Don't think you'll be saved too, dog! Don't think your litter at home are going to be spared when that ivy goes crawling over the forest. She's using you, that Dowager! She'll cast you all aside as soon as she's got what she wants."

Dmitri grumbled something in response and turned his back on Seamus, scraping a paw idly over the dregs of his bowl.

But Seamus's temper had been sparked, and he began shaking

at the bars of his cage. "Free Wildwood!" he shouted, then louder: "FREE WILDWOOD!"

The other bandits joined in, hitting their tin bowls against the wooden bars. The cavern was alive with the chaotic sound, the metallic clang echoing through the chamber. Suddenly, the warden appeared at the doorway below with a pair of armed guards.

"Keep it down in here, maggots!" he yelled. "Or we'll start using ye for target practice." One of the accompanying guards, as if to grant credence to the warden's threat, raised his rifle to his eye and began aiming it indiscriminately at each dangling cage.

Septimus the rat jumped up from his reclining position and scrambled up the side of Curtis's cage. Grabbing hold of the rope, he looked back down at Curtis and whispered, "This is where I take my leave! Catch you later!" And he was gone up the rope.

One of the bandits, concealed in his cage, yelled a muffled insult to the warden.

"That's done it!" shouted the stout warden. "No breakfast tomorrow!"

The bandits groaned loudly in mock protest.

"And no lunch!"

Finally, the prisoners fell quiet, the only sound being the creaking of the cages on their ropes. "All right, then, lights out!" The two guards separated and began snuffing out the torches that lined the cavern wall until the chamber was consumed in darkness. "Good night, maggots!" shouted the warden, and he was gone again.

Once he'd left, Cormac put his face against the bars and addressed the prisoners from his cage. "Mark my words, lads," he said in a raspy whisper, "as long as Brendan, our King and comrade, walks this earth, Wildwood *will* be free. I swear it."

The prisoners responded with a quiet cheer.

"He's comin' for us, boys," hissed Cormac. "He's comin' for us and we'll burn and bludgeon our way out of here. Mark my words. And no dog soldier or Dowager Queen will stand in our way."

CHAPTER 16

The Flight;
A Meeting on the Bridge

Prue was flying.

The feeling was *incredible*.

She'd flown in planes, but that had been a sterile sensation, a mediated experience that gave the illusion of flying—replete with the jarring complaints of gravity and the television-screen-sized windows broadcasting pictures of fluffy clouds and miniaturized cities. It was nothing compared to this, this true feeling of soaring: the dome of sky above her, the verdant sprawl of the forest below. Her arms were now safely wrapped around the General's fleecy neck, and her shoes had found footing at the joint where the eagle's tail feathers fanned out from his body. She could feel his powerful back muscles heaving and contracting with every wing beat, and the cool, damp morning air assaulted her skin, blowing her hair straight back and bringing tears to her eyes. The dawning light was pervasive now, crowning the tops of the fir trees with a golden glow. The horizon burned rosy and bright, reflecting off a bank of clouds in the distance, perhaps heralding a coming storm.

Below them, dotting the treetops, was a multitude of nests, large and small. Some were elaborate, multileveled affairs connecting the topmost branches of a given tree with a series of nests, aeries, and landing platforms. Many of the nests looked like common robin's nests, all straw and small branches, while others spanned whole boughs, their walls built of sizable tree limbs, their floors plastered with a smoothed gray mud. Several cedars towered above their neighboring firs, and Prue could see small cities of swallows' nests built against the bark of the trees, a dizzying network of little mud abodes. It was breakfast time, and from Prue's high vantage she could see the little holes, the entryways, to these nests crowded with the outstretched beaks of expectant chicks. As the morning progressed, she noticed that the air above this veritable metropolis of nests was growing more and more active as birds of all size and feather darted in and out of the massive blanket of trees, carrying worms and beetles, twigs and grass to succor their demanding broods.

"It's beautiful!" shouted Prue.

"The best way to see the Principality!" the General shouted back. The high wind whipped at them noisily; it was difficult to talk above the din. "From the air!"

Suddenly, the General banked left and carved a diagonal line down to skirt the tops of the trees. Prue felt her stomach drop. She gave a yelp as she felt the green newborn shoots of these gargantuan conifers brush her knees. A flock of adolescent peregrines, out for a morning flight, fell into the General's draft and began chasing him for sport, wheeling in and out of his flight path, badgering him to go faster and try to lose them.

"On an important mission, lads!" he shouted. They wouldn't have it; they continued to toy with him until he took a deep breath and, warning Prue to "hold on!" he corkscrewed up into the air, briefly stalling in midflight, and plummeted headfirst into the dense foliage of the trees. Prue screamed. She clutched his neck feathers tightly. Before he got too low, however, he expertly pulled from the tailspin and began flying through the thick jungle of tree boughs, masterfully weaving through the branches that hampered their way. The peregrines tried to keep up as best they could, but barely five minutes had passed before they were forced to give up pursuit. Once their pursuers had been lost, the eagle shifted his tail feathers and soared upward, out of the thick of the tree boughs. When they returned to their initial altitude, Prue saw something extraordinary. "Wow!" she exclaimed.

"The Royal Nest," explained the General, guessing the object of her amazement.

Before them towered a single tree, a majestic Douglas fir, which dwarfed its neighboring trees by sheer size. The trunk, even at this lofty height, was the width of a small house—Prue could only guess what its width would be at ground level—and the topmost branches soared fifty feet—easily!—above the nearest tree. The most extraordinary thing about the tree, though, was the impressive network of aeries that filled the high branches. An immense series of smaller nests occupied some of the lower branches, each inhabited by droves of sparrows and finches; above them, a smaller number of larger nests, these sheltering flocks of hawks and falcons—all leading up to a single, massive roost crowning the topmost branch, the pinnacle of the tree. It was solidly thirty feet in diameter and made of a diverse collection of every source of vegetation imaginable: fir boughs and raspberry brambles, ivy vines and coltsfoot stalks, flowering nasturtium and maple vines. The bowl of the nest was caked in a smooth layer of mud and looked to be the most inviting nest one could imagine—but, alas, it remained empty.

"The Crown Prince's own roost," explained the eagle solemnly.

"What will you do now Owl Rex is gone?" shouted Prue over the roar of the wind. They circled the complex of the Royal Nest a few times before resuming their northward flight.

"His nest will be tended and kept till he is returned. If South Wood refuses to do so, however, it will be war." The eagle arched his wings back and picked up speed as the city of nests below them grew sparser within the trees.

Prue was troubled by the eagle's response. "But how will you fight two wars at once? Assuming that the coyotes keep attacking you from the North?" she hollered. "And what will happen to Owl Rex?"

"We have no choice, Prue," was the eagle's loud reply. The General heaved a few wing beats, bringing them to a higher altitude; the blanket of dark green below them fell away, and Prue could feel her ears pop.

"Keep an eye peeled for hazards," came the General's instruction. "We're crossing over into Wildwood."

Prue squinted and scanned the crowns of the trees; here, the forest seemed wilder, untamed by any single colony. In the understory, deciduous maple and alder trees fought for dominance of the canopy alongside their larger coniferous cousins, the hemlock, fir, and cedar trees. They seemed packed closer together, their growth unhindered in this wild country; indeed, trees were not the only vegetation that sought the concentrated light at this height—fantastic vines of ivy had clambered to the top of several unfortunate maple trees, seemingly suffocating their hosts in the attempt to reach the blue of the sky.

"Looks clear!" shouted Prue.

As they flew on, the trees began to grow taller and wider, and they overshadowed the lesser deciduous trees around them. The tops of these trees seemed to scratch at the sky, the wind swaying their high branches. The General was forced to ascend even higher, and Prue could feel her lungs beginning to struggle for air at this elevation. From the new altitude, she could see how the dense patchwork of trees below them stretched on, seemingly endless, into the horizon. The borders of the Wood appeared impossibly vast. Forgetting herself and the thrill of her flight, she was suddenly overtaken by a feeling of hopelessness at her task. From this vantage, looking out over the massive expanse of wilderness below them, she thought, for the first time, that she might never find her brother. As if for comfort, she hugged the eagle's neck tightly and buried her head into his feathers.

And so she did not see the coyote archer.

She did not see him steady himself on the topmost limbs of a great fir and carefully nock an arrow in his bowstring. She did not see him pull the string back taut, and then release. She did, however, hear the singing whistle of the arrow as it sped toward its mark, and she felt the weight of the shaft as it hit its target, sinking with a sickening *thunk* into the breast of the eagle. And she saw the tip of the arrowhead exit from between the General's shoulders, mere inches from her cheek, its metallic point stained red with blood.

"NO!" she screamed.

The General gave out a single, impassioned squawk and then he

Prue was flying.
The feeling was incredible.

was silent, his head dipping low into his breast. His wings, by reflex, contorted around his body, and Prue and the eagle began to plummet from the air.

Prue, in absolute shock, began fumbling with the arrow in his chest, trying to pull it out, but it was held fast. "General!" she yelled desperately. "Don't! No, no, no!"

His wings suddenly contracted and he began shouting garbled protests to the skies; he beat his wings just enough to keep them from crashing straight down to earth. They skimmed the tops of the trees, Prue clutching to his neck feathers as he violently canted to either direction in flight, threatening to pitch his rider at any turn. The eagle valiantly carried them a good distance from the archer's position until he finally could labor no more; he gave one last cry, and, his wings falling limp, his body dropped from the air.

Prue shrieked and closed her eyes as they went crashing through the canopy of the trees. The thorny branches of the firs tore at her clothes and skin, attacking her body with the force of a thousand lashes. She pressed her face into the blood-wet back feathers of the eagle to guard from the whipping branches, and she felt the stillness of his body against her cheek. Finally, one stout tree limb broke their forward momentum and they toppled straight down, she and the eagle, cartwheeling through the leaves of the trees until they plowed into the ground, a rain of broken branches showering on them from overhead.

Prue was thrown several feet from the eagle, but luckily landed in the soft, rotted remains of an ancient tree trunk. Her fingers and face stung; she lifted her hands to see them crisscrossed with red scratches and abrasions. Her clothes hung in tatters from her body, and a wide patch of crimson red stained the front of her shirt. *The General's blood*, she thought. She jumped up to return to the eagle when she heard the sound of movement in the trees, the distinct crunching noise of footfalls in the undergrowth. She stopped in her tracks, guardedly searching the words around her.

Slowly, imperceptibly, the dense vegetation shifted, and a circle of human figures emerged from the woods. She was surrounded.

"Don't . . . move . . . a muscle," commanded one of the figures.

Prue froze. These men and women wore an eclectic array of clothing: brigadier uniforms, khaki scrubs, fine silken waistcoats—but in disrepair. The elbows of their coats were frayed, their undershirts stained with dirt, and everything looked to be fairly ill fitting. More significantly, they were armed to the teeth: antique pistols and rifles, swords and bowie knives. And they were pointing them at her.

"Where did you come from?" asked one of the men.

Prue slowly lifted her arm and pointed to the sky.

Her assailants were aghast. "What, you flew?" one asked, in disbelief.

Prue nodded. Her head was spinning, and she was beginning to feel faint. A searing pain was growing in her chest.

A voice came from behind the crowd. "What is going on here?" shouted the voice, gruff and authoritative. Pushing a few of the figures aside, a man appeared in the clearing. He had a deep red beard and wore a dirty officer's coat. A sash over his shoulder carried a sizable saber at his hip, and his forehead was tattooed with a design Prue couldn't immediately decipher. He towered over Prue, his curly red hair gaining him another six inches, easily, and glowered down at her. "Who are you, and where did you come from?"

"I'm—I'm Prue," she faltered. "And I was flying . . . on the eagle back there . . . and we were . . . we were shot down." Sputtering those last few words, she suddenly collapsed in a heap on the ground.

※

When she came to, Prue was moving. A kaleidoscope of sunlight and tree leaves wheeled above her. She was lying down and yet, strangely, hovering over the ground, traveling horizontally at a fairly fast speed. She lifted her head slightly and saw how this was possible: She'd been laid in a makeshift stretcher—two tree boughs with some ropes threaded between—and was being carried through the woods by the strange people she'd just encountered.

"The General!" she shouted, pushing herself up by her elbows. "The eagle! Where is he?"

The woman's voice came from behind her. "He didn't make it."

Prue tried to crane her body around to see the woman who'd spoken. "He's . . . dead?" she asked falteringly. The woman nodded, and

Prue's stomach plummeted. A jolt of pain shot up her neck from her chest, and she fell back against the twine beneath her. She grabbed at her ribs. "Ouch!" she cried.

"Looks like you took a pretty bad fall," said the woman, her breath heaving fast as she and the other stretcher-bearer ran through the woods at a near sprint.

The man at the front of the stretcher yelled over his shoulder. "Don't move. We have to get you to safety. Never seen a coyote marksman that far from the warren. There may be others."

Prue looked to one side and saw that the stretcher was accompanied by the rest of the people who had found her. They ran nimbly through the undergrowth, barely disturbing the bushes and bracken as they went.

"Who—who are you?" Prue asked. Her mouth was dry; it was difficult to speak.

"Bandits, kid," responded one of the runners. "Wildwood bandits. You're lucky we found you."

"Oh," said Prue. The world swam above her and a fog suddenly overtook her vision and she lost consciousness again.

🌿

Bap.

"Hey!"

Bap.

Prue, her eyes still closed, was suddenly alerted to a smacking noise, as if someone's back was being slapped.

Bap.

There it went again! she thought. It suddenly dawned on her that she felt a sensation accompanying each slapping sound—the feeling of someone hitting her cheek, gently, with an open palm. She opened her eyes, slowly, and started. Directly above her was the man she'd seen in the clearing, the red-bearded one with the forehead tattoo. His breath smelled very sour; his hand was poised for another slap.

"There you go," he said, satisfied. "Wasn't sure if you were going to die or not."

Prue was shocked. "No, I'm not going to die!" she said defiantly. "I was just . . . sleeping, I guess."

"Good," said the man. "Besides, you'd be a mite bit embarrassed if you died of a bruised rib and a sprained ankle, that's for sure."

"A bruised rib?" she asked. "How did you . . ."

"Ah, those South Wooders would love to sell us bandits as know-nothings, but we sure ken our bruises and breaks." He paused for a moment, thinking. "But you don't look like you're from South Wood. And you're no North Wooder neither. You're an Outsider, ain't ya?"

Prue nodded.

The bandit sat back, and Prue had an opportunity to take in her surroundings. She appeared to be in a lodge of some sort, rudely constructed of unfinished logs and brambly branches. The ceiling was made up of leafy fir boughs, and a simple handwoven rug covered a large section of the earthen floor. Shifting slightly, Prue realized that she was lying on a kind of rustic canvas mattress in the corner of the hut.

"Very peculiar," said the bandit, chewing thoughtfully on a dried cinnamon stick. "I never met an Outsider before in my life and then, in the span of two days, I see two."

Prue's eyes went wide. "Two? You've—you've seen another?"

"Yes, in a skirmish with the coyotes," said the bandit. "Only yesterday. A young lad, probably the same age as yourself. Fought alongside the Governess—and a good fighter, too! Rather crafty." The bandit suddenly came to a realization. "You ain't . . . you ain't in the employ of the Dowager, is ye? She's not made some dark alliance with the Outside, has she?" His hand instinctively went to the saber at his hip.

"NO!" shouted Prue, pain spiking at her chest. "I swear! I've never met her; only heard some terrible things."

The bandit lifted his arm from his side. "As you should. Evil woman, that Dowager Governess."

"But this other Outsider you saw," asked Prue. "What did he look like? Did he have curly black hair? And . . . and glasses?"

The bandit nodded.

Prue was flummoxed. "I can't believe it!" she said. "He's okay!

And he was actually fighting! With the Governess! It can't be true!"

"'Tis true," the bandit replied. "Knocked out our finest howitzer, too. Turned the tide of the battle single-handedly, he did. Lost a lot of men that day." The bandit shook his head dolefully. "But here I'm shooting my mouth off—haven't even introduced myself. I'm Brendan. Folks call me the Bandit King."

Prue blushed. "King!" she said, embarrassed. She had no idea she'd been addressing royalty. "Very good to meet you, Your Highness. My name's Prue."

Brendan batted the air. "Oh, don't start with the Highness stuff. It's mostly a title I use to scare people. Tends to work fairly well, too."

"So," began Prue, "if you're bandits, then why didn't you try to rob me? Isn't that what bandits do?"

Brendan tilted his head back and laughed. "Oh, aye, that's the truth. But robbing little girls who fall out of the sky ain't necessarily our forte. We go for rich folk, delivery drivers and the like—folks plying the Long Road between North and South Wood. We like to think we're liberators. Liberatin' money from folks who take it all for granted."

Prue smiled politely, though the bandit's reasoning struck her as funny. She chose to change the subject. "This other Outsider, his name's Curtis, I have to find him! We came in together, and we got split up when the coyotes found us, but that was before I saw Richard and made it to the Mansion, but then I—"

"Whoa, whoa there," chided Brendan. "Slow up, you'll bust that rib going on like that. First things first: Why are you here in the first place?"

"My brother," said Prue calmly. "My brother was abducted by crows. And brought here. Somewhere in Wildwood."

"Whew!" whistled Brendan. "You lost *two* Outsiders? Bad luck there."

Prue shook her head sadly. "I know," she said. "I don't know what I'm going to do. I was on my way to North Wood, you know, when we got shot down. Now I'll never make it."

The Bandit King nodded. "It's a long ways," he said. "To North Wood. And it's unforgiving territory, too. The coyotes are crawling over these parts."

Prue looked at the King imploringly and said, "Can you help me? Please? I'm just so terrified that something horrible has happened. And now Curtis has joined in with the coyotes? I'm just so confused!" Despite herself, she began to cry.

Brendan frowned. "I don't know what to tell you, Prue. We've got our hands full here, what with this war on. I can't be helping little girls find their brothers."

A knock came at the hut's doorframe.

"Sir!" shouted the bandit at the door. "Coyotes! On the perimeter!"

Brendan leapt up. "What?" he shouted, alarmed. "How far out?"

"Second sentry line!" was the response.

The King whispered a curse under his breath. "There's no way they could find us—they've never been this far out. Unless . . ." He stopped and looked down at Prue.

"You're coming with me!" he shouted, kneeling down and throwing Prue over his shoulder as if she were an empty duffel bag. She shrieked at the pain of her bruised rib colliding with his shoulder blade. He ran from the lodge, into a clearing surrounded by rustic huts and lean-tos. The camp, built into the shallow of a deep, wide draw, was alive with activity: Men and women milled about the periphery at various labors, children played with little wooden toys near a central fire pit.

"Aisling!" he shouted. "Saddle up the brown mare, Henbane, and bring her to me!"

"What are you doing?!" called Prue.

"Getting you out of here," responded Brendan. "They've got your scent. They're after *you*. And you're about to lead the whole coyote army down on us."

🌿

Henbane was a lithe chestnut mare, and she whinnied excitedly when Brendan vaulted astride her and threw Prue on her flank behind him. Prue winced, the horse's quick movement painfully jarring her delicate ribs. Brendan grabbed a fistful of Henbane's mane in one hand

and pointed to the camp with the other.

"Get the children inside!" shouted Brendan to the throng of bandits. "And arm up. We've got coyotes on the perimeter!" The horse reared, and Prue desperately threw her arms around him, pulling herself in close to his back. Brendan briefly surveyed the actions of the bandits, all scurrying to follow his instruction, before kicking the horse into a gallop. They sped down the ravine, away from the camp.

Prue watched the camp disappear behind her as they arrived at the mouth of the draw and took a sudden right turn onto flat ground. The huts and lodges seemed to melt away into the green of the foliage, undetectable. Brendan shouted a loud "HYAH!" to the mare, and they vaulted through the underbrush, dodging brambles and leaping fallen tree trunks. After a moment, the bandit pulled back on Henbane's mane, and, coming to a shimmying stop, he looked up into the overhanging tree branches. "Where are they?" he shouted.

A voice came from above. Prue squinted to see a bandit, hidden in the boughs. "Farther south, sir! One hundred yards. By the split oak!"

Brendan gave no reply but spurred the horse instantly back to a gallop, and they drove through the woods as fast as the mare could carry them.

"Are you just going to turn me over to them?!" shouted Prue over the crashing of the horse through the bracken. How was it that she was single-handedly bringing all this danger on top of everyone she met? She felt like the world's most effective bad luck charm.

"That'd do me no good!" he shouted back. "They'd still be on the perimeter, sniffing around! I can outrun them, but I need them to follow me." He whistled and shied the horse to avoid a giant mossy berm. "And you're my bait, Outsider!"

Suddenly, they broke through a wall of blackberry brambles and landed directly in the middle of a squad of coyote soldiers, easily fifty in number, knocking over several who stood in their way.

"The girl!" barked one of the coyotes.

"The King!" shouted another.

Brendan, with an expert twist of his wrist, turned the mare eastward and kicked her flank. "HYAH!" he shouted, and the horse burst into speed. Prue gripped Brendan's waist tightly, her body jolting against Henbane's bare back. They tore through the underbrush, the bushes and boughs whipping at their skin.

The coyotes, in a desperate, baying lather, tore after them. A pursuit troop broke away from the main group, sprinting on all fours, their uniforms ripped away by the sheer power of their strides. Reduced to their base animal instincts, they joyously barked and snapped as they gave frantic chase.

Henbane was heaving, her muscles churning with every leap. But she knew the terrain; Brendan barely had to direct her as she deftly flew through the forest.

"Faster! Faster, Henbane! On!" Brendan cried hoarsely.

The dogs gained ground. A few managed to catch them and sprinted alongside, snapping at Henbane's ankles. Seeing this, Brendan yanked at the fistful of horse's mane in his grip and they angled sideways, into a grove of salmonberry stalks. Just beyond, a shallow ravine opened up and a brook cut a noisy path downward. With a swift spur of his heels, Brendan commanded the horse into a long leap, and they made the other side in a fleet second. The dogs that had been so intent on taking the horse down by her ankles dropped with a whining scream into the rushing water.

Prue cast a cautious look back and saw that, while they lost a few pursuers to the ravine, the majority had made the jump and were gaining on them.

"They're still on us!" she shouted.

Brendan urged the horse faster, and they zigzagged through the forest, the horse's hooves pounding the soft earth.

"Almost there," Prue could hear Brendan whisper.

Suddenly, the brush cleared and a short, steep slope led down to a massive road cut into the side of the hill. Henbane scrambled briefly for footing before stumbling down onto the gravelly surface.

"The Long Road!" Prue shouted.

The coyotes behind them leapt the incline and landed squarely in the middle of the road, their hackles bristling, their teeth angrily bared.

Brendan gave them a brief look and shouted, "Come on then, dogs!" and they were off again, sprinting down the road. Their speed on this level surface was even greater than in the forest, and Prue could feel Henbane begin to really stretch into the run. She could also feel Brendan temper his spurring; he wanted the coyotes to keep up, drawing them farther away from the hidden camp.

Prue looked ahead over the rider's shoulder and saw, fast approaching, two ornate columns on either side of the road and the weathered wooden planks of a bridge just beyond. As they drew closer, Prue could see that the earth fell away at a dramatic angle below the bridge,

creating the rocky walls of a deep canyon. She gave a shriek as Henbane's hooves hit the bridge and she could look down into the ravine; the depth looked to be bottomless.

All of a sudden, Brendan pulled back at the mane and the horse came skidding to a stop midway across the bridge. "Oh boy," he rasped below his breath.

Prue looked up and saw on the far side of the bridge a tall, striking woman, dressed in a kind of buckskin gown, astride a coal-black horse. A long, thin sword was sheathed at her side, and her copper-red hair hung in a pair of braids to her waist. She smiled when she saw them and walked her horse onto the bridge.

"Well, hello, Brendan," she said icily. "Fancy seeing you two days in a row!"

Brendan said nothing.

"That's . . . that's the Governess?" whispered Prue.

He nodded gravely. Reaching to his side, he slowly, deliberately pulled his saber from its scabbard and pointed it at the woman. "Let me pass," he said.

Their coyote pursuers arrived behind them and stopped at the first plank of the bridge, pacing and pawing at the dirt, their snarling lips quivering.

The Governess laughed. "You know I can't let you do that, Brendan," she said. She rode slowly closer and craned her neck to see who was riding behind him. "Who's your partner, Bandit King?"

Prue stuck her head out from behind Brendan's back and stared at the woman. The Governess's eyes shot open wide. A flicker of recognition drifted across her brow. "An Outsider!" she exclaimed. "You've got yourself an Outsider!"

"And where's yours, witch?" Brendan scoffed. "Last I saw you, you had one in your thrall."

"Gone, sadly," she said. "He went home, back to the Outside. Wasn't suited for Wildwood, apparently."

A wash of relief fell over Prue—had Curtis made it home? Had one of her rescue missions been solved? At that moment she felt a tinge of envy for Curtis; she imagined him safe at home, his parents lovingly tousling his curly hair.

The Governess urged her horse forward; she drew closer to them. Brendan did likewise and the two horses faced each other, mere feet apart, at the middle span of the bridge. The coyotes growled and yapped behind them. The Governess kept a steady eye on Prue; it was unnerving.

"Little girl," she said. "Sweet little girl: You don't know what you've gotten yourself into. This is nothing for a child to witness. You should be home with your parents!"

"Quiet!" shouted the Bandit King. "Stop your toying!"

Alexandra glared back at him, a wry smile cracking across her lips. "And what will you do, O King of the Bandits?"

Brendan snarled and raised his saber. "I'll run you through, is what I'll do. So help me gods."

"And what would that possibly solve?" she asked, unbowed. "My soldiers would tear you to pieces before the sword was withdrawn. Your people, your scrappy followers, deprived of their fearless leader. Who will protect them?"

The King spat on the wooden planks and said, "No matter how many of my people you kill and imprison, you'll never find us. You don't know these woods as we do."

"All in due time, Brendan," she replied. "All in due time. Your 'people' will be sorry they didn't come out and join me, when the day is at hand. And it won't matter what little cesspit they may be hiding in presently."

Brendan was losing his temper. "Draw your sword, Governess," he said calmly. "We'll settle this now."

"Not so simple," was Alexandra's stoic reply. She put two fingers to her lips and let out a loud, bright whistle. Suddenly, the far side of the bridge behind her filled with coyote soldiers, each training a rifle directly at Brendan and Prue.

Brendan gaped. Prue squeezed his waist tight and buried her face into the damp cloth of his shirt.

Alexandra took this moment to finally draw her sword from her sheath. "Drop your weapon," she commanded, the tip of her sword pointing steadily at Brendan's face. The sound of metal clattering on wood followed as Brendan's saber fell from his fingers, and the pack of coyotes behind them, still breathless from the pursuit, came clambering up and dragged the two riders from their horse.

"Take the King to the cages!" shouted the Governess. The coyotes barked in approval. "But bring the girl to me."

Alexandra gave one final look at Prue; she then sheathed her sword and drew the reins on her horse, guiding him at a trot away from the bridge and back into the forest.

CHAPTER 17

Guests of the Dowager

Curtis woke to the sound of gnawing. It came from above his head, and he cracked one eye open to try to identify its source. A few of the torches in the cavern had been relit and Curtis could see, dimly, the hanging shapes of his neighboring cages.

Looking up, he saw Septimus, the rat, busily chewing on the cable connecting his cage to the root system. He'd taken a sizable chunk out of it; barely half remained. Curtis shot a quick look down to the ground below the cage—a distance of some sixty feet led to a cavern floor piled with jagged rocks and strewn with fractured bone—before scrambling to his feet.

"Septimus!" he hissed. "What are you doing?"

The rat jumped, surprised, and momentarily stopped in his labors. "Oh!" he said. "Good morning, Curtis!"

Curtis, agitated, repeated his question. "Septimus, why are you chewing on my rope?"

Septimus looked over at the rope, as if unaware of the activity. "Gosh, Curtis," he said, "I don't know. I just do that from time to time—feels good on my teeth."

Curtis was furious. "Septimus, there's like a *huge* fall to the ground here, and if you break that rope, I'm dead!" He jabbed a finger downward, pointing to the bones that littered the ground. "Look at those bones!"

Septimus looked down. "Oh," he said. "I see."

"Now . . . buzz off!" Curtis shouted.

"I think they throw those bones around down there just to make it look scarier," said the rat calmly.

"Septimus!" yelled Curtis.

"Got it," said the rat. "Loud and clear." He shot up the rope, scampered across a root tendril, and leapt onto the top of another cage, setting it to swaying. The bandit in the cage he'd jumped to, Eamon, was awake and was quick to shoo the rat from his rope. "Don't even think about it, rat," he said.

Septimus huffed grumpily and disappeared into the dark crevices of the root-ball.

One of the bandits, Curtis couldn't make out who, grumbled something in half sleep. Another snored. Pushing himself up into a seated position, Curtis kicked his legs across the floor of his hanging cell. His lower back was killing him; if it weren't for the fact that he'd been so incredibly exhausted, he wondered if he'd have slept at all. He stretched his arms over his head, feeling a *crrrrack* in the midsection of his spine as he did so.

Suddenly, a commotion from the hallway disrupted the relative calm of the morning; a coyote soldier came rushing into the cavern, waking the warden, who sat slumbering against the wall, with a kick of his paw. A few words were hastily exchanged and the warden, getting stiffly to his hind paws, followed the soldier out of the room. Shouting could be heard from the tunnel and then, to Curtis's great surprise, a small troop of coyote soldiers was led into the cavern, a rope-bound man in their custody. Curtis immediately recognized him from the battle the previous day.

"Brendan!" Eamon shouted, anguished. "My King!"

Brendan stared stoically up at the cages. His red beard and mop of crimson curls were matted and wet with sweat—it looked as if he'd been through some arduous labor before arriving here.

The other bandits were roused and took to the bars of their cages, staring down in disbelief as the warden gave his rote speech to the new prisoner: "The distance to the ground, unjumpable. Abandon hope. Abandon hope." Brendan looked on into space, his face betraying no emotion.

"YOU'LL PAY FOR THIS!" screamed Angus, desperately shaking his cage.

Eamon and Seamus had picked up their tin bowls and were dragging them across the wood of the bars, making an unholy din.

Cormac merely sat cross-legged on the floor of his cell, quietly murmuring to himself as he watched the proceedings. "We've lost," Curtis thought he heard him whisper.

The warden attempted to quiet the prisoners by shouting them down, but it was no use; the bandits kept up their deafening protest. Pulling the ladder from where it rested against the wall, the warden grumpily hooked it to the bars of an unoccupied cage, and the Bandit King was released from his bonds and forced at swordpoint up the ladder and into the dangling cell. His fellow bandits fell into a shocked, reverent silence as the key was turned in the lock and the

entire scene was over as soon as it had begun: The ladder was returned, a few shouted epithets were thrown at the prisoners, and the warden and the soldiers walked from the room.

It was quiet for a time in the cavern. The rope above Brendan's cage wheezed under the weight of the new occupant. Brendan sat in the middle, still blankly staring straight ahead.

Finally, Seamus hazarded a word. "King!" he said softly. "Our King! How did you . . . ?"

Brendan, not breaking his stare, simply said, "The war ain't over, boys."

"But what about the—did they find the—" stammered Angus.

"The camp is still hidden," replied Brendan. "They'll not be finding it. Everyone is safe."

Cormac, still sitting in shock, said, "We're lost."

This simple declaration caused Brendan to erupt from his sitting position. Both hands gripping the bars of the cage, he shouted to Cormac, "Don't for a moment think that. This war is a long shot from being over. We've still got blood in us yet!"

The cavern fell silent. No one said a word.

🌿

Prue's head was spinning. She realized, as she was marched through the woods by the coyotes, that she'd not actually stood on her own since the crash landing, and she was noticing that there was a distinct, needling pain in her ankle as well as her chest. The abrasions on her skin were scabbed over and lined with bright red welts. She'd never felt like such a mess. Her thoughts just before the arrow had downed the eagle were replaying endlessly in her head. Now they seemed like a prophecy come true: *My task is hopeless. My brother will not be found.* She desperately fought the images that were crowding into her mind's eye, macabre pictures of what might happen to a baby in a wild forest, unfed, a captive to a flock of violent crows. Perhaps the worst had passed. Perhaps he was at peace.

The coyotes, under instruction of their commander, were thankfully lenient, and she was allowed to move at a slower pace, hobbling along on her one good ankle. After they'd traveled for a time, they arrived at a wide cave opening dug into a large hillock, nearly covered by overhanging ferns, and they instructed her to walk inside. A tunnel led down into the earth, root tendrils hanging overhead. The air was cool and damp and smelled like dog. Finally they came to a large, cavernous opening where a few coyote soldiers milled about. A cauldron boiled in the center. She was led through an open door in the wall and entered what looked to be some sort of rustic throne room.

In the throne sat the Dowager Governess. "Come," she said, waving a finger. "Come closer."

The few coyotes that had flanked her fell away and left the room, and Prue carefully limped forward until she was within feet of the throne.

The Governess looked at her fondly. A warm smile had spread across her face. "But I'm forgetting myself," she said. "We haven't been properly introduced. My name's Alexandra. Perhaps you've heard of me."

"The Dowager Governess," croaked Prue. "Yes, I have." She found it difficult to get the words out; her voice sounded alien to her, all raspy and weak.

Alexandra nodded, smiling. "Would you like a seat?"

Prue was relieved when a coyote attendant came forward, bearing a stool fashioned out of rough-hewn tree boughs and tanned deer hide. She gratefully sat.

"I'm hoping only good things," continued Alexandra.

"What?"

She clarified: "I'm hoping you've heard only good things about me."

Prue thought for a moment. "I don't know. A bit of both, I guess."

Alexandra rolled her eyes. "Such is the nature of fame."

Prue shrugged. She was exhausted. In normal circumstances, she could imagine being terribly intimidated by the beautiful woman in the throne, but now she was just too tired.

"And your name?" prompted the Governess.

"Prue," said Prue. "Prue McKeel."

"Very nice to make your acquaintance," said Alexandra. "I trust my soldiers have treated you gently?"

Prue ignored this question. "Where's Brendan?" she asked.

Alexandra laughed quietly, running her finger along the armrest of the throne. "He's gone somewhere where he'll never be able to hurt people again. You know, don't you, the man is quite honestly a menace to society."

"What's he done?" asked Prue, dubious.

"Terrible things," explained Alexandra. She paused, eyeing Prue quizzically, before continuing: "I know he might seem the charming rake, this so-called Bandit King, but I can assure you he is a *very* dangerous individual. You were lucky we found you when we did; there's no telling what may have befallen you had you stayed in his clutches."

"I was fine," said Prue.

"He's a murderer, my dear," said the Governess, suddenly serious. "A murderer and a thief. He's a blight on inter-Wood commerce and a plague to common goodness. An enemy of man and woman, human and animal alike. He's caused more harm and pain in this country

299

than any civilized person would countenance. Now that he's behind bars, we're all the safer for it."

Prue chewed on this information thoughtfully; perhaps the Governess was right. She'd barely spent an hour in his company—she knew better than to jump to conclusions about people she'd met in this strange country. Her misplaced trust in the Governor-Regent had taught her that much.

"I'm just here for my brother," said Prue finally. "I don't want to get involved."

Alexandra raised an eyebrow. "Your brother is here in Wildwood?"

Prue took a deep breath. The speech was beginning to feel pretty mechanical. "He was abducted. By crows. They brought him here. And I came looking for him."

The Governess shook her head ruefully. "The crows, you say. I can tell you that the crows happen to be my next priority: bringing them in line. They've done some horrible, horrible things, those crows, since they broke away from their Principality."

Prue's face brightened slightly. "You've seen them? The crows?"

"Oh, we've seen them. Out in the woods. Like those nefarious bandits, the crows are an element in Wildwood we are trying to . . . how shall I say . . . *mitigate*. Like an illness. Or a particularly irritating insect. You follow?"

"I guess so," said Prue. Her ankle burned from the weight it'd been forced to bear on the walk into the warren. A dripping noise could be heard distantly; the sound of chattering soldiers. "But my brother. Have you seen him?"

Alexandra thought for a moment before replying, "I'm very sorry to say that we haven't. It would've been a notable discovery, a baby Outsider boy in Wildwood. We've expanded quite a bit, our humble army, and we've seen much of this wild country—but there is much more to cover. I imagine we'll be running into those crows once we get closer to the Avian Principality. Perhaps we'll—"

Prue interrupted her. "But you *are* near the Principality. Your soldiers are all over the border; the General said so. And we were barely into Wildwood before one of your coyotes shot us down, me and the eagle." She was beginning to lose her train of thought. The image of her baby brother, pale and silent on a bed of moss and branches, continued to haunt her. "And now that eagle is dead. Why? Why did you have to shoot him?"

"An unfortunate casualty. Call it collateral damage."

"I call it coldhearted."

The Governess cleared her throat. "The rules of engagement, dear. Wildwood is a no-fly zone for military birds. It may have been sold to you as a simple ride, gratis, from a kind old buzzard, but I can assure you, more suspect intentions were at hand. Fly-bys, midnight raids, eagles and owls picking up defenseless coyote pups and dropping them to their deaths—that is the MO of the Avians. I believe it's called *cleansing* in your land."

Prue stared at the Governess. She then shook her head, her eyes cast down at her sneakers, now soiled brown with mud and dirt. "I can't believe it," she said under her breath.

The Governess watched Prue intently. "How *old* are you, dear?" she asked.

"Twelve," said Prue, looking up.

"Twelve," repeated Alexandra, pondering the fact. "So young." She shifted in her throne, sitting upright. "If I may be frank: I find it incredibly admirable that you would come in here, to what must be such a strange world to you, in order to find and protect your baby brother. Very admirable for such a young lady. Your courage is uncommon. I would hate very much to be the party responsible for your brother's kidnapping! You would prove an *indefatigable* foe, no doubt." Her wandering fingers found a steady grip on the ends of the throne's armrests. "However, a young girl as bright as you must understand the danger of becoming involved in affairs that are beyond your realm of experience. Things are rarely as simple as they appear—at first glance, a clan of bandits can seem fairly sympathetic, that whole 'steal from the rich to give to the poor' platitude; a colony of birds blithely 'defending' their border. I ask you to see the flip side of that coin: a group of bloodthirsty amoral murderers and a society bent on expanding their borders in a savage, greed-driven landgrab. Which is it?"

Prue suddenly realized this was not a rhetorical question. The Governess was waiting for her to answer.

"I . . . ," she stumbled. "I don't know." Her mind churned over the events of the last few days, swimming in a haze of exhaustion, sleep deprivation, and fear. She imagined her mother and father, beside themselves with grief and worry, bereft not just of one child, but both. Her bruised rib radiated a dull pain through her chest. She looked down at her hands, at the network of lacerations that graffitied her skin, at the little dried spots of blood hardened in the crevices of her knuckles.

Alexandra moved in for the pounce.

"Dear, go home," she intoned. She said this calmly yet forcefully, her voice betraying no emotion. "Go home to your parents. To your friends. To your bed. Go *home*."

Prue stared, a tear welling in her eye. "But . . . ," she protested. "My brother."

Alexandra, her face softening, placed her hand to her chest. "I swear to you," she said, "on the grave of my only son. As a woman and a mother." Alexandra's eyes, too, appeared to be filling with tears. "I will find your brother. And when I do, I will charge my soldiers to return him, *immediately*, to your home and your family."

Prue sniffled at a tear. Her nose was beginning to run.

"You will?" she trembled.

"Pssst! Curtis!" The voice came from above the cage. It was Septimus.

"I said: I don't want you chewing on my rope! That's final." The midmorning tedium had cast a pall over the cages. The prisoners were silent, no doubt contemplating the hopelessness of their circumstance.

"No, no!" whispered Septimus conspiratorially. "Your friend—she's here!"

Curtis looked up. "Who?"

Septimus, exasperated, shot a wary look down at the warden, who was noisily napping on the cavern floor. "The sister of that baby! She's here!"

"Prue!?" shouted Curtis, before catching himself and whispering, "You mean Prue?"

The warden shifted in his sleep. He was curled around a stalagmite, his face buried in a pile of old rags. "Yes!" whispered Septimus. "I saw her—in the throne room!"

"What was she doing? Was she captured?"

"I don't know, but whatever it is, it must be serious. The Governess is giving her a good talking-to."

"She came in with me," came a voice from below them. It was Brendan. He spoke flatly, not attempting to hide his voice from the warden. "We found her just past the Old Woods. She'd been shot down riding an eagle; she had coyotes on her tail. We didn't realize that until we'd gotten back to camp, but by that time the dogs were practically on us. I tried to get her away, but we were stopped on the Gap Bridge."

Septimus and Curtis both stared down at the speaker.

"You're Curtis, ain't you?" continued Brendan, peering up through the bars of his cage. Curtis nodded. "The girl's looking for you," the King said. "She was worried about you. Said you guys got split up."

"And now she's captured?" asked Curtis. "Great. Both of us locked up in here."

Brendan shook his head. "No," he said, "I have a feeling the witch has other plans. She brought me straight in here—but had Prue brought to her chamber. It's strange, but I get the distinct feeling the Dowager is *afraid* of this girl. Whatever the case, I don't think she'll be letting on that you're in here."

"Of course not!" rasped Curtis. "If Prue only knew what she was up to . . ." Here he paused and looked over at the rat. "Hey, Septimus: How'd you see her?"

Septimus nonchalantly eyed his claws. "Oh, I have my ways. There's a whole circuit of tunnels that ain't big enough for anyone but me in this place."

"Can you get back there? Find out what they're doing?"

Septimus leapt up and saluted. "Recon? I'd be happy to." And with that, he scurried back up the rope and disappeared.

🌿

"So you promise," said Prue. "You promise to find him. How can I possibly know if I can trust you?"

305

"Dear girl," said the Governess. "There's little benefit in me lying to you."

Prue studied the woman carefully. "And you'll bring him straight back to me, back home. Just like that?"

"Absolutely," responded Alexandra.

Prue's vision blurred a little and she paused, trying to measure her words. What could she say? "Do you need my address?" asked Prue faintly. The prospect of returning home was growing more and more attractive by the moment.

Alexandra smiled. "Yes, you'll have to give that to one of my attendants before you leave."

"And you'll let me go, just like that?"

"I'd insist, for your safety, that you be accompanied to the border of the Wood by a small detail of soldiers—nothing serious, just to make sure you're not hurt on the way. This is, as you no doubt know, a very dangerous neck of the woods." The statement was spoken with an illustrative twirl of her finger. "We did the same for your friend Curtis. He was most appreciative."

"And you swear," repeated Prue. "You swear on the grave of your son. To find my brother."

Alexandra looked at her guardedly. "Yes," she said after a moment.

"I know about your son," said Prue. "I know what happened."

The Governess arched an eyebrow. "Then you know how I have been wronged. How those madmen in South Wood—my home country—have cast me out and put in place that puppet government. You were flying from there; tell me, how is my old homeland?"

Prue shook her head. "Terrible. They're rounding up all the birds and imprisoning them. For no reason. Though . . ." Here she paused, thinking about the Governess's earlier words. "Now I don't know."

"*Exactly,*" said the Governess, leaning forward. "Prue, listen to me. *I'm* the force for good in this land. *I'm* the one who can set these things to rights. Let the South Wooders and the Avians battle and imprison one another, fighting suspicion with suspicion—I will throw them both. Things have reached a boiling point. No one is safe until the entire place is brought back under proper leadership. Under *my* leadership." She sat back in her throne. "If you know of my son, then you know of my husband, my late husband, Grigor. We ruled together, the three of us, in harmony. The Svik doctrine was one of liberty and fidelity among all species of the Wood. It wasn't until the deaths of my husband and my son that those relations spiraled out of control. And it is my intention to renew that harmony."

Prue nodded, silent.

"But these things shouldn't concern a girl of your age, much less one from the Outside," said the Governess. "I can assure you, Prue, that we will prevail. We *will* be victorious. And we will return your brother to you and your family. You can expect to return home today, safe in the knowledge that your family will be united once more."

Prue nodded again. Her whole world seemed to be spinning

about her, flipping on its axis; up was down, right was left. It was as if everything, her entire worldview, had abruptly switched polarity. "Okay," she said.

ᴥ

Curtis's frantic pacing in his cell as he waited for Septimus to return had elicited the interest of his fellow prisoners, and they whispered among themselves, venturing guesses as to Prue's fate.

"Oh, she's a goner, as sure as I'm standing here," whispered Seamus.

"Aye," concurred Angus. "She's vulture meat, for sure. They'll hang her from a hemlock, let the birds sort out the rest."

"Oh, it'll be much simpler than that," surmised Cormac. "I'm thinking a quick decapitation. Bang. Over."

Curtis stopped his pacing and glared at the bandits, each in turn. "Come on. I mean, seriously."

Brendan gave a quiet stutter of a laugh, the first show of emotion since he'd arrived. "Ease up, lads," he said. "You'll drive the kid to ruin."

A scraping of claws on wood announced the return of Septimus as he scampered out of a crack in the root-ball and launched himself onto the top of Curtis's cage.

"Well?" prompted Curtis. "What did you see?"

The rat was nearly out of breath, and it took a moment before he could manage a word. "She's there . . . in the throne room . . . I saw her . . . black-haired girl . . . looks pretty scraped up."

"Scraped up?" asked Curtis. "Like, what way? Did they hurt her?"

Brendan spoke from his cage. "She's got a bruised rib and a sprained ankle, I think. One of our lads had a look at her in the camp. She crashed from the sky, remember, riding a dead eagle. No doubt she's scraped up."

Septimus nodded before continuing, "But they've mostly just been talking. I can't hear much—there's a fair amount of noise from the main chamber—but it's sounding like the Governess is going to let her go."

"What?" asked Curtis, shocked.

One of the bandits murmured, "Didn't see that coming."

"Yeah," said Septimus. "Says she doesn't know where the baby is, but she'll look for him. Lying through her teeth, basically."

Curtis was outraged. "Someone has to tell her! Septimus! You have to tell Prue that she's being lied to!"

Septimus was taken aback. "Me? Just outright yell that the Governess is a liar? You've got to be kidding. I'd be on a coyote's skewer, a-roasting over an open fire, before you could say 'rodent rillettes.' And your friend would be thrown in here, likely. Or worse . . ." Here he ran his finger across his throat.

"But . . ." Curtis objected. "But . . . we can't let her get away with this!" He had forgotten the volume of his voice, and he heard the warden grumble loudly in half sleep, "Keep it down up there!"

Curtis glared down at the warden, incensed. "And what are you gonna do, huh?" he shouted. "Cancel my dinner? Take away visitation rights? No television for six weeks? Things can't really get much worse, man!"

The warden had stood up by this point and was staring up at Curtis, his arms akimbo. "I'm warning you . . ."

"Oh, spare me," shouted Curtis before holding his face in between the bars of his cage and hollering, in the direction of the tunnel leading from the cavern, "PRUE! PRUE! DON'T BELIEVE HER! SHE'S LYING TO YOU!!!"

The warden's face became beet red, and he began scrambling around, trying to find a way to quiet his insolent prisoner.

"MAC IS HERE!" Curtis shouted again, his voice cracking at the volume. "YOUR BROTHER IS HERE!"

"GUARDS!" shouted the warden, finally, and a group of coyotes came tramping into the room, their rifles raised to their shoulders.

🌿

"Well, I guess that's it," said Prue. She glanced briefly out the open door to the chamber beyond; some sort of ruckus had erupted, and a group of soldiers was being directed down one of the far tunnels. Alexandra followed her glance, curiously watching the activity before motioning to one of her attendants to close the door. The room was quiet again.

"Yes, I suppose that is," said Alexandra. "It was very nice to meet you, Prue. It's not often I have a chance to meet Outsiders." She stood up from her throne and walked to Prue, extending a hand to help her from her seat. Prue winced to have weight on the ankle again, and Alexandra gave a concerned look, saying, "Ooh. That poor ankle. Maksim!"

One of her attendants walked swiftly to their side. "Yes, madam."

"Why don't you pack our guest's sprain in a poultice before she goes. Turmeric and castor leaves." She looked back down at Prue. "Should be good as new."

"Thanks, Alexandra," said Prue, accepting Maksim's proffered elbow.

"Let's post a troop at the hillside overlooking the Railroad Bridge; if there's some sort of rift in the Periphery allowing free passage into Wildwood, now would be a good time to step up the security," Alexandra instructed. "We don't want any more Outsiders stumbling in here and getting hurt. Enough damage has been done to these poor children; heaven forbid more should be lost in the Wood."

Maksim nodded.

The Governess continued, "And Maksim: Take the side exit. There seems to be some sort of tumult in the main chamber. Best not to disturb the dear girl any more."

"Aye, madam."

As Prue was led from the chamber via a side door, she could see Alexandra calling a group of soldiers to her and, whispering hushed instructions, following them through the opposite door.

"What's going on?" asked Prue, hobbling unsteadily over the uneven ground.

"Nothing of note, I expect," replied Maksim. "Likely just some tiff between soldiers. Here, let's make it to the pantry, and I can tend to that ankle of yours."

"Thanks," said Prue. It tasted bitter, this sudden surrender, but the anticipation of returning home was sweeping over her like a breeze on the first clear spring day.

*

"Shut those prisoners UP!" shouted the Commandant, having arrived at the growing group of soldiers standing on the cavern floor, staring up at the cages. The bandits had joined in with Curtis, screaming the girl's name over and over, batting their cage bars with their empty bowls. The noise was deafening, echoing endlessly off the tall cavern walls.

The frantic warden was babbling, "I don't know what's come over them! I don't know!"

The Commandant glared at the warden before turning to his soldiers and instructing them to raise their rifles. "Fire at will," he said firmly.

Curtis had his eyes on the crowd of soldiers below them, and when he heard the Commandant's directive, he yelled to the other prisoners, "They're going to shoot!"

"Swing your cages, boys!" shouted Brendan. "Give 'em a moving target!"

Immediately, Curtis and the bandits began running from side to side in their cages, sending them into a jostling sway. The hemp ropes holding them to the root branches moaned and creaked under the violent action.

The soldiers began firing indiscriminately, and the cavern was alive with the crackle of gunfire, the acrid smoke from the powder filling the room.

"Keep swinging!" yelled Brendan. "Faster!" Curtis heard a bullet whiz by his cheek and he set to swinging his cage even harder.

A woman's voice came through the cloud of smoke that was billowing up from the soldiers' rifle barrels. "STOP!" she commanded. The firing abruptly ceased. Curtis stopped his running, his stance spread across the cage floor in an attempt to slow its swinging. Finally, the smoke began to clear and Curtis could make out the figure of Alexandra, walking toward the cages. Her face was flushed red.

"Insolent children!" she shouted, waving a hand in front of her face to dispel the smoke. "Insolent, bratty ruffians!"

Dmitri, the coyote, demurred from his cage. "*I* wasn't doing anything."

"Shut up, you," dismissed the Governess.

"Where's Prue?" shouted Curtis, out of breath from the swinging. The smoke in the chamber clawed at his throat and stung his eyes. "What have you done with her?"

"I sent her home," said the Governess. "She's gone. Back to the Outside. So you all can stop your racket now, thank you very much." She looked directly at Curtis and said, "She's in bad shape, you know. She's been through a lot."

"You lied to her!" Curtis yelled. "She doesn't know your plan!"

"She's a smart girl, that Prue McKeel," responded Alexandra calmly. "She knows when she's in over her head. Unlike certain *other* Outsiders of my acquaintance."

Here Brendan interceded. "Let the children be, witch," he said, his gruff voice emanating angrily from his cage. "What kind of woman chooses children for enemies?"

Alexandra directed her glare toward Brendan. "And what kind of king abandons his people at the slightest intrusion, hmm? Your compatriots should know that you were intercepted trying to retreat into the woods, away from your precious hideout. The first sight of the enemy, and you're off to save your own hide."

Brendan laughed. "Tell them what you will, Dowager. Your words ring hollow."

Curtis, in despair, had thrown himself down on his cell floor. He stared dolefully into space. "I can't believe it," he murmured. He felt abandoned.

Brendan glanced sympathetically over at Curtis before shouting down to Alexandra, "What have you done with the girl's brother? The baby?"

"The baby is safe," said the Governess. "He is well kept."

"She's going to feed him to the ivy!" said Curtis. "On the equinox!"

Brendan stood in his cage and stared down at the Governess, his hands gripping the bars. His face was blank. "Oh, Dowager," he said softly. "Say it's not so. Not the ivy."

Alexandra smiled up at Brendan, almost beaming with accomplishment. "Oh yes, Bandit King. We've arrived at a deal, myself and the ivy. The plant requires infant blood. I require domination. One thing for another, quid pro quo. Seems like a decent partnership, yes?"

"You're mad, witch," said Brendan. "The ivy won't stop till everything is wiped out."

"That's precisely the idea," responded Alexandra. She calmly waved her hand, a horizontal slice through the air, a dismissal, a negation. "Everything. Gone."

"We'll stop you," said Brendan, the emotion rising in his voice. "We have numbers yet, the bandits. We can still bring you to your knees."

"Unlikely," said Alexandra. "What with their 'king' being imprisoned. However, since I do expect that your remaining ragtag group will continue to harry my forces, I would insist that you give me the location of your little hideout. Posthaste."

Brendan spat on the ground. The glob of spittle landed feet away from an observing coyote soldier, who grimaced and stepped away. "Over my dead body," said the King.

Alexandra smiled. "That can certainly be arranged." She then turned to her cohort of soldiers and barked a command: "Bring the King to the interrogation chamber. Elicit the location of the bandit camp. By whatever means necessary." She began to walk from the chamber but stopped at the tunnel entrance. She turned back to the cages and smiled. "Good-bye, Curtis," she said. "I don't expect that

I'll see you again. This is where you will find your end, sadly. I wish it could've worked out differently, but alas, such is the way of the world."

Curtis stared, aghast.

"Good-bye," she repeated, and left the room.

At the Governess's instruction, the warden pulled the ladder from the wall and, braced by a coterie of coyotes, removed the Bandit King from his cage. Proud and defiant, he climbed down the ladder to the floor below, quietly allowing his captors to place manacles at his wrists. The bandits in the cages watched the proceedings wordlessly, and Brendan cast a single steely look up at them before he was led from the room.

"Be strong, boys," was all he said, and he was gone.

CHAPTER 18

On Returning;
A Father's Admission

T he poultice, a thick layer of a yellow-green paste enclosed in a wrapping of oak leaves, felt cool against her ankle as Prue was led from the warren by two silent soldiers. The remedy appeared to be surprisingly effective; she was able to walk, albeit with a slight limp, almost immediately, and didn't require the arm of one of her attendants.

The coyotes wordlessly led the way; they traveled for a time down a shallow gully where a path, worn into the bracken, wound through the hanging ferns and blankets of wood sorrel on the forest floor. The light had grown dark since they'd first arrived at the warren; a layer of clouds had blown in from the southwest, and the air was cool and damp. The patter of a first wave of raindrops could be heard, assailing the outstretched leaves of the trees and the ground cover. After a while, the path opened up onto the Long Road, the muddy gravel of the surface speckled with rain, and Prue followed the coyotes along the road. They arrived at the Gap Bridge, spanning the dark void below it, and crossed. At the far side, the coyotes left the road and began following a hidden trail, imperceptible to Prue's eyes, down through a wide field of enormous sword ferns and into a glen suffused with the spidery branches of vine maples. Prue fell into a kind of rapt meditative state and began to lose her sense of direction entirely.

Finally, after what must have been several hours, the coyotes arrived at a break in the trees and there, looming darkly over the span of a wide gray river, were the twin spires of the Railroad Bridge. The little wooden houses of St. Johns could be seen on the far banks of the river, snuggled cozily within the manicured trees of the surrounding neighborhood. The soldiers stopped at the tree line and gestured for Prue to continue. She nodded and took her leave from her escorts, scrambling down a slope, brambly with blackberry vines, to arrive at a shallow gully that ran along a stretch of railroad tracks. She gave a quick look over her shoulder to see if she could still see her entourage—she wondered how many soldiers would be stationed here,

watching over the bridge—but saw nothing. If they were there, they were safely camouflaged by the trees.

She walked along the tracks toward the Railroad Bridge and, after a time, came upon the wreckage of her bike and the Radio Flyer wagon. They lay untouched in the tall grass of the gully. She groaned at the pain in her rib as she pulled her bike from the ground and set about untwisting the frame from the wagon. Her initial estimate had been true: The front wheel was hopelessly bent, but the rest of the bike seemed to be in decent condition. She righted the wagon, straightened out the stem that attached it to the bike, and began walking the entire ensemble through the Industrial Wastes and back across the Railroad Bridge. A loud, distinct *shhhhhh* noise came from behind her, and she turned to see a gray wall of rain descend on the hill of trees above the bridge. Within seconds it was upon her, and she was almost immediately soaked to the skin.

"Figures," she murmured to herself, and continued pushing the bike and wagon across the bridge.

Reaching the other side, she made her way up a gravel road that switchbacked down from the bluff. Following this, she soon arrived back in the tidy maze of cordoned streets, fresh-mowed lawns, steady humming traffic, and quiet dark houses of her neighborhood. She breathed a long, sorrowful sigh of relief.

The world seemed to have continued on without her fairly handily; the few pedestrians to be caught in the sudden shower were huddled beneath umbrellas and were jogging briskly to their destinations. A few cars whispered over the wet pavement, their windshield wipers busily in motion, but no one gave Prue so much as a second look, despite her haggard appearance, her torn clothes and tangled hair.

It was awhile before she arrived at the front door of her house. She briefly considered going to Curtis's house first, to check on him and see how he'd made it out, but decided it would be best to find her parents. She only hoped that her sudden reappearance would somehow temper the inevitable trauma they would experience upon learning of their son's vanishing. Prue knew she would have to tell the truth, no matter how crazy it would sound.

A single dim light was on in the living room, barely cutting through the afternoon's gloom and sending a small ray of light onto the front stoop. Prue could see through the window and into the kitchen; the rest of the house was dark, as if a cloud had passed over it. She could make out the figure of her mother slouched on the living room couch, her shock of curly hair as unkempt as the tangled mass of yarn she was staring into. Prue's dad was nowhere to be seen. She dropped her bike and climbed the few steps to the door, her ankle smarting at each step.

"I'm home," she called wearily into the darkened house.

With a shout of surprise, her mother was up in a flash from her seat on the couch. The mass of yarn on her lap spilled to the floor.

She ran to her daughter and engulfed her in an embrace that only a bereft mother could manage. Prue let out a cry as her mother's powerful arms squeezed her delicate ribs and a swell of pain overcame her, nearly causing her to faint. Hearing the cry, her mother released her and cupped her hands around Prue's cheeks, searching her face for signs of harm.

"Are you okay?" she managed.

Prue squirmed in her grasp. "Yes, Mom," she said. Her mother's eyes were red and guttered with deep, dark wells. She looked like she hadn't slept since Prue had left.

"Where's—where's Mac?" her mother stammered.

An enormous wave of tiredness and despair overcame Prue. She could feel her knees beginning to buckle. "He's gone," she said. "I'm sorry."

Her mother erupted into tears. Prue collapsed into her arms.

🌿

"So that's it, huh?" It was Seamus, pacing his cage and setting it to shaking. "That's it. No trial, no torture, no execution—nothing. Just left to rot." They had been left alone in the chamber. The warden and his two prison guards had been conspicuously absent for a few hours now.

Cormac sighed and said, "Sounds as much. Though I expect the King is getting the brunt of it. Tortured and *then* left to rot."

"Disgusting dogs. All of 'em," hissed Seamus.

Angus piped up, "And what did she say? She's feeding the baby to the ivy when? On the equinox?"

Curtis, his legs curled to his chest, replied, "Yep. The equinox."

Angus rubbed his forehead thoughtfully. "That's, what, two days from now? Ye gods, we don't have much time left."

"We're done for—though at least we'll outlast our brethren back at camp." This came from Cormac. "Don't expect they'll see it coming when the ivy takes over. That'll be a quick end."

"Aye," said Angus. "Y'know I took a nap once, down the Old Woods, in the ancient glen. Right down in a bed of the stuff, the ivy, that is. Not but two hours pass when I wake up and a little tendril of the stuff is all coiled around my big toe, sure as I'm standin' here." He paused and spat. "No telling what it'll do once it's in the control of that evil witch. And all drunk on baby blood."

Curtis grimaced at the thought.

Cormac continued, "Nah, we're better off starvin' down here, lads. At least we'll die a natural death, not have ivy a-snakin' into our eyeballs. Only hope that the camp catches word in time and gets somewheres safe—underground or somethin'."

Seamus laughed. "Nah, they'll all be done for long before that. You heard the Dowager—Brendan's done abandoned them. As soon as the dogs were on the camp, he hightailed it. If they haven't found it by now, no doubt he's spillin' the beans to them coyotes as we speak. He ain't bein' tortured, boyos, he's sitting down with the witch herself, havin' a glass of chilled juniper gin and laughin' about how we're just a bunch o' fools."

Cormac leapt up from his cage floor and raged from between the bars, "You take that back, you mongrel, you son-of-a-skunk. You can bet that Brendan's not betrayed us—he's got more courage in his pinkie fingernail than you ever showed!"

Seamus took up the challenge, shouting, "Aye, we'll see about that, Cormac Grady. You may be deceivin' yourself. I suspected for a long time that he was givin' in to the dogs. He was losin' his edge, for a damn sight."

"Watch your words, traitor!" yelled Cormac.

"Cormac," said Angus, "don't waste your breath. Who knows what's happened? In the end, it don't rightly matter much, us wasting away in here."

"You!" countered Cormac. "You too! And what with your old lady waiting at home. You'd throw in the towel just 'cause she's got a bit of a rovin' eye and is likely warming the tent of some other bandit."

This got Angus's hackles up. "Don't bring my girl into this," he yelled. "And no, she don't got no rovin' eye. She's as honest a woman as—"

"SHUT UP!" shouted Curtis. "For once: Please, please just stop arguing."

"Thank you," snorted Dmitri.

The bandits fell silent. A gloom fell over the cavern's inhabitants.

One of the torches on the chamber wall flickered and went out.

A jingling noise caught Curtis's attention. It was coming from above, from within the root-ball. He looked up to see Septimus, sitting on a snaking limb, casually picking his teeth with a shiny piece of metal. Something about the gleam of the metal caused Curtis to stand up and try to get a better look. Indeed, it wasn't just a single piece of metal, but rather a cluster of metallic *things*.

"Hey, Septimus," Curtis called out.

The rat paused and spat out a loose bit of food.

"What's up?"

"What are you chewing on?"

Septimus raised his eyebrows and looked at Curtis sideways, as if the question had never occurred to him. "What I'm chewing on? You mean these old things?"

He was holding a ring of keys.

"Where did you find those?" asked Curtis frantically. They looked incredibly similar to the ones that the warden carried.

The rat held the ring of keys at arm's length and studied them, as if for the first time. "Gosh," he said, "I don't rightly remember." He paused and thought, his tiny index finger poised at his chin. "Now that you mention it, I think I got them from the warden. *Ages* ago. He had two sets, see, and I figured he wouldn't miss 'em." He nodded and looked down at Curtis. "They feel really good on my teeth."

Curtis let out a jubilant laugh, which he quickly tried to suppress, looking out into the chamber. "Give them here, Septimus!" he whispered to the rat. Septimus dutifully dropped them down into Curtis's cage.

"A lot of good it'll do us," said Seamus, above. He was watching the proceedings intently. "We get out, sure, but we'll drop to our deaths."

Curtis waved him away impatiently. "Hold on," he said. "I'm thinking."

He stood up and looked over at the long, spindly ladder that was leaning up against the cavern wall. It was too far to leap—even from a swinging cage. Curtis gauged the distance carefully. To his eye, the closest cage to the ladder—Angus's—at its farthest-out swing would allow too much of a gap for even the boldest jumper to clear. If there were only some way of lengthening the rope, maximizing the swing . . .

He struck on something. "You guys!" he hissed. "I think I can get us out of here!"

The bandits, forgetting their earlier disagreements, all scrambled to attention.

❧

Prue's father arrived at the reunion sopping wet. He'd been out in the rain, and his yellow slicker was clinging to his wet skin. In his hand, he carried a stack of papers, matted with water. Made hastily on their home computer, the sheets featured photos of Mac and Prue above supplications for help printed in a large, bold typeface that was now smeared from rainwater.

Like her mother, Prue's dad had hugged her tightly until she'd been forced to push him away by the nagging pain in her rib. On discovering that his son was still gone, he sat down heavily on his reading chair and held his head in his hands. Prue and her mother looked on helplessly. Finally, her mother spoke.

"I suppose you should tell your father what's happened," she said.

And she did. She told him everything, as she'd told her mother moments before. It all spilled out of her in a fountain of regret and sadness. She finished this fantastic monologue, compulsively, by saying, "And now I'm just so tired. So very, very tired."

When she finished, both parents were completely silent. They gave each other a quick, meaningful glance—Prue, in her state, was unable to read it—before her father stood and, walking toward her, said, "Let's get you to sleep. You're exhausted." And Prue had crushed her face into her father's chest, feeling his strong arms lift her into a cradled position. Prue's father walked her upstairs, shushing her like a small child, and she was asleep before she'd reached her bed.

When she woke, it was dark.

She felt the familiar softness of her goose-down pillow against her cheek, the cocoon of her down blanket nestled closely around her body. Cracking one eye open, she lifted her head from the pillow to see what time it was. The clock at her bedside read three forty-five a.m. She kicked her legs out, stretching her weary hamstrings, and realized the poultice at her ankle had been removed. In its place, her parents had wrapped a conventional gauze bandage. She turned over, shutting her eyes again, but then realized she was desperately thirsty.

Getting out of bed, she quietly opened the door and walked out into the upstairs hallway, testing the strength of her ankle as she went. She was in her pajamas now, though she had no memory of putting them on. She climbed down the stairs, mindful to avoid the particularly creaky steps—she didn't want to wake her parents. She couldn't imagine what emotional turmoil they must be in. However, once she'd made the ground floor, she was surprised to see that a light was still on in the kitchen.

Sitting at the kitchen table was her father. He cradled a glass half full of water and was staring at a small black container, the size of a large jewel box, resting on the table's surface.

"Hi, Dad," Prue whispered as her feet hit the cork of the kitchen floor. She squinted at the overhead light.

Her father startled on hearing her approach. He looked up, surprised, his eyes tired and glazed over. It was clear he'd been crying.

"Oh, hi, honey!" he said. Initially, it seemed as if he were going to feign normalcy, put a brave face on things, but he soon lapsed back into despair. "Oh, sweetheart," he moaned, his eyes downcast again.

Prue stepped forward. "I'm so sorry," she said, her voice freighted with sadness. "I'm so, so sorry. I don't know what to say. This whole thing is crazy." She scooted out one of the four red chairs that surrounded the table and sat down. "I know this whole thing is my fault. If only I'd taken better—"

Prue's father interrupted her. "No, it's not your fault, dear. It's ours."

She shook her head. "You can't blame yourself, Dad, that's crazy!"

Her dad stared at her, his eyes puffy and red. "No, you don't understand, Prue. It *is* our fault. It's always been our fault. All along. We should've known."

Prue's curiosity was piqued. "Should've known . . . what?" She reached over and took a sip from his glass of water.

Her father rubbed his eyes and blinked rapidly. "I guess . . . ," he began, "it's best that you know. What with all you've been through. We should've told you earlier, but it just never seemed like the right time."

Prue stared at him. "What?"

"This woman you met," her dad said slowly. "This Governess. Your mother and I, we've met her before."

"What!?" Prue shouted. The sudden interjection sent a shower of pain from her bruised rib.

Prue's dad raised his hands in an effort to quiet her. "Shhh!" he said. "You'll wake your mother. Someone in this house has got to get rest."

"You met her? Alexandra?" hissed Prue, quieter this time. "When?"

"Long, long ago. Before you were born." He shook his head sadly. "We should've known." Heaving a deep sigh, he looked back up at Prue and continued.

"When your mother and I married, we were so excited to have children, to start our family. We bought this house and immediately began envisioning which room would be whose—always keen on the idea of having a boy and a girl. A brother and sister. But, as these things sometimes go, our hopes were never realized. We tried and tried, but no baby was coming. We saw doctors, specialists—went to holistic retreats and acupuncture sessions. Nothing. Even the most radical approaches seemed to be hopeless for us—we just couldn't have kids. Your mother, she was heartbroken. It was a very sad time. We tried to get our heads around the idea of being a family without kids, but it was just so . . . so impossible." He sighed again.

"One day, though, we were at the farmer's market—you know, downtown—and I was off getting, I don't know, rutabagas or something, and I came back looking for your mom and she's at this weird booth—one I didn't remember having seen before—talking to an old, old woman. The woman must've been in her eighties, she was selling trinkets and strange beads, and she had a whole shelf of weird bottles of tinctures behind her. Anyway, your mom was in a serious conversation with this woman when I came up, and your mother, she turned to me and said, 'She can help us. She can make us have kids.' Just like that. Well, at that point, we'd tried everything. I was starting to lose patience, but I knew it meant so much to your mother, so I said, 'Okay.' For a small price, she sold us this little box here."

He picked up the small black container on the table. It looked to be made of painted teak; hinges on the side of the cube suggested a clam-shell opening. A baseball could be comfortably concealed within. He continued:

"She instructed us to go to the bluffs, near the center of St. Johns—just down where that restaurant is—and, well, cast these runes." Here he lifted the lid on the box and poured six smooth pebbles onto the Formica of the kitchen table. These sigils, varied in color, had each been inscribed with a different strange runic character.

"When we cast the runes, she said, a bridge would appear. But not just a bridge, the *ghost of a bridge*. Apparently the apparition of some bridge that had been there long ago. And once that bridge had been called into existence, we were to walk to its middle point and ring a bell, and a woman would appear. She said we would recognize the woman because she was tall and very beautiful and she would be wearing a headdress of feathers. Well, naturally this all seemed like a bunch of hooey, really, but we were desperate and figured it was worth a shot, and if it didn't work we could just have a good laugh about the whole thing. So that night, when it was late and the streets were deserted, we walked out to the bluff and found this little stone slab, and we emptied the pebbles onto the stone. And the next thing you know, this big mist appears over the river and a giant, green bridge—with these cables and towers—just appears in front of us. I mean, it was incredible. Never had seen anything like it before. And we walk out to the middle of the bridge and, sure enough, there's a bell, a little antique-looking bell, just hanging from one of the columns, and we ring it a few times. So we wait there, and we wait a long time. Just the two of us, standing in the middle of this 'ghost bridge.' All of a sudden, a figure appears on the other side of the bridge walking toward us out of the mist. It's a woman, and she's wearing this funny headdress.

"She doesn't introduce herself, she just says, 'So you need a baby?' And we nod yes. And she says, 'I'll make you with child but you have to agree to something.' And we say, Okay, what is it? And she says, 'If you ever have a second child, that child belongs to me.'"

A chill came over Prue. She stared at her father.

Her dad, sensing her amazement, gulped loudly and continued, "At that point, Prue, we were desperate. We just wanted a kid, you know? So we said yes. Since it seemed impossible that we would have another child, it seemed like a good deal. Her end of the bargain would probably never happen, right? And this woman, this weird woman, steps forward and just lays her palm on your mother's stomach and that's it—she turns around and walks away. We walk back home over the bridge, and the bridge disappears behind us as soon as we've stepped off. Your mom, she doesn't feel much different, and we figure the whole thing was some sort of elaborate hoax until a few weeks later when we were at a doctor's appointment and it turns out, your mom *was* pregnant—with you!"

Clearly, her dad intended this to be a heartwarming moment, but it was lost on Prue. She was feeling fairly disturbed.

Her father clocked her response with a sorry grimace before he went on, saying, "So that was it. You were born. And there never were two people more happy than your mom and I. We were over the moon. You were the sweetest baby anyone could've imagined. And we never for a moment thought we'd have another kid—we'd been through hell and back to have one, after all—we were done. Single-kid family. That was us. Besides, as your mom and I got older, we figured it would be just impossible. Then, out of nowhere, some eleven years after you were born, your mom gets pregnant again. Out of nowhere. No way we saw that coming. Well, we figured that it had been long enough and that woman we met on the bridge had probably forgotten about the whole thing, so we went through with it. And that was Macky."

He sniffled a little, his eyes downcast. "So that's it. We brought this on ourselves." said her father. "That woman came back for her side of the deal."

There was silence in the kitchen. Outside, the rain had stopped, and a soft breeze rustled the oak branches in the backyard.

"Prue?" her dad asked after she'd sat silent for a few moments. "Are you going to say anything?"

Footsteps in the entryway alerted Prue to the presence of her mother. She had just arrived at the door to the kitchen. She padded over to Prue and rested her hands on her shoulders. "Hi, babe," she whispered. "We're so sorry. We don't blame you at all; there's nothing you could've done. It was our mistake. Our stupid mistake."

Prue's father nodded. "You see, Mac never really belonged to us. As terrible as that sounds—it's all clear now. But if not for that woman, this Dowager Governess, we'd never have been a family. We'd never have had *you*." He looked directly into Prue's eyes, tears welling up at the lip of his lower lashes. He reached out his hands and grabbed Prue's and squeezed them.

Prue stared back at her father. Her hands didn't move. Her mother's fingers burrowed into her shoulder muscles. Prue's ankle pulsed with a quiet pain. Her mind fumed.

"I'm going back," she said.

Her father's eyes widened. His mouth slackened. "What?"

Prue gave a quick shake of her head, as if loosening herself from a dream. "Back. I'm going back." In a decisive motion, she freed her hands from her father's and picked up the black box on the table. She scooped the rune stones back into their container and snapped the lid shut. "I'll be taking these," she said. Her mother's hands had dropped from her shoulders, and Prue scooted the chair back from the table. Standing, she briefly tested the strength of her ankle and, feeling less pain than she'd had since the accident, walked out of the kitchen.

"Wait!" shouted her mother, finally. Prue paid her no mind. She was already at the stairs and climbing, her mind quickly itemizing everything she'd need to do before leaving.

"Don't be rash!" came her father's voice from the bottom of the stairs. "Think this through. It's not safe!"

Prue was in her room, attempting a superhero-like quick change into her clothes. She shoved the box of runes into the midsection of the hoodie's pocket. The stones clattered from within. She knew that the Governess's coyotes would be guarding the Railroad Bridge; she'd have to call this Ghost Bridge. It was the only way to cross the river. She turned to see her parents at her door.

"Think about this, Prue," said her mother, desperate. "This is bigger than you. You're only going to get hurt!"

"Listen to your mother," said her father sternly.

Prue stopped briefly and looked from one parent to the other. Their faces were full of concern. "No, I won't," she said. She squeezed between them and began walking back down the stairs. They were frozen at the top. She heard their furtive whispers. "Do something!"

came one. "I'm trying!" came another.

She'd barely set foot in the kitchen when she heard her parents stomping down the stairs after her. Her father's voice boomed from the entryway. "Prue, as your dad, I'm telling you to stop. You are *not*, I repeat, *not* going back into those woods."

She felt his strong fingers grasp her upper arm, and she was jerked backward.

A stunned silence followed as Prue and her father stared at each other; he'd never acted so forcefully with her before. The color had drained from his cheeks. Screwing up her courage, she shook her arm free and faced down her parents.

"Don't," she said, glowering. "Don't you *dare* tell me what I can or can't do. Not now. Not after what you've done."

Her father's face was drawn. He began to stammer an apology, but Prue angrily waved his words away.

"Listen, I love you both," Prue continued. "So, so much. I should be hating your guts right now, but I'm not. I don't." The anger she was feeling gave way to a kind of bewildered pity for the two adults as they stood, speechless, in the entryway. They suddenly looked to Prue like two confused and terrified children. "But you really screwed this up, didn't you? I mean, *what were you thinking?*"

Finally, her father spoke up. "Let me go," he said. "It's my fault. I'm the one responsible here. Just tell me where to go. I'll get him back."

Prue rolled her eyes, exasperated. "Wish you could," she said. "I would *totally* make you go. But you can't. Long story, but I think I'm able to go in there when other people can't. Something about a Periphery magic. Whatever. Besides"—she looked back and forth between her parents—"I figure I have Mac to thank for my even being alive. If it weren't for him, I'd've never been born, huh?

"I'm going to go get my brother back," continued Prue, her voice now loud and commanding. "And that's that."

She turned and walked briskly through the kitchen and out into the backyard, where her derelict bicycle stood, resting limply on its kickstand. Reaching under the porch, she found her father's red metal toolbox and began combing through it. She could hear her mother crying, faintly, from inside the house. Her fingers finally came upon the crescent wrench, and she set about removing the misshapen front wheel of her bike.

She jostled the tire loose from the fork, and reached for one of her old bike wheels; she'd had the rims replaced last spring in anticipation of a busy summer of bike riding, though her old ones were still decent enough to warrant saving. She was thankful for this bit of foresight as she pulled it out, dusted it off, and began threading her bike's front fork dropout over the threads of the wheel hub. Within minutes, the bike was back in riding shape.

Her father appeared at the back door, his body casting a shadow from the porch light across the lawn. Prue squinted up at him, a dark silhouette against the doorway.

"Don't do this, Prue," said her father. His voice was weak, tired. "We can be happy, the three of us."

"Bye, Dad," she replied. "Wish me luck." She climbed aboard her bike and pedaled out into the street.

·

CHAPTER 19

Escape!

"Now, you're sure about this, yeah?" asked Septimus, eyeing the twisted rope warily. It was already half-chewed; only part of the rope remained.

"Yes!" hissed Curtis impatiently. "Just do it. And quick! We don't know how much time we have before the warden comes back."

"I've got a hold, rat, don't worry," said Seamus. He spoke with some difficulty, as he was belly-down on his cage floor, his arms uncomfortably extended out between the bars, his hands gripped around the upper bars of Curtis's cage. It had taken some time getting into this position, but after a few minutes of hardy swinging, the cage had come within Seamus's grasp, and now his fingers were locked tight around the knotty wood of the bars.

Septimus cast a glance over at Seamus before shrugging an okay, and in a flash he was at the rope, busily gnawing at the remaining material. Curtis stood, his legs spread, bracing himself against the bars of the cage. He intently watched the rat at work.

"How close?" he asked after a moment.

Septimus stopped and, leaning away, eyed what was left of the rope. "Not much," he said. "Frankly, I don't see why it hasn't—"

He was interrupted when the rope broke with a low, almost polite snap and the cage was loosed from its mooring, leaving the rat dangling from the nub that remained attached to the root tendril. Curtis gasped as he felt the cage swing into a free fall. The floor seemed to wheel upward, the stones and the bones calling for his blood—when, with a jerk, his downward motion was stopped short and an agonized moan issued from Seamus's cage. Curtis looked up; Seamus's fists were still snarled around the bars of the cage, his knuckles white from the pressure.

"OOOOOF!" grunted Seamus loudly. "This ain't as easy as it looks!" He worked his fingers over the wood of the bars, searching for a better grip.

"Hold tight, Seamus," instructed Curtis. "Now, if you can just start making your way to the rope."

Seamus began moving his grip, one hand over the other, toward the joint where the rope met the cage. The cage gave little quakes with Seamus's every movement, and it was all Curtis could do to keep himself from eyeing the bone-strewn cavern floor. Finally, Seamus arrived at the eyebolt where the rope was fastened and, with a quick heave, let go of the cage bars and grabbed the rope, giving a groan again when the weight of the cage tightened the slack.

The groan twisted into a laugh, however, as Seamus rasped, "Ha! Think I'd let ye fall, kid?"

Curtis, his heart rate beating a frantic tap dance in his ears, tried on a nonchalant laugh and found it did not fit him at the moment. His voice broke at the first chortle.

Seamus grew serious, his face beet red. "Okay, so off to Angus?" he asked.

Curtis nodded.

Seamus puffed up his red cheeks into blowfish proportions and began swinging Curtis's cage by the nearly ten-foot length of rope remaining. Curtis's stomach dropped out with every swell as the arc of the swing started small and grew. At the crest of every upswing he could see Angus, some five feet above him, belly-down on his cage floor, his arms extended to catch.

"And . . . NOW!" shouted Curtis.

Seamus gave a bellowing cry as he heaved the cage airborne and Curtis, aboard this flying vessel, was thrown toward the waiting hands of Angus.

Angus, his eyes bulging, threw his arms forward, his hand grasping at the bars of the cage.

First grasp: missed.

Second grasp: missed.

In this moment, every fraction of a fraction of a fraction of a second felt like it lasted minutes, hours, eternities.

Third grasp: both hands extended, flailing for the cage, and Curtis's free fall was stopped with a sudden jerk as Angus's hands gripped at the rope.

Angus let out a heroic sigh of relief. It sounded like an ocean breaking a flood wall.

"Oh. My. God," intoned Curtis.

Seamus laughed from behind them. "Your god's got nothin' to do with it! Them's a bandit's nimble fingers! Nice catch there, Angus!"

Angus was silent. His eyes were closed. "I think I may've wet meself," he whispered.

Curtis allowed himself now to look down at the cavern floor. There was easily a fifty-foot drop remaining. A pile of rocks topped by a particularly jagged-looking boulder lay directly underneath his cage. He looked over at the ladder leaning against the wall. He hadn't been much of a hand at physics—at least the introductory chapter they'd studied in the last week of sixth-grade life science—but if his estimates held true, if Angus was able to swing Curtis's cage to its highest arc and get his own cage swinging as well, Curtis would be able to make the leap to the ladder.

"And then I'll just climb down," he said aloud.

"What's that?" asked Angus, his voice straining as he concentrated on his hands' tight grip of the rope. He'd managed to get the end looped once around his wrist—it looked to be a solid hold.

"I said I'll just climb down the ladder," said Curtis. "Once I've jumped to it." He looked up at Angus. "But you've got to swing me as high as you can—and get your own cage swinging too."

"That's goin' to be the easiest part, boyo," Angus said, smiling. "As for you, ye've got a bit of a jump there."

Curtis nodded seriously. "Okay," he said. "Here goes nothing." Using Septimus's keys, he began testing each one in turn in the lock of his cage door. A long silver skeleton key turned out to be the one; it undid the bolt with a dull metallic *click*, and Curtis was able to swing the door open. The ground swayed far below him; was that a skull dashed on those jagged rocks? He closed his eyes to the sight and focused on the task at hand. He secured himself in the now-open doorway, the balls of his feet positioned on the cage floor edge, his hands gripped to the outside bars.

"Okay," he instructed.

Angus took a deep breath above him, and with a grunt began swinging Curtis's cage. It moved in small, quick arcs at first but soon began gathering speed and swing. Angus's cage began swinging as well, and soon the two cages were a long, articulated pendulum, sailing through the air of the domed cavern. Curtis judged the distance to the ladder with each upswing.

"A little higher, Angus!" he shouted.

"Aye!" responded Angus, his sinewy arms flexing with each arc. After a few more swings, Angus reported, "Think that's as high as you're goin'!"

Curtis looked at the ladder as he swung toward it. It was a little farther away than he'd hoped, but no matter.

"Okay, Angus," he shouted. "When I say 'go,' I want you to toss the cage with all your strength."

"Got it," said Angus.

Eamon, several cages away, offered this encouragement: "'Tis like the hammer-toss, Angus—you've done it a hundred times!"

"Aye, but I never done the hammer-toss lyin' flat on me belly!" He waited for his command.

"Okay . . . GO!" shouted Curtis, and in a flash, the cage was airborne. He waited until it had reached its highest point—it happened in the blink of an eye—and with a heave, he pushed away from the cage, his arms and legs vaulting him from the open doorway. Before

344

he knew it, he'd cleared the distance and his hands were scrambling to find a grip on the top rungs of the ladder. His body slammed against the rough wood, and his left foot landed squarely on the sixth rung from the top. He was about to holler a report of success when he suddenly felt gravity shift under his weight, and the top of the ladder began to pull away from the cavern wall.

"OH, OH, OH!" he shouted as the ladder, all sixty rickety feet of it, began tipping backward.

"Oh boy," said one of the bandits flatly.

Time moved comically slow as the top of the ladder, with Curtis affixed, fell away from the wall. It balanced momentarily as it came perfectly perpendicular to the floor and then began its quick descent backward.

The floor sped toward Curtis.

The scattered bones on the cavern floor seemed to cheer what would be the newest addition to the collection.

But then the ladder stopped. Suddenly, violently. Curtis was now upside down, his back facing the ground below, his left arm desperately linked to one of the ladder rungs. His left leg was wrapped over another, the wood biting into the crook of his bent knee. His eyes were tightly closed.

He heard a swell of laughter from the bandits: throaty, relieved laughter.

He opened his eyes to see that the ladder had landed squarely against Angus's cage, the metal hooks extending from its top rungs conveniently hooked into the bars of the bandit's cage door.

"Well, that'll do, boyo!" shouted Angus between snorts of laughter.

Curtis breathed deeply. "That's . . ." His voice cracked. "That's what I meant to do."

🌿

A sheen of water remained on the top of the pavement, and Prue's bike tires hissed over the slick black surface. The red Radio Flyer wagon bounced noisily behind her.

The downtown of St. Johns seemed abandoned in this early morning quiet. A haze of dimmest blue tinted the sky. A few dogs howled in welcome to the new day. A single car waited helplessly at a dormant traffic light; even in this otherworldly hour, the rules of the day applied. A figure huddled at the bus stop in the center square was a faceless pile of parka and knitted cap.

Prue turned the corner at the old clock and headed toward the river. The street ended at a sudden cul-de-sac; a line of cement bollards provided a barrier between the pavement and an unkempt field of raspberry brambles and yellow-trumpeted Scotch broom. Here, she dismounted her bike and walked it over the curb, past the barrier, and into the field of weeds. The river was a low rush of noise ahead of her,

346

past where the ground sloped away to arrive at the lip of the bluffs.

She hadn't gone far, however, before she came to a small clearing in the weeds. In the midst of this clearing lay a large slate-gray slab of stone, just as her father had described. Mere feet beyond the slab was the steep embankment of the bluff; here the earth fell away to the grassy bank of the river far below. A thick pall of fog had settled over the river valley, obscuring it entirely. Prue carefully laid her bike amid a crop of knapweed and walked to the stone. Kneeling down, she pulled the little box from her hoodie pocket.

Opening the lid of the box, she stared at the contents, at the six multihued pebbles and the strange inscriptions etched into their smooth faces. "Uh," she whispered to no one in particular, "I'm not sure if I'm supposed to say anything, but . . ." She emptied the pebbles on to the stone, watching them clatter and roll against the cold, hard surface. "Abracadabra? Open sesame?"

The pebbles wheeled and spun on the stone until they each found a resting place, the alien sigils faceup in a curious pattern. Prue caught her breath and waited. A sudden breeze tousled the surrounding thicket of weeds.

From the direction of the river, Prue heard a distinctive metallic lowing, an ancient groan of a hundred thousand tons of metal and iron settling into place.

She looked up to see that the fog over the river had erupted into a dense plume of cloud; it towered above her, blotting out the dim blue of the early morning sky. Slowly, shapes began to emerge from the cloud: a distant green arch, a giant coiling cable. The cloud of fog began to dissipate, revealing more and more of this hidden structure until a massive bridge stood before Prue, spanning the distance from the bluffs to the far shore. Its vast span was interrupted by a pair of wide, flat towers, hundreds of feet high, each inset with a series of cathedral-like arches of varying sizes. On either side, tree-trunk-sized cables anchored the tops of the towers to the bridge's span.

Prue looked around her quickly to see if anyone else was witnessing this spectacle, but saw that she was alone in this cool dawn of the morning. The fog continued to fall away from the bridge until it pooled just beneath the surface of the span, revealing the awesome edifice in its entirety. The river remained covered in mist. Satisfied, Prue ushered the rune stones back into their container and, snapping the lid shut, picked up her bike and began walking it across this ghostly bridge.

The beginning of the span was marked by two lampposts, their glass glowing with a spectral light. Prue stepped gingerly onto the pavement of the bridge, testing its surface before venturing farther: It held her weight firm. Indeed, this "ghost" pavement felt no different from real pavement. Prue confidently set about making her crossing, the clacking of her bike and wagon the only sound disturbing the morning's quiet.

Upon arriving at the middle span of the bridge, she saw a single brass bell hanging from a small hook. Curious, she walked over to it; its metal was deeply tarnished, a kind of gray-green, and it was simple in design. The clapper hung down from the center of the bell by a leather cord.

Prue instinctively reached up and put her hand around the cord. She imagined her parents standing there, some thirteen years before, their hearts burning with fear and curiosity and wishfulness. She imagined her father's hand grasping this same cord, the look he must've given her mother before he gave the bell a few pealing rings. At that moment, she felt a surge of sympathy for her parents, for all that they'd risked for their two children. Would she have done the same in their shoes? Overcome by a sudden boldness, Prue flicked her wrist and sounded the bell; three firm tones rang from the brass of the bell. The sound pierced the soft, misty air and echoed against the wall of trees on the other side of the bridge.

I'm coming, witch, thought Prue. *I'm coming for my brother.*

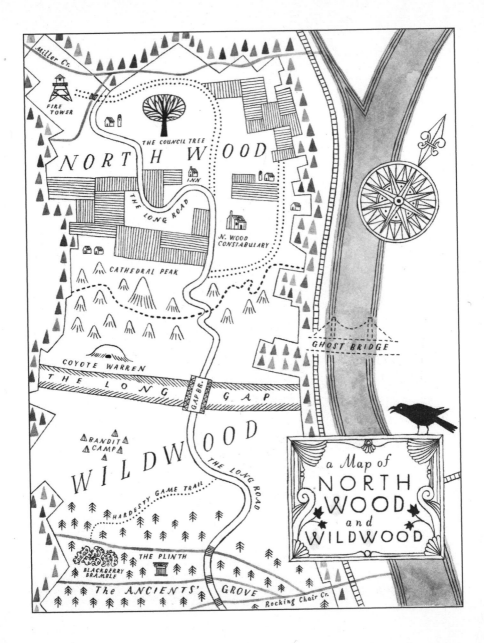

a Map of
NORTH
WOOD
and
WILDWOOD

PART THREE

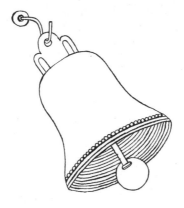

Three Bells

*A*lexandra stood on the dais in the throne room, staring up at the snaking tendrils of plant roots that dangled over the chamber. They seemed to tremble and shimmy in the flickering torch-light. The clamor of the soldiers surrounded her: crates hammered shut, walls of halberds and rifles loaded onto wagons, tenting being struck.

The roots spoke.

"When, O Queen?" said the roots. "When will we feed?"

Smiling, the Governess reached her thin hand to the cave roof and ran her fingers through the fine fringe of the pale root hairs.

"When the time has come," she replied. "When the equinox is here. You will have your succor. We move on the Ancients' Grove tonight."

"Yesssss," hissed the roots. "Yesssss." They quivered like so many hungry, lapping tongues.

Ring.

Alexandra dropped her hand to her side.

Ring.

A hot flush blemished her cheek; her eyes flew open wide. Her brow knotted.

Ring.

Silence.

"Three bells," said the Dowager Governess, before her lips cracked into a wicked smile. "That stupid, stupid girl."

✿

Curtis was awestruck by how ably the bandits made their way down the long, spindly ladder. He stood at the bottom, anchoring the ladder with a foot, while each bandit in turn undid the padlock to his cage and nimbly capered down the ladder's rungs. Within a short span of silent minutes, all four bandits had arrived at the cavern floor. Only Dmitri, the coyote, remained a prisoner. He was sitting in his cage with his back to the bandits. They'd been cajoling him in hushed voices the entire time.

"C'mon, man!" whispered Seamus loudly. "Think of your family."

Dmitri stood on his hind paws up against the bars of his cage.

354

"But . . . ," he objected. "So you guys go free. Me, I'll be court-martialed if I'm ever caught! That's a hanging offense for sure."

Cormac stepped forward: "Then don't get caught. You're a fool to stay here. They'll probably hang you anyway, as a party to our escape. You ain't necessarily raising a warning, are you?"

Dmitri thought about this for a moment before shrugging his shoulders and saying, "Yeah, I guess you're right. Okay: Throw up the keys."

The ring of keys was tossed, the padlock undone, and in a moment, Dmitri was gingerly making his way down the ladder to the floor. "All right," he said once he'd arrived. "What do we do now?"

"You lead us out," said Eamon, stroking the tussocky scruff of his black beard. "Septimus will scout ahead. You know this warren well enough?"

"Pretty well," said Dmitri, his snout angled high as he snuffed the air. "I think I can find my way."

Angus grabbed the remaining lit torch from the wall—it sent a shower of sparks skyward as he pulled it from its sconce—and called up to the rat, "Let's fix a meeting point."

"The armory. There's a side passage that is usually empty. If we follow that we can skirt the central chamber and leave by the back entrance to the warren," whispered Septimus from his nook in the ancient root-ball.

"But not before we free the King," Cormac reminded the group.

"We're not leaving without Brendan."

The four bandits, even the former dissenter Seamus, all nodded in resolute agreement.

"Very well," said Septimus. "The interrogation chamber's not far from the central hall. Do you know the way, Dmitri?"

Dmitri nodded, and Septimus continued, "I'll scout it out. If there's any trouble, I'll head you off before you arrive." The rat disappeared into the tendrils of the tree root, and this unlikely band of escapees—a coyote, an Outsider, and four bandits—left the prison chamber without looking back.

The air in the tunnel leading from the chamber was close and wet; the bandits' footfalls made no noise. Only Dmitri's and Curtis's footsteps disturbed the quiet stillness. Curtis did his best to mimic the soft, quick movements of the four bandits but found it to be very difficult: The bandits' dexterous motion seemed inbred, a natural instinct. After a time, they arrived at an intersection.

"Dmitri?" called Cormac quietly. "Which way?"

Dmitri squeezed his way to the front of the pack and pointed his muzzle down each of the four potential pathways. "We go right," he said, finally. "To the armory. Straight ahead would take us to the central hall." He heaved a swift inhale. "I smell dead campfire. They've put out the hearth. Curious."

"Why?" asked Curtis.

Dmitri looked back. "I've never known the fire to be out. It's always raging. I had the unfortunate task of keeping it stoked for a fortnight. No fun."

"Never mind," whispered Cormac. "Let's keep moving."

They took the right turn, Angus leading the way, with his sputtering torch casting a yellow globe of light along the corridor walls. Plant roots and knobby boulders vied for space along the ceiling; the loose, brown dirt of the floor was pockmarked with paw prints.

Curtis, falling behind momentarily, tripped over a leather strap from his boot that had come loose. He caught himself before hitting the ground but issued a loud "OOF!"

"Shhhh!" hissed Seamus. "Keep those footsteps light. We don't want the whole coyote army coming down on us."

"Sorry!" whispered Curtis. "I'll try." A look on Seamus's face, however, belied a kind of puzzlement. It was strange that they had yet to hear any sound from their captors; the warren tunnels were surprisingly silent.

Finally, they arrived at another intersection and, at Dmitri's behest, they took a smaller corridor that led off to the left. This snaked around for a time before ending in a cramped chamber.

"Hold up," instructed Angus quietly. He hefted the torch, and the light illuminated a short wooden door in the wall of the chamber left slightly ajar. "I hear something."

The band of escapees held their collective breaths. A scurrying noise could be heard breaking the silence, the sound of small feet on the dirt floor.

A rat's whiskery snout appeared around the corner of the door. It was Septimus. Using a single forepaw, he shoved the door open with a loud creak.

Cormac threw his finger to his lips reproachfully, reminding the rat of the need to stay silent, but Septimus was undeterred.

"It's empty, lads," he said. "The warren's abandoned."

"What?" asked Cormac, instinctively whispering.

"Gone. Vanished. *Whoosh*," said Septimus, splaying the bony fingers of his paws before him. "Don't need to be quiet. No one's gonna hear you."

"But . . . ," came Dmitri's voice from the back of the group. "They were just going to—to leave me there? In that *cage*?"

"What about us, you mutt? We were gonna be left too," said Seamus.

"Well, I know but . . . I mean, you guys were the enemy," explained Dmitri.

"Looks like the Dowager cares as little for her soldiers," said Angus. The overall posture of the bandits had relaxed considerably. Seamus leaned against the earthen wall, picking dirt from a fingernail.

Dmitri was gutted. "I guess so," he said slowly. "And I was only in there for 'general insolence,' whatever that means."

"Capital crime, apparently," said Angus.

Septimus interjected, "But you're still looking for that Bandit King of yours, yes?"

Cormac's face lit up. "Did they leave him? Where is he?"

"Follow me," said Septimus, and he disappeared around the corner of the doorway.

Angus swept the sparking torch upright, and the four bandits, Curtis, and Dmitri followed the rat down the darkened passage.

As soon as the last bell peal had echoed into oblivion, Prue was on her bike and pedaling madly across the remaining span of the bridge— she was already beginning to regret her own impudence at ringing the bell. A wind had picked up, and she could feel the cold air from the river surface crest the lip of the bridge and sway the uppermost cabling of the suspension, causing it to whine noisily. The pavement seemed to shift underneath Prue's bike tires, and, mindful that the bridge was in fact *spectral*, she set her eyes on the ground at the far side, intent on her crossing.

The rear tire of the Radio Flyer wagon had scarcely touched the earth on the other side when the mist reared once again into a massive thunderhead of fog and the bridge was consumed by the clouds. Prue slammed on the brakes and turned to watch the green steel towers dissipate in the mist, and then the smoke cleared to reveal the empty river valley yawning below her, uncrossable.

Prue turned back to the hill, gazed up at the looming barrier of trees before her, and shivered. The sun, now rising, glowed moodily behind a heavy curtain of clouds, its light a blue-gray sheen against the topmost firs and cedars of the forest. A chorus of birdsong was being taken up, and the air grew clamorously melodic. Looking down the hill, she saw that a dirt path had been worn in against the slope, leading away to the North and parallel to the river. Holding the handlebars of her bike, she cautiously scampered the few feet down to the path and began following it.

After a time, the ground became considerably less steep and no longer cut such a severe angle into the hillside; it ambled through the short trees that made up this sort of forest boundary-land. Prue found she was able to comfortably ride her bike along the path, the red wagon raising a considerable ruckus as it clanged along behind her.

When she felt like she'd gone far enough, she stopped and gauged her position: Looking south, St. Johns was a distant speckle of rooftops, and the Railroad Bridge was all but lost to the shifting layers of mist on the river.

"Back we go," Prue sighed.

She studied the hillside, looking for an opening in the bracken; an obliging break between two stands of twiggy dogwood allowed her deeper into the brush. She navigated her bike and wagon for a time through this low-growing vegetation, grimacing at every sticker bush that caught the leg of her jeans, until the underbrush began to thin away and was replaced by a stately grove of fir trees. The gaps between the trees became windows to wide glades of ground cover: wood sorrel, salal vines, and wildflowers. As she traveled farther, and the gray light grew more pervasive, she noticed that one of the forest meadows she'd passed had been lined with garden rows, a tangled muss of twining pumpkin vines and bean stalks. A quiet gravel lane opened up before her and she began to follow it; it wound through a series of similar glades, the wildness of the ground cover tamed by these tidy garden plots. Prue began to see small, ramshackle houses nestled in the far trees, tendrils of smoke drifting from their stone chimneys. Curious at this new development, she set the kickstand of her bike and walked closer to one of the garden plots to investigate. No sooner had she left the path when she heard a voice explode behind her.

"Go. No. Farther," came the voice, low and steady.

Prue froze.

"Show your hands," it instructed.

Prue raised her hands above her head.

"Now, turn to me. Slowly. I'm armed and unafraid to use force," cautioned the voice. "So."

Gulping, Prue slowly wheeled around to face her captor, away from the garden patch and back to the dirt lane. Before her stood a rabbit. A hare with a pitchfork. And what appeared to be a colander on his head.

"Disarm yourself," said the rabbit.

Prue stared. He was a mottled brown hare and, reared on his hind legs as he was, came up no higher than her knee. The colander on his head splayed his long ears down the side of his face in what looked like an uncomfortable fashion. He apparently recognized Prue's wonder, as he embarrassedly adjusted his helmet. A single ear poked out of the side handle of the colander. He brandished the small pitchfork angrily.

"I said, disarm yourself!" he shouted, baring two white, flat teeth.

"I'm unarmed!" said Prue, finally. She shook her hands. "See? No weapons."

The hare, satisfied, sniffed at the air. "Who are you and what is your business in North Wood?"

"My name's Prue. I'm from the Outside." She paused before adding, "I'm here to see the Mystics."

The hare raised an eyebrow. "An Outsider? I thought there was something funny about you, so. How'd you get in here?"

"I came from the river, from St. Johns. I walked in," she explained. "Can I drop my hands now?"

"Okay," acquiesced the hare. "But you're coming with me."

The hare led Prue farther down the earthen lane, following close behind with his pitchfork tines pointed at Prue's back. A small break in the overhanging clouds cast little rays of light across the wooded meadows they passed; the garden plots that dotted the surroundings sucked in the brief sunlight before it was swallowed again. Here was a field of poppies, a mosaic of naked blue bulbs garlanding a hilly meadow. More small houses appeared, nestled into the trees. They were more rustic than any house Prue had seen in South Wood, appearing to be made with whatever materials were at hand, be it tree boughs, rock, or mud plaster. The roofs were thatched with bundles of yellow hay. Prue, after they'd walked a while, hazarded a question.

"Is that a colander on your head?" she asked.

"What?" asked the hare incredulously. "No. It's a helmet. So."

"Can I ask who you are? Like, what's your title?" asked Prue, not wishing to challenge the hare's response.

"Constable to the People's Collective of North Wood," responded the hare proudly. "And it's my job to keep the roads clean of riff-raff like yourself." He then added, clearly unconsciously, the single word, "So."

The lane widened. They began to pass more and more travelers, animal and human alike. Many walked; others rode rickety bicycles or slow, slope-backed donkeys. A brightly covered caravan wagon, drawn by a pair of tasseled mules, lumbered along the road ahead. Prue watched it curiously as it passed them. The wagon itself was like a small house on wheels. Prue was shocked to see that it was being driven by a coyote. Her mind flashed to the scene, only a few days prior, of Curtis's abduction at the hands of the coyote soldiers. However, as the caravan drew closer, the kind look on the coyote's face immediately put her fears to rest. The coyote nodded at the constable as they passed. Apparently coyotes lived amicably among their fellows in this part of the Wood.

Finally, the hare led Prue down a smaller road off the lane, and they arrived at a small wooden house in the middle of a wide meadow. A sign above a ramshackle porch read N. WOOD CONSTABULARY. A fox in a pair of faded dungarees and a half-buttoned linen shirt sat in a chair on the porch, smoking a pipe.

"What ya got there, Samuel?" asked the fox.

The hare stamped the handle of his pitchfork on the ground and saluted. "An Outsider, sir," he said. "Found her on the boundary. Says she wants to see the Mystics. So."

The fox looked up. "An Outsider? How the heck did she get in?"

"Probably Woods Magic, sir. She must be a half-breed," was the hare's reply.

"What?" Prue interjected.

The fox studied Prue intently before answering, "Yep, seems like she is. Don't see much of that anymore."

"What do you mean, half-breed?" asked Prue, intrigued.

The fox waved away the question. "What do you want, coming in here?" he asked, stepping up from his chair. He tapped the remaining ash from his pipe onto the ground. "We don't need for trouble."

"I'm here to see the Mystics," explained Prue. "I was sent by Owl Rex, from the Avian Principality. The Dowager Governess is back and she has my brother. She's raised an army in Wildwood, and I don't know what she means to do, but I know I need my brother back."

The fox stared at her a moment before saying, "Sounds serious enough. Samuel, let's take this half-breed to the Mystics. They'll know what to do."

Samuel saluted and gave his pitchfork another quick stamp on the ground. The fox was lazily stepping away from the house when the hare cleared his throat. "Um, sir," murmured the hare quietly.

"You'll want your weapon. Official constabulary business, right?"

The fox looked directly at the hare for a moment, chagrined by his deputy's impudence, before turning and walking back into the house. In a moment, he returned with a pair of pruning shears stuck in the belt of his pants.

"Okay," said the fox. "Let's go."

Wildwood Revisited;
A Meeting with a Mystic

They'd heard the groaning long before they arrived at the interrogation chamber, eerily echoing through the low tunnels of the warren. They no longer needed to follow Septimus; they were able to find the location of the Bandit King by the sound of his agonized moans alone. Turning a sharp corner just beyond the abandoned central hall, its giant soot-black cauldron toppled sideways, they stopped short to see the King hanging from his ankles by a thick cable anchored to the ceiling of the tall chamber. A burlap sack had been put over his head, cinched at his neck by a leather cord. Angus ran up to his leader and, with a swift flick of his wrist, flung the sack from Brendan's head.

"My King!" he shouted as the rest of the bandits ran to his side.

Brendan cracked a blackened eye at the gathered crew. A bit of crusted blood darkened his lower lip, and his hair was matted with sweat.

"Hey, boys," he said, his voice labored and rough. "Mind getting me down?"

Within moments, they'd pulled him down from his hanging position; Septimus sped up the rope and gnawed it clean through, letting Curtis and the bandits ease Brendan to the rocky ground. A simple tether holding his arms behind his back was quickly undone, and the Bandit King sat on the chamber floor, rubbing his reddened wrists.

"What happened?" Seamus asked finally.

"Oh, they knocked me around a bit," Brendan replied, regaining his voice. "They were keen on the location of the camp, the mongrel dogs." He briefly surveyed his rescue party, his eyes falling on Dmitri. "What's that one doing here?"

Dmitri threw up his paws. "Hey, I'm with you."

Brendan squinted his good eye at the coyote suspiciously.

"Well, did you?" asked Seamus. "Did you tell 'em anything?"

Brendan shot his gaze over at Seamus, his eyes set in a deep, studied glare. Curtis could see a deep sinew in his neck tense and shiver. He spoke in a slow, deliberate voice. "What do you think?"

Seamus cracked a mischievous smile and held out his hand to the King. "Good to have you back, Brendan." Brendan returned the smile and accepted the bandit's outstretched hand; he winced a little as he stood.

"The dogs bruised me up a good bit," he hissed, hobbling uncertainly on his feet. "But I'm good to keep pace. Where's that witch? She's mine, boys."

"They're gone, Brendan," Angus explained. "Just all up and gone. No one's here."

Brendan scanned the room, nodding. "Figured as much. They weren't done with me, I don't think, before they just left me there, hanging like a possum."

"Where do you think they're going?" ventured Curtis. "You think they're on their way to do the thing? The thing with Mac?"

Brendan stared at Curtis. He walked slowly toward him, his pace hitched by a slight limp, until he was standing within inches of Curtis's face. He stood easily a foot above Curtis, and his skin was fair and freckled, his forehead tattoo faded by sunburn and sweat. The hollow below his left eye was darkened by a deep purple shiner. Curtis could smell the sourness of his breath as he stood and stared down. "You," he said. "Outsider. Now that we're here, now that we're free . . ." He reached down and tangled his fingers into fists around the lapels of Curtis's uniform coat. "I can tell you what I really think." Brendan flexed his arms, and Curtis could feel his boot heels lifting from the cavern floor. The Bandit King leered menacingly as he brought Curtis's face up to his.

"I ought to tear you limb from limb," he whispered. "For what you've done. You fool kid, you meddling Outsider."

Curtis began to whimper helplessly. "I didn't know!" he objected, the fabric of his jacket in Brendan's fist constricting his throat. "I thought she meant well. I didn't know."

"Whoa!" shouted Cormac, coming to Curtis's side. He placed his hand on Brendan's arm. "He's okay. He's a friend."

Brendan's grip relaxed slightly, and Curtis's feet met the floor again.

Cormac continued, "He risked his life for our escape, Brendan. He's one of us." Brendan let go of Curtis's lapels, firmly smoothing the fabric back into place. His right eye was bloodshot and wide. Cormac held him off, away from Curtis.

"One of us, huh?" Brendan asked the room.

The group of four bandits nodded in unison, their steely faces glinting in the low torchlight.

"Very well," said Brendan. He staggered backward, his knees buckling under him. Eamon leapt to his side and caught him by the arm, helping him to stay on his feet.

"Brendan!" shouted the bandits, each clamoring to his aid.

The king waved them away. "A momentary weakness, lads," he said. "Let me just catch my breath."

The fog continued to fall away from the bridge until it pooled just beneath the surface of the span, revealing the awesome edifice in its entirety.

The room was silent. Curtis felt a tug at his pant leg and looked down to see it was Septimus. Curtis gestured with his head, and Septimus clawed up the fabric of his worn uniform to sit comfortably on his shoulder, staring at the Bandit King. The four bandits stole quick looks at one another, their faces tarnished with worry.

"We move," said Brendan, finally. "We go back to camp." He lifted his head, the blood returning to his face. "I can only hope that my little gambit with the Outsider girl got them far enough away from the scent. There, we gather our forces."

Visibly gaining strength, Brendan lifted his chin high and let go of Eamon's shoulder, limping to the center of the room on his own.

"If the witch is doing this thing, this sacrifice of the Outsider child," he said steadily, "then the whole army must be marching on the Ancients' Grove now; by my reckoning, the equinox is tomorrow." He looked over at Curtis. "We'll stop her. By my oath, we'll stop her in her tracks. And the only blood that ivy'll be feeding on will be her own." A malicious smile spread over his face as he turned back to the bandits. "Don't know about you lads, but I'm a bit antsy to get out of this stinking pit and back aboveground. Let's move."

The bandits chorused their approval. The group moved on toward the exit of the warren.

*

The hare and the fox traveled very slowly, and it was all Prue could do to keep her pace in check and not speed ahead of them. They had embroiled themselves in a heated argument about what was the best weather in which to grow Anaheim peppers and how to place them so as to maximize their spiciness, and when a finer point needed to be made, one or the other would stop in the path, their little fingers gesticulating in the air. At one instance, they diverged from the path completely, leading Prue on a meander through the underbrush because the hare had, earlier that week, discovered a healthy-looking patch of morel mushrooms and was curious to see if it remained untouched.

After what seemed like an eternity of this slow travel, Prue ventured an objection. "Hey, it's really important that I see these Mystics, and soon. I don't know how much time I have."

This interjection was met by a stony silence from her hosts. They shared a disdainful look before the fox replied, "We're  moving just as fast as we can, missus. Need I remind you, you are in the custody of the North Wood Constabulary, and we move at the pace we feel is necessary per the circumstances." However, after Prue's complaint, they ceased talking quite so much and regained their earlier speed.

The countryside here was peaceful and calm, a remarkable change from both the wildness of Wildwood and the metropolitan busyness of South Wood. The air was clear and slightly tinged by the smell of burning leaves and peat. There were no towns per se in this rural landscape, just small gatherings of wood-and-stone hovels through which the wide dirt lane would wander; occasionally, a hanging sign above one such cottage would advertise drinks and food. Another had the picture of a winged envelope carved into the wood, suggesting a post office. They passed many fellow travelers as they walked, all of whom seemed to be moving at a similarly leisurely pace and greeted the constables warmly as they passed. After a time, they rounded a bend in the woods and arrived at a small inn, neat puffs of peat smoke drifting from its earthen chimney. Several small tables had been placed outside the front door, and the fox bade Prue to sit.

"The Council Tree isn't far," said the fox. "I'll go ahead and make sure they aren't in meditation. Besides, you must be famished."

"I am, in fact," replied the hare, "so."

"The girl, Samuel," castigated the fox. "The girl."

Prue smiled. "I guess I wouldn't mind a bite," she said. "Though when you see them, the Mystics, please let them know this is very, very urgent."

The fox nodded. "Of course, though I won't make any promises. The Mystics' judgment doesn't often come quickly." He arched an eyebrow and walked away from the inn, down a path that broke away from the main road.

Prue set her bike up against the wall of the inn and sat at the table across from the hare. A young girl came out with menus and, seeing Prue, blanched. She hesitated at the door before the hare waved her forward. "She ain't gonna bite," said Samuel. "Least not on my watch." The girl blushed and walked forward, handing them the paper placards. "A bottle of water for the girl to start," said the hare, eyeing the menu. "And I'll have a glass of your poppy beer." The girl nodded and walked back into the cottage.

The afternoon ebbed warmly. Prue kept one eye on the path down which the fox had disappeared. The girl came back with a clear decanter of water for Prue; she set a mug of brackish beer in front of Samuel. The hare, who had been studying the menu the entire time, peeked up and ordered, "I'll have the braised greens and lentils." He looked over at Prue. "You? It's on the Constabulary."

Prue gave a quick glance at the menu before replying, "I'll have the squash dumplings. And some bread."

The waitress smiled sheepishly, curtsied, and walked back into the inn.

The hare watched her go. "You make quite a stir, you know, coming in here," he said, taking a sip from his beer. "We're not used to this sort of upset, so."

"I know, I know," said Prue. "I'm really sorry for that. I really don't mean to." She paused before volunteering an observation. "This place is really different from the other places in the Impassa—I mean, the Wood."

"And thank the earth for that," said Samuel. "Couldn't imagine living down there in South Wood—I've got a cousin in the Mercantile District, and I get letters sometimes, so. Crazy folk, down there. Glad we've got all of Wildwood as a buffer twixt them and us."

Prue nodded before asking, "And we're going to the Council Tree? Didn't the fox say something about that?"

"Mm-hmm," responded the hare, wiping a thin film of foam from his furry lip. "The Council Tree. Oldest tree in the Wood. They say it was here before anyone, any animal or person. It has roots, I guess, that stretch miles in all directions, like a fungus. It knows the Wood unlike any other living thing here. That's where the Mystics meet, so. And all issues and petitions of the North Wood have to be put to the tree before any decision is made."

"The tree . . . talks?" asked Prue, remembering the picture she'd seen on the wall of her room in the Mansion—the figures linked in a circle around the massive tree.

"Talk, not so much," he said. "That's why the Mystics are there. They're the ones who can hear it and can translate its thoughts for the rest of us. Though, the way the Mystics tell it, it's not only the Council Tree that talks: It's everything." He waved an arm above his head. "Every tree, flower, and fern." He shrugged. "But I don't know. I haven't heard anything myself, though I don't quite find the time to practice as some folk."

"Practice?" Prue asked.

"Meditation. That's the key, supposedly. Calming your mind in total silence. Understanding your connection to the natural world, and all that. You do that, and you can hear it. All the talking." He took another swig from his beer. "But between the big brood in my warren and that damned fox yapping my ear off all day, I hear enough talking as it is. Don't need my tomatoes yammering to me, so."

"Really?" Prue asked. "Just meditation?" This "practice" was not unfamiliar to Prue: Prue associated it with sneeze-inducing incense, sweaty yoga mats, and the smell of brewer's yeast, of all things. "That's their . . . magic?"

The hare didn't have a chance to respond before the girl came out with a pair of pewter plates in her hand. She set them down on the table: Prue's dumplings were topped with chunks of white cheese and looked delicious. She thanked the waitress and, tearing a hunk of bread from a small loaf the waitress had set on the table, began eating. The hare pushed his colander-helmet back and dug into his meal with enthusiasm. The time passed in silence between them as they ate. Prue never got her answer about the Mystics' practice. She assumed that Samuel had interpreted the question as being rude, so she didn't bring it up again.

Prue had just finished wiping the remnant sauce from the bottom of her bowl with a hunk of bread when the fox reappeared. "Okay," he announced. "They can see you."

The narrow path led away from the main road between two long, neat rows of stately cedar trees—to Prue's eyes, they seemed almost manicured in their orderly appearance. At the end of the path, the tree rows fell away and the wood opened into a great, grassy meadow surrounded by a wall of towering fir trees. The tall grass of the meadow shifted under the disturbance of a cool breeze, though the entire ecosystem of vegetation in the meadow seemed to heave toward a central point: a gigantic tree of indeterminable variety, exploding from the center of the meadow, its massive, gnarled trunk twisting upward to burst into a joyous eruption of vast arteries of leafy branches, a canopy that spanned nearly the entirety of the meadow's breadth and towered in the air over the surrounding trees, where its topmost spires grew hazy against the cloudy sky. Prue's eyes widened at the sight. She immediately recognized it as the same vista rendered in the painting in the Mansion. The awesome size of the tree was made even more incredible when Prue saw the gathering of creatures at the base of the trunk, meandering in the shadows of the tree's branches like so many ants below a skyscraper. As she grew closer, she saw that the figures were her size, animals and humans, and they were dressed in simple, flaxen gowns. Some stood chatting in the field of grass; others lay in respite on some of the roots that snaked away from the tree. As Prue, the fox, and the hare walked closer, a single figure stepped away from the crowd and approached them.

"Hello there," said the figure, a wizened human woman, hiking her robe as she walked to keep its hem clear of the wisps of grass. As she came closer, Prue saw her face was lined with deep wrinkles and her hair was long and gray, falling away from her head like silvery strands of wire. "Welcome to North Wood." A beatific smile lazed on her tawny face, and she extended a hand in greeting. "I am the Elder Mystic. My name's Iphigenia."

Prue took her hand and shook it; it felt worn in her grasp, the inner skin of her hand smooth as tanned leather. "I'm Prue," she responded.

"I know," said the Elder Mystic. "I'd heard of your coming. The tree"—here she gestured back to the enormous tree behind her—"has been following you. All along. It has informed us of your travels." Her hand moved to caress Prue's cheek. "You've suffered, my girl. You've endured great hardship. Come." She wrapped her hand around the crook of Prue's elbow. "Walk awhile with me."

Iphigenia waited as Prue set down her bike before leading her away from the two constables, her arm locked in Prue's. The distinct smell of lavender hovered over the Elder Mystic, and her touch was warm. Prue immediately felt calmed in her presence. A group of children, similarly bedecked in robes, played a frenetic game of tag in the meadow. Prue and the Mystic fell into a distant orbit of the giant tree, and Prue couldn't help but marvel at its immensity. The flesh of the tree was a great knot of sinews spiraling upward, and its base was easily fifty feet across. A small galaxy of knotholes disrupted the wide grain of the trunk, some of them big enough to swallow a human whole. A tempest of birds circled the high canopy, enriching the sky with their colorful plumage.

Iphigenia marked Prue's wonderment, saying, "Incredible, yes? You're not the first Outsider to see the Council Tree, though very few have braved the journey."

"So, others have been here? Other Outsiders?" asked Prue.

"Oh yes," replied the Elder Mystic. "But long, long ago. Before the invasions and before we wove the perimeter trees with the Boundary Magic—the very spell that you are so able to disregard." She smiled warmly.

"And how did I do that? I didn't mean to, believe me," said Prue.

"Of course you don't mean to," said Iphigenia. "It's nothing you've done. Rather, it's something that you *are*."

Prue began to understand. "The constables, they called me a halfbreed. Something about being of 'Woods Magic.' What does that mean?"

"It means that you belong here," said Iphigenia matter-of-factly. "That you are part of the Wood. For whatever reason, the germ of your being is tied to this place."

Prue nodded. It was peculiar that no one else in the Wood had recognized her as being a half-breed, and yet everyone she'd met in North Wood saw it immediately. "My parents made a deal with a woman from here—from Wildwood. She made it so they could have me." Her stomach knotted at the thought. "In some ways, I guess, she made me *be*."

Iphigenia gripped Prue's arm and looked at her. The Mystic's frame was bent with age and her eyes met Prue at the same height. "Alexandra, yes. Very sad, that family. Great tragedy. But such is the case: She has imbued you with Woods Magic. You are a child of the Wood. For better or worse."

"So you must know about my brother, Mac," said Prue. "I need to save him."

The Mystic frowned and looked at the ground as they walked. "Alas," she said, "I'm not sure I can be of help."

Prue felt her heart sink. "Why?" she asked. "I've come all this way; you're the only hope left to me."

"My dear Prue, we are the inheritors of a wonderful world, a beautiful world, full of life and mystery, goodness and pain. But likewise are we the children of an indifferent universe. We break our own hearts imposing our moral order on what is, by nature, a wide web of chaos. It is a hopeless task."

Prue didn't quite follow.

Iphigenia smiled. "These are difficult issues for a young girl to grasp. Needless to say, I must respect the order of the universe and the paths that each of us, as individuals burdened with free will, has chosen to follow. For your parents, that path was to have a child, at all costs. They were granted their wish. They must now face the consequences of their actions. I would upset the balance of nature if I were to intercede. This, I cannot do."

Prue was speechless. "There's nothing you can do?"

The Mystic shrugged. "Nothing is absolute, my dear. Perhaps I will put it to the Council and we will gather in meditation. We will ask the tree."

Prue stopped their walk and turned to the old woman, holding her hands. "Oh please, please. Anything you can do. I just need help, that's all."

Iphigenia nodded thoughtfully. "Come," she said, finally. "We won't gather in Council for another few minutes. I'll need all my energy about me for a sit of this kind. Let's continue our walk. These knees need some movement. Tell me of the Outside; I've not heard in many years."

"I wouldn't know where to start," said Prue.

"Begin with your parents; describe them to me," said the Mystic. So Prue did.

🌿

When the escape party arrived at the door to the warren, they collectively sucked in a massive breath, delirious to be in the air of the aboveground world once again.

"All the sweeter," said Seamus, "after bein' in that hellhole. Praise be the trees and the air of the woods!"

Cormac turned to Dmitri. "This is where we part ways, friend," he said. "I expect you'll be heading back to your pack."

Dmitri frowned. "What's left of it, I suppose," he said. "But I can't wait to see my litter—those pups'll be grown by now!" He extended his forepaw in thanks, and the bandits and Curtis shook it in turn.

"Bye, Dmitri," said Curtis as the coyote grasped his hand.

"Ah, Curtis," said Dmitri, "if ever you're in need of a fresh-scavenged meal, you know where to find me. My warren's west of the Long Road, by the headwaters of Rocking Chair Creek, in the Old Woods. Look for the broken stone. Call out for me, I'll come find you."

Curtis grinned and thanked him.

"Don't get too wealthy, Dmitri," said Seamus playfully, "or our paths will cross again. We bandits quickly return to our true nature."

"And likewise: Don't let your babies wander too far in the night," replied Dmitri, "or they'll be dinner."

Brendan laughed. "Get goin', dog, get home to your pups."

Dmitri nodded and, dropping to his four paws, began trotting into the underbrush. Before he'd disappeared, however, Curtis saw him stop and glance down at the tattered uniform that still clung to his frame. With a quick jerk of his muzzle and a shake of his hindquarters, he'd thrown it off, and it fell to the ground in a dirty lump. He gave a quick, joyous howl and vanished into the trees.

Curtis felt a hand grip his shoulder; it was Brendan. "And I suppose you'll be heading home now. Huh, Outsider?"

He thought for a moment before replying. The events of the previous days unspooled in his mind. He found the whole recollection a little dizzying. "No," he said, shaking his head. "No, I want to come with you."

Brendan looked him squarely in the eye. "You know what you're getting yourself into? This is a lot bigger than you, kid."

"I came here to find Mac. I came this close"—here he held up his thumb and forefinger, nearly touching—"to finding him. Prue's gone home—she's given up, for all I know. I have one last chance. I can't go home now. No way."

"Very well," Brendan said. "Follow us. But don't never say I didn't warn you. You may forfeit your life here, boyo."

Curtis nodded gravely. "I know," he said. He peered at Septimus the rat perched on his shoulder. "What about you, rat?" asked Curtis.

"I'm with you, kid," replied Septimus. "There's nothing left for me in that warren. No coyotes means no food to scavenge." He smiled toothily. "I go where the food is."

Ahead, Angus was already scanning the ground cover; the low-lying ferns and clover that carpeted the forest floor here was trampled flat in great swaths.

"An army," he said, "has passed here. The whole blasted army must've massed here for the march. Look." He pointed to a wide path that had been beaten into the forest, leading south. "Must've been hundreds of them."

A discarded bayonet, rusty from misuse, jutted from a stand of ferns. Brendan picked it up and studied its steely edge. "Yep, boys, this is it. Let's move back to camp. Whatever that Dowager plans on doing, she's gonna have to fight her way through us to do it. Let's go."

He tossed the bayonet into the trees, and the band of freed prisoners made their way toward their home.

¥

Prue sat calmly in the meadow, watching the robed figures gather. No call was issued, no signal given, but the Mystics, each engrossed in their own contemplative activity, began slowly arriving of their own volition at their stations. They eventually made a giant circle around the base of the great tree, each figure separated from their neighbor by a distance of roughly fifteen feet. Suddenly, and without a word, the robed Mystics all sat down on the ground, crossing their legs beneath them as they did so. Prue could see Iphigenia, sitting between a similarly robed rabbit and deer, stiffen her back and straighten her neck, her eyes closed in deep concentration. The entire circle breathed in unison, and Prue could hear their collective breaths, sweeping beneath the low roar of the wind's blowing.

The meditation had begun.

¥

The pace was fast; the bandits moved quietly and stealthily through the trees. After a time, they came to the Long Road. Checking to see that no sentry had been posted, they began running southward, beckoning Curtis to keep pace. They arrived at the Gap Bridge and crossed, none of them besides Curtis giving so much as a glance to the deep and fathomless darkness of the ravine it spanned. When they came to the other side, they swiftly left the openness of the road and dove headlong into the treed canopy of the forest.

Septimus rode on Curtis's shoulder, ducking the odd low-hanging tree branch that threatened to knock him from his perch. "What do you think the plan is?" he whispered into Curtis's ear.

Curtis could barely catch his breath to speak, the bandits traveled so fleetly. They followed paths that were undetectable to his eyes, traced against the forest floor like invisible ink. "I don't know," he hissed back at Septimus. "We're gathering an army, I think."

Septimus whistled between his teeth. "I don't know about that, kid," he said. "Sounds dangerous. I happen to know that that woman's army is pretty massive. They've been gaining recruits hand over fist. And how do I know this? I eat their garbage. And they make a *lot* of garbage."

"Okay," said Curtis, focusing intently on the distant figure of Angus, crashing through the brush.

"What I mean to say is this: It's hopeless. I don't know how many bandits there are, but I doubt it's enough. It ain't gonna be pretty."

"Thanks, Septimus," said Curtis. "Thanks for the vote of confidence. Listen, if you're gonna ride on my shoulder, you can at least keep those kinds of thoughts to yourself."

Septimus huffed. "Okay," he said. "But don't say I didn't warn you."

The bandits' momentum came to a stop when they arrived at a small clearing. Brendan stood in the center, searching the treetops. "Strange," he was saying as Curtis caught up. "No lookout. Where's the cussing lookout?"

Curtis followed Brendan's sightline. He saw nothing but strata upon strata of green oak tree leaves and the branches that supported them. Silence filled the glade, disrupted only by the slight rustle of the fern fronds around the bandits' boots.

"Let's go," commanded Brendan, visibly concerned. His step was slightly lopsided from his limping, but he still was able to move as swiftly as any of his bandit cohorts. After a short distance, the group followed Brendan around the slope of a hillock that masked the mouth of a shallow ravine. Soon the gully became a small, brook-bottomed valley. Through the underbrush ahead, Curtis saw that the ground leveled into an enormous natural cul-de-sac. As the bracken cleared, an entire camp of canvas tents, rugged lean-tos, and smoldering campfires came into view, populated by a small contingent of milling figures. As soon as the escapee party arrived at the clearing, the camp flew into a commotion: A group of children who had been busy at a game of marbles came running over, men carrying a load of firewood dropped their cargo and hollered for joy. Women began to appear from within the little domiciles, clearly overjoyed to see Brendan and the bandits approach. Embraces were shared, stiff handshakes were exchanged. Sloppy, lovelorn kisses between reunited husbands and wives were enjoyed. Only Brendan stood away from the group, eyeing the camp.

"Where is everyone?" he said at last. "Why are we so few?"

A young man in a frayed white button-up shirt and suspenders stepped forward. His face showed a deep sorrow. "Sorry, King. We done our best in your absence."

"What's happened?" demanded Brendan.

The man spoke again: "Yesterday evenin'. The sentries picked up dog soldiers on the perimeter. We sent out a troop. Only Devon returned."

Devon, his arm set in a splint, came forward. He walked with some difficulty, his thin frame supported by an improvised tree-bough crutch. The rapturous atmosphere of the bandits' reunion had fallen away, and a pall descended over the camp. Devon nodded. "My King," he said.

Brendan stared, glassy-eyed.

"My King," continued Devon, "the far sentry saw 'em, a few dogs just shy of the Periphery. So we went out to give 'em a little taste. Turned the corner by the fern glade, down the old creek bed, and ran into the whole army." Devon sniffled a little here, visibly troubled

387

by the memory of the incident. "We fought best we could, but we weren't no match for them. They was hundreds of 'em, sir, hundreds. All comin' from all directions. Never seen so many in my life. We couldn't get away—they had us surrounded. Brin, Loudon, and Maire. All dead. So's Hal. We lost thirty-five in total. They stalked me down and let me live. Gave me this"—here he pointed to a jagged claw mark that made a series of three parallel red streaks across his cheek. "Said I should let my kin know to stay clear." The young man's voice was freighted with grief. "I'm so sorry, King. I know I let ye down."

Brendan stood, his jaw set firmly in concentration. "Have we lost so many?"

An older man, his brown beard flecked with ribbons of gray, stood apart, his hands on his hips. "Aye, King," he said. "Between losing those men and all we'd lost in the battle over the ridge, we're in no fit shape to go anywheres. Barely've got enough to keep the camp guarded."

Remembering himself, Brendan walked up to the wounded man, Devon, and gripped the back of his neck with his hand. He gently pressed his forehead into Devon's, his eyes wet with tears. "They won't have died in vain," he said slowly, quietly. "We'll avenge their deaths. All of them."

A woman stepped from the small crowd at the foot of the clearing. Her coal-black hair was closely cropped, and her earlobes were garlanded with large metal hoops. A saber hilt jutted from a wide wrap of silk around her waist, and she rested her ringed hands on the pommel as she spoke. "And how do you expect to do that, Brendan? With what army? We've not enough bandits to rob a country squire's coach-and-four, let alone take on the whole of the Dowager's coyote army." A few of the milling bandits nodded in agreement. "No," she continued, "we stay put. We wait this out. We've seen as troubled times as this in the great history of our band; we can make it through this."

Brendan stepped away from Devon and faced the crowd of bandits. "There's nothin' to wait out. This is it." He accentuated this statement with a pound of his fist against his open palm. His voice was steely, direct. "The Dowager's set to raze this whole place. The whole blasted Wood. She's feeding the blood of a human Outsider child to the ivy. The ivy, lads. And once she's done that, she means to command the vines to consume the whole Wood, North and South. And Wildwood. Gone. Just a big patch of ivy, when she's done."

A collective murmur of fear erupted from the gathered bandits. "What?" cried one. "How do you know this?"

Brendan limped to Curtis's side. He put his hand on the shoulder that wasn't occupied by Septimus. "This one," he said stonily. "This Outsider."

For the first time since their arrival at the camp, the bandits recognized Curtis. A tempered uproar of objection began to rumble among them. Brendan hushed them, saying, "He fought for the Dowager, yes. Indeed—he was a confidant of the witch! But when he was told of her plan, he broke away. And was imprisoned."

Angus spoke from the crowd. "We met him in that slop bucket of a prison. He aided in our escape. He's a friend."

"His friend is the sister of this child," said Brendan. "This baby the Dowager plans to sacrifice. If it were not for him, we would not have this information."

Someone called from the crowd, "But if she controls the ivy . . . she'll kill us all!"

Another: "And pull down every tree, drown every plant!"

"And that's what she means to do," said Brendan. "She's a mad-woman, this Dowager Governess. She means to lay waste to the whole wood, and she'll take us all down with her." His voice grew calm, and he limped forward and away from Curtis, closer to the bandits. "So we've got two options. One"—he held up a single finger—"we stay. And at the dawn of the equinox, tomorrow mornin', we are swal-lowed up whole by the ivy. Every one of us, dead. Man, woman, and child." He stared down the rapt crowd, making quick, deliberate eye contact with each bandit.

"Or two," he continued, holding up a second finger. A tattooed snake wound its way around the central knuckle. "We fight. We give them everything we've got."

"And we die," said the earringed woman, her face suddenly resolved and still.

Brendan nodded. "Yes, Annie. We die. But we die in the fight. And that's a sight better than waiting for the ivy to come and do the job."

Quiet settled over the camp. A log of cordwood buckled and popped in one of the fire pits. The sun disappeared behind a haze of cloud. The patter of raindrops descended on the high branches of the surrounding trees.

Brendan's tired, desperate eyes traveled over the faces of his compatriots, searching for their answer. Finally, one came.

"We fight," said Annie solemnly. The gathered bandits looked to her and back at Brendan. After a moment, each in turn nodded and intoned those words as well.

"We fight."

C H A P T E R   2 2

A Bandit Made

A premature dusk settled over the grassy meadow as the sun ducked behind an encroaching cloud. The telltale sound of distant raindrops foretold the coming rainfall; the Mystics, in their wide circle, did not move. They'd been sitting in silence for hours now, Prue guessed, and there seemed to be no indication they'd be leaving soon. The rain began to fall, pelting the grass in torrents. Prue sat for a time, trying to match the Mystics' resilience, but in the end gave up and ran to the cover of a nearby oak tree. Wringing water from her hair, she sat against the tree's rough bark and continued to wait.

And wait.

The rainstorm was momentary—it passed within half an hour, and the meadow was barraged by an explosion of sun as the rain clouds melted away, leaving the dew-dappled grass in a glistening sheen that looked almost diamond-studded. The late afternoon gave way to early evening; Prue walked back out from underneath the oak and returned to her seat, still watching the unchanging circle of Mystics intently.

It was clear that the robed children she'd seen earlier were acolytes of some sort. They had partaken in the sit briefly, lasting an impressive hour or so until the youngest among them became too fidgety and respectfully stood up and ran off to some other distraction. After a time, all of the acolytes had shrugged off the meditation and were back to the prior activities: playing tag and ring-around-the-rosy; studying bugs in the tall grass; daydreaming. One of the acolytes, a young girl, peeled away from her group, having kept an eye on Prue the entire time. Overcoming her shyness, she approached Prue and sat down a cautious five feet away.

Prue waited for the girl to say something and when she didn't, she smiled and said, "Hi."

"Hi!" said the girl, apparently overjoyed to have gained Prue's attention. "I'm Iris. What's your name?" Prue introduced herself.

"You're from over the boundary, huh?" asked Iris.

"Yep," said Prue.

"What are you doing here?"

"I'm hoping the Mystics will help me find my brother," said Prue before adding playfully, "What are *you* doing here?"

Iris blushed. "I'm learning. I don't know if I'm any good, though. It's hard to sit still. I'm only a second-yearer, though. They say I'll get the hang of it by sixth year. My parents said I have the gift." She shrugged. "I don't know, though."

"The gift?" asked Prue.

"Yeah," said the girl. "To be a Mystic. I didn't think anything of it; I just like to sit in the garden and talk to the plants."

"Do they talk back?" asked Prue.

Iris crumpled her nose and laughed. "No, they don't talk," she said. "They don't have mouths!"

"Well," said Prue, a little embarrassed, "then why do you talk to them?"

"'Cause they're here. They're all around us. It'd be rude to just *ignore* them," said the girl. "Watch."

The girl shifted onto her knees and, placing her hands calmly at her sides, closed her eyes. A tuft of grass before her began to waver, as if a breeze had suddenly picked up and was thrumming through its blades. Prue noted, however, that the air around them remained still. As she watched, the individual blades of grass started to quiver and then, to Prue's amazement, began wrapping themselves around their neighbors. Before long, the grass on the tuft had created a little forest of perfectly braided strands. "That's incredible," she whispered.

The acolyte's brow was wrinkled with concentration as the grass continued to weave together—but the uniformity of the braids slowly grew more chaotic and messy until the woven patterns became indistinguishable and the tuft of grass had knotted itself into a tangle of quivering green wires.

"Phooey!" shouted Iris, her eyes opening. "I *always* mess that up."

Her attention withdrawn, the leaves untangled themselves and returned to their previous incarnation: a simple tuft of meadow grass.

A makeshift soccer ball made of twine came bouncing between them. Two acolytes, a boy and a raccoon, apologized as they ran to get it. Iris, belying her age and attention span, immediately forgot Prue and leapt up to chase it, to get to it before her playmates did. She'd run only a few yards, though, before she stopped and turned to look at Prue. She jogged back to where Prue sat and placed a hand on her arm.

"Don't worry," she said, "you're going to find your brother." And

she ran off to join the other robed children.

Prue stared at the young girl as she ran away, thunderstruck by the display of power she'd just seen. *You do that,* she thought, *through meditation?* The Mystic had said that she, Prue, was of Woods Magic, or at least partly. Why shouldn't she then be able to make the grass do her bidding? She briefly stared back down at the tuft of grass and willed it to move. Nothing happened. She gritted her teeth and thought as loudly as she could: *Move! I command you!* Still nothing. Prue huffed in disappointment. She looked back up at the milling children, the sitting Mystics, and the looming tree. *What power!* she thought. If anyone could help her, these people could. And what had Iris said before she left? That Prue *would* find her brother? She was struck by the honesty of the young girl, how plainspoken she'd been—how *certain* her voice was. She found that she was smiling, a small ray of hope eclipsing the desperation of her predicament, if only for a moment. She watched the acolytes at play, watched a few older robed figures appear from the woods and whistle to them. Hearing the whistle, they all immediately dropped what they'd been doing and gathered in single file. A second whistle came and they began walking toward the whistler, their feet in a loose lockstep. Before long, they'd disappeared beyond the wall of trees.

Prue sighed and trained her eyes back on the Council Tree and the static circle of Mystics encircling it. The light began to fade. Prue hiked her knees to her chest and burrowed her chin into the inside of her elbow. And waited.

The grass at her feet rustled slightly.

🌿

"You're really gonna do this, aren't you," said Septimus in disbelief. "I mean, you're really gonna do this? You're going to go to war. With these people."

Curtis, sitting on a rock in front of the campfire, nodded. He was busy scraping a flinty whetstone against the chinked blade of a saber. With each drag of the stone along the blade, the gouges that marred the edge grew shallower and shallower. He'd been given the job by Seamus, and he found it was oddly satisfying. The dusk had lowered over the camp, and the air was tinged blue.

"You're crazy," declared Septimus, shaking his head. "You're nuts. Don't you have a family at home? Back on the Outside? Like, parents and things?"

Curtis nodded again. "I do, yeah."

Septimus held out his paws. "Then why, man, why? Why don't you go home to 'em? Forget about the whole thing? Go back to your life!"

Curtis paused and looked over at the rat. He was perched on an upended chunk of firewood in front of the crackling campfire. "That's what you're going to do, I take it," said Curtis. He held the saber at arm's length and eyed the blade. Satisfied, he tossed it on the pile of weapons beside him and called to Septimus, "Another one, please."

The rat hopped down from the log and scrambled over to another pile of weapons: swords, bayonets, and arrowheads. He grabbed a long dagger by the hilt and dragged it over to Curtis. Curtis picked it up and began the process anew: scraping the whetstone carefully over the blade.

Septimus climbed back up onto the log and pondered Curtis's question. "I don't know, rightly," he said. "Haven't given it that much thought."

"Don't you have family?" asked Curtis.

"Nah, not me," said Septimus, puffing up his chest. "Not I. Single man, me. Untethered."

"So there's nothing stopping you, then," said Curtis. "No reason you can't join the fight." He scraped the flesh of his thumb against the blade, feeling the sharpness. "Right?"

Septimus laughed. "Listen to you," he said. "Mister Big Britches all of a sudden."

Curtis colored slightly. "All I know, Septimus, is that I came in here to do something. And I don't feel like I should leave until I at least *try* to finish what I started, you know? I was *this* close, Septimus, *this* close. I had Mac in my arms. I could've . . . I could've . . ."

Septimus interrupted, "What, just run him out of the warren? Just like that? With all them crows and the Governess standing right in front of you?"

Curtis sighed. "I don't know. I guess I just want to make good on a promise. That's all."

Their conversation was interrupted by the approach of Seamus. He'd ditched his irretrievably torn prison attire for a handsome green velvet hussar's uniform, which hung a little loosely on his thin frame. "Curtis," he said, "let's go."

"What's up?" asked Curtis.

"Brendan. He wants to see you."

"What about?"

Seamus rolled his eyes. "Flower pressing," he said sarcastically. "What difference does it make? Important business. Come on."

"Okay," said Curtis, standing up. "Septimus, see if you can't, I don't know, finish things up here."

Septimus, nonplussed, looked at the whetstone. It was easily half the size of his whole body. "Okay, but I—"

"Thanks, man," said Curtis. "Guess I'll . . . see you in a bit."

Curtis, followed the bandit over to a lodgelike hut at the far end of the clearing. The light of a candle illuminated the interior of the building, casting a glowing orb of light across the overhanging branches of the fir-bough–shingled roof. Brendan sat on a small, upturned barrel at a rude desk. He looked up when he saw Curtis enter.

"How are you, Curtis?" asked the Bandit King.

"Good, thanks," said Curtis. "What's up?"

Brendan gestured for Seamus to stand by the door to the hut. He looked directly at Curtis, his steely blue eyes catching the flicker of the candle. "The boys were giving me the lowdown on what happened, back there in the Dowager's prison. Seems you really showed your mettle."

Curtis smiled sheepishly. "I don't know," he said. "Guess someone had to do it. It just happened that my cage was the right one—to make it to the ladder, that is."

Brendan stood up from his seat and walked a tight circle around the half-barrel chair. Opening a small trunk in the corner of the hut, he pulled an ornamental dagger from its insides. He turned it over in his hand thoughtfully. A gilded snake wound its way across the hilt from the guard to the pommel.

"The lads have come to me with a petition," he said. "And I have to say, I tend to agree with 'em. You've been nominated to take the bandit oath."

Curtis's eyes widened. "Really?" He cast a glance over his shoulder at Seamus at the door of the hut. The bandit gave him a quick, proud nod.

"Yep, and it's not something to be taken lightly. Very few men and women, if they ain't first born into the camp, get the opportunity to do so. And, as far as I can reckon, you'd be the first Outsider to be elected to it."

"What does it mean?"

Brendan walked toward Curtis and stood within inches of his face. Curtis's nose barely came up to the middle buttons of the bandit's shirt. "It means to be a Wildwood bandit," said Brendan, "through and through, till your dying day."

The conifer branches of the lodge's roof shook a little in a quiet breeze. The sound of the bandits' hubbub in the camp could be heard beyond the walls, a steady clamor.

"Okay," said Curtis, after a moment. "I'd be honored."

He was jarred by a sudden slap to his back. It was Seamus. "That's my lad."

Brendan walked to the front of the hut and yelled out into the milling crowd of bandits. "Angus! Cormac! He's ready."

The four bandits, Angus, Cormac, Seamus, and Brendan, led Curtis away from the hubbub of the campsite and over to where a few torches illuminated a narrow, switchbacking trail that cut its way up the side of the ravine. After a short time they came to a small glade. In the center of the clearing was a carefully stacked pile of slate stones, standing about three feet high, protected from the rain by a small wooden shelter. The bandits urged Curtis forward; they fanned out to make a semicircle around the altarlike stack. Walking closer, Curtis saw that a thick, dark film stained the gray face of the altar's headstone.

"Stand by the stone, Curtis," said Brendan.

Curtis glanced back down at the altar. Little stripes of the dried black liquid descended the length of the altar. A dark clot of the stuff had pooled in a little divot in the face of the top stone. Suddenly, Curtis heard the ominous *swik* of a dagger being drawn. He turned quickly to see Brendan, his face awash in the torchlight, approaching. He held the ornamental knife in his hand.

A momentary panic passed through Curtis's chest. Was this some sort of trap? Had they really not forgiven him for his involvement in the other day's battle? He was about to issue a frightened plea when he saw Brendan do something wholly unexpected: He brought the blade of the knife to his own palm and, gritting his teeth, drew it across the flesh. A bright streak of red appeared on his palm, and he walked to the side of the stone altar, letting the blood drip onto the rock. Turning to Curtis, he flipped the knife in his uncut hand so that the handle faced out, toward Curtis.

"Cut your palm, stain the altar stone with blood," explained Brendan, bright drops of red dripping from his open palm.

Curtis took the knife from Brendan and gingerly held the blade to the smooth skin of his palm. "Just like this?" he asked.

Brendan nodded.

He held his eyelids shut and pressed the cold metal into his skin, feeling a pang of pain as the blade cut through. A little bubble of deep-red blood emerged from the wound, and he quickly held it over the stone, letting the few drops fall on the altar. He watched as both his and Brendan's blood rolled down the shallow bowl of the stone to well together in the little divot, conjoining into a unified dark blot. Brendan smiled and nodded.

"Now the creed," instructed Brendan.

"Incredible, yes? You're not the first Outsider to see the Council Tree,
though very few have braved the journey."

Angus stepped forward and began to recite the oath, which Curtis repeated after every line.

I, Curtis Mehlberg, do solemnly swear to uphold the bandit code and creed.
To live by my own hand and to challenge all forms of authority before
the code
To protect the freedom and interests of the poor
To liberate the wealthy from their wealth
To put no person's labor before another's
To work for the communal good of my fellow bandits
To hold no allegiances over my fellow bandits
To hold all plants, animals, and humans as equals
And to live and die by the bandit band.

A quiet overcame the glade, broken when Angus spoke. "There you go," he said. "Step forward, Bandit Curtis."

Brendan slapped Curtis on the back. "Congratulations, boyo," he said, taking the knife back and sliding it into its sheath.

Curtis smiled and said, "Thanks." He held his palm to his mouth, tasting the sharp saltiness of the blood on his tongue.

Curtis was surrounded by the rest of the bandits, each shaking his hand and patting his shoulder in congratulations. "You'll make a fine thief," said Seamus. "I knew it as soon as I'd laid eyes on you."

A stir in the ring of vegetation bordering the glade announced the approach of a pair of bandit sentries. "Sir," one said, his face etched with concern, "the scouts have returned. The coyote army has crossed the Gap Bridge and is marching on the Old Woods."

Brendan frowned. "Sooner than I expected," he said, knitting his brow. "They'll be at the Ancients' Grove by morning." He looked back at Curtis and the bandits who stood by the stone altar. "Ready yourselves," he said. "We march tonight."

The clearing was immediately emptied of bandits as they ran back down the trail toward the camp. Only Curtis remained, standing frozen in thought by the stone altar. He held his palm to his mouth and sucked at the little cut. Pulling his hand away to inspect the wound, he heard himself say, "What did I just do?"

ⵣ

A bitter wind tonight, thought Alexandra as she trotted the horse across the dark boards of the bridge. The winds blowing down the ravine set the horse's bit to rattling. The sea of soldiers extended out before her, unending, the noise of their myriad boot steps a rhythmic drumbeat against the silent

forest. *This bridge*, she thought, *will be gone when the ivy comes. This ancient bridge. How long has it spanned the Gap? Since before the Svik dynasty, before the Mystics fled South Wood. The last unbroken remnant of the Ancients' great civilization, its wooden boards laced with magic. But as the Ancients fell, so will the usurpers of South Wood.*

How they will fall, she thought, *how they will beg for forgiveness. Little Lars, my beloved's idiot brother. What gall to assume that he could succeed me. That he could succeed my darling Alexei. And send me into frozen exile. He will be the first to pay.*

The tree branches moaned against the wind, a new shower of dead leaves drifting like snow on the neat columns of uniformed soldiers. The baby in her arm kicked at its swaddling and babbled.

This is how I will show them their impertinence, she thought. *This.*

🌿

Prue woke with a start. She'd had a dream: A low bell tone sounded and she found herself standing on a great bridge. She tried to run

across, but the wooden surface disappeared below her feet, and she fell to the rushing river water below. The sensation dragged her from her deep slumber. A bunched stand of grass had etched little dimpled lines into her cheek, and her clothes felt damp from the cold dew that spangled the meadow. It was pitch-black. The moon's glow shone from beneath a wide curtain of clouds, and shades of mist clung to the high treetops at the meadow's edge. She sat up, wiping sleep from her eyes, and looked down toward the Council Tree. Several torches had been lit around the meadow, and they cast flickering shadows on the ground. By the tree, one of the Mystics had stood and was running a wooden striker around the bowled interior of a brass bell, creating a long, sustained peal that covered the entire meadow—the very sound from Prue's dream. At the sound, the Mystics began to move from their seated positions.

As Prue watched breathlessly, she saw Iphigenia stir and open her eyes. The Elder Mystic began searching the surrounding meadow. When her look landed on Prue, she stood up and began walking toward her. Prue leapt up and ran to meet her.

"Young girl," Iphigenia began saying before they'd even met, "dear girl, we have work to do."

"What work?" asked Prue. "What are you talking about? What did the tree say?"

"A great wrong is unfolding," said the Mystic, her voice devoid of its earlier easiness, "a threat to every living thing in the Wood."

"What's happening?" asked Prue. "Did it say anything about my brother?"

Iphigenia paused and stared into Prue's eyes. "Oh, dear," she said, "I'm afraid the news is very bad." She gripped Prue's hands in her own. "The Council Tree is the foundation of the Wood itself, its roots entwined into every inch of soil beneath us, from North to South. And so, it feels every perturbation in the fabric of the Wood, from the topple of an ancient oak to a moth's wing beat. It has felt the ivy waken and has for some time. Something has been disrupting its slumber. It is now clear; the ivy thirsts for blood. A great army marches on the Ancients' Grove, the ruined heart of a long-dead civilization, where the taproot of the ivy sleeps. At the head of this army rides the exiled Governess, and she carries with her an infant human child, a half-breed Outsider like you."

Prue stared. "What's she going to do?"

Iphigenia shook her head sorrowfully. "Something more terrible than you can imagine: She means to feed the child to the ivy. The blood will revive the slumbering plant and make it subject to the Governess's will. Gaining that, she means to wipe out everything, every plant and animal in the Wood."

"She's—she's going to *kill* him?" Prue could feel the color drain from her face. Her knees began to wobble. She hadn't known what to expect, but this was certainly the worst she could imagine. "No," she said, leaning into the Mystic for support. "She . . . can't."

407

Iphigenia nodded, her knobby fingers pressing deeply into Prue's palms. "Such is the madness of this woman," said the Mystic. The other Mystics, their golden robes rustling the meadow's grass, approached and stood behind Iphigenia.

"This is our task," said Iphigenia slowly, looking at each of her fellow Mystics in turn. "We must stop this aberration from happening."

The Mystics each nodded gravely.

Iphigenia continued, "The trial before us, however, may be impossible. While there are protocols in place for such an event, rarely in the history of North Wood have we faced the need to muster an army. Nonetheless, this is what we must do now. And quickly." Here she addressed her fellow Mystics directly: "When the sun rises to its highest point on this day, this autumnal equinox, the child dies. We have little time." She turned and spoke to one of the Mystics, a slender doe. "Hydrangea," she said, "call the constabulary. We must ring the bell."

The doe nodded and loped away from the gathered Mystics.

"You have an army?" asked Prue.

"No, not as such," Iphigenia replied. "The North Wood charter decrees that all citizens of North Wood are duty bound to militia service, should the need arise. We are a peaceable people, my girl, but even we, in the course of our history, have been called to defend our community." She knitted her brow and frowned. "Though I can't rightly speak to the condition of our volunteer militia at present. Nine generations have gone and passed since we've had any need for an army. This is all very distressing." She sighed and glanced back at the massive tree in the center of the darkened meadow. "But if it is the will of the tree, then we must abide."

"Oh, thank you, thank you!" said Prue.

"If we are successful in stopping the Governess, your brother being saved would be a fortunate consequence of our actions, dear Prue," said the Mystic. "We will involve ourselves for the sake of the Wood. For the sake of our home." She looked to the space where the trail broke an opening into the bordering trees. "Look: The constables approach. Let's walk to them. We have little time to waste."

☙

The campfires were fed wood until the flames licked at the overhanging boughs, illuminating a throng of activity among the bandits—bindles being packed, provisions stowed, and arrows refeathered. A line of men and women stood inspecting ancient-looking rifles; another line carefully poured black gunpowder into leather pouches. Curtis quickly finished up the last of the weapons he'd been tasked to sharpen and was about to help load a brace of rifles into an awaiting cart when Brendan called him over.

"Yes?" asked Curtis as he approached.

"A newly christened bandit of your stripe, we'll need to outfit you right." Brendan brushed Curtis's coat. "That'll get tarnished over time—though ye've got a good start to it. How're your boots?"

"Fine, I think," said Curtis, shifting his feet as a way of inspection.

"Good, 'cause we ain't got any more boots," said Brendan. He paused before saying, "Trying to remember—you were more of a tactical-ops man in that battle we fought, when you was with the coyotes, weren't you?"

Curtis blushed at the mention. "Not really," he said. "I wasn't supposed to fight at all, actually. I kind of fell into it. *Literally.* I mean, I was up in this tree—"

Brendan interrupted: "Got it—no time for battle stories, boyo. We've got bigger fish to fry. Now: What'll it be? Pistol or cutlass?"

Curtis chewed on the options for a moment. The question had brought that old quandary fresh to the surface: He was going to have to fight. The battle he'd fought with the Governess leapt back to his mind, and it seemed to him that he'd been incredibly lucky; it didn't strike him as likely that that sort of luck would hold out again. The cannon fire, the dead tree trunk falling into the howitzer crew— he saw it in his mind's eye as if it were a dream.

A wry smile had cracked across Brendan's face. "I get ya," he said, reading Curtis's silence. "Both it is." He turned and walked into a nearby tent and returned holding a rugged leather belt. An ivory-handled pistol and a long, curved saber jutted from a holster and sheath attached to the belt. He threw it to Curtis, who gingerly caught it in his arms.

"You're a hard man, Curtis," said Brendan. "A hard man. Go see

Damian for munitions. And keep your head high! Remember: You're a bandit now."

Curtis, unsure of himself, gave a quick salute.

"And don't salute," reproached Brendan. "This ain't the army."

"Okay," said Curtis, his arm falling awkwardly to his side. "Thanks, Brendan."

He began walking toward the munitions tent, carefully dodging the insistent traffic of busy bandits: a leap to avoid a barrel-chested man with an armload of cutlasses, a pinwheel to avoid tripping two bandits carrying a wooden crate. Passing one campfire, he felt the familiar tug of Septimus grabbing hold of his pant leg and climbing to his shoulder perch.

"You really like it up there, don't you?" asked Curtis, when he felt the weight of the rat on his left epaulet.

"It's nice, yeah," responded Septimus. "I like the view. Besides, I prefer being up above things. It's every rat for himself down there on the ground. Had my tail stepped on twice already tonight."

"They're not used to having a rat in the camp," said Curtis.

"Guess not," said Septimus. "Hey: Where'd you run off to there? Looked ominous."

"I'm a bandit now, Septimus. Officially. Took the oath."

"Wow, kid, wow," said the rat. "I mean, impressive. How does it feel?"

Curtis shrugged. "I don't know. Guess I feel the same."

"They could use all the manpower they can get. I count just under a hundred. Ninety-seven bandits. With you? Ninety-seven and a half." He chortled at his own joke. When he saw it elicited no response from his host, he continued, "Whatever. Come tomorrow night, there ain't going to be any bandits. Zero."

"Septimus," said Curtis sternly. "What did I say?"

"Right: No bad-mouthing the bandits. Got it."

They arrived at the munitions tent, a large canvas structure nestled up against the ravine wall. A grizzled-looking bandit, Damian, with a cheek full of tattooed tears, stood at the front flap, doling out bullets and powder to a line of waiting men and women. The line moved quickly, each bandit peeling away when they'd received their allotment. Curtis was nearly at the front when a ruckus broke out between Damian and the bandit in front of Curtis.

"Sorry, Aisling, that's what ye get," Damian was saying stoically.

"C'mon! I mean, I'm fourteen!" said Aisling, a girl. She wore her sandy yellow hair back in a ponytail. A brightly colored skirt ruffled above a pair of tall boots; a pin-striped vest covered an ash-stained white blouse.

"Exactly," Damian rejoined. "You'll get your pistols at sixteen. Next, please!" He motioned for Curtis to step forward.

As Curtis excused himself and scooted to the front, Aisling clapped her fuming eyes on him. "But," she sputtered, "he's no older than I am! And he's got a pistol AND a cutlass."

Curtis, taken aback, could only apologize. "Sorry," he said. "I didn't really have anything to do with it."

Damian eyed him suspiciously. "Where'd you get that stuff?"

"Brendan," explained Curtis defensively, "Brendan gave 'em to me. I didn't ask for them. He just gave them to me."

Aisling, in disgust, blew a puff of breath at a dangling strand of her hair. "Figures. Brendan. Oh, it's okay for a *boy* to have pistols before his sixteenth. But me? No way. Hold all plants, animals, and humans as equals, my *shoelace*. What a bunch of squirrel scat."

Damian shrugged his shoulders apologetically before disappearing into the tent and coming out with two pouches of powder and bullets. Seeing this, Aisling gave in with a loud *"Hrrumph!"* and stalked away to a nearby fire circle. Curtis watched her leave curiously. He was jolted back to attention by the munitions officer.

"Hey!" he shouted. "Kid!" He snapped his fingers just inches from Curtis's face.

"Oh, sorry," said Curtis, blinking.

"You know how to use this stuff?" asked Damian impatiently.

"Um," said Curtis, "not really."

Damian rolled his eyes. "It's simple," he said. "Just watch me closely." He proceeded to give Curtis a quick demonstration of how to load the pistol and set the flint. Once he'd finished he handed the pistol, unloaded, back to Curtis. "Got it?"

Curtis didn't really. "I think so," he lied.

"Good. Next!" He waved Curtis away. Perplexed, Curtis wandered away from the munitions tent, studying the strange, archaic mechanics of the flintlock pistol.

"Careful with that thing," said Septimus, shying away.

Curtis looked up and saw the girl Aisling sulking on a nearby

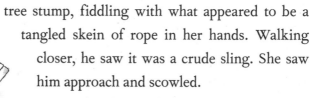

tree stump, fiddling with what appeared to be a tangled skein of rope in her hands. Walking closer, he saw it was a crude sling. She saw him approach and scowled.

"What do you want?" she asked, before adding, *"Outsider."*

Curtis stopped in his tracks as if he'd heard the rattle of a snake.

Aisling looked back down at the sling in her hand. Picking up a pebble, she placed it into the sling's cradle and fired it haphazardly into the ground. "I just want to do my part," she said mournfully.

Looking over his shoulder quickly, he said, "Hey, do you want to use this instead? I'll trade you." He held out the pistol, handle first.

Aisling eyed him suspiciously. "Really?" she asked.

Curtis nodded. "I'm not much of a gunner, myself," he said. "I'm more of a, you know, *tactical-ops* man."

The girl's face brightened. "Tactical-ops, huh?" she said, impressed. "Cool." She took the proffered pistol and bounced it in her palm, as if weighing it. She held the rear end of the barrel to her face and, pinching one eye closed, inspected the sight. "Nice," she said, offering her appraisal. "Thanks." She looked up at Curtis. "You want the sling?"

"Sure," said Curtis. Taking it, he attempted a weapon inspection as well: He stretched out the rope to an arm's reach and self-consciously stared one eye down the length. "Pretty nice one," he concluded.

Aisling laughed. "Thanks," she said, "tactical-ops man."

Curtis's face reddened. He tried to cover his embarrassment by holding out his hand and introducing himself. "I'm Curtis," he said. "You're . . . Aisling?"

The girl reached up and shook his hand. "Yep, nice to meet you, Curtis," she said. A spray of freckles bridged her nose from cheek to cheek. "Who's your friend?"

Septimus bowed low from his shoulder. "The name's Septimus Rat, ma'am. Pleasure to make your acquaintance."

"He's just there, y'know, temporarily," Curtis explained. "Said I'd give him a lift. We met in the coyote prison." He did a quick check to make sure the last phrase had registered with Aisling—a girl would undoubtedly be dazzled that he had been a member of the great escape party. He was rewarded when she made a half-impressed face. She then studied him as he awkwardly tried to think of another thing to say. He took a deep sigh and, arms akimbo, took in the busy camp.

"Pretty crazy," he said, finally, gesturing toward the camp. "All this."

Aisling nodded and continued to fiddle with the hammer of the pistol.

"Can't wait to get some coyotes in my sight," said Curtis, hefting the sling and swinging it casually in one hand. Glancing to make sure Aisling was watching, he reached down and picked up a small rock and set it into the cradle. "All this time, just sitting here." He began rocking the sling. "I'm pretty ready to get back into—" With an unintended flick of his wrist the missile in the sling went flying. "BATTLE!" he squeaked, watching the rock fly over the bandit camp and into a neat stack of earthenware bowls. They crashed to the ground in a shower of terra-cotta shards, and the entire camp stopped their activities to stare at Curtis.

"Oh God," he said, blushing deeply, "I'm so sorry. I really didn't mean to . . ."

Aisling was belly-laughing, rocking on the tree stump.

"Maybe you should stick to tactical-ops," said Septimus.

Curtis snapped at the rat, "I'll get the hang of it, just wait." He was about to fume off when Aisling waved him over.

"That's good," the girl said, between fits of laughter. "Things were getting a little too serious around here anyway. Nice work."

Curtis smiled and shrugged. "I do what I can," he said.

The sound of a horn penetrated the din of the camp's activity, its one long sustained note sweeping over the ravine. Curtis looked up to see the bandits snap to attention.

"Guess this is it," said Aisling, turning solemn. She stood up and fitted the pistol into her belt. Brendan had appeared at the mouth of the ravine, his sword clasped to his side and a long blunderbuss strapped over his shoulder. His left knee was shrouded in a layer of gauze, but it was obvious that his previous strength had returned.

"Ladies and gents," he shouted to the attendant throng. "Bandits, all. The morning approaches. Fall in. We march on the Ancients' Grove."

The bandits wordlessly stepped into two neat rows on the ravine floor and began their march from the camp. Sabers were set into sheaths, their blades newly polished and sharpened; rifles were slung over shoulders. Teary good-byes were exchanged between sweethearts, husbands, and wives. Several of the younger children began to cry, separated from their parents, and were comforted by the few attendants who had been left behind to mind the camp. Aisling and Curtis began to walk toward the marching column.

"Good luck," said Aisling as she disappeared into the crowd, "tactical-ops man."

CHAPTER 23

Call to Arms!

"An army?" asked the hare, wiping sleep from his eyes. He'd apparently been woken from a deep slumber; his colander-helmet was set askew on his head and his constabulary uniform was in disarray. "We—we've never done that before."

"What Samuel is trying to say, madam Mystic," explained the fox, looking equally discomfited, "is that it's, well, it's been *ages*, really, since we've had to do that. I mean, we're a peaceful people, right?"

Iphigenia was trying hard to suppress her frustration. "I under-stand that, Sterling, but you'll have to improvise. This is of utmost importance."

Sterling, the fox, stood and studied the Mystic. Prue, standing next to Iphigenia, grew impatient. Her toes were fidgeting in her shoes. The fox finally continued, "I suppose this would involve ringing the bell."

Iphigenia rolled her eyes. "Yes, it would, Mr. Fox. And if you wouldn't mind stepping to it, we have a half-crazed woman and her host of coyotes to stop before they lay the whole Wood to ruin."

"Well, that's just the thing, ain't it," the fox said. "The bell is in the old fire tower. And, well, the fire tower is locked."

"So, unlock it," said the Mystic.

The fox smiled uncomfortably. "No key." He displayed the open palms of his two paws, as if showing them empty was some condo-lence.

The speakers were silent for a moment; the Elder Mystic inhaled a long, dramatic breath of air. "Mr. Fox," she said, finally, "I am a woman of infinite patience. I have devoted my life to the prac-tice of meditation. I have sat and watched a stone, a single stone, gather moss over the course of three weeks. You, however, are trying this seemingly limitless patience." The admission seemed to ease her temper, and her tone changed: "If there is a lock, Mr. Fox," she said calmly, "and there is no key, then the obvious solution is to break the lock. The bell simply must be rung."

Sterling, suitably cowed, threw his paw to his forehead in a salute. "Yes, ma'am!"

"We will follow," said the Mystic, waving for Prue to stay by her. "To make sure these things are done to satisfaction." The first filigree strands of dawn appeared on the horizon, the edge of the clouds touched with a glowing pink. The constables stalked off toward the path, whispering between themselves, and Iphigenia and her entourage—Prue and the other Mystics—fell in after them.

After a brisk walk, they arrived at the fire tower. Standing atop a high hill, it was a rickety wooden affair: a small, domed hovel built at the top of a haphazard maze of cross-bracing beams, circumvallated by a narrow walkway. A stepladder, nailed to the side, led to a small door in the hovel, and it was to this door that Sterling the fox climbed, his pruning shears at the ready.

"See," he explained to the crowd below as he, with some difficulty, mounted the ladder to the door, "security is of utmost priority in this sort of situation. Hence the lock. Left unlocked, you can expect that the fire bell would be the prized object of every prankster in North Wood."

Iphigenia, from below, urged the fox onward. "Come on, Sterling, we've not got all day."

"Easier said than done, Madam Mystic," Sterling said as he

brandished his pruning shears and carefully wedged the blades into the keyhole of the lock. "This lock is of the finest South Wood crafts-manship; I myself oversaw its installation. It is very doubtful that I'll be able to . . . oh." An audible metallic *click* sounded. The lock fell to the ground. Sterling blushed.

"What happened, fox?" asked the Mystic.

"It, uh, appears to have been *unengaged*," replied the fox.

Iphigenia shook her head. "Well, get in there and ring the bell!"

The fox did just that; a jarring series of deafening clangs issued from the fire tower, the peals echoing out over the surrounding forest meadows and thickets.

The placid farmland, quiet in the early dawn, came to sudden life.

Figures in the trees and among the rows of crops began to show themselves; cottage doors were thrown open, their occupants step-ping out on to dawn-dappled verandas and looking curiously up at the small crowd gathered at the base of the fire tower. Brightly hued caravan wagons appeared from the woods and began trundling their way toward the hill. Shovel-laden farmhands paused in the day's first labors and walked from their tidy fields, their eyes set on the old wooden tower. Before long, a sizable crowd had gathered at the top of the hill.

Iphigenia turned to Prue. "You wouldn't mind helping me here, would you?" she asked, gesturing to the stepladder that led to the top of the fire tower. Prue smiled, said, "Of course," and mounted the ladder, holding her hand behind her so that Iphigenia could grip it on her ascent to the walkway. Once she'd arrived at the top, she looked out at the gathering crowd. Prue stood at her side. The serene countryside of North Wood stretched out beneath them, a maze of alder groves and patchwork garden plots. Little hamlets, their few quaint huts spewing peat smoke, nestled into far-flung hillsides; a single wide, meandering road—Prue guessed it to be the North Wood tributary of the Long Road—carved its way through the landscape like a wild river, disappearing finally among the wooded hills.

"Step forward, please," the Elder Mystic instructed the crowd. "Let the folks in the back in a little closer. I can only speak so loud. Sterling, make sure the smaller animals can be seated at front: the moles and the squirrels. Dears, if you're taller than four feet, please keep to the rear of the crowd. Mm-hmm. That's good."

She paused for a moment as a new flurry of witnesses arrived, swelling the crowd considerably. The two constables, Sterling and Samuel, busily walked the perimeter of the expanding assemblage, doing their best to keep people calm and attentive. The low hum of the crowd's chatter swarmed the scene like a hive of bees. When Iphigenia was satisfied with the hill's capacity, she spoke.

"Are we all here?" she asked.

A sea of moving heads, some nodding, some shaking. A voice

from the outer rim of the crowd sounded, "Folks up Miller Creek are on their way."

Another: "Kruger and Deck Farms are in the middle of hay baling. Can't make it."

Iphigenia nodded. "We'll make sure word spreads. For now, this will have to do." By Prue's estimation, three hundred fifty souls were gathered—a dizzying menagerie of creatures: stoats, coyotes, foxes, humans, and deer. A family of black bears in overalls towered above the crowd in the center; the antlers of a cluster of bucks jutted from the left side. A group of skunks, motioned forward by Samuel, made their way to the front.

"The reason we've called you here," said Iphigenia, her voice firm and resounding, "the reason we've rung the bell, is that a great trial is at hand. An army is on the march in Wildwood, an army intent on the destruction of the entire Wood. We have meditated through the night at the Council Tree and we have reached a unanimous decision, with the tree's consent, to gather arms against this foe. The North Wood volunteer militia will muster."

The quieted murmur of the crowd burst open afresh, the whispers turning to desperate chatter. "What do we care about what happens in Wildwood?" called one of the bears. "That's no business of ours."

Iphigenia frowned, responding, "The thing that threatens Wildwood threatens us all. The ivy has been awakened. The exiled Dowager

Governess of South Wood promises to feed the blood of a human child to the plant and thereby gain its control. We have this girl, this Outsider, Prue McKeel, to thank for first bringing this to our attention." She waved for Prue to come forward. Prue did so shyly, giving a little half curtsy to the teeming crowd.

"What's an Outsider doing here?" called a faceless voice from the crowd.

Another voice corrected the first: "She's not just some Outsider, she's a half-breed!"

The crowd seemed to collectively attempt a closer inspection of Prue as she stood on the tower's walkway. Satisfied, many in the crowd nodded. "It's true!" Prue heard someone say to his neighbor. Iphigenia gestured to Prue, an open palm extended in invitation. Prue's eyes widened.

"You want me to say something?" she whispered.

Iphigenia nodded. "Yes," she said. "It would be best if they heard it from you."

Prue gulped and took another step forward, resting her hands on the rail of the walkway. She stared out at the crowd. "My brother," she began. "My brother, just five days ago—"

"Speak up, then!" someone shouted from the back.

Prue cleared her throat and spoke louder. "Five days ago, I saw my brother taken by a flock of crows. From a park in St. Johns—the Outside. So I came in here to find him. I've asked the people in South

Wood for help—they did nothing." She was gaining confidence. "I asked Owl Rex, the Crown Prince of the Avians, for help—and he was arrested! He told me to come here, to speak to the Mystics. He said they'd be my last hope."

Iphigenia stepped to Prue's side. "The crows are in the employ of the Dowager," the Elder Mystic said. "They have fallen away from the Avians to do her bidding. Once the ivy is similarly under her command, there will be no stopping the swath of destruction that will follow. Every tree will be toppled, every glade consumed. Your crops, houses, and farms will be laid to ruin. The ivy knows no boundaries. It will consume and consume until it is instructed by its commander to cease. And clearly, its commander is nothing short of a madwoman, bent on the complete annihilation of the Wood as we know it."

The audience emitted a murmur of fear. The Mystic continued:

"It is clear from our meditations with the Council Tree that this is our calling. To gather our army in defense of the Wood. There is no other choice." Iphigenia paused and took a deep breath. "Mr. Fox," she called, "would you mind saying a word?"

Sterling, standing at the foot of the stepladder, nodded and climbed to the walkway. He held a tattered and yellowing scroll in his paw. Unfurling it, he began to explain to the crowd, "The Decree of Muster dictates thus: that every man and woman, animal or human, of able body, in the event that the Decree is instated, must take up arms and join the ranks of the militia. For this, he or she will be compensated from the community stores for labor lost."

"But we have no weapons!" came a voice.

Sterling rolled the scroll tight and patted the pruning shears at his belt. "Then you must use whatever is at hand. Farming implements, cooking utensils—whatever you can find."

The crowd collectively heaved a worried grumble.

Iphigenia stepped forward. "Go now," she commanded, "and find your families. Gather your weapons. Meet back at this point in an hour. You have an hour, no more, to do this. Our time is very short. The Governess intends to commit this sacrifice at noon this day. Remember: Our very lives depend on this."

The crowd of farmers, dismissed, moved into distressed splinters as they each ran home to their cottages, farms, and families.

Prue turned to Iphigenia. "Will you come? Into Wildwood?" she asked.

The Elder Mystic nodded, brushing a few strands of her silvery gray hair from her lined forehead. "Yes," she said, "I will represent the Order in this journey. The others will stay behind and remain in meditation. However, when I took the robes, I was sworn to do no harm, pledged to a life of nonviolence. Whatever fighting must be done, I will be unable to take part in it. But there are other ways that I may help."

Prue watched as the crowd continued to dissipate, its individual figures disappearing into the copses of trees and small hovels that peppered the landscape. "How many," she asked, "do you think there'll be?"

Sterling the fox grumbled under his breath. "We'll be lucky if we have four hundred," he said.

Iphigenia, her face set, looked at the fox. "It will have to do."

"That's it?" Prue asked. The number seemed far too small.

"You saw the crowd," said Sterling defensively. "Even if we get everyone—all the farmhands and homesteads on the far side of Miller Creek—we won't get many more than that. This is a quiet country; we're not accustomed to these upsets."

Iphigenia sighed. "And yet, the Council Tree has decreed it. We have little choice in the matter."

"What about—what about—" Prue's mind whirred desperately for options. "What about other creatures—in the Wood? What about all the animals in Wildwood—wouldn't they want to ally with us to do this? I mean, their homes are in as much in danger as yours are."

Iphigenia shook her head. "Impossible," she said. "The creatures of Wildwood, what we know of them, belong to loosely tied packs and families. It's truly a wild country. Getting each of those disparate packs to come together would be impossible."

Prue struck on something. "The bandits," she said. "What about the bandits?"

Sterling's eyes widened. "Those bloodthirsty hooligans? Are you kidding? No one in their right mind would ally with those anarchic hoods. We'd all get our throats slit and our purses taken."

"I don't think that's true," Prue objected. "I don't think that's true at all. I've been there—to the bandit camp."

"You've been to their camp?" asked a surprised Iphigenia. "How on earth did you manage that?"

Prue sighed. "Long story. I was lying on the back of an eagle when I was shot down by a coyote archer. They found me and brought me to their hideout. It's up a really deep ravine—totally hidden from sight. I wasn't there long, though, before they'd spotted some coyotes nearby—they were following my scent, you see. So their King, I think they called him, rode me out of the camp and away so as not to lead them right into the hideout. That's when I was captured by the Governess."

The fox was momentarily speechless. "They didn't rough you up, did they? I mean, that's what they do, right?"

"No, they were very gentlemanly," said Prue.

"I'd always suspected as much," said Iphigenia. "That the bandits were a sympathetic crew, however anarchic they might be. One thing is certain: They would be the strongest and most organized of the many tribes and packs of Wildwood. A formidable ally, if we were able to gain it."

"No way," said the fox angrily. "There is no way I will march alongside a bunch of Wildwood bandits. It's a miracle we're able to stay alive, what with their pilfering our shipments to and from South Wood."

"But Mr. Fox, you forget that for every shipment that is waylaid, others are allowed passage. They've always allowed enough through for us to live very comfortably," said Iphigenia. She turned to Prue. "Do you think that you'd be able to find this camp, this hideout, again?"

Prue thought for a moment. "I don't think I could get to the hideout itself," she said, "but I could get *close*, I think. It's just south of that big bridge—the one that crosses the ravine."

"The Gap Bridge," Iphigenia corrected. "Yes."

"And west," continued Prue, her memory busily retracing her flight from the hideout. "Yes, that's it: west of the Long Road. And I know they post sentries everywhere around the camp. If I were able to make enough of a racket, no doubt they'd nab me, right? And I know they'd recognize me from before—I could explain what's going on!"

Iphigenia nodded. "I can only imagine they'd be as concerned as we are. This threat endangers all of us."

"Let me go," Prue said, feeling a wave of determination rise in the cavity of her chest. "While you wait for the militia to regroup, let me ride into Wildwood. I've got my bike—I can take the Long Road—and maybe I can make it to the bandits and convince them to join by the time the North Wood army is on the march."

Iphigenia was thoughtful. "It's a dangerous gambit, my dear," said the Elder Mystic. "You certainly are risking running afoul of the bandits. Perhaps they would think it was a trick, to lead them from their hideout. There's no telling how they'll respond."

"Do we have a choice?" asked Prue. "I mean, if we have them with us—there must be hundreds of them!—we at least stand a chance against the Governess." She looked desperately back and forth between Iphigenia and Sterling. The fox crossed his arms and huffed. Iphigenia, after a moment, nodded.

"Yes," she said. "Go. Ride to the bandits. Tell them of our plight. Of *their* plight. In the meantime, we'll muster our arms and set out. And we will meet you at the Gap Bridge—before the sun has ascended to the midday mark." She looked up and gauged the height of the sun, its glow dampened by the strands of clouds above the horizon. "Go now. Ride quickly. We have very little time."

Prue dashed down the stepladder and leapt astride her bike, kicking it into motion.

Curtis could feel his tiredness deep in the heels of his feet. The little sleep he'd had the night before—a few fitful naps by the side of a campfire—was scarcely adequate to prepare his temperament for a long morning march, at the end of which, undoubtedly, would be his own personal end. The gravity of the situation was slowly unfurling, creeping over him like a chill. He found himself longing for the comfort of his own bed, his overcrowded bookshelf, the abrasive chime of his alarm clock, the endless footfalls of his two sisters crowding the hallway outside his door. He ran the rope of the sling through his fingers as he walked, feeling the pilly grit of the hempen cord and the smooth leather of the sling's little cradle. The six finger-wide smears of paint that a fellow bandit had striped across his face still felt fresh and cool against his skin.

The two long columns of marchers had fanned out as soon as they'd left the enclosure of the hideout ravine, and Curtis could see the dark forms of his fellow bandits making their way skillfully through the underbrush. While they traveled as fleetly as ever, a certain energy seemed to be drained from them. The reality of their doomed enterprise hovered over them like a dense fog, unbreakable. Curtis attempted to distract his own feelings of helplessness by searching the ground for good, usable missile projectiles for his sling. He stuffed them in his pockets as he found them, and he could feel the weight of the pocketful of rocks and pebbles with each step.

"Keep up, Curtis!" hissed a bandit ahead of him, noticing his slowed pace as he stooped to pick up a nice-looking stone. It was Cormac. Curtis heeded him, shoving the stone in his pocket and jogging ahead. They were getting farther and farther from the camp; the wood smoke was no longer even a hint on the air. Septimus had left his regular seat on Curtis's right shoulder and could be seen occasionally, leaping from tree bough to tree bough above their heads. After a time, the troop spilled out onto the Long Road. Brendan, having donned his viney crown, stood at the head of the crowd of bandits, waving them forward.

"We'll follow the Road," he explained, once the army had amassed around him. With a long, knobby stick, he began drawing a rough map in the wet dirt of the road. "Till the Hardesty game trail—then we'll go backwoods. Numbers ain't gonna cut it in this battle—we're well outgunned—but we can try to make up for it in stealth. An army of that size, I have to assume that they'll be on the Long Road as long as possible; they'll probably cut west off the Road between the north and middle fork of Rocking Chair Creek." He drew a long, snaked line with the stick and placed an *X* at the end. "We'll come at them from the northwest, just above the Plinth. That's the best we can do." He looked up at the gathered bandits. "Is that clear?"

A chorus of "ayes" was the reply.

Brendan's jaw was locked in firm determination. "Let's move," he said.

The army of bandits began their march down the Long Road. Curtis strayed to the rear, still glancing around at the ground below his feet for rocks. Something caught his eye: a flash of shiny metal in the underbrush near the side of the road. He peeled away from the columns of marchers and kneeled down. Pushing aside a small cluster of thistle stalks, Curtis was surprised to see his house keys. "My keys!" he said aloud. He pulled the keys from the undergrowth and shook them in his hand momentarily, reveling in their familiar jangle. Septimus, falling behind the bandit parade, scrambled to his side.

"What's that?" he asked.

"My house keys," responded Curtis. "They must've fallen out of my pocket when I was being carried by the coyotes."

"Fascinating," said Septimus wryly. "Now we shouldn't get too far behind. We have our own suicides to attend to."

Curtis smirked. "Right," he said, pocketing the keys. "It's just crazy to think that, like, straight that way, down through the woods, is the Railroad Bridge. And beyond that, my home. This was where I came in." He shook his head as if dispelling an enchantment. "Crazy."

The bandit army was farther down the Long Road now, the

midsection of the column disappearing around a bend. Septimus began hopping along the gravel surface, looking over his shoulder at Curtis. "C'mon," he said.

"Right," said Curtis. "Coming." He gave one last look to the wall of trees, the bunch of thistles that had held his keys, and jogged after the bandit host to catch up.

✿

Never in Prue's life had she been so focused on her riding, so tuned into every churn of the pedal assembly, the springy contractions of her quads as they powered the quick, rhythmic motions of her calves and ankles. She rode lightly on her bike seat, her weight off center on the back of the saddle in order to better absorb the incessant hammering of the bumpy road. That selfsame bumpy road, however, played havoc with the red Radio Flyer wagon trailing behind; it leapt and shivered manically as she rode, and made a terrific banging noise. Prue let the noise echo on; it felt defiant. Besides, if anything was going to catch the attention of the bandits, surely the clatter of a metal wagon would do the trick.

The encroaching trees loomed over the road, casting cool shadows across the smooth dirt. She'd long left the pastoral fields and tree groves of North Wood; a wooden gate had marked the border between the quiet farmland and the untamed country of Wildwood. A pair of constables, a human and a badger, had thrown the gate open for her—she hadn't even stopped to thank them. And now she was in the depths of Wildwood, and the roadside brush and bramble seemed to reach out to her like a million leafy arms. The wind whipped at her face and whispered through the heavy cotton of her hoodie, sending shivers through her body with each breath of wind.

"Faster!" she urged her legs. "Faster!" she willed the bike, the wheels, the chain.

Her eyes remained locked on the farthest point of the Long Road, and she snaked her bike handily around its many twists and turns. She knew time was running out.

Suddenly, a squirrel darted out in the road in front of her and Prue screamed, jamming on the brakes. The squirrel had stopped directly in front of her and was eyeing this strange metal contraption that was flying toward him. The brakes yelped and her rear tire began to skid, sending the Radio Flyer wagon into a contorting fishtail. The squirrel, instantly recognizing that he was about to be run over, yipped and leapt out of the way, just as Prue's bike skidded sideways and she was thrown from the seat. She hit the ground with a pained "*oof,*" her hands bearing the brunt of the fall. The bike clattered to the ground behind her. The squirrel shot into the trees without a backward glance.

"Watch it!" Prue yelled after him. She picked herself up and, wiping the grit from her palms, ran back to her bike. Inspecting it, she was relieved to find that it had suffered little damage other than a few scrapes on the frame. She picked it up, climbed back aboard, and pedaled off, pushing hard to regain her previous speed.

I can't afford another wreck like that, she thought. *If this bike gives out on me, I'm screwed.*

Her heart pounded in her chest, and she could feel her lungs working like bellows to keep up with her every heaved breath. Finally, her eyes caught sight of two distant tall shapes on the horizon, where the road straightened out and the landscape seemed to buckle and fall away into a massive ravine: the ornate columns that marked the near side of the Gap Bridge.

"Come on, Curtis!" shouted Septimus. "They're about to make the turn into the woods!"

"I'm coming!" Curtis called, though his steps felt slower—as if he was compelled to dally. The ring of keys in his pocket—what a miracle that had been!—rang quietly with his every step, each single *clink* reminding him of his home, of his bed. In his mind, he heard his father's wheezing laugh, cracking up at some lame sitcom joke from the TV. He smelled his mother's cooking—something he'd never considered to be anything extraordinary, but now, in this environment, it took on a kind of God's-own-ambrosia aspect. Even the boxed mac and cheese she'd serve up for a quick lunch on a summer afternoon seemed like a gourmet meal. He could hear his older sister, the sound of her dancing footsteps pounding through the ceiling below her room as she cranked her stereo and cast herself as whatever pop star she was currently obsessing over. It was all waiting for him. *I could just go*, he thought. *Right now. I could just go.*

He gazed again behind him, to the bend in the road that was beginning to obscure the place he'd recognized as being the spot where he'd first encountered the Long Road, when he'd been strapped to the back of the coyote and the forest had gone racing by on their way to the warren. Had it only been a few days before? It felt like an eternity. And now here he was, involved in this foolhardy scheme to try and wrest this baby boy from the hands of a crazed woman—and likely die in the trying. Did it matter so much? At what point had he arrived at this juncture? When had the retrieving of this kid—someone he wasn't even related to—become something worth losing his life over? Prue hadn't even stuck around. She'd left, gone back to her safe and happy home. She was enjoying her parents' cooking now, undoubtedly, catching up on her schoolwork, seeing friends, watching television. For all he knew, her life had returned to normal. And perhaps, eventually, the McKeel family would just learn to forget, and the grief of losing a child would dissipate. Why should he sacrifice himself as well?

"Psst!" hissed Septimus from ahead. "Curtis, what are you doing?"

Curtis realized he'd stopped in the middle of the Long Road, his hands in his pockets, his fingers rubbing the cool metal of his house keys. "Septimus," he began, "I don't know how to say this, but . . ."

He paused. Septimus cocked an eyebrow and waited for him to finish.

"I think I . . ."

A sound came from behind him, cutting his speech short. It was a distinctly metallic sound, disrupting the serene quiet of the woods. It grew louder and louder, a clanking noise that seemed to be lumbering toward him. Curtis froze and listened.

It was the sound of a bicycle.

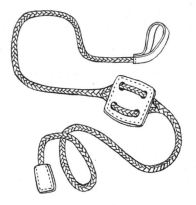

C H A P T E R   2 4

Partners Again

"**P**RUE!**"

It had sounded initially like the hoot of an owl. Prue's
focus was so intent on her front wheel and the navigating of
a particularly rough section of the Road that she'd ignored the sound
as being just another note in the unending symphony that was the forest's many noises. But it came again, louder, closer:

"PRUUUUUUE!"

It was, undoubtedly, someone calling her name. She looked up
and saw, standing in the middle of the road, a short figure wearing a

dirty brigadier's uniform. The figure had the hair and spectacles of Curtis, but her reasoning refused to allow her to believe it. As she came closer, however, the fact was indisputable. Curtis was not home in St. Johns. Curtis was not safe with his parents. Curtis had not left Wildwood. Curtis was standing right in front of her. And she was about to run him over.

"CURTIS!" she hollered as her fingers mangled her bicycle brakes and the back tire skidded and swerved against the dirt of the road. The wagon kicked up violently from behind and slammed back down on the ground with a tremendous *WHAANG*. Curtis leapt out of the way, diving headlong into the brush by the side of the road. Coming to a sliding stop, she jammed the kickstand down with her heel and vaulted from the seat, running to where Curtis had landed.

"Curtis!" she cried. "I can't believe it. I can't believe it!" Curtis was pulling himself from a small shroud of raspberries, the stickers clinging tenaciously to his uniform. She threw out her hand and he accepted it. Together, they stood on the side of the road staring at each other in amazement.

They both began speaking at the same time. "I thought you . . . !" "How did you . . . ?" Unable to get a word in, they let out a unified holler of joy and fell into a long, happy hug.

Emerging from the embrace, Prue was the first to speak. "I thought you'd gone home! That woman, Alexandra, said so."

Curtis shook his head. "No, I was in the warren when you were there. I was locked up!"

Prue cursed, her face pinched in anger. "That evil, evil lady. I can't believe that! All the lies she's told—"

"But you!" interjected Curtis. "They said *you* had gone home."

"I did," explained Prue. "But I turned around and came right back. Oh, Curtis, so much has happened since I saw you last—I can't even begin to explain."

Curtis slapped his palm against his chest in excitement. "Me too! You wouldn't believe it."

"But I don't have much time," said Prue, remembering her charge. "I'm riding ahead of the North Wood army—I have to get help."

"The North Wood army?" asked Curtis. "What's that?"

"Not really an army," Prue corrected herself. "More like a few hundred farmers and their pitchforks. I'm riding ahead to try and get help from the Wildwood bandits—I figure with their help, we stand a chance."

Curtis smiled.

"What?" asked Prue quizzically. "What are you smiling about?"

"You found 'em," he said.

"What?"

"The bandits. You found 'em. You happen to be looking at a Wildwood bandit, signed and sworn," said Curtis proudly, his arms at his hips.

"You?" she asked. "You're a bandit now?" She threw her hand to her forehead.

"Yep," continued Curtis. "The whole bandit band is right behind . . ." He swiveled as he spoke, but was stopped short to see that the road behind him was empty. "They *were* just there." He looked back at Prue, smiling apologetically. "Hang on," he said, holding a finger in the air. "I'll be right back." He turned and began jogging down the Long Road, the gold fringe of his epaulets swinging. When he'd arrived at a bend in the road, he stood on the forest's edge and yelled something into the trees. After a moment, a figure appeared. They spoke briefly, and the figure disappeared back into the trees. Curtis turned to Prue and waved his hand in a circle, rolling his eyes. Suddenly, the dark green underbrush gave way and dozens of armed men and women, dressed in an array of ragtag uniforms, stepped from the shadows onto the clearing of the road. A man Prue recognized to be Brendan walked to the front of the crowd, and with Curtis walking alongside, they all approached Prue as she stood, speechless, by her bike.

"Prue, this is Brendan, the Bandit King," said Curtis when the band of bandits came close. "I believe you two have met."

"We have!" shouted Prue, making a slight, embarrassed bow.

"Oh, Brendan. I'm so happy to see you're okay."

Brendan smiled. "How are your ribs, Outsider?" he asked.

"Fine, thanks," she said, blushing. "Much better."

Prue scanned the crowd of gathered bandits; their number was fewer than she'd anticipated. Apparently, her face said as much, because Brendan spoke up in explanation, his face suddenly sullen. "Our numbers have been decimated. We are not the hale band you encountered when you last fell into our midst. But no matter: You have found us on the march to confront the Dowager Governess once and for all. We plan on giving her the hiding of a lifetime—even if we die in the trying." The crowd behind the King murmured in resolved approval.

"But listen, Brendan," said Curtis, his voice quaking in his excitement, "Prue has an army too!"

"What?" Brendan stared at Prue.

Prue took a deep breath. "Since I saw you last, I went to North Wood and spoke to the Mystics there. They've agreed to help, to fight the Governess. They've called their militia together. The whole country of North Wood is mustering to the defense of the Wood. They're on their way now—they can't be far behind me. I rode ahead to find you, the bandits, in the hope that you would join us."

A collective furor erupted from the gathered bandits. "Allies!" one shouted. "Our number grows!"

Another reprimanded the first: "Those bumpkins? Are you kidding me?"

"No bandit has fought alongside a civilian—that's unthinkable!"

Brendan turned and, waving his arms in the air, attempted to quiet the unruly bunch. "Shut up, all of you!" he commanded. When the band had quieted, he turned back to Prue. "What kind of army are you talking about?" he asked.

"Four hundred," said Prue, "give or take. Human and animal. Armed with farm implements, mostly."

"Oh boy," remarked one bandit from the middle of the crowd. He was immediately shushed by his neighbors.

Brendan chewed on the information. "Not ideal, but the measure of a fighter is in his skill, not his weapon," he said, stroking the coarse hair of his red beard. "An old bandit adage goes, 'A bell is a cup until it is struck.'" He turned to the amassed bandit crowd and called for their attention. "We will fight alongside the farmers," he said, and the crowd exploded into objection.

"We steal from them, we don't fight with them!"

"My granddad would be spinnin' in his grave to know that a daughter of his would be fighting alongside a North Wooder!"

"Quiet!" shouted Brendan. "I'll take no objections! I didn't call for a vote on the matter; this is final!" Once the bandits had ceased their clamor, he continued, "The creed and code of the bandit clearly states 'to hold all plants, animals, and humans as equals.' Never in the history of our band have these words rung more true." His voice grew steely and hard, as he pointed a tattooed finger in the direction of the woods. "This threat we face is shared by every living thing in this Wood. By allying with North Wood in this fight, we not only uphold our code, our *oath*, but we make it stronger. Stronger by *living* it." He flared his nostrils and eyed the crowd. "Is that clear?"

He was met by silence.

"I said, is that clear?" he repeated, his voice ringing out through the narrow clearing of the road.

"Aye," said a bandit. A few more fell in as well: "Aye, King." Finally, the entire crowd chorused their approval, and Brendan nodded. He turned to Prue.

"Okay, girl," he said. "Take me to this army of yours."

🌿

Prue had pedaled her bike to the northernmost plank of the bridge and, resting its frame against the railing, had hopped off and was currently pacing the distance between the two columns. Occasionally, she would look sidelong at the farthest point of the road, hoping that soon a few shapes would appear out of the hazy distance—perhaps the ears of a rabbit or the arched roof of a caravan that would be a harbinger to the arriving army, but so far, the road remained empty.

The entire bandit band occupied the span of the bridge. They'd arrived sprightly and full of vigor, but the time that had elapsed between their arrival and the current moment had drained their energies. They meandered the boards of the bridge aimlessly, and Prue was hyperconscious of their eyes as they looked to her for direction. Curtis mirrored her steps as she paced; they would meet at each halfway point and share a look. The darkness of the deep ravine spilled out below them.

Brendan leaned against the railing, a weed protruding from his lips. He chewed on it thoughtfully as he stood.

Finally, he spoke. "Prue," he said. "We can't afford much more time."

Prue stopped in her pacing. She glanced back down the Long Road. It remained, as ever, empty. "I don't know," she said, fretfully. "I didn't think they'd be that far behind me."

"And you know for certain this army was being gathered?" asked Brendan.

"I swear," said Prue. "I was there when the instructions were given. The Elder Mystic—she told me to go, to find you. And she said to meet here, on this bridge. Oh, *dang* it all!" She stomped her foot, hearing the sole of her shoe echo against the wooden plank.

Brendan looked away, over at the milling band of bandits. Several of them had their weapons out—pistols, rifles, and cutlasses—and were engaged in a kind of time-killing inspection. "We've got to move," he said, "if we're to stop this woman. The time is fast approaching."

"Sir," one of the bandits called, squinting into the distance, "them

North Wooders, here they come."

Both Brendan and Prue jerked their heads in the direction the bandit had been staring; sure enough, far off, around a bend, the first few figures were appearing. They walked in a loose formation, and what first seemed to be scattered groups of marchers soon grew until the wide expanse of the Long Road was filled from side to side with an ocean of creatures. They were rabbits and humans, foxes and bears—each wearing the dirty and worn costume of farm laborer: coveralls, overalls, button-down gingham shirts, and plaid flannels. In their hands and paws they carried every known farm implement under the sun, and they walked with a kind of gritty determination Prue had not anticipated. The crowd was broken here and there by the presence of ox- and donkey-drawn carriages, their bright paint jobs a striking contrast against a background of the forest's million shades of green. Prue recognized Sterling the fox at the head of the marching crowd. She smiled widely when she saw him.

"You made it," she said, relieved, as the crowd came closer.

Sterling extended his palm in greeting. "It took some doing, yes," he said. "But here we are."

She turned to Curtis. "Sterling, this is my good friend Curtis. He's, well, he's a bandit."

Curtis made a low bow. "How do you do," he said.

Sterling looked at him suspiciously. "Are you their leader?" he asked, his eyes falling over the gathered band of milling bandits.

"Oh no, no," said Curtis, stepping away. "That'd be Brendan. The Bandit King."

Brendan walked forward, his hands resting on the pommel of his saber. His chin was held high, his crown of salal vines tangled dramatically in his curly red hair. "Hello, fox," said Brendan.

Sterling puffed up his chest at the arrival of the bandit. His eyes widened. "Hello, Brendan," he said, his tone frigid and firm. "Didn't think I'd be seeing your wretched face again."

Alarmed, Prue looked at Curtis. Curtis shrugged.

Brendan smiled. "Funny circumstances, to be sure. But it's all water under the bridge at this point, right, foxy?"

"I'm of the mind to arrest you, right here and now," said Sterling. "For all you've done."

Prue stepped forward. "Arrest him? Are you crazy? We're allies, remember?" The fox glared at Prue. "You didn't say anything about this *psychopath* being involved." He pointed a jagged claw at the Bandit King, his teeth bared. "This *man* is responsible for more shipments of produce lost than any single bandit in the Wood. He's a wanted man in all four of the countries. I personally have put my share of a season's harvest up as reward for his capture, dead or alive." He looked back at Brendan. "Last time we met, you were lucky to get away with your life—I intend to be more thorough this time."

"Oh come now, fox," said Brendan demurely. "Let's not quibble over administrative details. Bigger things are afoot."

Sterling was fuming. The thick red fur of his face seemed to take on a deeper hue as his eyes narrowed in anger. His hand went to the pruning shears at his side; he began to draw them from their sheath.

"Okay, foxy," Brendan said, "if you must." The silvery blade of his saber started to emerge from his scabbard. "Make your move, *constable*."

A voice erupted from the crowd of farmers behind the fox: "Stop this!" came the voice. Prue turned to see Iphigenia, the Elder Mystic, shoving her way through the crowd. Arriving at the bridge, she put her wizened hand on the fox's arm. "Constable Fox, I *command* you to stop this nonsense."

Brendan hadn't moved, his hand still positioned on his sword. "Listen to the old lady, foxy," he said. The fox's hackles rose; a bright spine of fur jutted from the back of his neck.

"You too, son," Iphigenia said, glowering at the Bandit King. She walked forward and, putting her hand on top of Brendan's, shoved the emerging sword hilt back into its scabbard. Having stayed the two combatants, Iphigenia stepped back and eyed the group warily. "Sorry we didn't make it sooner, dear," she said to Prue. "These old bones don't move as fast as they used to."

"No big deal," Prue said, exhaling a deep, relieved sigh. "Just glad to see you all."

Iphigenia smiled before raising her head and squinting up at the sky. The two armies squared off silently as the Elder Mystic gauged the position of the sun. Satisfied, she looked back at Brendan.

"King," she said, "we offer our services. We are a humble army, but what we lack in arms we make up for in number. We have five hundred strong here, farmers and ranchers, and all very able with a scythe and pitchfork. If you'll march with us, I think we should make a formidable force."

Brendan's face had softened in the presence of the Mystic. His hand fell away from the pommel of his sword, and he bowed deeply to the old woman. "If you'll have us," he said, "we'd be honored."

"No need to bow, King," Iphigenia said, blushing. "I understand your people's creed." She turned to face the gathered farmers. "People of North Wood, listen close. Today, on this bridge, an alliance has been struck—albeit temporary. Today, we march with the bandits of Wildwood for our common good. We go as allies." Turning to Sterling the fox: "Now, I would appreciate it, for the sake of our enterprise, if you would shake hands in good faith with the Bandit King."

The fox grumbled something under his breath before turning to Brendan. "Very well," he said. "If it's for the 'good of our enterprise.'" He held out his paw. Brendan took it readily and shook it. When a few shakes had transpired, the fox jerked his paw away and nodded gravely. "It is done."

"Okay, bandits," Brendan said loudly. "We march with the North Wooders."

Prue saw Iphigenia exhale a deep breath. She reached over and grabbed Prue's hand, saying, "Our little plan is working. Let's hope our good fortune holds out."

Prue smiled. "Let's do."

Curtis sidled up next to Prue and reached out his hand. "Hi," he said earnestly. "I'm Curtis. I'm Prue's friend. I'm a bandit, too."

Iphigenia turned to Curtis and began to smile politely when a look of surprise appeared on her face. "Well, that's quite a coincidence."

Prue and Curtis exchanged glances. "What's a coincidence?" asked Curtis.

"Another half-breed," explained Iphigenia, gripping his hand. "Having only ever seen a few in my lifetime, it's quite remarkable to meet two in the span of a day."

Prue was speechless. Curtis looked back and forth between Prue and the Mystic. "What does that mean, half-breed?" he asked.

Iphigenia reached up and patted him on the cheek. "No time for idle chitchat," she said, turning away into the crowd of farmers. "We have work to do."

🌿

The long wooden suspension bridge creaked noisily as the army crossed over the creek's ravine, and Alexandra's horse whinnied, reluctant to set his hoof on the first boards of the bridge.

"Shhh," quieted the Dowager, patting his thick neck. She urged him forward with a swift kick of her heels against his flank. The baby murmured in her arms. The crossing was slow; the bridge swayed under the weight of the line of bodies it supported. Once on the other side, Alexandra cantered the horse up the hill to monitor the rest of the army's crossing. The cannon teams were forced to cross on their own, so great was the weight of their munitions. Groups of four soldiers apiece slowly pushed the great metal behemoths across the complaining boards of the suspension bridge.

Alexandra was impatient.

She glanced up at the gloomy sky. The sun was slowly approaching its highest point. Noon was only a few hours away. She eyed the ravine that the creek cut through the hillside.

"Captain!" she hollered. A coyote ran to her side. He wore a peaked miter cap, and his uniform was a deep scarlet. He saluted as he approached.

"Send a sentry team up the north side of the creek," she commanded.

"We should establish a perimeter on the north side of the Grove. I don't want any surprises. I'll need all my energies about me to weave the incantation."

"Yes, Madam Governess," replied the captain, and he jogged off to organize a troop.

Alexandra watched the last of the artillery team make their way gingerly to the other side of the bridge. When the army was amassed in the road, Alexandra called for their attention.

"Here's where we leave the Road," she commanded. "Into the woods. Follow me."

"Of Woods Magic?" asked Curtis, still perplexed. "I just don't know what that means!"

The conjoined armies of the bandits and the North Wood farmers marched in single file up the narrow, winding path that was the Hardesty game trail as it snaked along a steep hillside. Curtis walked close behind Prue and her bike, peppering her with questions.

"I've told you everything I know, Curtis," said Prue. "It's something called Woods Magic. It just means that you, like, are kind of from here. Or something."

"And you're 'of Woods Magic' *how?*" he asked.

"I told you: Alexandra made it possible for my parents to have kids," she said, exasperated. "So that makes me of Woods Magic. I guess."

Curtis shook his head in disbelief. "I mean, I just don't know how that would be possible. We didn't even move here till I was five."

"Search your brain," offered Prue. "Do you have any strange relatives? Maybe one of them came from the Wood."

"I guess my aunt Ruthie was always a little weird," Curtis surmised. "She lives right on the edge of the Impassable Wilderness—the Wood—and she really keeps to herself. My parents say she's just a little batty."

Curtis, in this haze of concentration, had neglected to keep pace with the rest of the marching column. One of the farmers, a black bear armed with a pair of loppers, grunted angrily when Curtis fell back and nearly tripped over the bear's massive paws. "Sorry!"

"Just watch where yer going," growled the bear.

Curtis jogged to catch up with Prue as she continued to push her bike and wagon up the steep incline of the path.

"Well, there you go," said Prue. "Your old aunt Ruthie."

"I don't know," said Curtis, shaking his head. "Come to think of it, most of my relatives would fit that description: a little batty."

Suddenly, a whisper began cascading down the line of marchers. "Shhh!" A wave of an arm followed, passed from soldier to soldier, instructing the marchers to get down on the ground. Curtis waved to the black bear behind him, passing on the command, as he and Prue eased themselves quietly to the ground.

"What's up?" he whispered to Prue.

"I don't know," she responded. Prue slowly, silently laid her bike against the slope of the hill. She tapped the soldier in front of her, a female bandit in a muddy blue uniform with a thick coil of rope across her back. "What's going on?"

The bandit shrugged, crouched low amid the sword ferns that dangled over the small clearing of the trail. After a moment, more information was passed down the line in a series of whispers. The bandit, receiving the intel, turned to Prue.

"Coyotes," she whispered. "On the far ridge."

Prue looked over at the other side of the ravine. The ample vegetation spilled down the side of the hill, falling to an empty creek bed where the two slopes met in a deep V.

"Where?" she whispered. "I don't see any."

Curtis was searching the far hillside as well. Finally, the *crack* of a broken tree limb in the bracken announced the approach of their enemy. Within moments, the woods seemed to disgorge a troop of thirty or so coyote soldiers, their heads barely above the massive copses of maidenhair ferns that surrounded them. The going was tough; they laboriously made their way along the hillside slope.

Prue looked up the long line of crouched bandits and farmers, searching for some sort of guidance. She saw Brendan's head emerge from the line. He was gesturing to a few of his fellow bandits at the front of the column. The hand signals he made were indecipherable to Prue, but the bandits to whom they'd been directed nodded quickly in understanding. Walking crouched, he made his way down the line toward Prue and Curtis, stopping at the bandit in front of Prue. He made a kind of curlicue motion with his index finger and pointed across the ravine. The bandit nodded sharply and pulled the coil of rope from her shoulder.

"What's the plan?" hissed Curtis from behind Prue. "Can we do anything?"

Brendan shook his head. "Sit tight," he whispered. "Just archers and grapplers for this job."

"I've got a sling," suggested Curtis.

Brendan looked at him blankly. "Ever used one before?" he asked.

"No," said Curtis.

"Like I said: archers and grapplers only," Brendan repeated. "Hold your position."

Minutes passed. The coyotes on the other side of the ravine, unaware of the danger that lurked on the opposite bank of ferns, continued their cautious march along the ridge. The bandits in the hidden line on the game trail watched for the sign from Brendan.

Suddenly, the wind shifted and swept down the hillside above the hidden army. One of the coyotes, the jangling medals at his breast suggesting a superior rank, held his muzzle high, sniffing the air. His eyes widened as he caught their scent.

"Enemies!" he shouted, whipping a saber from his hip. "On the far ridge!"

No sooner had he voiced this warning than Brendan gave the signal from the front of the line. About twenty bandits, in various places along the column, stood up and prepared for action. Half the bandits juggled coils of rope topped with grappling hooks in their hands, while others drew back the string of tall yew bows and took careful aim at the opposing ridge.

"Archers, NOW!" shouted Brendan, and the air above the ravine became an aerial show of flying arrow shafts.

Several of the arrows found their mark, and dozens of fern stands were mowed low by the coyotes, tumbling lifelessly down the hillside. In that instant, the troop of coyotes was easily halved in number, and the ones that remained began yapping in panic. "Hold the line!" barked the coyote captain, still standing with his saber drawn. "Fusiliers! Fire at will!" The soldiers to whom the command had been directed began desperately fumbling with their long flintlock rifles, jamming powder and ball down the iron barrels. The bandits let loose another fleet of arrows, and the few poor coyotes who had not found cover fell under the barrage before any of their rifle shots were fired. The captain remained standing, defiantly glaring at the opposite ridge.

"Retreat!" he cried. "Back for reinforcements!"

Brendan seized the moment to signal his grapplers to throw. The ridge, in an instant, became crisscrossed with taut rope lines as the barbs of the grappling hooks found purchase in the overhanging tree boughs. The bandit in front of Prue had thrown such a line and, testing its strength momentarily, she leapt into the air and sailed across the gully with the fluid ease of an acrobat. Prue watched as she arrived on the other side and, drawing her saber, quickly dispatched three coyotes with a series of lightning-fast maneuvers. Along the ridge, several more grapplers had swung the distance between the ridges and were engaged in heated battle.

The coyote captain, enraged at how quickly his troop had been defeated, gave a quick, angry bark to the bandits and farmers on the far ridge, sheathed his weapon, and turned to run. Curtis was the first to witness the captain's retreat, and he quickly pulled the sling rope from his belt and began setting a rock in the sling's cradle.

"I got him," he said.

Prue looked at him sideways.

Curtis squinted one eye and began carefully swinging the sling, feeling the weight of the stone arc the sling assembly in a whipping circle around his shoulder. He gauged the distance between himself and the uniformed coyote, who was now disappearing into the underbrush, his bicorne hat bouncing just below the lowest-hanging branches. Before his navy-blue uniform had vanished, however, Curtis gave a great yelp and let loose the sling. Time seemed to slow to a stop.

Curtis watched the stone as it flew into the air above the creek.

And followed it with his eyes it as it fell with a mighty *plop* into the creek bed below.

He looked back up, crestfallen, to bear witness to the captain's escape into the underbrush. Suddenly he heard an arrow whistle across the ravine and land with a dead *thud* into the captain's back. The coyote fell, disappearing into the deep green brush with a crash.

Curtis looked up the line of figures to see Brendan standing with his bow drawn, the string still quivering from the released arrow. He glanced back at Curtis and smiled. Curtis felt his face flush red.

Brendan turned and eyed the far ridge, inspecting the terrain for stragglers. All was quiet. Satisfied, he waved for the column of marchers to continue up the trail.

"Nice shot," whispered Prue over her shoulder.

"Like to see *you* try it," snapped Curtis.

CHAPTER 2 5

Into the City of the Ancients

The trail cut southward when the ridge became too steep to climb; it crossed the trough of the ravine and carved up the opposite hillside in sharp switchbacks. Beyond the ridge, the ground leveled out and soon led to another shallow ravine where a second creek, this one much larger, cut a wide swath down the hillside. A small wooden bridge crossed the creek here, and beyond, the trail zigzagged up the hill on the other side. The trail opened up at the bridge, and the collected army of bandits and farmers paused at the clearing.

Prue and Curtis made their way into the milling crowd around the bridge and the creek. Curtis dipped his hand into the babbling water of the creek bed and ladled the cold liquid into his mouth. Prue stood alongside, her hands at her hips.

Brendan approached. "I noticed you travel unarmed, Outsider," he said with a cock of his eyebrow. "I respect a man or woman who fights with their bare hands, but you don't look the type."

Prue frowned, saying, "I hadn't really given much thought to it, actually. I thought maybe I could be some kind of nonviolent support, if that's okay with you."

"Very well," said Brendan. "You and Curtis, come up to the front of the column. I may well be able to use you to carry orders down the marching line."

When the soldiers had had their fill of the creek water, Brendan gave a quick, shrill whistle and the column fell back into position, weaving its way up the hillside just beyond the little bridge. Curtis and Prue jogged to the head of the line, Prue carefully pushing her bike by the handlebars, until they were just behind Brendan and Sterling the fox.

"How far till this place—what's it called?" asked Curtis after they'd topped the ridge.

Brendan monitored the column as it arrived above the switchbacks, motioning for the crowd to follow the crest of the ridge eastward. "The Ancients' Grove. Just east of here. An hour's march, maybe less."

Prue asked the next question: "What's the Ancients' Grove?"

"The site of a forgotten civilization," responded Sterling, falling in behind Prue and Curtis. "No one knows much about them. But it's believed that all of Wildwood was once a thriving metropolis, full of philosophers, farmers, and artists. It's said they perished centuries and centuries ago, a flourishing culture wiped out within the span of a few decades. Victims of a ruthless barbarian invasion."

Brendan, from ahead, grumbled, "I see where you're going with this, fox."

The fox ignored him. "The only remnant of this vast civilization, so advanced for its time, is this single grove of ruins that we are now marching on—and the descendants of the barbarian horde that extinguished it."

"Who'd that be?" asked Curtis.

"You're marching with them," said the fox. "These 'honorable' bandits."

"That's completely unproven," retorted Brendan. "And besides, who knows: Maybe those Ancients got what was coming to them."

"Believe what you will, hoodlum," said the fox. "Believe what you will."

There was a crackling in the surrounding vegetation that silenced the marchers, and the line seized at Brendan's frantic wave of an arm. He relaxed, however, when he saw it was Septimus the rat, scurrying out from under a thicket of ivy. Arriving at Brendan's feet, he shivered.

"Eegh," he said. "That stuff gives me the creeps."

"What's up, rat?" asked Brendan. "What have you seen?"

Septimus shook his head. "Blackberries. Blackberry brambles. As far as the eye can see. Just beyond that grove of alders there." He was winded from running and paused to catch his breath. "Impassable," he concluded.

Sure enough, as the long column of farmers and bandits made their way through a peaceful stand of tall alders, their leaves a kaleidoscope of yellow and green hues, they arrived at an impressive snarl of blackberry bushes that stretched like a wall in either direction, seemingly impregnable. Brendan cursed under his breath.

"Men!" he hollered to the line. "We'll have to cut our way through."

The army dove into the brambles headlong, their swords, scythes, and hacksaws a blinding flash of iron against the green of the bushes—but to no avail. The farther they were able to cut themselves into the dense thicket of briars, the more the bushes seemed to fall upon them, catching their uniforms and clothing in their sharp, clawlike thorns. Brendan finally pulled away, returning to the grove of trees. He'd hiked the sleeves of his tunic up to his elbows, and his forearms were laced with red scratches; a few leaves clung to his beard.

"Blast it all!" he swore. "I should've known this—it's been years since I'd been to the Grove. This must've seeded and grown in that time."

"Iphigenia," said Prue, remembering Iris, the young acolyte, and the braiding tuft of grass. "We should get Iphigenia."

Brendan looked at her askance. "What is she gonna do? Meditate them away?"

"Trust me," Prue said. "Just let me go get Iphigenia."

Brendan set his hands on his knees and briefly held his head down—sweat was pouring from his brow and glistening against the strange tattoo on his forehead. "Okay, Outsider," he said, adding, "But move quick. We're running out of time."

Prue engaged the kickstand on her bike and set off down the trail at a swift sprint. The line of soldiers extended back to the switchbacks leading down to the creek bed, and they all stared as she whipped by them. She cut the last few switchbacks in two short leaps and bolted over the small bridge to arrive at the cluster of caravan wagons that were laboring their way up the narrow path.

"Iphigenia!" she shouted, arriving at the first wagon.

A small door behind the driver's seat opened and the Elder Mystic's head peered out over the shoulder of the driver, a robed badger. "What's the matter?" she asked. "Why have we stopped?"

Prue paused to catch her breath from the sprint. "They need

you . . . ," she sputtered. "At the—at the top of the ridge."

"What's happened?" asked Iphigenia.

"Blackberry brambles," explained Prue. "We can't go any farther. I thought maybe you could, you know, ask them to move."

"What's the meaning of this?" asked Iphigenia when she arrived at the top of the ridge. "We are quickly running out of time. The sun is reaching its zenith."

"Apologies, madam," said Brendan, "but we've hit a snag. This bramble of berries is impassable—and to make our way around it would waylay us for far too long. The girl has suggested that you might be of some assistance in the matter."

Iphigenia harrumphed and stamped her foot beneath her flaxen robe. She stomped forward to take in the wall of brambles.

"This bramble has been here for many, many years—why did we not take a different path?" she asked.

Brendan reddened. "I was not aware that the bushes were here," he said, attempting a gentle diplomacy with the aged woman. "At least not in this *density*. I would've surely chosen a different path, but this is the only one afforded to us now, considering the time."

"Would you have your own camp, your bandit hideout, moved, torn apart and scattered, at the insistence of the . . . what . . . perhaps the trees?" asked Iphigenia unsympathetically, her hand waving toward the canopy of branches above them.

"I don't even know how to answer that question," responded Brendan.

Iphigenia glared at the King for a moment before capitulating. "Very well," she said. "I will ask the blackberries if they will move."

"What?" he asked, agog. "I'm not sure I heard you right. Did you say you were going to *ask* the brambles to move?"

"You heard right, Bandit King," was Iphigenia's response as she hiked up her robe and prepared to sit cross-legged on the forest floor. "I can only ask. I make no promises. If they deny this request, there's little I can do." She squinted sidelong at the tangle of vines before them. "Blackberries tend to be rather stubborn."

Brendan was speechless. He looked over at Sterling the fox and stared, searching for an explanation. Sterling lifted his shoulders in a shrug. Iphigenia, the dirty hem of her sackcloth robe gathered about her crossed ankles, sat on the ground and began to meditate. Curtis shot a questioning glance at Prue.

"Watch," Prue said quietly, confidently.

A calm breeze fluttered through the alder grove, scattering the mosaic of fallen leaves around the bent knees of the Elder Mystic. A brief sun break cast rays of golden light through the alder boughs, and Prue squinted to feel the warmth of the sun against her cheek. Iphigenia breathed deeply and loudly, the rhythm of her breaths providing an odd soundtrack to the late morning. Brendan, having suffered the quiet meditation session for a few minutes and borne witness to no results, made an angry curse below his breath and started to stalk off.

A gasp arose from the crowd of soldiers on the ridge.

The blackberries had begun to move.

They moved slowly at first—a few snags in the tangle of thorny vines separated, as if an unseen force was moving its way through the bramble—before picking up speed, and the bush disentangled itself from itself like the tentacles of some vast octopod. Where the vines were anchored to the earth by a rooted stalk, the capillary tendrils snaked to the ground and the bush widened, opening like a great, thistly flower. Before too long, the motion of this long horizon of brush came to a gentle stop, and a great thoroughfare had been laid through the deep grove of briars.

Iphigenia's loud breathing softened and ceased. She opened her eyes and, looking at the bramble, nodded a wordless thanks. She then stood up, with some difficulty, tottered over to Prue, and grasped her elbow for support. Brendan, standing at the edge of the tree grove, blanched.

"Now, Bandit King," said the Elder Mystic reproachfully, "if we can avoid such displacements in the future, I—and the forest—would greatly appreciate it."

🌿

The army walked quietly through the Grove, surrounded by the bone-white stone of the toppled columns and colonnades, this ancient city bearing silent witness to their every movement. Alexandra rode in the middle of the coyote host, the ocean of uniformed canine bodies spilling out into the clearing around her. The baby was asleep now, nestled against her chest, calmed into slumber by the gentle rocking of the horse's stride. The ivy made a deep bed of green here, suffocating nearly every other living thing in the vicinity; only the marble and stone ruins that jutted from its clutches seemed to defy the plant's supremacy in the Grove. Here was a wide slab of white, block-hewn stone—perhaps the foundation for a market square; there were the teetering remains of a columned archway, a central auditorium. On a squat ridge above the clearing stood the remnants of a long colonnade.

What a waste, thought Alexandra. So much knowledge, lost to the ages.

A soldier disrupted her reverie. He was a young coyote, barely older than a pup, and his gold-ornamented uniform hung loosely at his shoulders. "The Plinth, ma'am," he informed her. "Just ahead— above that little hill, in the ruined basilica. I've been instructed to tell you so."

"Thank you, Private," said the Governess, searching the horizon. "You've done well."

Here they were. The moment was close at hand. The sun was approaching its highest point. Soon it would be the noon hour. She could sense the *ivy seething below the horse's hooves. The dark green leaves and their little snaky fingers seemed to lick at her ankles.*

"Patience, my darlings," she whispered. "Patience."

🌿

The scout returned breathless. "The Grove," he finally spouted. "Just ahead! The coyotes have beaten us there—but just barely."

Brendan received the news silently. The army of bandits, Mystics, and farmers stood in wait. Behind them, the blackberry bramble had tangled itself back into its previous impassable shape when the last of the soldiers had made their way through; now the entire army had amassed in the shade of a vast collection of ancient fir and cedar trees. Between two of the tallest and thickest trees of this glade lay the first evidence that this had once been a tamed country: a single fluted column—not unlike the ones Prue envisioned littering the landscape of Rome and Athens—had toppled here, creating a bizarre contrast to the wildness of its surroundings. It was in the shadow of one of the column's shattered sections that Brendan gathered his captains together: Cormac, Sterling the fox, and Prue.

"Why am I here?" was Prue's first question.

"You'll be our messenger," explained Brendan. "A very important function."

"Okay," said Prue, leery. She was a little uncomfortable with the designation. People's lives were at stake here.

Brendan spoke quietly. "The Plinth is in the old basilica, in the center of the Grove. The basilica's made up of three separate levels—think three giant steps cut into the hillside. The Governess's army will be marching into the lowest level—it was some sort of gathering square. The third tier, nearest us, is the clearing where the Plinth is. We'll meet the coyote army at the middle tier. That's where we'll have our fight. That way, if we get pushed back, we can still defend the Plinth."

He looked each of the captains in the eye before continuing. "We split into three units," he explained. "Two flanking units and a spearhead. Cormac, you'll carve northward. Sterling, south. I'll lead the central unit from above, coming in from the west, across the third tier. You'll be positioned on either side of the middle tier, north and south. Move on my command. Hopefully, we'll be able to split their forces in half between the first and middle tier—where the Plinth is. In the end, though, we have one goal, and one goal only: keep the Governess from reaching the Plinth." He turned to Prue. "We'll be split apart—and communication will be of the utmost importance. This is where you come in, Prue. You'll need to relay information between the units. Is this clear?"

Prue nodded, desperately tamping down the fear that was beginning to rise from the depths of her belly. She wondered if her tennis shoes were up to the task. She'd wished she'd worn her cross-trainers, the bright pink ones her parents had bought her for her birthday. She'd abjectly refused to wear them, they were so ugly. That consideration seemed awfully petty now.

Brendan heaved a momentous sigh. "We've got about six hundred fighters. Against their one thousand. This won't be pretty. But if we can just keep that Plinth protected and stop the Governess from completing this ritual, any lives lost will not be in vain." The sun broke through its veil of clouds, and Brendan glared defiantly at its cast light.

"Now," he said.

With a sudden jump, he'd leapt to the top of the fallen piece of column and gave a low whistle to the awaiting crowd of soldiers.

"Men," he began. "Women. Animals, all."

The army of farmers and bandits murmured in acquiescence as they gathered around the speaker.

"Once, in these quiet groves," Brendan began in a resonant voice, "a great civilization thrived. A city of momentous proportion graced these grounds, full of life and thought. Today, it is no more. But its ruins stand as a stark reminder to those of us who have survived whatever ravages befell it—a reminder that nobody is safe from the machinations of those who, at any cost, wish to destroy the advances of brotherhood and civility."

He paused, surveying the crowd.

"Brother and sisters," he continued, "humans and animals.

Today, we forget whatever grievances we may have with one another in an effort to combat a greater evil, an evil that threatens to undo us all. Today, we are not the Wildwood bandits. Today, we are not the unassuming farmers of North Wood. Today, we march together. Today, we are all brothers and sisters. Today, let us together be the Wildwood Irregulars, six hundred strong, and let the mighty Wood strike fear into the hearts of anyone who dares stand in our way."

The crowd exploded into a cheer.

Prue walked back to Curtis, who was waiting along with the rest of the soldiers for their orders.

"What's happening?" he asked. "Why'd you get to go over there?"

"I'm the messenger," she said. "I'm supposed to run communications between the units."

"Ah," said Curtis, knowingly, "communications-ops."

Brendan, having jumped down from the fallen column, began disseminating orders to the gathered soldiers. He split the large crowd of soldiers into three sections; Curtis was placed in Sterling's unit. While the soldiers were receiving their marching orders, Curtis walked over to Prue.

"So this might be it," he said dolefully, holding out his hand.

Prue shook it. "Yep."

The host around them began to take shape under the direction of their captains: What had been a single, milling crowd became three taut blocks of eager soldiers, their ragtag display of weaponry brandished at the ready. The two outside blocks peeled away from the central one and began to make their way to either side of the Grove ahead. Curtis watched his troop on the move and quickly turned back to Prue.

"If I don't see you again," he said, "maybe you'll just let my parents know that I did this for a good reason; that, at the very end, I was truly, truly happy? I mean, I really found someplace where I felt I belonged. Will you tell them that?"

Prue felt tears rise in her eyes. "Oh, Curtis," she said, "you can tell them that yourself."

"It's been nice knowing you, Prue McKeel. For real." His eyes began to water, and he ran his uniform sleeve across his nose.

Prue leaned over and kissed him on the cheek. His show of emotion made it easier, somehow, for her to forget her own fear. "Likewise, Curtis," she said.

He sniffled back a tear. "Bye, Prue," he said, and jogged away to join his troop.

Prue stood watching the column of soldiers disappear into the thick of the forest. When they'd gone, she turned and saw Iphigenia emerge from one of the caravan wagons and wave her over.

"Stay with me, dear," she said, "until you are needed."

Prue climbed aboard the carriage, sitting down next to the Elder

Mystic on the driver's bench. She was attempting a half smile when the dam broke on her emotions and she began sobbing. Warm tears poured down her cheek; she could taste their saltiness on her lips. Iphigenia, surprised, began rubbing her back.

"There, there," she said, consolingly. "Why the tears?"

"I don't know," babbled Prue through her sobs. "This is just all so overwhelming. Just to get my brother back. I mean, me just being here. I feel like everyone I come in contact with, I'm ruining their lives."

"You needn't wear it all on your shoulders. Bigger events are in play, my dear," Iphigenia said, "far bigger than you. Your brother's disappearance was merely the catalyst to a long chain of events that has been waiting to tumble since the first seedling sprouted in this forest. You had as much control over your own involvement in these events as a leaf does in the time of its falling. We must only follow, we must only follow."

Prue sniffed and carefully wiped a few tears from her cheek with the sleeve of her hoodie. "But if I hadn't come here—or—or," stammered Prue, "if my parents had never made their deal with Alexandra and I was never born—we wouldn't be here! All these sweet people and animals wouldn't be putting their lives at risk."

"There's as much benefit to wishing the world away as there is in demanding a bud to bloom," responded Iphigenia as she patted Prue's hand gently. "It's better to live *presently*. By living thus, perhaps we can learn to understand the nature of this fragile coexistence we share with the world around us."

Prue straightened in her seat and tried to gain control of her feelings. The Mystic's words, while being comforting in their way, seemed to open up a greater mystery. "Where will you be in all this?" she asked.

"I will stay behind," explained Iphigenia, "My order decrees this. I will sit in meditation until the battle has ceased. The victor will be clear; the forest will inform me of this. If the Governess prevails, and the ivy is let loose, then I will simply become a part of the forest. To me, this is not a horrible fate. It is an inevitability."

Prue squinted at the Mystic, puzzling at the peaceful resignation in her face. If she were to spend more time with the old woman, she was going to *have* to get used to the Mystic's sometimes startling frankness.

In the wide glade, Brendan waited for the two flanking units to depart. He spent the time sizing up his troop; satisfied that enough time had passed, he jogged over to where Prue sat.

"It's time," he said. "I'll need you by my side."

Prue nodded and hopped down from the carriage, swallowing her remaining tears. She gave a final look to Iphigenia, smiling, before turning to walk toward the waiting soldiers.

Something made the Dowager Governess pause as she slowly walked her horse through the ankle-deep banks of ivy that blanketed this ancient ruin. A thought, like a mild warm breeze on a cold day that dissipates as soon as it's arrived, fell over her. A suspicion. A hitch of unease.

But why, she thought, in this moment of my victory, this moment of fruition?

It had been so easy.

There had been no resistance.

And yet, she'd felt something. Something deep in her bones. Something whispered among the trees, perhaps, a quiet murmur from plant to plant. As if the forest was intending to rise up against her.

She laughed the thought away. Even the North Wood Mystics, in all their power, could not bring the forest, this lawless cosmos of greenery, to their side.

The baby was waking. She looked down at him and cooed. He smiled in response, wiping the sleep from his eyes with two balled fists. He blinked at the brightness of the sun, the sun that had nearly climbed to its highest point in the sky.

That was when the forest broke open.

Brendan was the first to give the command.

"Center column," he began.

Prue stood at his side as they looked over the embankment at the oncoming horde of coyote soldiers, the tall, implacable figure of the Dowager Governess astride her horse in the center of the multitude.

In her arms was a swaddled baby.

My brother! My baby brother! The thought blocked all others from Prue's mind. She fought the urge to scream his name.

"Attack," Brendan finished levelly.

The conjoined army of the bandits and the North Wood farmers, the Wildwood Irregulars, broke through the line of trees above the ruined center of the ancient city, and the eerie silence of the ivy-strewn clearing was instantly shattered by their full-throated, impassioned voices.

※

Prue saw Alexandra's horse rear in surprise, nearly bucking its rider from her saddle, and screamed.

"MAC!" she cried, giving in to her instincts. Her heart surged with protectiveness for her baby brother.

The spearhead, the center column of the Wildwood Irregulars, led by the copper-haired Bandit King, descended the hillside like a great wall of water being released from a dam and crashed into the unsuspecting army of coyotes with a loud explosion of sound: bodies colliding, iron clashing. Their battle cries, yelps, and howls erupted into the air and echoed off the marble stone of

the ruined city. The coyote fusiliers had been caught off guard, their muskets unloaded, and they were forced to defend themselves by bayonet. Even the coyote swordsmen had to struggle with their sheathed swords in the chaos of this initial melee, gaining the Irregulars an acute tactical advantage until the coyotes were able to wrest themselves free of combat long enough to draw their weapons.

Alexandra wheeled her horse in the middle of the throng and, kicking his flank, shot past a pair of dueling soldiers to arrive at a safe distance on a stone platform. There, she took the baby in her hands and placed him, upright, in a saddlebag. His pink face peered out from the top of the leather bag; Alexandra took hold of the reins with one hand and drew her long, silvery blade with the other.

"Coyotes!" she hollered. "Attack!"

A wave of coyote reinforcements crested the hill into the bowl of the clearing, smashing headlong into the crowd of warring soldiers with a loud crash. They had come prepared, their sabers flashing amid the tight scrum. A long line of fusiliers appeared behind them and began packing their musket barrels with powder and ball. The Irregulars, despite their earlier advantage, appeared to be losing ground.

"Prue!" came a voice from below the ridge where she was positioned. It was Brendan. He'd run halfway up the hillside and was carefully engaged in a delicate swordfight with a particularly large coyote soldier.

"Yes?" she called.

"Get to Sterling's unit!" he shouted over his shoulder between saber clashes. "Tell them to move in!"

"Got it!" yelled Prue, and she leapt up from her crouched position.

🌿

The soldiers, huddled as they were in the deep green carpet of ivy, heard the telltale sounds of the battle cresting the ridge. Curtis winced at the shouting voices, the sound of clashing steel, and the *crack* of gunfire. His heart started racing in his chest. Sterling lay sidelong against the sloped ground, listening to these first salvos of war, his eyes flickering with anticipation.

"Blast it all," he muttered. "Why don't we just attack?"

The sound of footsteps in the underbrush eclipsed the distant noises of the battle.

"Prue!" shouted Curtis, seeing his friend approach at a sprint. She was crouched low as she ran, and her clothes were decorated with fallen leaves and strands of spiderweb.

Sterling jumped up to meet her. "What's the word?" he asked frantically, as she slid into the underbrush beside the gathered soldiers.

"Go," she said, fighting for her breath. "Brendan says to move in."

A glow erupted in the fox's eye. "Finally," he said. He turned to the two hundred men, women, and animals that lay hunkered down behind him and said, "Let's move."

Prue and Curtis shared a quiet glance before the soldiers on the hillside, with a great collective holler, leapt up from their positions and stormed the crest of the ridge.

Good luck, Prue mouthed as Curtis was carried by the wave of soldiers over the ridge and into the battle below.

CHAPTER 26

The Wildwood Irregulars;
A Name to Conjure With

At the fox's instruction, Curtis, along with the archers and riflemen, after scrambling to the top of the ridge, held their positions behind the charging unit at the higher ground above the bowl of the clearing. He watched as the rest of the Irregulars tore into the heated melee below. A black bear wielding a threshing flail was laying into the tide of coyotes with a surprising enthusiasm, a wide swale of unconscious coyotes littering his wake. A bandit, armed with two short sabers, was engaged in a fierce skirmish with a coyote swordsman; the coyote seemed to be getting the better of the bandit until Curtis saw a rabbit, his haunches covered in blue denim, snaking between the feet of the coyote, stretching a tangled web of twine. Before the coyote had any idea what was happening, the twine cinched at his ankles and he went crashing down to the earth in mid sword thrust. The figure of the Dowager Governess, astride her horse, towered over the warring hordes, and she laid an impressive swath of destruction wherever she leapt her horse: bandits and farmers fell at the flashing steel of her long sword. Every attempt to unhorse her seemed to fail; her skill at swordplay was clearly unparalleled in this field of battle. Curtis watched her with rapt fascination as she made her way through the crowd, her eyes set on the far staircase that would lead to the third tier of the basilica: the clearing where the Plinth lay. A barked instruction woke him from his spellbound stare—Samuel the hare stood at the end of the line of soldiers on the ridge and made his command: "Long-range fighters, ready your weapons!" Curtis dropped a large stone into the cradle of his sling.

A loud whistle emanated from the midst of the combat below; it appeared to come from Alexandra, her fingers poised between her lips. Within an instant, a deafening sound of screeching tore through the air, and the sliver of sky to the east of the clearing was blotted by a throng of jet-black birds.

"The crows," Curtis, whispered to himself in awe.

Samuel seemed to be in the grip of the sight as well—the scores of these flying birds like spatters of ink against the tree line as they dove down into the skirmishers below—but finally returned his attention to his charge. "FIRE!" he shouted.

The ridge came alive with the *crack* of gunfire and the *swish* of arrows. Curtis let fly the rock from his sling and watched it arc lazily toward his intended target. He was dismayed to see it fall well short of its mark, lost in the ocean of ivy that carpeted the ground of the clearing.

A bandit standing next to him, repacking the barrel of his musket, saw the shot. "Swing harder," he suggested. "Put more arm into it."

"Yeah, okay," Curtis said as he grabbed another rock from his pocket.

A few crows had fallen during this barrage, but more arrived to take the place of their fallen kin—a dark cloud of birds funneled up the wide valley from the first tier of the basilica. The clearing was awash in the noise of clanging steel and the warlike shouts of the combatants.

Prue watched briefly as the fox's battalion made their charge over the ridge into the wide valley below before she turned and ran back to her station—at the little stand of trees that stood between the middle and upper tiers of the open-air basilica. The valley in which the ruin sat was masked by the hill of ivy and trees, and as she ran back up the ridge, she had to roughly gauge where her initial position had been. Guessing at a break in the trees, she dove through the underbrush at the crest of the ridge and, losing her footing, tumbled down the hillside, her fall softened by the rich bed of ivy. Standing up to brush herself off, she saw the Plinth standing in the center of a clearing, its fluted base covered by fresh shoots of ivy vines. She began to walk toward it—she wanted to touch it, to feel the cold, austere stone—but was reminded of Brendan's instructions when the sound of a thousand screeching crows sounded beyond the wall of trees.

She ran to her previous position, behind a squat stand of salmonberry bushes, and looked down at the heated battle below. She watched, aghast, at the teeming murder upon murder of black crows as they wheeled over the clearing.

Brendan, flanked by two bandits, stood on the bottom step of the wide stone flight of stairs that led up the slope to the top tier of the basilica. The three bandits were in a bitter struggle with an ever-growing crowd of coyote swordsmen. Brendan and the bandit to his right stood with their sabers flying, desperately holding the coyotes at bay, while the bandit to his left busily crammed ammunition into the muzzle of his rifle. While Prue watched, Brendan gave a swift kick to the chest of one coyote assaulter while shoving another away with the flat of his saber blade. Given a moment's respite, he glanced back to see Prue ducking her head out from behind her covert.

"Good job!" he cried, leaping backward, step by step, up the flight of stairs. "Now quick: Get to Cormac's unit. I want them to come down the ridge, regroup in the lower tier, and sweep up the slope from the east. Catch them in the rear flank. Is that clear?"

"Got it," she said, preparing to run.

Brendan wiped a streak of blood from his brow. His beard was clumped with perspiration. "If we can hold them a little longer," he said, eyeing the field of battle, "I can maybe get to the Dowager. But I'll need those reinforcements to set up the distraction." Prue dove off into the brush. The ivy was impossibly dense here, in the space between the middle and upper tiers, and Prue's sprint was hampered by the vines—but she made it to the far ridge in a matter of minutes. Before she knew it, she was tearing down the lee side of the ridge, the low-hanging tree branches lashing at her face and hands. Farther down the slope, the third unit of the Wildwood Irregulars lay in wait.

"What's happening? Are we to attack?" asked Cormac frantically, when Prue came to a sliding stop amid the waiting bandits and farmers. His was the last unit to receive instruction, and Prue could tell that he was desperate to join the fray. The sounds emanating from the valley beyond the little ridge came loud and fierce.

"He wants you to head down the ridgeline," she said, battling for breath. "Regroup in the lower clearing. And then come up from behind."

Cormac looked at her blankly. "How do we know we won't be surrounded once we're there? Does he know how many soldiers remain in the lower tier?"

Prue raised her hands apologetically. She could read the fear in the bandit's face. "That's what he said to do. He seems to have a plan."

"Very well," said Cormac gravely, turning to the gathered soldiers under his command. "Down the ridge, lads. We're to fall in from the rear."

Ducking low, the third-unit Irregulars jogged down the line of the ridge while the sounds of battle receded behind them. When they'd traveled far enough, Cormac instructed them to hold tight while he crawled up to the top of the ridge and looked over the lip. Prue waited with the rest of the unit, hearing their quiet, steady breathing and the sound of their weapons—iron, wood, and stone—as they turned them over, antsy, in their hands and paws.

Cormac returned from the ridge. His face was pale and serious.

"There's a whole army down there," he said stonily. "Waiting to funnel up those stairs to the second tier." He looked over at Prue. "It's an impossible feat."

"What do you want me to do?" Prue asked, searching the bandit's worn face for an answer.

"Nothing," said Cormac finally, shaking his head. "Tell the King we done what he told us. Tell him there are four hundred more in the lower clearing. There's a line of heavy artillery—I'd say twelve cannon—just about up the slope. They'll need to contend with that. As for us, we'll do our best."

Turning back to the gathered soldiers, Cormac gave his orders. "Over the top, lads," he said, and, with a great yell, the third-unit Irregulars crested the top of the ridge and ran howling down the far side. Prue remained in the protection of the low ridge for a time, listening to the cries of the soldiers and the loud baying of the coyote army they engaged, before she took a deep breath and went running back through the bracken, up the line of the ridge.

Arriving back at the stone steps above the middle clearing, Prue was surprised to see that Brendan had left his prior position on the stairs. Momentarily panicked that he'd been struck down, she crouched low and crawled to the head of the steps and looked out over the tumult of the warring armies in the wide square. She could see Alexandra in the center of the crowded melee, her sword making wide arcs over the heads of her embattled soldiers. Mac's face, flushed and distorted in a terrified fit of crying, peered out from the horse's saddlebag. A tight ring of protective coyote grunts had made a circle around Alexandra as she slowly attempted to wade her way through the crowd. Occasionally, a squadron of crows would dive-bomb into the chaotic multitude and return to the air, a farmer's pitchfork or a bandit's saber clutched in their talons. Suddenly, Prue caught sight of Brendan's crown of vines in the midst of the crowd; he'd forced his way closer to

Alexandra and her guard of soldiers.

"Brendan!" Prue shouted.

It was impossible to raise her voice above the deafening clamor of the battle.

"BRENDAN!" she hollered again.

She saw him hesitate in his violent slog through the crowd. He searched the air for the source of the voice. She stood up and waved her arms in the air.

"CANNONS!" she shouted, pointing to the place where the ground sloped away to the basilica's first clearing. "THEY'RE MOVING IN CANNONS!"

He furrowed his brow, confused.

She pointed again to the far slope, this time with as much animation as she could muster. He looked where she pointed in time to see the great black muzzles of the dozen cannons crest the ridge. His face dropped.

🌱

Curtis was the first to see the cannons, their four-coyote artillery teams laboring to push the massive guns up the slope of the hill. There must have been more than ten of them, all lined up along the lip of the clearing, and he was disturbed to see the artillery crews, once they'd set the cannons in position, swivel them to point at the line of archers and fusiliers who manned the ridge he currently stood on.

"Samuel!" he screamed, not taking his eyes from the line of cannon.

"What?" called Samuel, his musket raised to his eye as he took aim at the crowd in the middle of the clearing.

"Cannons!" said Curtis, pointing to the artillery.

Samuel dropped his musket to his side and stared. He gulped. "Hold your line, boys."

"Are you kidding me?" asked Curtis.

"Hold the line," repeated Samuel as he hefted the musket back to his shoulder, this time aiming at the artillery teams as they began to load the cannons. "Let's see if we can't take some of 'em out before they get a shot."

The line of archers and fusiliers turned and aimed into the row of coyote artillery and fired, the ridge exploding with gun smoke and rifle fire. Curtis looked to see several coyote artillery officers fall, only to be replaced by reinforcements from the slope behind them. While the Irregulars reloaded, shoving muskets full of powder or pulling arrows from their quivers, the coyote artillery completed their task and let fire the cannons.

The world erupted around Curtis.

The explosion instantly silenced the noise of the warring armies, and Curtis's hearing was reduced to a single high-pitched whine. The ground below his feet seemed to fall away, and he was showered in a wild spray of earth as he fell back, tumbling into a seemingly endless, bottomless void.

🌿

Prue screamed to see the cannon fire rip into the ridge of archers and riflemen, knowing that Curtis had been positioned there. The ridge had practically disintegrated under the awesome power of the artillery, leaving a wide slope of craters where the leafy hillside had once been. The displaced soil from the barrage rained down on the warring armies in the square. What was left of the ridge was empty of its prior occupants.

In the middle of the tumultuous crowd of fighters, Prue saw Brendan, his saber swinging in a wild circle around his head. Having witnessed the dizzying spectacle and the devastation that the line of cannon had wrought, he gave a long, defiant whoop before diving back into battle.

As the coyote artillery team prepped their guns for another fusillade, a fresh wave of coyote infantry came roaring up the slope from the lower tier. Prue watched in despair, understanding the implication of this new assault: that Cormac's unit had been unable to hold back the reinforcements. Like a basin overfilled with water, the bowl of the clearing could not contain the amount of bodies it was now carrying, and the fighting was forced up onto the adjacent hillsides as the vastly dominant coyote army began their systematic routing of the Wildwood Irregulars.

❧

Curtis emerged from unconsciousness to the thunderous sound of a million pounding footsteps all around his ears. His hearing was still impaired; the world sounded as if it were veiled in a thick fog. He was half-buried in earth and, as he took in his surroundings, he realized that he had awoken some twenty feet away from where he'd initially lost consciousness. The footsteps, he quickly gauged, were of the conjoined forces of the coyotes and the Irregular infantry, the fighting having been forced over the cannonball-cratered ridge. Curtis, gaining his bearings, covered his head with his arm in an effort to avoid being trampled. Protecting himself thus, he began crawling away from the throng of fighters, toward a little thicket of plum trees.

He'd no sooner arrived in the safety of the trees than he heard a *click* behind him, the distinctive noise of a pistol's hammer being engaged. He turned slowly, still on his hands and knees, to see a coyote sergeant, his uniform stained with dirt and blood, standing over him, his pistol cocked and at the ready.

"Hello there, turncoat," said the coyote, immediately recognizing Curtis from his time in the warren. "This is a pleasant surprise." He grinned, his face carved from jowl to jowl by a string of long yellow teeth. He held the pistol jauntily in his paw, prolonging the moment. "I'm going to enjoy this. I'm going to enjoy this very much." He paused and scratched his snout with the muzzle of the gun. "Might be a promotion in it for me—I'll be a decorated war hero. Sergei, turncoat slayer. That's what they'll call me."

"Please," said Curtis, backing up against the trunk of a tree. "Let's talk this through. You don't need to do this."

"Oh, but I do," corrected the sergeant. "I really, really do." He held the pistol at arm's length, carefully taking aim at Curtis.

Curtis squeezed his eyes shut, waiting for the shot.

Plonk.

The noise came suddenly, and Curtis quickly opened his eyes. Another *plonk*. The coyote, his pistol still outstretched, was being assaulted from above by plums.

"What the devil?" shouted the coyote, searching the branches of the plum tree. The snout of a rat appeared from behind a curtain of yellow leaves.

"Hey, mutt!" cried the rat. Curtis saw that it was Septimus. "Up here!"

The coyote, enraged, had lifted the pistol and was beginning to take aim at Septimus when Curtis spied his chance. He leapt from the ground and bowled into the coyote sergeant with all the force he could muster. His head connected with the coyote's belly, and Curtis could feel it deflate like a balloon, the air escaping through the coyote's mouth with a loud *"Oof!"* The coyote crumpled at the force, and the two of them went tumbling to the ground. Curtis reached for the pistol, and the coyote, regaining his senses, struggled to keep the gun from his attacker. Finally, in the chaos, Curtis was able to get his hands cupped over the coyote's grip on the pistol handle and began trying to wrest it away. The coyote began kicking his hind paws into Curtis's stomach, and he could feel the claws scratching painful scores across the skin under his uniform. The coyote, above him now, yelped in frustration as he tried to regain control of the gun. Curtis pulled it toward him, the cool metal of the barrel pressing up against his cheek.

BANG!

Curtis flinched. Had the pistol gone off in his hand? Had he been shot?

The coyote's strong grip on the pistol loosened, and his paws fell away. Curtis saw that his eyes had rolled back in his head and his tongue lolled out of his mouth like a fat slug. The coyote collapsed, lifeless, on top of Curtis.

Shoving the sergeant's body aside, Curtis jumped up and looked around him. He was surprised to see Aisling standing not far off, a little wisp of smoke drifting up from the muzzle of her pistol. She wore a shocked look on her face.

"I—" she stammered, "I—I hadn't—I hadn't used it yet."

A whistle sounded from the plum tree boughs. "And not a moment too soon," complimented Septimus.

Curtis, sympathetic to the girl's shock, walked over to her and took her hand. "Thank you," he said. "I don't know what would've happened."

Aisling forced a smile. "Well, there you go," she said. "Good thing you gave me this."

The clamor of the fighting behind them arrested them from their conversation, and they gave each other a final, fleeting look before Curtis ran back into the battle. Aisling remained, motionless, in the Grove, looking down at the pistol in her hand.

⚝

The tide had clearly turned for the worse. Prue stood on the top stair of the ancient steps, staring out over the clearing as the coyote reinforcements poured in from the far side. She'd seen a small wave of Cormac's unit appear at the lip of this slope, being pressed backward by the crush of coyote soldiers. Before long they were forced into the middle tier and were reunited with Brendan's unit, though both troops had been badly diminished. The Wildwood Irregulars appeared to be hopelessly separated, with the conjoined soldiers of Brendan's and Cormac's units surrounded in the bowl of the middle tier and the remnants of Sterling's troop having been chased over the edge of the south ridge.

The Governess, seizing her moment, began careening her horse across the sea of bodies toward the steps that led to the upper clearing. Brendan saw her move and yelled something at the few bandits who fought at his side; they, together, began fighting their way toward Alexandra's intended path.

Prue didn't see how it happened—the action in the clearing was much too fast and chaotic to see clearly—but in the few seconds between Brendan's sighting of Alexandra and his arrival at the spot in front of her horse, a shot had been fired from somewhere far off.

Prue couldn't tell if it had been a coyote sharpshooter, lodged in a tree somewhere, or perhaps a misfire from a fellow Irregular, but its object was clear: Brendan's head flew back in an agonized yell and he fell away from the charging horse, a bright splash of red suddenly appearing on the shoulder of his white shirt.

Seeing the Bandit King struck low, the surrounding soldiers, human and coyote alike, paused in their fighting to watch him stumble backward and fall to the ground. The bandits howled in anger and despair, but no sooner were they able to bear witness to the King's wounds than a fresh wave of coyote soldiers fell on them, and they leapt with a renewed ferocity back into battle. Brendan, abandoned, lay in the trampled ivy vines of the clearing floor, his fingers clutching at his shoulder.

"NO!" shouted Prue, and without thinking, she dove down the marble steps into the horde of battling soldiers.

In the frenzy of the battle, she was able to slip through relatively unnoticed. One coyote grunt, having dispatched his opponent, spotted her as she made her way toward Brendan and dove to intercept her. He was stopped short when one of the Irregulars, a stoat in coveralls, swung the iron blade of a shovel in front of him and the two fell into fierce combat. Another coyote turned to see her as she crawled between the backs of two battling soldiers, and aimed the long barrel of his rifle at her; an arrow *thunk*ed into his chest and he fell, yelping, to the ground.

Brendan was crawling helplessly across the ivy-strewn stone of the clearing when Prue finally arrived at his side. He'd made little distance; the green leaves of the ivy were spattered with his blood, making a dotted trail of crimson red behind him.

"Brendan!" she shouted, grasping for his arm.

He turned his face to her. His eyes were glassy and his beard was matted with dirt, sweat, and blood. His white shirt was now soaked red, and his hale coloring was slowly disappearing from the skin of his face.

"Outsider," he croaked, his cracked lips forced apart in a wry smile. "Sweet girl." He glanced over at the wound in his shoulder and spat angrily on the ground. "Fifteen generations of bandits," he said. "Fifteen kings. And I'm felled by a cursed gunshot." He looked back at Prue. "I don't want to die," he said, his face soft and quieted. "I want to keep here. Help me keep here."

Prue, her face streaming with tears, tore her hoodie off and packed the cotton fabric against the flow of blood from his shoulder. The green of the hoodie turned brown as the cloth became soaked in the blood.

"You'll be okay, King," said Prue. "We've just got to stop this bleeding."

Desperately scanning the clash of the battle behind them, Prue searched the crowd for another bandit who might be able to help; her first aid knowledge was woefully little. "Help!" she cried.

"The King! He's been shot!"

Suddenly, a long shadow fell over Prue and the prone form of the Bandit King. Prue squinted upward to see Alexandra, steeple-tall in the saddle of her black stallion as the horse reared dramatically, his forelegs sending up a spray of earth. Her sword was drawn, and she held it above her head, the blade wet with blood. The baby in her saddlebag wailed.

"Your time is over, Bandit King," she said. "A new era in Wildwood has begun."

Without a further word, she spurred the flanks of her horse and vaulted over the two of them, Prue and Brendan, in a single leap, galloping toward the unguarded marble stairs that led to the ruined basilica's upper tier.

C H A P T E R   2 7

The Ivy and the Plinth

The tattered and disjointed remains of Sterling's troop were easily corralled down the slope of the hill away from the basilica, though many continued to fire quick, errant shots back into the horde of pursuing coyotes as they went. Those who survived the routing found cover on a wide granite promontory built atop a large pile of massive boulders. The ruins of a felled tower were here; only the foundation remained. As Curtis sprinted toward this refuge, ducking a fresh hail of gunfire from the coyote fusiliers, he saw Sterling, waving him forward.

"Come on!" he cried. "Quickly!"

He shot up the broken staircase and threw himself down on the stone floor of the promontory. A short rock wall, the scant remnant of the ancient foundation, made a kind of low palisade around the edge, and it was behind this that the small troop of Irregulars found cover. Behind the promontory, the ground fell away to a deep ravine.

Curtis crawled to the wall and peeked out over the top. The sloping hillside was awash with coyote soldiers, a seemingly endless supply pouring down from the ridge above. The promontory held around fifty bandits and farmers, sitting with their backs pressed to the wall. They took turns popping up over the edge of the wall and firing into the onslaught of coyotes. The close air was sharp with the smell of sweat and gunpowder. A bandit, his leg badly wounded, was being comforted by a fellow soldier in the corner of the foundation. The grime-streaked faces Curtis saw inside the low walls of the ruined building were sorrow-laden, the troop desperately demoralized.

The approaching coyotes heeded their captains' orders and dug in behind whatever cover was available to them in the terraced sculpture garden. Their numbers grew and grew as more reinforcements, freed from the fighting in the basilica, joined their compatriots on the hillside. The tree branches became leaden with the weight of the scores of black crows, watching the scene play out from above.

One of the coyote captains stuck his head from behind his cover and cried out, "You're surrounded! Give yourselves up! There's nowhere for you to go!"

Sterling, his back against the edge of the wall next to the staircase, eyed the huddled group of farmers and bandits. "Well, folks," he said. "It's come down to this." He paused his clawed fingers working over the handle of his pruning shears. "I don't blame you if you want to give yourselves up. Any man, woman, or animal who wants to do that, I suggest you go now."

No one moved. The distant sound of gunfire could be heard up over the ridge.

Sterling nodded. "All right then," he said. "Unto the breach, it is."

The gathered remnants of the Wildwood Irregulars nodded in agreement.

The fox took a deep breath. "On my mark," he said. "One . . . two . . ."

🌿

"My King!" shouted a voice from behind Prue; she turned to see a bandit sprinting to their side from among the clashing soldiers in the basin of the clearing. Prue had Brendan's head cradled in her lap, and she was using all the strength she could conjure to hold the blood-soaked hoodie to the fallen Bandit King's deep wound. "What happened?" asked the bandit frantically.

"A shot—I don't know where from," Prue sputtered. "A bullet. In his shoulder." She peeled her jacket away to reveal the torn fabric of his shirt, saturated with blood, clinging to the skin of his chest.

The bandit grimaced. "Hold on," he said. He reached into a leather bag at his hip and pulled out a little tincture bottle. Dripping a few droplets of a hazel-brown liquid onto a clutch of torn ivy leaves, he packed the poultice against Brendan's shoulder, using Prue's sweatshirt as a secondary bandage. Brendan winced when the liquid came in contact with the open wound, and the bandit grabbed his hand and gripped it.

"Breathe into the pain, Brendan," the bandit said calmly. The battle still raged behind them. He looked up at Prue. "Erigeron cinnamon," he explained. "Strong stuff. It should help stop the bleeding." Brendan's eyes were fluttering as he battled to stay conscious against the rush of pain.

"I've got to go," said Prue. "Stay with him?" She knew that Alexandra would be moving on the Plinth. There was no one left to stop her.

The bandit nodded and Prue jumped up, running for the stone staircase to the third tier of the basilica.

She leapt the stairs, two at a go, until she'd made the top of the slope and her feet met the tangled carpet of ivy. In the middle of the clearing, Alexandra was dismounting from her horse and pulling the wailing baby from the leather saddlebag. The Plinth, its base all snaked with ivy, stood in the center of the square. Prue stood at the top of the stairs and opened her mouth to scream.

"Alexandra!"

The voice had not been hers. Instead, it came from the other side of the clearing. Prue, her mouth clapping closed, stared across the wide ivy-strewn plaza to see Iphigenia, the Elder Mystic, making her way through the dense ground cover toward the Governess.

"Put the baby down," she demanded.

The Governess stifled a laugh.

"Iphigenia," she said archly. "Dear Iphigenia. I should've known that your hand was in this little bagatelle you set for my armies—those poor farmers you've sent to their deaths. Well, you've arrived just in time. The ceremony will soon be complete."

"You will only mark yourself as a murderess," said Iphigenia flatly.

"I am freeing a natural force from its imposed slumber," replied Alexandra. "Allowing it to once again assume its prior dominance in the wild world. To a godless naturalist such as yourself, this must seem a real setting to rights."

"It will consume you when it's finished tearing down every tree in the forest; don't think you're immune. And the coyotes, that innocent species you've conscripted, do they know the true consequences? Have you told them that their warrens will be invaded and their waiting broods, their wives and pups, will be smothered?"

"Pish," dismissed the Governess. "Those hapless dogs? The

illusion of power is manna enough for them. I've given them more in the last fifteen years than they've ever enjoyed in the history of their breed. When they are extinguished, at least they'll die an elevated species. As for me, I wouldn't concern yourself with my outcome. I'll have slept the ivy long before it can get its vines around me."

Iphigenia frowned, her face set with worry. "Don't assume it's so easy to control. Once you've started this wheel in motion, there's no stopping."

The Governess laughed. "Can I assume that I have your sanction, then, to continue? Or are you going to keep distracting me from the task at hand?"

The Mystic spoke, but Prue couldn't make out the words. It was something intoned to herself, as if she were assuring herself of her own beliefs. The Governess looked at her askance, before striding the short distance to the waiting Plinth. With her free hand, she drew a long dagger from her belt. Prue, desperate, jumped forward.

"Please, Alexandra!" she cried. "Don't do this!"

Alexandra stopped and looked over at Prue. She flared her eyes. "Please, if you don't mind," she said, "I hadn't expected an audience to this. This is a great moment for me. I'd like it to not be ruined by the miserable mewlings of a little girl and an old woman."

"That's my brother you've got there," said Prue. "That's my

parents' only son. You don't know how much it would break their hearts."

"Then they shouldn't have made the deal," replied Alexandra. "They were foolish, those Outsiders, but they certainly knew what they wanted. They wanted *you*." Here the Dowager Governess pointed the knife at Prue. "And so they got *you*. Congratulations. You were born. I held up my side of the bargain. Come to think of it, if anyone is truly responsible for your brother's death and your parents' heartbreak, it's you. Your very existence, your parents' *need* for your existence, is the true root of this entire debacle. I'm merely a player in the drama." She moved a few more feet toward the Plinth; she was now within a few yards.

"Would you have fed Alexei to the ivy in order to assume such power?" This came from Iphigenia, her voice firm.

The Governess froze.

"Would you?" pressed the Elder Mystic. "He was a baby once, I'm sure you recall. Such a beautiful child, that one."

The color rose in Alexandra's pale face, and she turned angrily toward Iphigenia. "I told you, *old woman*, not to distract me from my purpose. You both are becoming very irritating."

"Poor Alexei," said Iphigenia. "Not even your magics could bring him back into the world of the living."

"But I did!" shouted Alexandra, her temper finally piqued. "I gave him life. *Twice*. I'd breathed life into that body once, why not a

507

second time? Why should that be any different? It was his choice to die the second time. He could not appreciate the labor that *I*"—she pounded the hilt of the dagger against her chest—"that *I* underwent to give him new life. Each time. My idiot nephew and his underlings gave him his second death; they killed him and then they used his death as a motive to throw me from power. And so they will pay. They will pay with their lives. And their families' lives." The Governess regained her composure, her dagger at the ready. Mac was still crying in her arms, his face a deep red. "It's really that simple."

Prue, unmoored from her fears, leapt forward at a sprint and dove into the space between Alexandra and the Plinth, pressing her back against the cold stone of the short edifice. "Stop!" she yelled.

Rage distorted Alexandra's porcelain features. She whipped the dagger in a clean arc across her body, slapping Prue on the cheek with the flat of the blade. The force of the blow sent Prue cartwheeling sideways into the plush tangle of the ivy. A sharp flush of pain burned at her cheek; a trickle of blood wet her lip.

"Do *not*," Alexandra said forcefully, "do *not* keep me from my task."

The sun had reached its zenith. It was noon. Prue could feel the ivy moving, slowly, underneath her.

☙

". . . three," intoned the fox.

The ragtag remnants of the Wildwood Irregulars on the stone

outcrop let out a collective howl and leapt up from their concealed position behind the low stone wall.

A barrage of bullets and gunpowder filled the air as they began this final assault.

Curtis whipped his saber from his scabbard and went bounding down the flight of stairs with a terrific holler.

The wall of coyote soldiers before them stood up from their cover and took aim at the advancing soldiers.

The crows in the neighboring trees launched from their perches and dove toward the fray.

A bandit sprinting next to Curtis took a bullet in his chest and fell back in a spray of dirt.

Another farmer tumbled to the ground, an arrow lodged in his furry gullet.

Curtis braced himself as he ran, ready for the hit that would send him, too, to the soil.

Time slowed to a near stop.

KEE-YEP! KEE-YEP!

Curtis looked up to see a vast fleet of eagles as they coursed over the Irregulars' heads, diving down from the air behind the promontory. The pale gray sky was obliterated by an ocean of birds in flight.

"The Avians!" shouted Sterling.

The wave of flyers crashed into the descending crows, the crows' terrible caws of fear and pain profaning the air above the fighters on the ground, all of whom had stopped in their warring, spellbound, to watch the amazing scene play out overhead. More birds came from the south; a tide of falcons and ospreys, owls and kestrels filled the sky. Their manifold voices, chiming their cumulative battle cry, were deafening.

Sterling was the first to shake himself from his shock. "Let's move in!" he shouted, and the Irregulars, renewed, continued their advance.

The army of birds dispatched the crows in short order—those who weren't torn apart by the raptors' fierce talons fled into the surrounding woods as fast as their wings could fly them—and turned their force to the coyotes below. The coyotes, petrified by this new army that threatened them, were caught trying to choose which advancing force to engage. Those who aimed their rifles into the blur of wings above them were cut down by the farmers and bandits who dove into their ranks on the ground.

One coyote, his eyes set on Curtis, dove into the fight, his cutlass flashing; Curtis threw the blade of his saber up defensively, feeling the weight of his opponents' weapon crashing into his own. No sooner had he done this than a pair of gnarled yellow claws appeared at the coyote's shoulders and the animal was lifted skyward in the clutches of an enormous golden eagle. Curtis tumbled backward into a pile of dead leaves, and watching the bird and his catch grow distant in the sky, he let out a loud, victorious *"WHOOP!"*

The air soon became a cloud of wheeling raptors, diving to the ground to pick up more hapless coyote soldiers and returning to the air only to drop them to their deaths on the ground below. After a time, avoiding this aerial assault of falling coyotes became more of a concern to the Wildwood Irregulars on the ground than actually fighting them. More birds crested the ridge, and the forces, the conjoined Irregulars and the Avians, cleared the hillside of coyotes and made their advance on the ridge and the basilica beyond.

🌿

The Governess heard the eagles' call. Her face whipped upward, staring at the sky. The sound was unearthly, a thousand birds crying out at once. Prue pushed herself up and scanned the horizon for the source of the noise.

"The birds," whispered Alexandra to herself angrily. "The cursed birds."

The Governess redoubled her focus on the task before her. Mac squirmed against her clutches as she placed him, roughly, on the headstone of the Plinth, his wails melding with the screams of the birds in the distance. Holding him flat against the Plinth with one hand, the Governess began her ritual. Her lips began to move, intoning the guttural sounds of some ancient incantation. With the tip of the dagger, she drew forth a single bulb of blood from the baby's outstretched palm. Mac screamed.

Prue let out an impassioned yelp and tried to lift herself from the ground but discovered she could not move; the ivy had entwined itself around her legs and wrists. She was pinned to the clearing floor.

Prue's mind raced as she struggled against the rippling vines of ivy. The tree branches above her swayed in the cold breeze, indifferent to the horror about to play out below them. *If only they would stop her*, she thought. *If only you would reach down your boughs . . .*

The Governess lifted Mac's body from the Plinth with her left hand, her fingers clutching the cloth of his jumper, and held him high in the air. The dagger in her right hand flashed momentarily in a brief break of sun. The blood on Mac's palm dripped down his finger, poised to fall at his fingertip to the ivy below.

"Stop. Now," came a voice.

It was Brendan, standing on the top of the stairs. His yew bow was stretched taut, an arrow nocked in the string and held to his cheek. His eye squinted down the shaft of the arrow as he took aim at his target. His face was drained of color, and the front of his shirt was soaked a dark red.

Alexandra turned to the bandit and cracked a smile. "Too late, O King of the Bandits," she said. She raised the dagger to strike.

If only you would, thought Prue.

Please. My brother.

Suddenly, a dark shape swept across the wide plaza, casting a moving shadow over the expanse of quivering green below. Prue looked up and saw that it was a pair of long, spindly fir boughs, arcing mightily toward the Governess's extended hand. Her attention momentarily distracted by Brendan and his drawn bow, she did not see the boughs as they descended on the baby in her hand. In a quick motion, they had snatched Mac from her grip and carried him aloft. Alexandra shrieked, twisting as she grabbed for the baby's feet.

Brendan released his arrow.

It sank home between Alexandra's shoulder blades.

The ivy licked greedily at her ankles.

A single drop of blood fell from the wound the arrow had made, falling to spatter against the leaves of the ivy vines. The dagger fell from her fingers. The Dowager Governess followed the droplet of her blood into the awaiting tongues of the ivy vines, and the entire glade of dark green leaves surged forward, consuming her long body in the span of a few short seconds.

Mac, cradled high above the scene in the spiny fingers of the fir bough, cried fitfully. The ivy quavered around Prue, its spiny tendrils still holding her fast. She screamed, terrified that the ivy would consume her next.

Iphigenia called out to Brendan from across the clearing.

"Bandit King, you've fed the ivy! They've feasted on the Governess herself!" she shouted. "The plant is in your thrall. You must command it to sleep!"

A flicker of recognition flashed across Brendan's tired face. Prue could see the realization pass fleetingly through his mind: He now had control of the most powerful force in the Wood. But no sooner had the idea occurred to him than he had cracked his bloodied lips wide and intoned the simple command:

"Sleep."

The ivy immediately stopped its pulsing movement and relaxed into the floor of the square, its many leaves twitching like a sleeper on the edge of slumber. In a moment, the glade had ceased movement entirely. The vines around Prue's wrists and legs released their powerful grip and she tore at them, quickly freeing herself from their bounds. The Bandit King, as if heeding his own command, slumped to the ground in a pile, his bow clattering across the paving stones at the top of the stair.

Iphigenia held a single hand above her head and gestured to the high branches of the fir tree, and Prue watched as the tree complied with the Mystic's request, dropping Mac gingerly from bough to bough like

Holding him flat against the Plinth with one hand,
the Governess began her ritual.

a multitude of hands juggling a delicate bauble slowly to the ground. Once the tree's freight had arrived at its lowest branch, the limb swung wide again, curving across the wide glade to deposit the baby softly into the lap of his sister.

Prue threw her arms around her brother and squeezed him tight to her chest. "Mac!" she cried. "I have you!"

The baby, recognizing his sister's voice, held back his crying and stared up at her. "Poooo!" he said, finally.

The tears came flooding as Prue kissed the soft skin of his brow over and over. Mac babbled merrily in her arms.

🌿

The quiet scene did not last long; a loud groan sounded from the far side of the clearing. "Brendan!" Prue shouted, remembering her friend. She ran toward his prone body, sprawled over the two top steps of the stone staircase. The ivy leaf poultice the bandit had made was barely clinging to his shoulder, and it was apparent that the act of drawing the bow and firing the arrow had opened the wound afresh. Brendan's eyelids were closed, though Prue could see his pupils moving underneath the thin veil of skin, as if he was searching for something, desperately, in the darkness of his unconsciousness.

"Help!" she yelled. "The King needs help!"

A broad swirl of gray and brown birds wheeled above the middle tier of the basilica, and the ground was littered with discarded

515

weapons and fallen soldiers. The surviving Irregulars and the seemingly endless tide of birds continued to pick off the last of the coyotes as the Governess's defeated army beat its retreat, the coyotes falling to their forelegs to run, casting off the coarse fabric of their uniforms as they went. The south ridge of the clearing still smoldered from the artillery barrage, and a great mantle of smoke hung over the ruined city. Prue heard someone approach; it was the Elder Mystic.

"Let me see," she said, her voice calm. She knelt down at Brendan's side and inspected the wound beneath the poultice. "Hmm," she said. "Blood lost, some flesh—a chance for infection." She lifted the King up by the shoulder and looked at his back. "An exit wound—it's gone clean through. That's good. Here." She reached over and tore a long swath of fabric from the hem of her robe sleeve and set about packing it against the wound. The pain of the Mystic's work woke Brendan from his unconsciousness and his eyes flew open, wide and bloodshot. He grasped at his shoulder; Iphigenia held him down. "Easy, King," she said. "You've had a bit of a hurt. Not major, but you surely shouldn't have been playing archer."

There was a clatter of footsteps on the staircase; Curtis, flanked by several of his fellow Wildwood Irregulars, was leaping up the stairs. "Prue!" he shouted. "Prue! You won't believe what's happened. It's all so—" He stopped short and stared at the baby in

Prue's arms. A wide grin broke over his face. "Mac," he said. "You've got him."

"Yep," said Prue, beaming. "I've got him."

He went to hug her but was again distracted by the supine body of the Bandit King below him. "Brendan!" he said. "How is he? Is he okay? What happened?"

Iphigenia, trussing the King's shoulder with the bit of tawny fabric, nodded. "He'll be all right. Might be laid up for a bit—he won't be robbing any stagecoaches anytime soon, but he'll heal in time. Important thing is that we get him to the circle of caravans, quickly. There are people there who can see to his wounds."

The several Irregulars standing next to Curtis vaulted forward at Iphigenia's request, and hoisting Brendan into a standing position between their shoulders, they walked him off toward the glade above the basilica.

The Elder Mystic wiped her hands on the hem of her robe while Curtis sat down on the top step next to Prue, who was staring down at the child in her arms. Her brow was furrowed, as if she were mulling over some important puzzle.

"Pooo!" the baby was saying.

"I can't believe it," Curtis said quietly. "We did it." He reached out his arms to the baby and Prue smiled, handing him the child. He bounced Mac on his knee, and the baby squealed happily.

Prue squinted over at Iphigenia. "That was amazing," she said.

"Really incredible. If you hadn't convinced the tree branches to swoop in and grab him—who knows what would've happened?"

Iphigenia nodded thoughtfully. "Indeed." She shifted a little in her seat and added. "But I didn't ask them."

Prue looked back at her blankly.

"It hadn't occurred to me, actually. I was distracted in the moment, as the Dowager was, by the arrival of the Bandit King. The trees, they seem to have done it of their own accord, which is very strange," continued the Mystic. "Or"—she paused—"they answered the request of someone else." She studied Prue intently. "But that is highly, highly implausible."

Prue shyly looked down at her shoes.

"So what's happened to the Dowager?" Curtis interjected, gesturing over at the glade of ivy behind them. There was no sign of Alexandra's body; it was as if she'd vanished completely.

"She's part of the ivy now, dear," replied the Mystic. "A fate this baby has narrowly avoided."

"Does that mean she's, you know," started Prue, "dead?"

Iphigenia shook her head. "Oh no," she said. "Not dead. Very much alive. But certainly incapacitated. She's . . ." The Elder Mystic searched for the right words. "She's simply changed form. Her every molecule has been absorbed by this plant, which is now returned to its soporific state. Quite incapacitated." Iphigenia looked off into the distance thoughtfully. "I suppose, now that you mention it, there would be a way to . . . well, hello, look who's come to see us."

At the bottom of the steps, a contingent of the Avian army had gathered. The largest of them, a golden eagle, stepped forward and climbed the first few steps of the staircase.

"Is one of you Prue McKeel?" asked the eagle.

Prue looked up. "I am," she said.

The eagle bowed low. "My name is Devrim. I'm the acting general of the Avian infantry. I understand you were flown, two days ago, by another eagle such as myself."

"Yes," she said. "We were shot down. He didn't survive."

The eagle's face was stoic. "It is as we feared."

Prue's heart sank and she began to stammer a desperate apology; all the calamity that she'd brought on these poor animals! But before she could speak, Iphigenia seemed to guess at her troubles and stepped forward.

"Good General," said Iphigenia. "How did you hear word of our . . . predicament?"

"A sparrow," replied the general. "A young sparrow named Enver. He took a particular interest in the young Outsider girl. He sought news from the birds of Wildwood as a way to follow the girl's progress. When the Dowager's army had amassed and began marching south, the news traveled very quickly. We knew that we had to intercede. Alas"—the general pecked at the underside of his wing thoughtfully, as a man might stroke his beard—"our numbers are fairly small. The persecutions of South Wood have badly diminished our standing."

The Elder Mystic nodded. "Perhaps then," she said, "our work is not completed." She turned to Prue and Curtis, snaking her fingers into the crooks of their arms and standing up. "Help me down the stairs, little ones," she said. "I've got an idea I'd like to put to the good General. I've a mind to set some things right. We do have an army at our disposal, after all."

CHAPTER 28

Wildwood Rising

A steady breeze picked up the tattered scraps of fallen leaves on the dirt paving of the Long Road and shuffled them around in little funnels. The trees were changing more and more each day; another autumn was reaching its height. Soon, winter would arrive with its steady gloom of rain and the occasional fall of snow. The people of South Wood were busy stocking their larders with the jarred surplus of the summer's harvest and eyeing their steep woodpiles while their begrudging offspring stacked it in tidy blocks in dry enclosures, away from their house walls, where the bugs could get in.

The two guards stood on either side of the wide wooden gate, leaning on their rifles. They'd been on the shift for more than five hours and were already looking forward to their reprieve for the evening. The sun was shifting downward in the sky; an early twilight was at hand. They could smell the first whiffs of the nearby houses' dinners being put on the hob, and it made their stomachs growl. In unison, in fact. Hearing it, they looked at each other and gave a laugh.

A noise sounded from the distance. A clattering noise. Something was coming toward them on the Long Road.

They stiffened. The evening's rush hour had long passed, and the road's travelers had become fairly sparse, as they always did at this time of the evening. Once the final shipments had made their way into the South Wood gates, the Long Road often had the feel of a deserted highway.

The clattering grew closer. The guards exchanged a glance and stood up from their leaning positions, both of them staring down the wide expanse of the road. The noise was distinctly metallic, like a chain being rattled or . . .

A bicycle.

It came around a distant bend, weaving under the weight of its passengers. On the front of the handlebars sat a young boy with a fountain of curly black hair atop his head. He was wearing a dirty, torn military uniform. As the bike came closer, the guards saw that the person pedaling the bike was a young girl with short dark hair; a small red wagon bounced along behind the bike, carrying a bald infant swaddled in a pile of blankets.

The bike came to a quick, skidding stop in front of the gates, and the boy on the handlebars hopped off. He pulled a sling from his pocket and began swinging it casually at his side. The girl dismounted from the seat and, after quickly checking on the baby in the wagon, turned to the two guards.

"Let us through," she said.

The guard on the left of the gate laughed, taking in the strange sight. "Oh yeah?" he asked. "What's yer business?"

"We've come to free Owl Rex and the citizens of the Avian Principality from the South Wood Prison," she said matter-of-factly. "Oh, and to remove Lars Svik and his cronies from power." She thought for a moment, adding, "Peacefully, if at all possible."

The guards stared, speechless.

The boy with the sling prompted, "Well? You gonna open up?"

The guard on the right tried to snap himself from his confusion. "I—I mean—we—you've got to be—I mean, NO! What are you talking about?"

"This is a coup," said the girl. "So if you wouldn't mind opening those gates, we'd greatly appreciate it."

The guard continued to sputter. "But—come on, now, little one. You and what army?"

The girl smiled. "This one," she said.

From behind them, around the distant bend of the Long Road, the horizon was suddenly filled with a multitude of birds, humans, and animals, a wall of figures moving toward the great gate.

⚘

It would be called "The Bicycle Coup" when, in due time, the history was written. It would be recorded as a perfectly peaceful overthrow, the existing South Wood army having already been at odds with the ever-expanding force of the SWORD, the government's nefarious secret police. As the combined force of the Avian infantry and the so-called Wildwood Irregulars marched through the streets of South Wood, they were met with open arms, the citizens and soldiers falling into step with them on the march toward Pittock Mansion. When they'd finally arrived at the doors of the Mansion, the major players of the Svik administration had either escaped, running into the surrounding woods to, presumably, find refuge in some damp gully in Wildwood, or were kneeling in supplication on the marble floor of the Mansion foyer.

There, the arriving revolutionaries issued their first demand: the keys to the South Wood Prison. The overthrown officials handed them over with no resistance. The revolutionaries then boarded the steam train that ran to the prison, a welcome respite since they'd spent the better part of the last twelve hours on a grueling march through half the country. When they'd arrived at the walls of the prison, the gates were thrown open and a pinwheeling collage of plumage erupted from within, funneling into the sky. The imprisoned birds of the Avian Principality were freed.

The last bird to exit the prison, it is recorded, was a very large owl, the Crown Prince of the Avians, and he was met with embraces from the lead revolutionaries. Together, they decamped back to Pittock Mansion and set about mapping out a new era for the Wood.

🌿

"Hold still," instructed Prue, her colored pencil poised over the page of her sketchbook.

Enver cocked an eye sideways and looked at her. "How much longer?" he managed through a half-open beak. He shifted his small talons on the railing of the balcony, trying to find a more comfortable stance.

"Almost done," replied Prue, lowering the tip of the pencil and drawing a rust-colored streak. The wisp of the bird's tail feather was complete. "There," she said. She placed the pencil on the stone of the railing and held the sketchbook at a distance, so the grainy details of the colored pencil blurred together to form the striped features of the sparrow.

Enver, freed from his frozen position, hopped over to take a look. "Very nice," he said. Prue wrote his name in capitals under the picture. Below that, she wrote the words *Melospiza melodia* in her best script.

"Song sparrow," explained Prue.

Enver chirped appreciatively.

"It's not improving on Mr. Sibley, or anything," Prue demurred. "And he didn't even have the benefit of being able to talk to his subjects. But it'll do."

Enver, antsy to move, leapt into the air and wheeled above the twin turrets of Pittock Mansion. Prue watched him sail against the charcoal-gray sky.

A skyline of dense trees defined the horizon below the sparrow's dizzying flight path: golden yellow maples and deep green firs. Beyond the shroud of trees, she knew, was Portland. Her home. From this vantage, Prue thought, Portland seemed like the strange, magical country—not the world she currently stood in, with its stately groves of tall trees and busy populace, plying their trades in a peaceful coexistence with the world around them. The lattice of Portland's freeways, clogged with cars and trucks, all the concrete and metal—these things seemed more alien to her now.

She shook herself from her thoughts: A long day's ride was ahead of her. She closed her sketchbook and collected the colored pencils, slipping them back into her messenger bag. The air was cool; fall had truly arrived. The smell was everywhere.

A door opened behind her, and she turned to see Owl Rex and Brendan, deep in discussion, approach through the wide French doors from the second-story sitting room. Brendan's arm was affixed to his chest in a tight sling, but he seemed to be moving about without much trouble. There had been quite a to-do the day before, when the Mansion nurses had insisted on his having a bath; the hallways had echoed with his roared objections. His clothes having been laundered and his skin freshly scrubbed, he was barely recognizable as the rake she'd met in the woods.

"How's it going in there?" she asked as the two walked to the railing of the balcony.

"There's little doubt that it will be a long and difficult process," said the owl. "So many species were given short shrift by the Svik rule of law; much recompense is due. The coyote dignitaries are expected today; their inclusion in the process will no doubt be controversial. Already, the bandits and the North Wood farmers are at odds; a few of my bird underlings staged a walkout over compensation to the families of the imprisoned Avians. Thankfully, lunch arrived early, and they were coerced back to the table with the promise of fresh pine nuts." He sighed. "One thing is certain: No process of government building is ever easy. There is, however, a striking feeling in the air, regardless of the petty disputes, that we will arrive at a solution in time, a solution that will see to the rights and needs of all citizens of the Wood."

Brendan massaged the bandage at his shoulder. "Aye, it's no easy thing," he said, his feet shifting against the brick of the balcony. "But the sooner we get to some sort of agreement, the better. All the paving stones around here hurt my feet. I'm antsy to get back to the woods, back to the hideout, back to my people."

"I'm sure it will all work out," said Prue. "You're all pretty able folks."

"There'd be a place for you, you know," said the owl, arching an eyebrow. "An ambassadorship, perhaps. Envoy to the Mystics? How does that title suit you?"

"Thanks, Owl," she said. "But I really have to get back. My parents—I bet they're tearing their hair out, wondering what's happened. Mac needs to go home. I need to go home."

The owl nodded in understanding. "Well, as you know, you'd be welcome back, anytime."

"Where's that little bairn now?" asked Brendan. "Your brother, I mean."

As if conjured by the reference, Penny the maid appeared at the open French doors, crouched over to hold the upstretched hands of Mac, helping him totter over the threshold onto the balcony.

"He'll be a walker in no time!" proclaimed Penny, beaming. "He's really getting the hang of it!"

Prue walked to meet them. She hoisted Mac up in her arms. "Thanks for watching him, Penny," she said. "I just needed a little moment to get ready."

The maid curtsied. "I guess you'll be leaving then," she said. "It was an honor to have met you, Miss McKeel."

"You too, Penny. Thanks for your help."

The maid turned to go but let out a little shriek when a figure came bowling out of the sitting room through the doorway, nearly knocking her over.

"Curtis!" shouted Prue. "Watch where you're going."

Curtis, neatly decked out in freshly pressed uniform, made a clumsy bow to the maid. "Sorry about that." he said before returning to his mission. "Owl! Brendan! There you both are!" exclaimed Curtis. He came rushing to the railing of the balcony. "You should really go back in there—hi, Prue— it's kind of a mess. The birds are in the chandelier, and they're refusing to come down till the South Wood contingent agrees to dismantle all check-points; the North Wooders are still arguing with the bandits on amnesty for poppy beer shipments, which the bandits have rejected, and Sterling is brandishing his pruning shears, saying he'll clip the trouser buttons off any bandit who disagrees."

"Ugly, ugly words," said Septimus, clucking his tongue. He was perched on Curtis's shoulder, gnawing on a medal he'd been awarded for bravery. The silvery surface was covered in little teeth marks.

The owl and the Bandit King exchanged a vexed look, and the two of them turned to go. "Good-bye, Prue," said the owl, shaking his head. "Maybe you're better off on the Outside."

Brendan held out his arms and gave Prue and Mac a long embrace. "Till next we meet, Outsider," he said, stepping back. Reaching into his pocket, he pulled out a small, shiny piece of metal, dimpled from having been hammered flat. He pressed it into her palm. "If ever you find yourself back in Wildwood," he said, "and you're waylaid by bandits, show 'em this." Prue turned it over in her fingers. On the back had been etched the words GET OUT OF HIGHWAY ROBBERY FREE, BY DECREE OF THE BANDIT KING.

Brendan winked and turned to leave.

Curtis started to follow the two of them back into the Mansion, but the owl stopped him. "Stay here," he said. "We'll handle things in there. Your friend is leaving. You might want a moment with her before she goes." He gestured to Septimus. "Come, rat," he said. "You never know when a rodent's perspective will be needed. Leave these two alone for a moment."

Septimus, easily flattered, leapt from Curtis's shoulder to the ground. "Bye, Prue," he said. She bowed slightly and watched as the rat scampered into the Mansion. The owl and the bandit followed, disappearing behind the French doors.

Curtis looked at Prue, his face falling. "Really?" he asked. "That soon?"

"Yep," she said. "I've got to get Mac back. To be honest, I've been missing my bed, my friends. I'm even missing my parents, if you can believe that. It'll be nice to be back home."

A wind picked up and coursed through the manicured estate of the Mansion, sending a fountain of leaves whirling about the tidy gardens below them.

"You sure you don't want to come with?" Prue asked.

Curtis nodded. "Yeah," he replied. "There's lots of work to do here. A whole government to rebuild. Since I spent that time with the coyote army, they're saying I might be a lot of help when the coyote ambassadors arrive." He paused and looked out over the horizon of trees. "Plus, I made an oath, Prue. I'm a bandit now. A real Wildwood bandit. I just can't go back on that. That moment on the Long Road, before you came up, I had the chance to leave. But I'm needed here, Prue. I *belong* here."

A silence fell over the two friends. The baby in Prue's arms filled the quiet with a string of babbling gurgles. Prue watched her friend Curtis, wondering if she looked as changed as he did.

"Okay," said Prue, finally, "I understand." She squinted up at the sky, the thin gray of the clouds beginning to glow as the morning sun continued on its upward arc. "Walk me to my bike?" she asked.

"Of course," said Curtis.

They made their way through the long, looming halls of the Mansion, down the wide curve of the grand staircase above the foyer and out through the front door to the grounds. They walked in silence, each of them lost in their own thoughts. Leaning against the stone balustrade of the Mansion's veranda was Prue's bike, and Curtis helped her make a little bed of blankets in the wagon for Mac to ride in. A carved wooden horse, given to Mac as a gift, lay where they'd left it on the floor of the red wagon, and Mac was overjoyed to be reunited with the toy.

"Come on," said Curtis, "I'll walk you as far as the start of the Long Road."

"So what are you going to do now?" asked Prue as they made their way lazily along the serpentine drive of the Mansion.

"I don't know," he said. "Once this is through, I guess the rest of us bandits, those who haven't already returned, will head back to the camp. There's a lot of work to do; we lost a bunch of bandits in that war. Gonna have to get used to sleeping under the stars, that's for sure."

"I'm sure you'll do fine," said Prue.

Standing in the middle of the driveway, just beyond the turnout in front of the Mansion doors, was a single brilliantly colored caravan wagon. A white rabbit was lying on his back underneath the axle of the wagon's front wheel, hammering at the assembly with a crescent wrench. A woman in a sackcloth robe stood over him, muttering instructions.

"Iphigenia!" shouted Prue as they came closer.

The woman turned and waved. Her face wore a look of bemused frustration.

"You're leaving?" asked Curtis. "Aren't you needed in the meetings?"

Iphigenia dismissively waved her hand in the air. "Bah," she said. "Who needs an old bag like me? I have no stomach for prolonged argument. There are folks younger than I who can uphold our interests. However, I'm not going anywhere till this blasted axle is fixed." She eyed Prue. "I suppose you're on your way, yes, half-breed?"

"Yep," she said. "Going home. What about you? You heading back to North Wood?"

"Yes," replied the Elder Mystic, "I'll be making my way there eventually. The Council Tree will need attending to. I imagine it will have a lot to say about our little adventures." She set her hands at her hips and lifted her chin, as if taking in the air. "I think I might take my time heading home, though," she said. "While it was not under the best of circumstances, I did so enjoy seeing the Ancients' Grove again. I'd not been there for many years. There are truly so many beautiful things to see in the Wood—the great falls at the headwaters of Rocking Chair Creek, the outlook from the top of Cathedral Peak. The very kind Crown Prince has invited me to stay with the Avians for a time, a personal guest of the owl. I think I'd like that very much. Then—who knows—perhaps I'll find my way to the Ossuary Tree, visit the tombs of my fallen predecessors, those ancient Mystics who managed the journey before me. And then? A long, steaming hot bath and a cup of tea in the comfort of my own little home. That'll be enough adventuring for me."

"Best of luck," Prue said. "That sounds like a wonderful journey."

"Good-bye, Prue," said Iphigenia, holding out her arms.

Prue set the kickstand of her bike and walked into the Elder Mystic's embrace. Her wiry gray hair caressed Prue's cheek and was bathed in the rich scent of lavender. "I don't know if I'll ever see you again," Prue said, choking back her tears.

The Mystic patted Prue's back. "You will," she said. "You will."

Leaving the caravan wagon behind, Prue and Curtis continued on their way. When they arrived at the junction of the Mansion's drive and the wide expanse of the Long Road, Curtis turned and extended his hand.

"Okay, then," he said. "Let's not make this all blubbery and emotional. Good-bye, Prue."

Prue stuck out her lower lip in mock seriousness. "Good-bye, Curtis. Coyote soldier, bandit, revolutionary."

They shook hands firmly.

Curtis's chin began to quiver. Prue marked this by saying, "Oh, come on." She reached out her arms.

Standing in the middle of the driveway, surrounded by a steady stream of traffic on the Long Road, the two friends shared a long hug. After a time, Curtis stepped back, wiping his nose with the cuff of his uniform. "Look what you did," he said. "My newly cleaned uniform, all snotty on the cuff." He looked up at Prue, his eyes wet with tears. "See you, Prue."

Without another word, Prue turned and walked her bike into the flow of traffic on the road. She gave Mac a quick kiss on the cheek and checked the connection between the bike and the wagon; all was well. Throwing one leg over the frame of the bike, she mounted the seat and set her feet into the pedals. Within a few moments, she was off.

"Hey, Prue!" Curtis suddenly shouted. Prue pulled the handle brakes to slow the bike and turned around.

"If I ever need you," he called over the hum of traffic, "I'm gonna come and find you, okay?"

"Okay!" responded Prue, moving farther down the road.

"Because we're partners!" shouted Curtis.

"What's that?" yelled Prue. It was hard to make out words in the din of the busy road.

"WE'RE PARTNERS!" yelled Curtis, at the top of his lungs.

Prue grinned widely, hearing him. "OKAY!" she shouted, and the Long Road made a jog around a bend and Curtis was gone behind her.

She'd traveled for a time, weaving in and out of the knot of traffic, before she arrived at the front gates. Seeing her coming, the guards threw open the doors and gave her a proud salute as she rode slowly under the arch of the wall. The Long Road stretched before her, leading off into the hazy distance. Standing up on the pedals, she kicked the bike into speed, the cool wind whipping at her cheek. Mac gurgled happily in the wagon and waved the carved horse above his head, as if it was itself riding wildly down the road.

"Let's go home, Mac," said Prue.

🌿

Prue and Mac's reception, when they arrived back at their house in St. Johns, was riotous. Her mother gripped her around the shoulders in a bone-crushing embrace while her father whipped Mac, laughing, from the wagon and threw him deftly into the air. The exchange of hugs and kisses was so lengthy that they soon lost track of who had hugged whom and which child had been kissed more. Even her parents spent several moments embracing each other as if they had been the ones lost, while Prue looked on, bemused. The afternoon rolled into evening and the celebrations did not cease: Prue's dad played DJ, pulling out all his favorite old rocksteady records, while her mother danced around the room, lost in a constant frenzy of indecision about which child should be her partner. In the end, she chose both, and the three of them spun about the house in a tight bunch, their arms clinging tightly to one another, their faces bright red with joy.

Prue's world, once again, returned to normal. Her absence from school during the week was explained away as a sudden extended illness, and her friends greeted her in the hallway with sympathetic faces.

"Chicken pox," Prue explained, when pressed. One friend pointed out that she'd already had chicken pox, that she remembered this because she'd been the one who'd given them to Prue. "Guess I got 'em again." Prue shrugged.

The weeks passed. Halloween came and went, notable only for the fact that it was pouring rain that day and everyone had to adjust their costumes accordingly. November ushered in an uncommon Indian summer, the rains having abated, and the McKeel family chose a particularly pleasant Saturday to head out to one of the farms on Sauvie Island to pick up some pumpkins for their planned Thanksgiving desserts. Prue milled about the apple orchard near the farm's open-air market while her parents went in, arguing over who had the best eye for squash. Mac, now walking unaided, tottered around the few picnic tables that dotted the orchard.

A group of figures making their way toward their car in the parking lot caught Prue's eye. They were a middle-aged couple and their two children, both girls. Prue recognized them in an instant as the Mehlbergs, Curtis's bereft family.

Before she knew it, she was walking toward them. "Mr. Mehlberg," she heard herself saying, "Mrs. Mehlberg."

The couple looked up. The two girls, one older, one younger than Prue, stared at her as she approached.

"Yes?" said the woman.

As Prue came closer, she saw such a sadness in the woman's face. Indeed, it was a sorrow that seemed to hover over the entire family like a dark cloud. Prue put her hand on Mrs. Mehlberg's arm.

"I was a friend of Curtis's," said Prue.

The woman's face lit up. "From school? What's your name?"

"Prue McKeel. I know him—I mean I knew him pretty well. I'm . . ." Prue paused. "I'm sorry for your loss."

The pallor returned to the woman's face. "Thank you, dear," she said. "That's very kind."

Prue bit her lower lip in thought. Finally, she said, "I just want you to know that . . . well, I believe that he's in a better place. I think, wherever he is, he's happy. Truly happy."

The Mehlbergs, the man and woman and their two daughters, stared at Prue for a moment before Mr. Mehlberg replied. "Thank you," he said. "We believe that too. It was very nice to meet you,

Prue McKeel." He opened the driver's-side door and climbed into his car. The rest of the family followed him. Only one of the girls, the youngest one, paused at the open car door and squinted up at Prue. "Tell him hello," she requested before climbing into the backseat of the car.

Prue, momentarily taken aback, replied, "I will," and watched the car as it drove out of the parking lot and away down the road.

The McKeels' trunk, when they arrived at home, was laden with squashes of every variety and size, and they'd had to make several trips to get the bounty into the kitchen. It was getting late, and Mac, having had a bowl of banana and avocado at the farm, was acting fussy from tiredness. Prue's mom was flustered.

"Hey," she said, "can you put that cranky kid to bed? We've got to start these pies if they're going to be ready for this week."

"Sure," said Prue, just now waking from the spell the encounter with the Mehlbergs had cast on her. She reached down and grabbed Mac, trundling into the kitchen for good-night kisses from his parents. Once he'd been properly smothered in hugs, Prue took him upstairs, ignoring his tired whines, and put him in his jammies. She set him in the middle of his crib and snuggled his stuffed animal owl into his arms. She gave him a peck on the bald crown of his head and walked to the door, hitting the lights on the way out. "G'night, Macky," she said.

She hadn't gotten halfway down the hallway when she heard her brother's mournful plea: "Pooooo! Pooooo!"

Stopping in her tracks, she sighed and rolled her eyes. Returning to the doorway of his room, she popped her head around the doorway. "What's up?" she asked.

Mac gurgled something in response.

"Can't sleep? Not tired? What is it?"

Another gurgle.

"You want a story, don't you?" she asked.

Mac's face widened into a smile. "Pooo!" he chimed.

Prue caved. "Okay," she said, walking to his crib side and pulling him from the mattress. "Just one story."

The two of them, the brother and the sister, sat in the rocking chair in the corner of the room. Mac nestled himself against her arm, and Prue looked out the window, as if pulling the story from thin air. Finally, she began.

"Once upon a time," she said, quietly, "there lived a little boy and his big sister." She paused, thinking, before continuing: "But before that, there was a man and a woman and they lived here in St. Johns and they wanted more than anything to have a family. But in order to have children, they had to make a deal with an evil queen, an evil queen who lived in a faraway wood."

Mac was riveted, a broad smile splayed across his face.

"The deal was that, in time, the evil queen would come for the second child, the little boy, and would take him with her into her forest kingdom. And one day she did. His sister, however, would have none of it, so she got on her bike.

"And took off after him . . .

"Into the deep, dark woods . . ."

In memory of Ruth Friedman

About the Author and Illustrator

COLIN MELOY once wrote Ray Bradbury a letter, informing him that he "considered himself an author too." He was ten. Since then, Colin has gone on to be the singer and songwriter for the band the Decemberists, where he channels all of his weird ideas into weird songs. This is his first time channeling those ideas into a novel.

As a kid, CARSON ELLIS loved exploring the woods, drawing, and nursing wounded animals back to health. As an adult, little has changed—except she is now the acclaimed illustrator of several books for children, including Lemony Snicket's *The Composer Is Dead*, *Dillweed's Revenge* by Florence Parry Heide, and *The Mysterious Benedict Society* by Trenton Lee Stewart.

Colin and Carson live with their son, Hank, in Portland, Oregon, quite near the Impassable Wilderness.

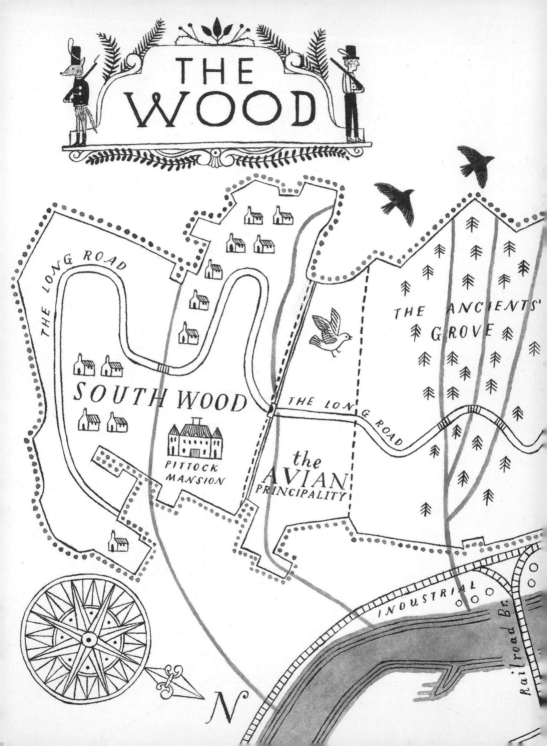

A Sneak Peek at

UNDER WILDWOOD

THE WILDWOOD CHRONICLES, BOOK II

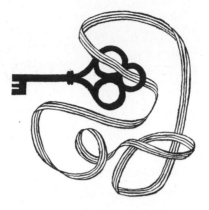

CHAPTER I

A Boy and His Rat

S now is falling.

Snow as white as a swan's feather, white as a trillium bloom. The whiteness is nearly blinding against the dark green and brown of the surrounding forest, and it lies in downy heaps between the quiet, dormant clutches of ivy and blackberry bushes. It is heaped against the bases of the tall fir trees, and it carpets the little trenches in the shallows around the wide cedar roots.

A road carves its way through the deep forest. It, too, is covered in an untouched shroud of snow.

In fact, if you didn't know there was a road beneath the snow, if you didn't know there were centuries of footsteps, hoofbeats and miles of weathered flagstones beneath the snow, you might just think it was a fallow stretch of woods, somehow left untouched by the forest's teeming greenery. There are no wheel tracks, no tire treads on this road. No footprints mar the delicate white of the snow. You might think it was a game trail, a stretch of ground where no tree could take root because of a constant traffic of silent walkers: deer, elk, and bear. But even here, in this most removed area of the world, there are no animal tracks. The more the snow falls, the more the road disappears. It is becoming just another part of this vast, unending forest.

Listen.

The road is quiet.

Listen.

A distant clatter suddenly disrupts this placid stillness; it is the sound of wagon wheels and the whinnying of a horse, pushed to the limit of its strength. The horse's hooves beat a mad rhythm against the earth, a rhythm dulled by the mute of the snow. Look: Around a bend comes flying a carriage, two of its four wheels lifting from the ground momentarily to make the turn. Two sweat-slick black horses are harnessed to the coach, and plumes of steam blow from their nostrils like smoke belching from a chimney. Perched above the horses is the coachman, a large man piled in black wool and a tattered top hat. He barks gruffly at the horses at their every stride, shouting,

"GYAP!" and "FASTER, ON!" He spares no strike of the whip. There is a look of deep consternation on his face. He spends the brief moments between the snaps of his whip eyeing the surrounding forest warily.

Look closer: Below him, in the simple black carriage itself, sits a woman, alone. She is dressed in a fine silk gown, and her face is covered in a shimmering pink veil. Rings studded with bright jewels glint on her fingers. In her hands, she holds a delicate paper fan, which she opens and closes nervously. She, too, watches the flanking walls of trees surrounding the carriage, as if looking for someone or something within them. Opposite her sits an ornate chest, its sides decorated with gold and silver filigree. A lock holds the chest's twin clasps closed, the key to which hangs at the woman's throat by a thin golden cord. Antsy, she raps at the ceiling of the carriage with the fan.

The driver hears the rapping and spurs the horses on, raining even more blows from his whip down on their heaving flanks. A sudden flash of movement on the road ahead catches the driver's attention. He squints his eyes against the blinding white of the falling snow.

A boy is standing in the middle of the road.

But this is no ordinary boy. This boy is dressed in what appears to be an elegantly brocaded officer's coat, like some infantryman from the Crimean War. His hair is black and curly and sprouts from beneath the coarse fur of an ushanka hat. He is idly swinging an emptied sling. There is a rat on his shoulder.

"STOP!" shouts the boy. "THIS IS A STICKUP!"

"You heard him!" shouts the rat. "Rein it in, fatso!"

The coachman hisses a curse under his breath. With a quick turn of his wrist, he has dropped the whip and has taken the reins in both of his hands. He snaps them eagerly, and the horses lean into their gallop. A cruel smile has appeared on the coachman's face. "HYA!" he shouts to the beleaguered horses.

The boy's face, formerly buoyed with confidence, falls. He swallows hard. "I—I'm serious!" he stammers.

The coachman's cracked lips have pulled back to reveal an astonishing row of yellow teeth. He is not slowing. The lady in the carriage gives a slight shriek as it careens along the snowy road. The boy quickly reaches down and pulls a rock from the ground. He wipes it clean of snow on his trousers and sets it into the cradle of his sling.

"Don't make me do this," he warns. It's not clear whether the coachman hears this; he is barreling toward the boy and the rat at an alarming rate.

With a casual expertise—he's evidently been practicing—the boy lets loose the stone from the sling, and it flies toward the coachman, who ducks just in time; the stone sails over his head to fall into the deep, snowy bracken of the forest. The boy does not have time to pick up another; the coach is so close that the boy can smell the sweat coming off the horses.

The rat gives a little *ulp!* and dives into the gully at the side of the

4

road. The boy follows him, and they tumble into a pile together. The carriage roars by. The horses, spooked at having so nearly missed hitting the two brigands, whinny noisily as they pass.

The veiled woman in the carriage clutches at the key at her throat. She gives a high-pitched warble of fear. The coachman, somewhat chuffed at his bravado, throws a look over his shoulder at the boy and his rat. "Better luck next time, suckers!" he shouts. His attention thus diverted, he does not see the cedar trunks as they fall, domino-like, in a crash of splinters to block the road ahead. Three of them. One after another. *Bam. Bam. Bam.*

The woman screams; the coachman swings his head to face forward and gives the reins a violent yank. The horses yawp. Their hooves scramble desperately against the slick surface of the road. The carriage tips and shimmies and emits a shuddering groan. Thinking quickly, the driver hollers an impassioned *"HYA!"* and deftly navigates the horses and carriage through the obstacle course of the fallen trees. Bodies, male and female, are appearing from the woods; they are dressed similarly to the boy, but their uniforms are mismatched. Some wear tattered shirts; some have bandannas covering their faces. They are all children. The oldest might be fifteen. They are staring with disbelief at the coachman's ability to thread the cumbersome carriage with its two panicked horses through their trap. Within moments, the coachman has cleared the obstacles and has returned to his whip, urging the horses on.

In the meantime, the boy and the rat have picked themselves up from the roadside ditch and have brushed the clinging snow from their clothes. The rat leaps back up to the boy's shoulder as the boy puts his fingers to his lips and gives a shrill whistle. From the dense scrub of the forest comes a horse, a dappled brown-and-white pony. The boy throws himself astride the horse, the rat holding tight to the boy's epaulet, and kicks it into a gallop. Arriving at the fallen trees, he leaps the horse and clears the three cedars. A spray of snow and mud flies up when the horse makes landfall. The children in the woods have shaken themselves from their shock and are calling their mounts; soon the road is filled with galloping riders giving chase to

the fleeing carriage.

The coachman, ahead, marks this. He curses the bandits' temerity. The wind is lashing at his face; the snow is now driving, icy.

Of the pursuing riders, the boy with the rat is clearly among the fastest. Many are unable to keep up the pace that the carriage is setting and fall away. Within minutes, only four remain: the boy, another older boy, and two girls. They draw closer to the speeding carriage and split apart, two on each side of the vehicle. The rat, holding tight to the boy's shoulder by a flap of his furry hat, issues a warning to the coachman: "Give up your gold," he shouts, "and you can go free!"

The coachman responds with a hair-raising curse that makes the

boy blush, even in this most hectic of moments. He is now level with the carriage. He can see inside: the veiled woman, the key at her neck, the clasped ornate chest. The woman watches him curiously, her large brown eyes glinting from above the shimmering cloth at her face. The boy is momentarily distracted by the scene. The rat shouts, "LOOK OUT!"

In an effort to unseat his pursuers, the coachman has feinted the carriage to the left, and the boy nearly runs his pony directly into the coach's traces. He catches a shriek in his throat and veers the pony off the road. The pony's hooves hit the soft underbrush of the roadside and it falters; the ground drops away here and slopes down to a rushing brook far below. The boy braces for the fall, but the pony is nimble. In a flash, the boy's steed has righted itself and finds its footing again on the road. The boy whispers a word of thanks in its ear. They are back in the chase.

The carriage leads them now by several horse lengths. The three other bandits are struggling to keep up. One of the riders, a girl with straw-blond hair, has grabbed hold of the roof of the coach and is attempting to climb aboard. It is a risky ploy; the girl's face is set in concentration. The other two bandits, a boy and a girl, have managed to spur their mounts to ride parallel to the coach's horses. The blond-haired girl grunts loudly and vaults from her horse; she barely manages to grab hold of the latticework that runs along the top of the carriage. Her horse veers away; her body swings against the carriage-side, eliciting another high-pitched scream from its passenger. The girl steadies herself and climbs to the top of the carriage, giving a triumphant whoop. She turns her head to the boy with the rat, who is still several horse-lengths behind.

"May the best bandit—" she begins. Her sentence is cut short when the carriage plows underneath a low-hanging bough and the girl is lifted from her perch in the blink of an eye. The boy with the rat must duck to avoid the girl's dangling feet as he gallops his pony toward the carriage.

"Win," finishes the girl, suspended from the limb of the tree.

The boy nods to the rat and grits his teeth in determination. There is now only he and the other girl. The other boy has fallen away from the chase, his mount limping into the underbrush.

"Aisling!" the boy shouts. "Get the horses!"

The girl, now parallel with the right-hand horse, has heard him. She is trying to get her hands on the horse's bridle, but the coachman's whip is foiling her every attempt. "Away, vile brigand!" shouts the coachman. The girl winces as the whip's leather tip leaves a red welt on the back of her hand.

"Septimus," hisses the boy to the rat, "think you could help out?"

The rat smiles. "I think I could do a little something." The boy is now even with the carriage. He can hear the mewling of the maiden within. The rat leaps from the boy's shoulder and lands on the nape of the coachman, who lets out a bloodcurdling scream.

"RRRRRATS!" he shouts. "I CAN'T STAND RATS!"

But the rodent has already crawled down the coachman's shirt and is busy practicing a kind of Irish step dance between his naked shoulder blades. The coachman hollers and lets fall both the whip and the reins; the coach's horses, confused, lose their gallop, and the boy and the girl are able to pull up even with them. With a quick glance at each other, the two bandits leap astride the carriage horses and pull them to a scrambling stop.

The coachman jumps from his seat and stumbles away down the road, his hands desperately clawing at his back. The girl and the boy watch him, laughing, before turning to the task at hand. The girl beckons graciously. "After you." The boy bows and walks toward the idle carriage, radiating confidence. He swings the door open.

"Now, ma'am," he says proudly, "if you wouldn't mind turning over . . ."

His words falter. Inside, the woman has removed her veil to reveal a shocking, tangled nest of auburn facial hair.

Also: There is the barrel of a flintlock pistol pointing at him.

"I don't think so," says the passenger, in a husky (and very unladylike) baritone.

The boy is crestfallen. "But—" he begins.

"Bang," says the passenger. He gives the boy a scolding rap on his forehead with the pistol barrel.

The boy stares and scratches at his temple, as if replaying the entire scene in his mind. He kicks his boots in the snow. The winter term of Bandit Training has begun. And Curtis has just failed his first test.

❧

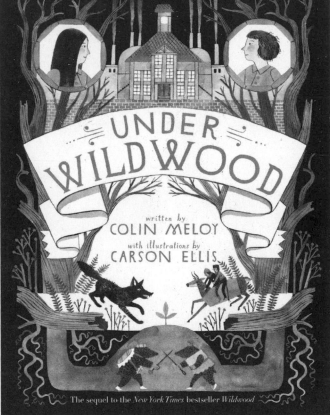